For Roger Llewelyn
Misbehaved all his life

CONTENTS

DEAD WATER vii

Prologue 1
Chapter 1 3
Chapter 2 9
Chapter 3 17
Chapter 4 27
Chapter 5 39
Chapter 6 49
Chapter 7 55
Chapter 8 72
Chapter 9 80
Chapter 10 98
Chapter 11 109
Chapter 12 119
Chapter 13 130
Chapter 14 146
Chapter 15 154
Chapter 16 163
Chapter 17 171
Chapter 18 187
Chapter 19 195
Chapter 20 206
Chapter 21 217
Chapter 22 225
Chapter 23 239
Chapter 24 247
Chapter 25 263
Chapter 26 272
Chapter 27 279
Chapter 28 286

Chapter 29 294
Chapter 30 304
Chapter 31 309
Chapter 32 318
Chapter 33 328
Chapter 34 333
Chapter 35 343
Epilogue 350

Acknowledgments 355
Coming soon... 357
Dead Man's Dive 359
Forensic File 369

DEAD WATER

Detective Inspector Rob Rego has just transferred to the southwest coastal county of Cornwall from Greater Manchester Police, even though he gets seasick just looking at a boat. Maybe leaving the city was a bad career move.

Tamsyn Poldhu already knows that life can be cruel, but on her first day as a student police officer in her home town of Penzance, she has no idea how tough it's going to be.

When a body washes up on a remote Cornish beach, DI Rego uncovers evidence of an organised crime gang operating in Cornwall. Time is running out to catch the killer – and Tamsyn's involvement in the case goes deeper than she could ever have imagined.

PROLOGUE

Gulls wheeled overhead, their wild cries echoing around the cliffs as the sun rose, promising a fine day.

The woman's hair moved gently with the ebbing tide, swaying like seaweed, her eyes sightless, her limbs soft and swollen.

In 35 minutes, a woman walking her dog would find her.

The gulls still had time.

CHAPTER 1

DI Robert Rego was nearing Exeter when his phone rang.

"Rob, this is DCI Finch. Where are you?"

"Nearly at HQ, sir, just approaching Middlemoor."

"Not today – I'm sending you to Penzance. I know you haven't finished your familiarisation training yet, but they've got multiple incidents down there, they don't have a DI and they're already short staffed. There's a serious RTC on the A30, an unexplained death at a hotel, and a body had been washed up somewhere on the way to Land's End. DS Stevens is a safe pair of hands, but he'll need all the help he can get today. Take the drowning; that'll be a good one to get your feet wet."

Rego's boss spoke without a trace of irony.

"We get a lot of suicides – people go to Cornwall to die. No one knows if it's because they've just run out of road or because they have happy memories of holidays here when they were younger. Could be both. Or maybe they want their final memory to be of somewhere scenic." His voice became business like. "It's not unusual to have as many as fifty unexplained deaths in the far western part of the county in six months. Be ready for a briefing at 12.00 with the Super." He paused. "Welcome to Cornwall," and DCI Finch ended the call.

Rego turned his car around and began the two-hour journey south west to Penzance, the last stop before Britain tumbled into the Atlantic Ocean.

As a newly promoted Inspector and a transferee from Greater Manchester Police, he should have had a couple of weeks to familiarise himself with Devon & Cornwall's Major Crime Investigation Team. A month ago, he'd never been further south than Birmingham (apart from a stag weekend in London), never sat on a beach in Devon, and he still hadn't been tempted to eat a Cornish pasty. But his learning curve had just been fast-tracked and it looked like he'd be boots on the ground instead.

That suited him fine.

Normal procedure would be for Rego to drive directly to where the body had been found, but he had yet to pick up a stack of new case books, evidence tags or full barrier clothing: paper suits, masks, shoe covers and gloves. From the sound of it, he'd need to get suited and booted for the body on the beach, and it was likely to be a Home Office pathology job.

Rego's first impression of Penzance was a mixed one. The granite buildings glittered as the rising sun reflected off the mica in the stone. Georgian and Regency terraces lined the steep high street, elbow-to-elbow with dreary modern buildings. It was an attractive town fallen on hard times with too many empty shops and a sprawling Poundland but compensated with a millionaire's view of the harbour and the castle of St Michael's Mount rising magically from the bay beyond.

The police station was tucked away off the main street,

an ugly concrete rectangle with all the charm of a Soviet era apartment block. Rego was used to that – not many police stations won beauty awards. It was also a lot smaller than he was used to, as well as being understaffed: a full complement should be an inspector, one DS, four DCs and an unknown number of uniformed officers and PCSOs. He also knew that in the whole of Cornwall, there were only twelve police officers of colour. As of today, Rego was lucky thirteen.

He parked around the back of the station, surprised that the area wasn't secured – only a sign warning members of the public not to proceed beyond that point. He buttoned his suit jacket as he climbed out of the car and clipped on his new ID.

Nerves and something like anticipation tightened his stomach. He needed this transfer to work – there was a lot riding on it, not least his marriage.

He'd already received a fob key to enter the station but it refused to work, the door staying stubbornly locked. He frowned as he tried again, then banged on the door a few times, but nobody came. He was about to go round to the public entrance when a young blonde woman with an identical fob key smiled at him uncertainly.

"Shall I try mine?"

"Do you usually let strangers into the police station?" he asked curtly, taking his irritation out on her.

Her eyes widened. "No! I mean, no, it's my first day."

Rego wished he hadn't snapped at her. Part of his job was to encourage young officers, not knock them before they'd even started, but that thought was several seconds too late.

"And you're wearing ID," she pointed out, glancing at the badge on his jacket. "Sir."

"Well spotted," he said, trying to sound less like an arse. "And you are?"

"PC Tamsyn Poldhu," she said more confidently. "I'm a student officer. It's my first day."

"Yes, you said. Well, it's good to meet you PC Pol ... doo," he said as they shook hands. "I'm DI Rego. So, if you could open the door?"

"Oh, yes! Of course. Sorry, sir."

She seemed so damned young. He hoped that this young officer would show more confidence in the job than she had with him.

Thankfully, she used her card with no trouble and Rego held the door for her as she stepped inside. She hesitated, clearly not knowing which way to go. Unfortunately, neither did he.

A short woman with brown hair, who looked about the same age as the young PC, was walking down the corridor.

"Tampax!" she laughed, a small, mean sound. "What are you doing here?"

Tamsyn flushed, her eyes flicking unhappily towards Rego.

"Hi, Chloe, I didn't know you worked here. I'm the new student officer." She straightened her spine. "PC Poldhu."

The other woman's lip curled. "Whatever, Tam*pax*."

Rego stepped forward. "I'm DI Rego. What's your name?"

The woman blinked. "Chloe Rogers."

"And what do you do at the station, Chloe?"

Her chin lifted. "I'm a civilian investigator."

Rego nodded. "We work best when we work as a team. I don't want to hear that sort of language again."

Chloe regarded him with her sloe-eyes and waited an impudently long time to mutter, "Yes, sir."

She wasn't a sworn officer and didn't have to call him 'sir', but Rego didn't tell her that. He continued to stare at her and Chloe looked away first.

"DS Stevens is expecting me. I'd appreciate it if you could take me to him."

Without a word, Chloe turned on her heel and headed down the narrow corridor, pointing at a conference room filled with a buzz of activity.

They both forgot Tamsyn was there.

She hesitated for a moment, wondering if she should follow, but then saw a sign for the toilets, so she took the opportunity to change into her uniform and tied her hair into a neat bun. Hell would freeze over before she asked Chloe frickin' Rogers where to find the women's locker room. She'd been a bitch at school, and it didn't look as though much had changed.

Tamsyn couldn't believe that the woman who'd made school a misery was here, already stirring, already spoiling the first day of her new job, her new life.

Pensively, she pulled out her Warrant Card, running her fingers over the braille inscription that spelled *police*. No, Chloe might be the same snarky bitch, but Tamsyn had changed in the last two years, growing into herself and becoming more confident. She wanted this; she'd wanted to be a police officer since she was ten years old. She hadn't thought she'd make it through selection, but she had and she was here. Now she had a job to do.

The toilet was small with a musty odour that someone had tried to mask with bleach. It was awkward changing in the enclosed space and Tamsyn didn't want to leave her sports bag on the wet floor.

She lifted on the heavy stab vest, fiddling with the straps until it felt less uncomfortable, then slipped on the utility vest that held her baton, torch, leg restraints, handcuffs and key, notebook and pens, gloves, surgical gloves, fob key, evidence bags, spit hood, tourniquet, and rough-cut scissors. Finally, she clipped her body-worn video onto the left and her Airwave police radio onto the right. With her private mobile tucked into a back pocket, she checked that her police Mobile Data Terminal was close to hand. These days, police and police cars were mobile offices, and the Mobile Data Terminal – a smartphone that she'd been issued with – could be used for accessing the PNC, issuing tickets, taking statements, and using a variety of online forms.

The equipment was a weighty reminder of this new page in her life.

Her private phone pinged with a message from her best friend, Jess:

> Good luck! Don't take any shit and don't arrest me if you see me! Love ya!

Tamsyn smiled, tapped out a quick reply then turned off her phone.

She stared at herself in the mirror, seeing but not recognising the woman staring back: the bright blue eyes and lightly tanned skin were familiar; the fair hair scraped tightly into a bun and the uniform were not.

Her eyes closed and she took a deep breath: *I am a sworn officer of the law.*

When she opened her eyes, she caught her nervous reflection.

"Oh, shit."

CHAPTER 2

The conference room was filled with uniformed officers and CID. It looked chaotic but Rego recognised that there was method in the madness. It seemed as if the briefing had just finished.

A broad man with a bald head appeared to be in charge, so Rego walked towards him.

"DS Stevens?" The man glanced up. "I'm DI Robert Rego."

The man's eyebrows lifted imperceptibly as his eyes scanned Rego's face and ID badge, but he held out his hand. Rego wondered if he was Penzance's first black officer.

"DS Tom Stevens. Good to meet you, sir. We're pretty stretched today."

He gave a succinct rundown of the incidents, introducing the rest of the team as he talked.

"This is DC Jen Bolitho," he waved at a capable looking woman in her forties.

The woman shook hands, giving Rego that same quick appraisal, that same quick look of surprise at the colour of his skin.

"Sir," her gaze flicked between the two men. "I'm off to Marazion – unexplained death in a B&B. The owner, Mrs Dennis, called the paramedics but the man was already dead. I'll have a chat with her and look at the deceased's room."

"Okay, I'll catch up with you later, Jen." Then the DS pointed at a man in his late twenties who had a phone clamped to his ear. "That's DC Jack Forshaw – he's heading out to a serious RTC at Crowlas – four injured, one critical – that's the motorcyclist. Also involving a Honda Civic and a 40-foot artic from Poland carrying bog rolls. He's working with a DS from Camborne." He glanced at Rego. "That's ten miles up the road from here on the A30 – the workshop for our cars is there, and the custody suite."

"You don't have any here?" Rego asked, surprised.

"No, sir. There used to be a couple of cells back in the seventies, I think. But they're storerooms now."

Rego was beginning to understand some of the logistical differences between policing in a major city and in a rural area across a wide geography.

"We have thirty-five uniformed officers across five teams: six PCs and a sergeant each. But right now, three-quarters of our officers are dealing with the RTC – that's why we're so thin on the ground this morning. We've also had a report of a body washed up near Lamorna. The Coastguard is attempting to recover the victim and there's a uniform there now."

"I'll take that one, Tom."

"That would be great, thank you, sir."

He introduced two more uniformed officers, then rubbed his eyes tiredly.

"DC John Frith has been taken ill – appendicitis – so I covered the night shift for him, but we're a DC down anyway. We've also got Sergeant Bryn Terwillis off sick. He's mentoring our student officers: we've got two of 'em starting today. Not great timing," he sighed, glancing towards the open door. "I reckon that's one of them now."

Tamsyn was hovering at the room's entrance, looking ill at ease. Rego saw that she'd changed into her uniform.

God, was I ever that young?

He felt every one of his thirty-four years.

Stevens was already striding across the room, shaking her hand and giving her a quick, reassuring smile.

"Welcome to the mad house, Tamsyn," he said. "We've had three incidents land in our laps this morning, so we're run a bit ragged." He paused. "There's supposed to be another student officer starting today. Have you seen anyone else lurking around?"

"No, sir. Just me."

"Hmm. Unfortunately, Sergeant Terwillis who would be looking after you and our other student officer is off sick today so..." he hesitated, looking about him as if wondering what he could do with her.

"Are you a local?" Rego directed his question to Tamsyn.

"Yes, sir."

"So you know where Lamorna Cove is?"

"Yes, sir. It's about five miles, probably a twenty minute drive." She saw the expression on his face. "The lanes are really winding."

"Right, let's go."

She stared at him for half a second, a deer in the headlights.

"Yes, sir!"

DS Stevens interrupted quietly. "Sir, PC Poldhu hasn't even double-crewed yet."

"I'm aware, but as you don't have your trainer, she can be my guide for today.

The DS hesitated.

"Yes, sir. If there's anything else you need..."

"Case books, evidence tags and some forensic suits."

DS Stevens nodded, clearly harried, running a hand over his bald head.

"We don't have any admin staff today, but there's Chloe – she's a civilian investigator on loan from Camborne. She'll know where everything is. You'll find her in the CID office upstairs. She's got brown hair and..."

"We've met," Rego answered shortly, turning to leave.

Tamsyn followed behind in silence.

They found Chloe sitting in front of a computer screen, a cup of coffee next to her. She watched them impassively, her face blank as Rego listed what he needed.

He followed her to the store cupboard, unsurprised to find it was a complete mess – they usually were.

"PC Poldhu will also need to be issued with her PAVA spray."

"What's that?"

Rego looked up from the store cupboard and frowned. "Incapacitant spray."

"We use Captor here," Chloe said sulkily.

"Okay, then please issue her with one of those."

Chloe disappeared into another part of the building without speaking.

Rego continued to rummage through the cupboard for forensic suits, gloves, exhibit bags and case books. He pulled out a pack of white suits but they weren't a brand he was familiar with. He'd just have to hope that 'large' fit well enough. They were a pain at the best of times: female officers usually ended up with a suit that hung off them, and Rego's was usually too small, got stuck up the crack of his arse and split the first time he bent over.

While Tamsyn was waiting for the canister of Captor spray, Rego called the Control Room for an update: the body had been recovered by the Coastguard and was being taken to the quay at Lamorna Cove where a paramedic, the undertaker and uniform were waiting.

Tamsyn hovered close by, compulsively checking her equipment.

"You're fine," said Rego without looking up. "Now, this is where we're at with the investigation: an incident log has been created with a unique reference number. All actions completed against that incident are to be recorded on that running log. I'm having it emailed to me so I can read the sequence of events so far. There's a uniformed officer in attendance and he is keeping a running scene log." He looked up at her. "Do you know what that's for?"

"Yes, sir. The scene log records times that people have either attended or left that scene."

He nodded.

"Tell me about the area where the body has been found."

It always helped to have as much intel as possible, but he'd asked so she had something else to think about other than first day jitters.

"It's a small fishing cove, sir, with a harbour and quay. Good for swimming. A few lobster pots, but not as many as there used to be."

He glanced up at her curiously.

"The cliffs aren't very high there," she continued, "but further round the coast path you could..."

She paused, as if unwilling to say that there were cliffs nearby that would be high enough to kill yourself if you jumped.

He Googled images of where the body had been found and saw what she meant: the cliffs above the harbour wouldn't be anyone's first choice for committing suicide, but either side of the cove, the cliffs rose sharply.

Chloe reappeared with the Captor spray, waiting while Tamsyn scrawled her signature to say that she'd received it.

"Thanks, Chloe," Tamsyn said, giving the other woman an insincere smile. "Great seeing you again."

Chloe didn't reply.

Rego frowned, but ignored the exchange. For now. He turned to Tamsyn.

"Okay, let's go."

As they headed for his car, he noticed that she was still carrying the sports bag he'd seen her with earlier. He glanced at it enquiringly and a light flush coloured her cheeks.

"I wasn't sure where the lockers are."

He didn't reply, hoping that she wasn't one of those new officers who needed their hand held and had to be told every little thing to do. He simply unlocked the car so she could drop her bag in the boot and slide into the passenger seat.

He set his SatNav automatically even though the young PC appeared to know the route.

She sat in silence for the short journey, and Rego didn't feel much like talking either. A body on the beach was the kind of thing a DC would usually deal with. He'd thought his role with Devon & Cornwall Police would be more strategic. It was simply bad luck that three incidents in the same morning had emptied the station of officers.

Tamsyn had been right about the narrow lanes down to Lamorna, and Rego swore under his breath as gorse scratched both of the car's wing mirrors at the same time.

As they dropped down the steep hill to the village below, the clear blue waters of the small cove sparkled in the sunlight, but the picture-perfect scene was marred by blue-and-white police tape and the Hi-Vis jacket of a uniformed officer who walked towards them as they approached the cordon of two road cones.

Rego flashed his ID as he climbed out of the car. "DI Rego. And you are?"

"PC James Smith," he said, glancing briefly at Tamsyn then back to Rego. "I go by Jamie."

The men shook hands, then Rego introduced Tamsyn.

"First day?" Jamie asked.

"Yes, sir."

He laughed and Rego smiled.

"You don't need to call me 'sir'; we're the same rank – Jamie is fine."

Jamie showed Tamsyn the scene log where he entered *REGO, R, DI,* time of attendance *8.07am*; then entered Tamsyn's details, as well.

"We want a tight cordon," Rego said when Jamie had finished recording their arrival, "but move it back another fifty metres to where the road comes down to the harbour. We want to keep any press away and to reduce distress to onlookers."

He glanced at Tamsyn as he said that.

"Yes, sir," she nodded, and picked up one of the heavy cones to move it back as Jamie took the other.

Rego introduced himself to the paramedic who was there to pronounce life extinct, and the undertaker who would transport the body. Then Rego stood and looked around him, taking it all in. He couldn't see any CCTV at the harbour but it was likely that some of these cottages were holiday homes or Airbnbs, and might have doorbell videos or other security, and he needed to know which of these homes were occupied or empty. He made a note to put those questions on the list for house-to-house enquiries which would come later.

The sound of an engine from the seaward side drew his

attention, and Rego turned to watch the Coastguard's rigid inflatable slowing down to bump gently against the buoys positioned along the sea wall.

Jamie went down to help them tie up.

"We're gonna need a bigger boat," said Rego, quoting his favourite film.

"It's a B-class ILB – an inshore lifeboat, sir," said Tamsyn, completely missing the *Jaws* reference. She spoke matter-of-factly. "Two-hundred horse power, 35 knots."

It was a foreign language to Rego, but he wasn't afraid to ask questions – something he encouraged in his teams.

"Only four crew?"

"Yes, sir. But it's used for all inshore call-outs."

"You know your boats."

For the first time she smiled warmly and seemed to relax a couple of degrees.

"My Grandad taught me. I grew up around them and spent every summer crabbing. Fishing has been in my family for generations."

Another foreign concept to Rego. He'd never met his grandparents and spent his summers underage drinking and thieving.

CHAPTER 3

Rego watched from a distance as Tamsyn checked the details of the paramedic and undertaker in the scene log. He smiled at her earnest expression, remembering his own first days in the job. He'd been a cocky little shit.

Rego cursed as he lost his balance struggling to climb into a forensic suit, the granite paving stones of the harbour slick underfoot.

One of the men from the Coastguard raised a hand and Tamsyn waved back. Rego glanced at her and she gave a small shrug.

"That's Bernie Ryder. He's friends with my Grandad."

"Of course he is."

Another difference policing in a small community.

The man who'd waved was in his late fifties, fit-looking, with a short beard, weather-beaten face and wearing Hi-Vis bib-and-braces overalls.

"Tammy! Are you in the job now, my lovely?"

"Yes, I am! It's my first day, Bernie. This is my ... this is DI Rego, PC Smith, Al Ross, and Mr Sellers is from the funeral home."

The man nodded at Rego, his hazel eyes assessing.

"Gents. I'm Bernie Ryder, Maritime Operations Manager. We don't usually expect to see the police on these jobs. Well, we recovered the body just down from that outcrop," and he pointed at a section of the cove that couldn't be accessed on foot. "Female. Been in the water at least a day, probably two."

"You're sure?" Rego asked sharply.

"Near enough. Bodies will float for a few hours after death, if that. Then sink. Bump along the bottom for one or two days. Gases of decomposition will make it rise and float after a day or so. Then it would be more subject to wind than tide."

Rego decided he'd check to see if the pathologist agreed with Ryder's estimated time of death.

The paramedic jumped onto the boat, staggering slightly as he caught his balance. He squatted down next to the body, pronounced life extinct, made a few notes and hurried away, calling over his shoulder that he'd be in touch.

Moving more cautiously than the paramedic, Rego climbed aboard, hoping the movement of the small boat wasn't going to make him seasick. To take his mind off that thought, he concentrated on the job, or rather the body – definitely female. Then he steeled himself for a closer look.

Just because you could get used to seeing a dead body, it didn't mean it was ever easy.

He snapped on a pair of disposable gloves and performed a brief body search, but there was no obvious cause of death: no bullet or knife wounds; no blunt force trauma, because from what he could see, the bones appeared to be intact. It was likely a suicide or accidental drowning. Maybe they'd get lucky with dental recognition.

The body's skin was mottled and the outer layer

beginning to slough away. As he rolled the body over, he saw that her eyes, lips and throat were gone along with some other soft tissue damage.

"Seagulls been at her," said Ryder. "Probably crabs, fish, lobsters, too."

Rego lost any appetite for seafood while he was in Cornwall. He crouched down to take a look at the victim's hands in case he could use his mobile scanner to take fingerprints. Fish had definitely had been nibbling at the epidermis, but he was hopeful that the pathologist could get some friction ridge detail from the underside. It was possible, but beyond what he could do with his phone scanner.

He was surprised to find Tamsyn peering down at the body from the quay. She seemed a little pale, but then again, everyone in Cornwall was pale compared to him.

"Is that a tattoo?" she asked, bending closer and peering at the woman's right ankle.

Rego had spotted it too, and was impressed that she had the presence of mind to notice it. He moved closer and knelt down, pulling out his phone to take a picture. The image was blurred as the woman's skin had begun to decompose, but Rego's pulse gave a sharp jump as he enlarged the photo. He'd seen that tattoo before, or one very like it. But where?

"Okay, the body can be taken from the scene."

Stepping back, he watched as the Coastguard crew and the undertaker worked together to place the corpse into a black body bag, then move it from the boat to the funeral director's van waiting on the quay.

He glanced at Tamsyn to see how she was doing. He was glad that she seemed composed.

"We always treat bodies with as much dignity as possible," he said.

She nodded slowly.

"I don't think there's much dignity in death, sir."

He met her gaze. "We do our best."

After a final word with Ryder, Rego turned to PC Smith. "Who found the body?"

"A Mrs Madeleine Polpenn who lives at Kemyell, that's half a mile up the lane," he said, pointing up the hill. "She saw the body when she was walking her dog at approximately 6.30am. Called 999. She was upset but not crying and all that."

"Okay, I'll go and debrief her in a minute. Are there any other roads down to this village?"

Jamie shook his head. "Just this one, sir. There's another lane above the pub, but that's half a mile or more. The coast path runs either side of the cove."

"So entry is by this road, by boat, or on foot?"

"Yes, sir."

"We need air surveillance," Rego said.

Jamie looked doubtful. "The helicopter is probably deployed to the RTC. We might be able to get another one down from Brixham. That's Devon, sir."

He said 'Devon' the way people in Manchester said 'Arsenal'.

Rego shook his head.

"No, we don't need a helicopter. Is anyone at Penzance trained to fly drones?"

Until recently, air surveillance would have meant a very expensive helicopter from the National Police Air Service – and they allocated helicopters to scenes on a priority basis, so if there was a critical incident or car chase, you probably wouldn't get a look in. But one of the things that had attracted Rego to this rural community was their innovative use of drone technology, and D&C Police had recently expanded the number of officers trained to use the equipment.

Jamie shook his head.

"No, sir, but they've got two drone pilots at Camborne."

Rego made a note of that.

"They'll need to search at least a mile up the coast path in each direction. But if we can't get drones up quickly, it'll have to be on foot. We're looking for clothes, shoes, a handbag, preliminary entry point; a suicide note, if we're lucky."

Tamsyn stood back and watched as Rego worked. She didn't feel as nervous or unsure now. Part of that was due to the Inspector treating her like a proper member of the team, and part of it was because she felt like she was actually being useful.

She wasn't sure what she'd expected from a Detective Inspector, but she hadn't thought he'd be so inclusive: orders, yes; explanations, not so much – but he'd been really good at clarifying what was happening and what she needed to do in her role.

Plus, he was pretty hot for an old guy.

She followed his gaze as Rego glanced up at the cliffs, then back down to where the body was being secured inside the funeral director's van. Nobody had asked Tamsyn's opinion but she didn't think the woman could have jumped from anywhere near the cove – the cliffs were sloping, not sheer. If she'd jumped nearby, well, she'd have hit rocks first – you'd be able to tell if that had happened. And it seemed weird that she'd have jumped naked.

"You okay there, Tamsyn?" Jamie asked.

"I was wondering about her clothes."

"The sea could have taken them if she's been out there for a while."

Although unconvinced, Tamsyn nodded. She'd lost her bikini top once when she'd been surfing so she knew the power of the waves. But for all the clothes to have disappeared? She wondered what had happed to the woman and why she'd decided to end her own life. It was all so random, so pointless.

It wasn't the first dead body that Tamsyn had seen. She'd been ten when her father had drowned, fallen overboard while running the lines on his lobster pots, and she still remembered the numb horror of seeing his wax-like body rolling free of the tarpaulin that her grandfather had tried to cover him with.

It hadn't seemed real, hadn't felt real. The shock, the overwhelming pain – that had come later.

Tamsyn glanced again at the DI then up at the cliffs again. She thought it was more likely that the body had drifted here. The whole of the bay between the Lizard peninsular and Land's End had very weak currents, but Lamorna was really tidal so it was harder to tell where the body might have come from. Her grandfather would probably be the person to ask. If she was allowed to tell him what she'd seen.

She decided her best bet was to let DI Rego do the detecting and for her to find out what PC Jamie Smith was doing.

"These are the fast track actions," Rego explained to Jamie and Tamsyn, but mostly for Tamsyn's benefit. "Identification: we need to identify the victim so that next of kin can be informed. We'll need house-to-house, search social media for miss-pers, as well as the missing person's database. If we don't get anywhere with that, we'll have to ask for information in a press release, but that's not a scenario we want if it can be avoided." He looked up at Tamsyn to make sure she was taking this in. "We don't want the victim's family hearing from the press that their loved one has died rather than hearing it from the police."

Tamsyn nodded as she took notes.

"We want to identify her as quickly as possible but we need to be prepared to have something ready for the local papers," *and get on the right footing with the journalists*, Rego thought to himself.

"That'll be *The Cornishman* and *The West Briton*," Smith said confidently.

"And *Cornwall Live*." Both men turned to Tamsyn. "It's online, so it's quicker," she added self-consciously.

Rego nodded, pleased that she was thinking for herself.

"And I'll need to organise a dedicated phone line for the press release if we have to go down that route."

He wanted a detective answering the calls on that.

"We also need to speak to local fishermen to ask if they've seen anything: clothing floating in the water..."

"What about the *Scillonian*, sir?" asked Jamie.

"What's that?"

"It's the ferry between Penzance and the Isles of Scilly. Maybe she jumped off there."

Tamsyn frowned. She thought it was more likely that anyone falling or jumping off the *Scillonian* would be swept up the north coast and not against the prevailing south-westerlies. Unless she'd jumped when the ferry left Penzance ... or was nearly back.

But she didn't say anything.

"Jamie, you go with the undertaker and hand over at the hospital which is...?"

"Rose Cottage, sir. That's West Cornwall Hospital in Penzance. But if a post-mortem has been requested, they get sent up to Treliske Hospital. That's in Truro – about 35 miles away."

Rego could see that he'd be spending a lot of his time

driving up and down the length of Devon and Cornwall. Even his new HQ was 120 miles away in Exeter.

He added to his list of jobs: speak to the Coroner and request a post-mortem then get one booked asap, this afternoon, if possible; he needed forensics to lift a clearer image of the tattoo and get that circulated, then…

His phone rang.

"Yes, Tom."

DS Stevens' voice hissed and spat, reminding Rego that he was in a poor signal area.

"We've been able to negate criminality in the RTC, sir, so we've handed over to the Specialist Road Traffic Policing Unit; and Jan has found medication for heart pills at the unexplained death in Marazion."

"Good, thank you."

Rego went on to list everything he needed from his DS, including personnel for the team.

"PC Smith is going with the body and I'm taking PC Poldhu to debrief the witness. I'm hoping to get a post-mortem this afternoon, so I'll bring Tamsyn back to the station then."

He glanced across to find her watching him. Her focus was slightly unnerving.

Rego finished the call as the funeral director's van left the quay. A couple of locals were waiting beyond the cordon, but there was no press interest yet.

Rego went to speak to them – it was always a good idea to talk to the people who lived near the scene to find out if they'd seen or heard anything. These two men were both stooped and white-haired but looked alert.

"Good morning, I'm Detective Inspector Rego. Do you live here?"

"Yes, both of us. I'm Arthur Evans and this is Bill Gwavas." The elderly man pointed at a whitewashed cottage a few yards back from the harbour. "That's me, and Bill is next door but one."

Rego made a note.

"Is it true that a body has been washed up?"

"Yes, we have recovered a body. I can't say more than that at the moment. Have you seen or heard anything unusual over the last couple of days?"

They discussed it between themselves for a few moments before declaring that they couldn't think of anything relevant.

"Do you know anyone in the harbour area who has CCTV?"

They seemed to find that suggestion surprising, maybe even shocking, shaking their heads vigorously.

Rego handed them each a business card in case they thought of something else, then walked back to Tamsyn and Jamie.

"Tamsyn, if any of the locals ask you what's going on, you simply say, 'A body has been recovered, an investigation is under way, but it's too early to say anything else'. And that's it, nothing else except to take their names, addresses and phone numbers. All communications will be dealt with by the Force Press Office, and they'll allocate a trained officer to deal with all press enquiries at this stage. Okay?"

"Yes, sir.

As he walked up the steep path from the village, he waited for Tamsyn to speak. After half a minute of silence, he realised that she was too inexperienced to know that she could ask him questions.

"What are your thoughts so far, Tamsyn?"

She looked surprised, then appeared to compose herself.

"Do you think you'll be able to trace that tattoo, sir?"

"Possibly. We'd circulate it with the press release."

"It looked a bit like a fancy V with vines," said Tamsyn.

"Or maybe ... maybe a goat skull. Wait, could those be sort of like ... seahorses ... or birds?"

A memory pinged Rego's brain; one with frightening possibilities. Could it be? Was that possible, in sleepy Cornwall of all places? No, no. It couldn't be. *But what if it is?*

He didn't tell Tamsyn about his *Oh shit* moment. Instead, he kept his tone conversational.

"Maybe," was all he said.

Tamsyn seemed to be waiting for him to say more, but Rego's brain was cycling through a previous case that he'd been involved with. The tattoo could be a coincidence.

Except Rego didn't believe in them.

CHAPTER 4

"What was the name of the witness who found the body?"

Rego knew the answer, but he wanted to see if Tamsyn been taking accurate notes. She immediately flipped open her notebook.

"Mrs Polpenn, sir, of Kemyell Cottage."

"Another Pol-something," he commented.

Tamsyn nodded. "Yes, there's a lot of us: *'By Tre, Pol and Pen, shall ye know all Cornishmen'*."

"Sorry, what?"

She smiled. "Loads of place names and older Cornish surnames start with those: *tre* is farm or homestead, *pol* is pool or lake, and *pen* is headland or hill."

"So Penzance is..."

"Headland of the saints."

"Saints?"

"Yes, they all came over from Ireland in, like, the fifth century or something. We did them at school."

Rego took in this new information. He hadn't even known

that there was a Cornish language. Then something occurred to him.

"Your name is Poldhu – so what does the *dhu* part mean?"

"Dark or black," she answered.

He thought for a second then started laughing. "So, you're telling me your name means *Blackpool*?"

She rolled her eyes. "Like I've never heard that before." Then she remembered that she was speaking to a ranking officer. "Sorry, sir."

"You're fine," he smiled. "Kemyell Cottage – this is it. I'll just be having a general chat with Mrs Polpenn. It's good to get some details while it's all fresh in her mind. I'll ask her to come into the station to make a formal statement tomorrow. Your job is to listen, take notes, and make a brew for her if she wants one."

"Yes, sir."

He studied her serious expression, nodded once, then knocked on the door.

They heard a high pitched bark and the door opened abruptly. An older woman wearing jeans and holding a startled looking Chihuahua stared at them wide-eyed.

"Mrs Polpenn? I'm Detective Inspector Rego and this is Police Constable Poldhu."

He pulled out his Warrant Card and Tamsyn scrabbled for hers, too.

"Can we come in for a chat?" Rego asked politely.

"Yes, yes, of course. That poor woman! Oh my God, I can't tell you what a shock it was."

She led them into a small living room lined with books, looking out onto sweeping views of the cove below. She perched on the edge of the worn settee, still clutching the small dog.

Rego settled opposite Mrs Polpenn and raised his eyebrows at Tamsyn.

"Can I make you a cup of tea?" Tamsyn asked gently, stroking the dog who licked her hand appreciatively.

"Oh, yes, of course," said Mrs Polpenn shooting up again.

"It's okay, I can do it while you have a chat with the DI," Tamsyn said soothingly. "Kitchen through here?" and she disappeared from view.

While Rego took Mrs Polpenn through the basics: name, address, contact number, how long she'd lived in Lamorna, Tamsyn listened through the open door, finding mugs, milk, a teapot and sugar bowl. She hadn't been told if she was allowed a cup of tea, but she was thirsty. She decided that it if was the wrong thing to do, she'd soon find out.

She carried the tray back into the living room and started taking notes.

"I was sitting in the widow's watch," continued Mrs Polpenn.

Rego looked up.

"It's what we call a little nook by a cottage window," she said. "The wives of fishermen lost at sea would sit there staring at the cold, grey water that had claimed their husband or sons."

Rego blinked. "Right."

Mrs Polpenn smiled at Tamsyn.

"That's so sad, isn't it? Perhaps I should rename it my reading nook. Well, I thought I could see something but I didn't know what it was, so I called Henry..."

"Henry?"

Mrs Polpenn pointed at the Chihuahua.

"My dog, Henry. I named him after my late husband."

Rego merely nodded.

"I see ... so, you called Henry and then...?"

"We went for our usual walk ... and that's when we saw it ... the body."

She shivered and looked down.

Half an hour later, they hadn't learned anything new.

Mrs Polpenn walked the same path every morning with her dog Henry. She hadn't heard or seen anything unusual until she saw the body. She was high up enough to have a mobile signal and called 999.

She knew everyone who lived in the small village but admitted that at least a third of the cottages were holiday lets so strangers came and went all the time, although it tended to be quiet until Easter.

Rego gave her his card just in case she thought of anything else and asked her to come into the station to make a formal statement.

As he and Tamsyn walked back to his car, he checked that she'd made accurate notes, which she had. Probably too accurate – she'd all but counted the number of books in Mrs Polpenn's library and the number of teabags in her kitchen.

He nodded solemnly as she regurgitated everything she'd seen and heard. She'd soon learn what was important and what wasn't.

But then she surprised him.

"I don't think the body came from around here, sir," she said.

"Why's that?"

"She couldn't have jumped from any of these cliffs for at least a mile in each direction without hitting rock on the way down and she didn't look like ... well, I don't think she had so..."

"Go on."

"Mrs Polpenn said she hadn't been able to sleep the last couple of days and she always has her window open at night –

she'd have heard if anyone was using a motorboat. Sound carries up in coves like this at night. And anyway, we'd have found the boat."

"Maybe the victim sailed here and we'll come across the boat somewhere..."

Tamsyn shook her head. "It's a difficult cove to sail into, sir. You'd really have to know what you were doing, especially at night, and it wasn't good weather Friday and Saturday. Most yachts coming into the harbour would stow their sails and come in under engine power. I mean, yeah, she could have sailed and fallen overboard somewhere, but it doesn't seem likely because any boat adrift would have been seen by now."

Rego was intrigued and well aware this was out of his field of expertise.

"What about if she was rowing?"

"It's pretty tidal here, sir."

"Which means what?"

"It would be really hard work to row against a falling tide. And anyway, where would she have rowed from? Even the gigs with six people rowing, it wouldn't be easy. And no one has reported finding a rowing boat or anything else."

"So what does that tell you?"

Tamsyn glanced at him sideways as if to check whether or not he wasn't humouring her.

"I think the body has drifted from further out."

"Like?"

"I'm not sure but my Grandad would know – I mean, not *know*, but he knows the currents around here better than anyone. We could ask him. I mean, if you want ... if you think..."

Her words tailed off but Rego nodded.

"Right, let's talk to your Grandad."

Tamsyn's hesitancy vanished. "He'll probably be working on the *Daniel Day*, that's his punt." She saw Rego's confused expression. "I mean his crabber – it's what we call the boats under 20 foot."

"Call him and let him know we're coming."

She grimaced. "He doesn't usually have his phone turned on."

"No problem. We'll surprise him."

With the car windows open, Rego could smell Newlyn harbour before he saw it. The odour of fish was strong as Tamsyn pointed out a huge shed with a corrugated roof that housed the fish market and ice house.

The harbour was quiet, certainly not the hustle and bustle Rego had expected, especially as Tamsyn had told him that it was one of the largest fishing ports in the UK.

There were fishing boats of all shapes and sizes in varying stages of rust and decay, as well as half-a-dozen sleek looking yachts bobbing on the water – racehorses next to old nags. It was a world and community that Rego didn't know or understand. He'd better start learning fast.

"Not many people about," he commented.

"Most of us go out just before first light," said Tamsyn, and Rego didn't miss the way she included herself in that statement. "Lobsters, crab and grouper are nocturnal, and anyway, we fish on the neap tides, which is two weeks out of every month. The bigger boats can go out whenever they want, but when it's rougher, you could get your gear washed away. You land your catch two or three times a week and put them in the stow pots, then sell them at the market when the orders come in."

She pointed at a small, worn-looking fishing boat, some 15 feet in length, with peeling paint and no wheelhouse.

"That's the *Daniel Day*," she said, "but I can't see Grandad. We can go down the pontoon and see if he's there."

They walked back along the pier, the breeze whipping the water into whitecaps beyond the harbour wall. Rego followed Tamsyn who seemed completely at home. He looked around the near empty harbour, but as they reached the pontoon where the larger boats were tied up, he saw a heavyset man in yellow overalls and matching boots staring at them, his gaze not quite hostile.

"Do you know him?"

"Oh!" Tamsyn said, relief tinging her voice as she turned to look. "That's Uncle George. He'll know where Grandad is."

The man smiled as Tamsyn walked towards him but his eyes remained wary when he glanced at Rego.

"Look at you, Tammy. I can't believe it. You a copper," and he shook his head as he hugged her.

"I know! I only started today. Cool, isn't it?"

Rego cleared his throat. He hoped she didn't make a habit of hugging people when she was in uniform.

"Oh, sorry, sir. This is George Mason. Uncle George, this is Detective Inspector Rego."

"A DI? He's your boss then, is he?"

Tamsyn looked uncertain.

Rego reached out to shake the man's hand.

"Good to meet you."

"Hope you're looking after our Tammy," he said, his voice cautious.

"We're looking for Grandad," Tamsyn interrupted quickly. "Have you seen him?"

"Gone Pirates for new plugs."

Tamsyn translated for Rego's benefit.

"Pirates Cave is the chandlery across the way." She saw

the continuing look of incomprehension on his face. "Where you can buy spares and that for your craft, for your boat."

"What you wantin' Ozzie for?" Mason asked.

"You're a fisherman, as well?" Rego said, avoiding answering the question.

"Lobster and crab, in the season, mackerel, some squid jigging. There's good money in bass, 'specially if you can tag 'em line-caught and sell 'em London. So, them and whatever swims into *Mari-morgans'* nets rest o' the time: pilchards, herring, dabs maybe."

"Have you worked here long?"

Rego pulled out his notebook and George glanced at Tamsyn before he answered.

"My whole life, boy."

Rego's eyes narrowed at being called 'boy', but Tamsyn was his weathervane for talking to locals and she hadn't reacted. He decided to let it go. This time.

"So you're experienced in these waters?"

"None better," he said proudly, then cast an eye at Tamsyn again. "'Ceptin' maybe Ozzie."

She smiled.

"Perhaps you could answer a couple of questions?" Rego said. "If something washed up at Lamorna Cove, where might it have come from?"

"Depends."

"On what?"

"Weather, tides, if the wind's onshore or offshore, time o' year, if it was floating on the surface." He shrugged.

Rego was frustrated by his own lack of knowledge. At least Tamsyn hadn't blabbed out that they'd found a body.

"Heard you found a body," Mason said, raising his eyebrows.

"Who'd you hear that from, Uncle George?" Tamsyn asked, sounding surprised.

"Word gets around," he replied, and Tamsyn nodded as if that explained everything.

"Who told you?" Rego pressed.

George glanced at Rego then directed his answer to Tamsyn.

"Gyp told me just now. Heard it from Ky Polpenn, and he heard it from his Aunt Maddie."

"That's the woman we interviewed," Tamsyn said.

"Yes, I made the connection, thank you, Constable," Rego said, failing to mask his irritation.

Tamsyn fell silent.

"Okay, so a body washing up at Lamorna Cove – where might that have drifted from?"

"Hard to say."

Rego felt like he was wasting his time here and wondered if Tamsyn's grandfather might be more forthcoming. He let the silence sit, hoping Mason would fill it, but he didn't.

"What's your best guess?"

"Police into guessing now, are they?"

"Could it have come from the Scillies ferry?" Rego asked.

Tamsyn automatically shook her head but Mason nodded slowly.

"Could be."

"Do you think so, Uncle George?" Tamsyn asked, looking puzzled. "Wouldn't it have been swept up the north coast?"

"The prevailing wind is sou'-sou'-west," Mason replied, rubbing his chin.

Tamsyn shook her head, her eyes bright and her expression earnest. "Not last night. It was a northerly, and the two nights before sou'-sou'-east."

"Are you sure?" Rego said. "Because this is important PC Poldhu."

She met his gaze without flinching.

"That's what Grandad said and he knows these seas better than anyone."

Rego didn't want his investigation riding on the word of someone's grandfather and made a note to check it out.

Mason seemed annoyed.

"Don't you go asking Ozzie about it! Bring back bad memories it will."

Tamsyn looked as though she might argue so Rego stepped in.

"Okay, thank you for your time, Mr Mason. If you think of anything else, please contact me," and Rego handed the man a card, watching as he pocketed it reluctantly.

"Bye, Uncle George," Tamsyn said quietly.

"*Chons da*," and he walked away.

"Sorry about him," Tamsyn said sadly. "He doesn't like the police ... or any authorities very much."

"Because?"

She sighed.

"I don't really know. Maybe all the EU rules? All the post-Brexit cr— stuff. But people around here go on about those all the time anyway. Grandad said he's always been a bit ... and that when Aunty Marie left him, he just got more..."

Her words died away.

"Is his boat named after his ex-wife? I saw that he'd called it *Mari-morgans*?"

Tamsyn laughed nervously.

"Kind of..."

He kept looking at her until she continued. It was a useful technique when interviewing suspects – most people rushed to fill the silence. Not that Tamsyn was a suspect, but after 14 years as a copper, Rego did it automatically now. His wife hated when he did it to her – and she was quick to point it out.

"Uh well, the *mari-morgans* are from Cornish folktales. They're female water spirits and, um, they're known for drowning men."

Rego's eyebrows lifted.

"Not an amicable divorce then."

Tamsyn wrinkled her nose.

"Not so much."

He paused, then glanced at his notebook. "And 'squid jigging'? I'm almost afraid to ask."

She gave him a quick smile.

"It's how you catch squid, but it's really messy."

"Because...?"

"Squid and cuttlefish are really popular with customers in France and worth quite a lot of money – we call it 'black gold' – but when you catch them, they start squirting black ink all over the deck. So, it just gets messy. You have to hose down your deck after."

Rego was glad to have an interpreter.

"And what did he say to you just now?"

"*Chons da?* It means 'good luck' or 'see you later' – that kind of thing."

"Do you speak Cornish?"

"Only a few words – stuff that they taught us at school."

Rego paused.

"Why didn't he want you to talk to your grandfather?"

Tamsyn hesitated, twisting her lips to one side.

"Because of my dad. He drowned at sea. Uncle George was the one who found him. He was Dad's best friend, so he's never forgiven himself. Not that it was his fault. A rogue wave tipped the boat and Dad went over – got tangled in his nets."

She looked up at Rego. “Grandad doesn’t like to talk about it. No one does.”

“How old were you?”

“Ten.”

“Must have been rough.”

She nodded and looked away.

Rego decided to change the subject.

“Where does the Scillies ferry sail from?”

“Penzance,” Tamsyn replied. “About half a mile from the police station.”

“We’ll go there next. Let’s see if they’re missing any passengers.”

CHAPTER 5

After a quick catch up with DS Stevens, Rego learned that there were no hits on the missing persons database or on social media, which meant they needed that draft press release as soon as possible. Then he made a call to brief the Super and DCI Finch on all three incidents that the station had been dealing with. Finch agreed to the dedicated phone line and gave him the email address of the Press Office which was made up of a team of civilians with media training, if and when he needed them – which was looking more likely with every passing hour. Not ideal, but you did what you could.

Then Rego drove back to Penzance and the offices of the Isles of Scilly Steamship Company.

He learned that there was only one sailing a day, leaving at 9.45am and taking nearly three hours in good weather to reach St Mary's, the largest of the small group of islands which lay thirty miles off the Cornish coast. The ferry then arrived back at around seven in the evening.

The booking clerk paled at the suggestion that they might have lost a passenger, especially when she admitted that although tickets were checked on embarkation, no one counted off the passengers at the other end. In other words, it was entirely possible that someone could have jumped or fallen overboard without anyone knowing.

Rego wasn't completely surprised by this information, but it didn't help him.

"Well, if you could send over CCTV of embarkation for the last 72 hours and of people leaving the ship," he said, handing over a business card with his information.

Then the Coroner's officer called, informing Rego that the pathologist had arranged the post-mortem for 3pm. Rego dropped Tamsyn at the police station and headed back up the A30 to Truro, the administrative seat for Cornwall.

Tamsyn watched him leave, raising her arm to wave goodbye but realising just in time that would be more than a little weird and a lot inappropriate. Gran had once told her that she had the eager-to-please personality of a Golden Retriever – although she wasn't sure that it had been meant as a compliment. She knew that she tended to be a people-pleaser, and she knew that she had to toughen up. But being known as 'the kid with the dead dad' had made her different, so she'd tried hard to fit in, especially at school. It had never quite worked.

She groaned when she realised that DI Rego had driven off with her gym bag containing her civilian clothes and a stack of sandwiches that her grandmother had insisted on packing her for lunch. She'd felt too nervous to eat breakfast, but now she was really hungry.

It had been an interesting morning to say the least, and her brain was buzzing with new information and ideas. Seeing the body had been a strange experience – somehow shocking but unreal, too. Over the years, she'd seen a lot of dead seals and dolphins that had been washed up, once even the carcass of a cow that had fallen off a cliff, but the body today had seemed so ... not human. It was as if her mind refused to admit that a walking, talking, thinking, feeling being had become *that*.

Her stomach rumbled, reminding her again that her sandwiches were on their way to Truro. Sighing, she made her away to the station's staff entrance and let herself in. She found an empty desk and typed up her notes with an account of what had happened and what she'd done. During training, she'd been surprised by how detailed these had to be, even things like having the right equipment, how you dealt with members of the public, considerations you used when taking a statement.

As a student officer, Tamsyn had to complete a long list of competencies – this report was just the start. Her tutor would then put his own comments on it, send it back to Tamsyn, and only then it would be sent to the training team. Tamsyn would face three years as a probationer while she completed her degree, and during that time she had to experience the full range of duties and responsibilities that an officer would come across. She'd be expected to work with different units such as Response, Neighbourhood Policing and Investigations, Crime, and Public Protection.

When she was finally finished, she wasn't sure what to do next so was glad when she saw Jamie walking up to her.

"Hi, Tamsyn! How'd it go?"

"Yeah, it was good, thanks. I mean ... not *good*, but interesting."

"Don't worry, I know what you mean. We'll be handing over to the late shift shortly and we always debrief so everyone is up to speed on who's been doing what. Have you written up your candidate's report?"

"Yes, I hope I've got it right."

"Good, next important thing – the kitchen is this way,"

and he led her upstairs to a small, cluttered area, with surfaces covered with used mugs.

"Each shift has our own kitty, and the coffee, tea and sugar is locked away. A- and C-teams are the worst – bunch of thieving toe rags," he said cheerfully. "Milk is kept in the fridge, so that's a free for all." He grinned at her. "The biggest squabbles are different shifts nicking each other's milk ... or someone leaving milk that's gone off and you accidentally pour it into your coffee."

Tamsyn smiled. "I'll remember to do the sniff test."

"Or drink it black," he suggested, pulling a face.

The cup of tea that she'd had at Mrs Polpenn's had been a godsend, but Tamsyn was hungry. Coffee would help. Sort of.

Mug in hand, Jamie led her to the conference room and introduced her to Sergeant Carter who'd been dealing with the RTC before Tamsyn had come on duty.

"Good to meet you, Tamsyn," he said. "I hear you were swept up by the new DI. First unexplained death – something for the response and investigations part of your portfolio."

The sergeant checked that each officer was accounted for, then introduced her to the rest of E-team and the other student officer, a massively built former Royal Marine called Jason.

"Your tutor, Sergeant Terwillis, will be back tomorrow, so, Tamsyn and Jason, he'll tell who you're double-crewing with. And I believe you'll get to meet our boss, Inspector Maura Walters, too."

Tamsyn knew that she couldn't expect to work on the DI's investigation but it was important and she'd felt like she'd been useful.

Sergeant Carter carried on with debriefing the other six officers, and Tamsyn heard that the RTC had been handed over to Traffic at Camborne when criminality had been negated.

As she listened to the other officers who'd dealt with two domestics, one attempted shop-lifting, theft of a caravan, criminal damage, one drug overdose and one homeless woman with mental health issues who was probably going to be Sectioned, she studied the men who were now her teammates, her backup. She was disappointed that there weren't any other women on E-team, although she knew there were seven others based in Penzance and she'd meet them eventually.

Jamie reported on the body at Lamorna Cove then Sergeant Carter turned to Tamsyn.

"Okay, Tamsyn, let's hear your debrief."

Flushed and feeling sweaty to be the focus of everyone's attention, Tamsyn reported back on the interviews with Mrs Polpenn and the office manager at the *Scillonian.*

She felt as if she'd babbled and stammered her way through it, but Sergeant Carter nodded and gave a small smile when she'd finished. Then he handed over to B-team and dismissed them.

"Pretty good first shift," Jamie said to her. "You okay?"

"Yeah, I'm fine," she said, yawning widely. "I'm really tired though. Hey, I didn't get around to finding the women's locker room this morning, can you tell me where it is?"

They both looked up as Chloe walked into the room.

"Great timing," Jamie smiled. "Chloe can show you."

"Show her what?" Chloe asked, her dark eyes flicking to Tamsyn.

"Where the women's locker room is."

Chloe smirked.

"I don't think being a detective is in your future if you can't even find the locker room."

Jamie laughed but Tamsyn was tired and irritated enough to snap back sarcastically.

"It's great being part of a team. Thanks for the warm welcome, Chloe."

As she walked out of the room, she heard Chloe say, "That girl is such a bitch," but missed Jamie's reply.

"Takes one to know one."

Tamsyn was annoyed with Chloe, but mostly with herself for letting the skank get to her.

"Hey, are you okay?"

A woman a few years older than Tamsyn was looking at her with a concerned expression.

"Oh, yeah, just..."

Tamsyn shook her head and the woman smiled sympathetically.

"Some days, yeah? I'm Jasmine Flowers, but they call me 'Rosie'. I'm on C-team but I had to come in early today. I guess you must be one of the new student officers."

"Yes! I'm Tam ... Tamsyn Poldhu. It's nice to meet you."

"Welcome to the team. Do you have a locker yet, Tam?"

Tamsyn shook her head.

"No problem, I'll take you. Anyway, someone should have shown you how to store your incapacitant spray safely. Where have you left your civvies?"

Tamsyn groaned. "I left them..." *in the boot of the DI's car* "in a patrol car."

She wasn't sure why she'd altered what she'd been about to say, but leaving your clothes in the boss's car sounded a bit suspect. Make that *a lot* suspect.

Rosie laughed, none the wiser.

"Easily done. Don't worry, they'll turn up. Maybe keep a spare set in your locker anyway. So, tell me about your first day..."

It took Rego some time to find his way across the sprawling hospital site at Truro to the mortuary where the post-mortem was to take place.

Dr Blake was the Home Office pathologist, an austere man with the appearance of an undertaker. The mortuary assistant was a heavy-set older woman with a strong Filipino accent who introduced herself simply as Lana.

Dr Blake handed Rego an apron, mask and gloves, then asked him to stand to one side while he switched on a video camera, beginning the painstaking work with an external exam.

"This is the body of an adult female, slightly undernourished, found in seawater at 6.35am, 26th March. She is 159cm in height and current body weight is 49kg. X-rays show signs of historic breaks in both arms, but nothing recent. We have also taken dental images for identification purposes." He paused and leaned in closer. "A visual exam of the anterior shows no evidence of knife wounds, bullet wounds, or puncture marks. Some predation of the soft tissue," and he glanced up at Rego. "Probably crabs and lobster."

"So I've been told," Rego said drily as he made notes in his day book.

"Peck marks from seagulls – possibly where the *bulbus oculi* have gone. Tearing around the eye sockets consistent with beak marks." He flexed one of the body's arms. "No signs of *rigor*."

"Can you tell her race?"

"Hmm. I'd guess white, but the pale colour could be the result of skin sloughing due to immersion in salt water. The skin's outer layer, the epidermis, that's where human pigmentation is contained." He turned to the mortuary assistant. "Can you help me turn the body please, Lana?"

Rego had never got used to the cold weight of a dead body, and watching as the woman's torso was turned face down was deeply unsettling.

"Posterior shows no outward wounds but mottling in the buttocks and shoulder blades is from *livor mortis*, suggesting she died lying down."

"On a hard surface?" Rego asked, surprise in his voice.

"Potentially," the pathologist said, without looking up. "These marks are interesting – the victim wasn't lying on something completely flat ... it looks like," he paused, "something slatted? A bench or a large crate, perhaps."

"Can you estimate the time of death?"

"I can *estimate*," Dr Blake said mildly. "There are three pathways to death, Inspector: putrefaction, mummification, and saponification which requires a cool setting and poorly oxygenated water. All three can occur separately or in combination." He still hadn't looked up from his work. "However, determining the post-mortem submerged interval is challenging. I will examine the decomposition stage of several areas of the body, but..." and he glanced up at Rego over his mask, "I have to consider water salinity, depth, tides and sea temperature, but..."

"But?" Rego encouraged.

"I'd say that this unfortunate woman has been dead between 36 and 72 hours." He acknowledged Rego's frustration. "I'll try to narrow that down for you but since she's been in cold water, time of death is more difficult to determine."

"Of course," Rego said tiredly.

"I do have something for you, Inspector," Dr Blake said, peering up at him over him mask. "Friction ridges on the victim's fingers are still evident so we should be able to get you some fingerprints. One moment..."

Rego had been to many, many post-mortems – it was a rite of passage for new officers to ensure that they could still function while seeing a dead body being autopsied – but even he had to look away when the skin on the victim's hand was removed and the mortician's assistant slipped her hand inside the discarded skin, wearing it like a glove.

"Voila!" said Dr Blake, very pleased with himself. "I'll have those fingerprints for you in a jiffy."

Rego swallowed. "Thank you."

Dr Blake continued his grisly work.

"Is there any bruising, doctor?" Rego asked.

"Hmm, yes. See here?"

Dr Blake pointed at some faint, finger-shaped bruises around the jaw line. The hairs on the back of Rego's neck stood up.

"Could those have occurred after death?"

Dr Blake shook his head.

"Bruises are a physiological process of trauma affecting the living body and cannot occur after death. Darker areas of haemorrhagic fluids that accumulate beneath the skin after death due to gravity are not bruises. Of course, I'll check."

"Any sign of sexual assault?"

"No bruising or tearing that I can see at present, but early days yet."

Dr Blake photographed the tattoo, before cutting it out to preserve so forensic scientists could use enhancing techniques to get a clearer image.

Rego's phone rang so he stepped away to take the call. DS Stevens reported that nothing had shown up on the miss-pers database, and a trawl of social media hadn't turned up any descriptions matching the dead woman. A draft press release had been emailed to him with a dedicated phone number for the public, but it still needed information of height, weight, hair colour and the tattoo.

Rego thanked him then glanced down at his notes as he spoke to the pathologist.

"No wounds, no breaks, no underlying health issues that you've been able to determine so far. No signs of sexual assault, and we're not even sure she drowned." Rego let out a long, frustrated breath. "No evidence of how she died."

"Oh, I wouldn't say that."

Rego glanced up as Dr Blake stood up straight, his expression above the mask tight.

"I'd say she bled to death and her body was later thrown in the sea."

The air in the room seemed unbearably still.

"I thought you said there were no knife wounds?"

"No surface ones."

"Then?"

The pathologist met his gaze.

"I'm halting this *post-mortem*."

"What? Why?"

"There is evidence of sharp force injury: her tongue was cut out."

CHAPTER 6

Rego felt a jolt of electricity rush through him. The atmosphere in the room had become charged, tense, and he felt a renewed sense of urgency. This wasn't suicide or an accidental death, this was murder. And although he was almost certain that he recognised the victim's tattoo as gang-related, he was determined to keep an open mind. But cutting out the tongue – someone was sending a chilling message.

It also meant that his budget was shot. The basic £2,000 post-mortem was now going to increase to £6,000 for a forensic post-mortem. And there was another problem: DCI Finch informed him that only three doctors in the whole of Cornwall could perform a forensic post-mortem.

Fuming at the delay, Rego worked from his laptop as a new pathologist was sought urgently.

He commandeered a table in the hospital's staff break room and ran through the actions that needed to take place.

He needed to inform the Major Crime Incident Team at Camborne and get them up to speed; then Interpol, and Border Force who checked passenger lists at Newquay airport and for the ferries; he wanted a drone at the scene where the body was first spotted to see if they could find an entry point for the body, although dumping at sea seemed more likely. He also needed information on the weather conditions, sea temperature and currents for the probable hours that the body had been in the water. He wanted to check one final time whether missing persons reports had thrown up any possible matches, and as a priority, the victim's fingerprints had to be actioned.

But before he could do any of these things, he needed to get his team in place.

He updated DCI Finch who told him that the Force Intelligence Bureau had assigned the case name 'Operation Volt'.

"Sir, I'll need a good analyst for all the data we'll be pulling on this one. Who usually does this at Penzance?"

"Tom Stevens has done the course, but he usually brings in DC Eagling from Camborne. She's very experienced, I'd use her."

Along with a detective's gut feeling, a good analyst could make or break a case: reading and collating statements, as well as other intelligence such as telephone billing, then assessing the questions that needed to be answered and running the data through sophisticated software programs.

She'd need to differentiate between single strand intelligence, their source and their credibility: had it been corroborated; was it intel that wasn't in dispute? She'd need to follow the national intelligence model, known as 5 x 5 x 5 which scored the credibility of the intel – and on the same basis, who would have access to it.

She'd need to pull together all the strands and disseminate it appropriately. And they'd need to feed in information from CrimeStoppers and Neighbourhood Watch programmes – you never knew where intelligence was going to come from.

Analysts would produce a sort of Venn diagram linking overlapping areas of intelligence. The charts were documentary exhibits, and could be challenged by the defence.

He hoped DC Eagling was as good as his boss said.

Rego was stunned when Finch further informed him that MCIT at Camborne were too busy to take the case and that DC Eagling would also have to be the Exhibits Officer, oh, and that Rego would be heading up the investigation.

Since when was MCIT too busy to take on a murder case like this? Then he reminded himself that he hadn't shared his other suspicions with anyone yet.

Irritated with himself, he called the Penzance station so that they could make space in the HOLMES room. He smiled grimly to himself – the police loved their acronyms. Home Office Large Major Enquiry System described the rooms which contained a complete computer system to manage all major incidents.

A woman having her tongue cut out and body dumped at sea definitely fell into that category ... even without Rego's additional concerns.

And he needed to order a fob key that worked.

Rego also hoped that forensics would be able to clean up the image of the tattoo – he had his own theory about that and had forwarded the blurry image to a friend at the National Crime Agency.

His phone beeped with a text to let him know the forensic pathologist had arrived. Anxious to be at the start of the new post-mortem, he strode down the corridor, frowning as his phone rang again.

"Rob! I thought you'd gone to Devon to enjoy a quiet life and clotted cream sandwiches."

Rego gave a sharp laugh as he listened to his friend's familiar Brummie accent.

"Not so far, and I'm in Cornwall. I wouldn't mind a clotted cream tea." *But I've definitely been put off seafood for life.* "A woman's body was found floating near Penzance this morning. First thought was a suicide but her tongue has been cut out. I'm on my way to the forensic post-mortem now. The pathologist says *livor mortis* indicates that the body was lying on its back for eight to twelve hours – possibly more – before being dumped at sea. The tattoo I sent you was on her right ankle." He took a deep breath. "The image is pretty blurry. I just want to know if ... if you see what I see," he said cryptically.

"I'm opening your email now."

There was a long period of silence and all Rego could hear was the rushing of blood in his head.

Finally, Vikram's voice came back on the line.

"It'll need to be cleaned up, but yeah," he paused. "It looks like a double-headed eagle on two pistol butts: the Hellbanianz."

Rego grimaced and unconsciously walked faster.

He'd come across the Hellbanianz on one of his last cases in Manchester. They were a gang of street dogs, dealers and enforcers affiliated to Albanian organised crime. Their logo was the double-headed eagle of the Albanian flag but shaped into the handles of back-to-back revolvers.

More usually found in London over the last twenty years, the Hellbanianz had recently begun expanding their territory. Rego wasn't a sailor and he had no idea how far the woman's body might have travelled while it was floating around the coastline, but it definitely hadn't come from East London, Manchester, or Liverpool – three Hellbanianz strongholds.

This was one time where he really didn't want to be right.

He'd held onto a faint hope that Vikram would tell him he was seeing things that weren't there. But now he'd had his worst fears confirmed.

"I was afraid you'd say that," Rego said tightly. "What the hell is an Albanian gang tattoo doing in Cornwall?"

"I don't think they're there to build sandcastles," Vikram said.

"Can you run dentals against any known miss-pers or affiliates?" He paused. "Or informants."

"On it," Vikram said. "I'll put the word out with our International Liaison Officers on the Far Europe Desk and let you know if we get any hits."

"Thanks, Vik."

"Watch your back, Rob."

It was good advice. People who crossed the Hellbanianz didn't usually live to talk. Rego wondered how the dead woman had been involved. Could she have been an informant? If she was registered, he'd soon know.

Back at the pathology suite, he was introduced to Dr Manners, a straight-talking woman with iron-grey hair and a ramrod posture. She went to work straightaway.

She conferred with Dr Blake, then began the Y-incision through the chest, removing, inspecting and weighing the organs.

"The stomach is empty except for gastric juice. I'd say she hadn't eaten for the last 12 hours of her life. I can't smell any alcohol, but I'll do a blood analysis, of course. Hmm, that's interesting."

She paused. Rego was standing far enough back that he couldn't be sure what the pathologist was looking at.

"What is?"

"There's no water in the lungs but there is some blood. Quite a lot of blood."

"Which means?"

"Not sure yet, but it's unusual. I'll send bone marrow for analysis."

She went on to examine the key blood vessels and nerves, then with a deft U-shaped incision from ear to ear, removed the scalp to search for blood or bruising, then checked the outer surface of the skull for nicks or fractures

Using a handheld surgical saw, she cut out a section of bone from the skull and removed it with an odd sucking sound. Rego looked away.

"No signs of epidural haematoma or subdural haematoma."

Rego interpreted that as no sign of blunt force trauma or that the brain had been rattled around inside the skull following a car crash, explosion, or anything with similar G-forces.

Once the brain had been extracted and preserved, Dr Manners pulled off her gloves.

"Her tongue was removed using a sharp instrument with a short blade – possibly a retractable Stanley knife, box cutter or utility knife." She paused. "And the victim inhaled so much of her own blood that she effectively drowned in it."

CHAPTER 7

As she walked home, Tamsyn fumed. She was annoyed that she'd let Chloe get to her and she was irritated with herself. Now they had to work together, and she hated to think what lies Chloe might be spreading. There was no point trying to get on Chloe's good side because she didn't have one.

Tamsyn hadn't seen her since she'd left school and it had been an unpleasant surprise to learn than the enmity was still there. But why? Was she jealous? Was it because a warranted Police Officer was higher in the pecking order than a civilian investigator? Even a newbie officer?

Whatever the reason, it boiled down to one point:

"Born a bitch and just grew bigger," Tamsyn muttered to herself.

All the same, it worried her. She needed to get along with the other officers. She needed to know that they had her back, and they needed to know that they could trust her the same way. She hoped Chloe would go back to the Camborne station sooner rather than later. Maybe she should try to talk to her – dealing with conflict resolution was a big part of the job.

Am I over-reacting? Am I being a wimp? Then she remembered how the Inspector had stood up for her, how he'd shut Chloe down quickly. Unfortunately, Tamsyn didn't have that sort of seniority, but his no nonsense approach was one she needed to emulate.

And there had been one other good part to the day – meeting Rosie Flowers. Tamsyn wished that she was on her team. Maybe she'd get to work with her at some point.

As she approached home, she was hyper aware of still being in her uniform. She glanced around her, wondering if anyone she knew had recognised her, and how long it would be before all the neighbours knew that she'd joined the force. One of her trainers had told recruits to keep it low key. In his strong Scouse accent, he'd explained:

"Not everyone likes the bizzies, but you also don't want neighbours knocking on your door on your day off to tell you about Mrs Jones down the road who's ignoring the hosepipe ban, or Mr Brown's grandson who always drives his souped-up Skoda at the speed of sound."

She'd taken the advice to heart and slipped through the front door like a thief.

Despite the early start and busy day, Tamsyn was still fizzing with excitement after her first shift as a police officer, but off balance, too. Someone had died, a woman, a young woman, and it must be wrong to feel so ... so alive. She was disappointed that the cottage was empty when she got home. Not even little Mo was there to greet her. She didn't know what to do with the energy firing through her body and the storm of emotions brewing inside her.

As she listened to the emptiness of the cottage, Tamsyn realised that she'd forgotten to turn on her personal phone and saw that she'd missed two calls from Jess. She made herself move, walk into the kitchen, make a cup of tea and phoned her back.

"Hey wench! I've been waiting to hear from you. So, how was it?" Jess asked sounding hyper the way she always did. "Did you arrest anyone? Were you nervous? Excited? Bricking it?"

"No, yes, yes and hell yes," Tamsyn laughed and pulled a face, a little surprised to hear that her own voice hadn't changed. "I was a bit nervous, but I just wanted to get started, you know? I feel like I've been waiting for this for so long."

"I bet you were amazing," Jess said encouragingly. "But I get it. I feel the same – I want to start my life, get my career going. Wait a sec," and the sound became muffled for a few seconds as Jess switched to a video call.

Tamsyn could see unfamiliar floral wallpaper in the background.

"I've only got a couple of minutes because I'm showing this house to clients in a few minutes. Ugly wallpaper, right? I know what I wanted to ask you: what are you going to do if you have arrest someone we know?"

"Oh, God! Don't even joke about it! That would be a nightmare!"

"Would you arrest me?" Jess grinned at her.

"Only if you start dating the bartender with the dodgy tache in Mangos who fancies you."

Jess laughed.

"So, how'd it go today?"

I saw a dead body.

"Pretty intense, but good, really good. I met the station's new DI and ended up going out to Lamorna with him."

"What was at Lamorna?"

Tamsyn paused then lowered her voice, not because

anyone was listening but because she felt she should. It felt respectful.

"A body had been washed up there."

Jess shrieked, and Tamsyn had to hold the phone away from her ear.

"Oh my God, seriously? A dead body? Like, really dead?"

"Yep, very dead."

Jess pulled a face. "Oh that's gross! Did you have to touch it?"

"No, it was just ... sad. I just kept thinking that she was someone's sister or daughter..."

"It was a woman?"

"Yeah, but I'm not really allowed to say anything else so you'd probably better not tell anyone. Actually, I'm not sure I'm supposed to tell you..."

Tamsyn's voice trailed off and she frowned.

"Yeah, you'd have to arrest yourself, and that would be bad," Jess laughed, unfazed.

"Seriously, Jess, you can't tell anyone what I said."

"Yeah, alright, keep your hair on," she said, sounding miffed. "I won't say anything. So, what were the other officers like? Any hotties?"

Tamsyn relaxed, back on more familiar ground. Ready to be *that* Tamsyn again, the one who joked with her bestie about guys and dates and which clubs to avoid in Falmouth.

"I guess, a few," Tamsyn admitted. "There's this ex-Royal Marine who's totally built. He's about eight or nine years older than us, but he's just started today, too. I didn't really get a chance to talk to him though."

Jess blew a raspberry at the screen.

"That's rubbish! I'd have been all over that!"

Tamsyn laughed. "I know you would. But I don't think it's a good idea for me to date anyone at work."

"You don't have to *date* them – just have some fun, surf and turf," Jess snorted. "Oh shit, I gotta go – my new clients have arrived. I'll talk to you later. Love ya!"

"Okay, later! Sell some houses."

But Jess had already ended the call and Tamsyn was left holding her silent phone, feeling oddly empty. She tried to shake off the feeling of unease, but it clung to her like a sea fog that rolls in on a hot summer day.

Jess worked for her parents who had an estate agent business in Porthleven. She didn't have to worry about working her way up the food chain of promotion because one day, she'd own it and be the boss.

Tamsyn was a little envious of Jess's certainty, of knowing her place in the world. Because although Tamsyn loved going fishing with her grandfather, they'd both known for a while that she wouldn't be joining the generations of Poldhus who'd spent their lives at sea.

Instead, she'd worked in hospitality for two years and as a lifeguard in the summer months, until her application to join the police had been accepted. She'd wanted it for a long time but had never felt that they'd take someone like her until she'd been to the Royal Cornwall Show and talked to a recruitment officer. He'd persuaded her that a trained lifeguard had a lot to offer the force. He'd even suggested that working in a pub was useful training. She'd certainly learned how to deal with drunks and shut down any attempts by them to hit on her.

Tamsyn settled in a chair with her mug of tea and read a few pages from one of her textbooks, but traffic regulations couldn't hold her attention. She kept seeing the dead woman's body, naked and vulnerable, but no longer animated, no longer a person – just an empty shell. Feeling unsettled, tired and wired at the same time, she decided to go for a run.

As she pulled on shorts and a t-shirt, her thoughts

returned again and again to the body on the beach. Who was she? Where had she come from? Was anyone missing her?

When she checked the *Cornwall Live* website on her phone, she saw that a press release had been issued with the basic details: a woman's body had been found near Lamorna Cove that morning; a request for information, and a Freephone number. Maybe that was enough. Maybe by the time she started her next shift, they'd have the answers.

And at least she didn't have to worry about Jess telling anyone now. Tamsyn knew that she couldn't run her mouth like that again, but it would be weird not being able to tell Jess about her days.

She knotted the laces on her trainers tightly, warmed up with a few stretches, then headed out, following the footpath upwards, past Trezelah Farm to the narrow granite spine that separated the north and south coasts, then looped around the ancient settlement of Chysauster.

She paused to take in the sweeping views and wipe the sweat from her eyes, wondering what challenges the officers on the late shift were facing, feeling a deep sense of pride that she was one of them now.

The sun was lower in the sky and Tamsyn turned back for home, loping downhill, following the stream.

Before, she'd run because she'd enjoyed athletics at school and was good at it; during her A-Levels she'd run to de-stress.

Now, she ran with a purpose: who knew when she might need to chase someone on foot, or maybe even – and she scared herself with the thought – one day she might need to out-run a psycho, one day she might need to run for her life. Sweat trickled down her back and she forced herself to run faster.

As she approached the village, she slowed to a jog, letting several cars pass her as she navigated the narrow lanes lacking pavements. Cornish hedges lining the fields and winding roads weren't vegetation but built from granite, and you could easily be smeared against one by vehicles going too fast.

She was nearly home and still deep in thought when she saw a guy waving at her from a beaten up old Mini. She leaned down to see if he needed directions.

"Tamsyn? Tam, is that you?"

She ran through a few possibilities but came up blank.

"It's Ollie! Ollie Garrett – I was at school with you."

The name rang a vague bell but she was having trouble pulling a face out of the mists of time. She smiled anyway.

"Hi! How are you?"

"Good," he nodded. "I always said I'd come back to Cornwall." He scanned her face for any understanding. "You know, after my parents divorced, I had to go upcountry with my mum."

A fleeting memory came back to her but it was slippery and insubstantial, so she just smiled again.

"It's good to see you, Tam. You look amazing. I didn't know you ran," and his eyes travelled down her long, tanned legs.

She shrugged. "Sometimes."

He glanced over his shoulder at his friends who were making kissy noises as if they were twelve, not twenty.

"Look, um, I'd really like to see you again. What are you doing tonight? Don't say no, yeah? Let me buy you a drink at least – old friends and that."

The weight of the day felt very heavy and Tamsyn thought doing something fun might be a good idea.

"Okay," she said, trying to sound more certain than she felt.

"Great!" he said delightedly. "Meet you in the Coldstreamer at nine."

"But..."

He was already accelerating away, the Mini belching smoke.

"Shit," she sighed.

That was pretty late for someone who needed to be up at 5.30am.

By the time she reached home, lights glowed in the windows of the old fisherman's cottage. She felt a soft swell of affection, of love, for her eccentric grandmother and often cantankerous grandfather.

The cottage had been her home for more than half her life and carried more than two centuries of history within its thick stone walls.

She opened the door quietly, glancing into the tiny living room where a fire crackled in the grate, sparks floating up the chimney. Tamsyn smiled as her grandfather's loud snores disturbed the small, hairy dog at his feet who grumbled and opened one eye, then raced into the hall when she heard Tamsyn.

"Hello, Mo," she said, scooping up the little dog into her arms and nuzzling the warm fur.

"Is that you, angel?" called her grandmother, appearing from the kitchen.

Her grandfather snorted and opened his eyes, looking annoyed at being caught napping.

"How'd your first day go? Was it all filing and making the tea?" her grandmother asked hopefully.

"Gran, it's the twenty-first century."

Her grandmother shook her head. "I can't believe you're old enough to be a police officer. It doesn't seem possible."

Tamsyn smiled but she'd always felt older than her years – her grandmother called her 'an old soul'. She sagged into a chair, Mo on her lap.

"It was really busy at work – there'd been a bad traffic accident on the A30, so it was all a bit hectic."

"At Crowlas? I heard about that on the radio. Is that what you were doing?"

"Um, not really. There's this missing person's case," she paused, uncertain how much she could or should say. "I was just kind of helping out," she finished lamely, but her grandparents looked relieved.

It wasn't that they didn't support her career choice, they just worried about her.

"You be careful out there," her grandmother said softly.

"I will. Promise."

A silent acknowledgement passed between them, then Tamsyn rose to her feet, yawning and stretching, and the small dog jumped down, her hopeful hazel eyes fringed by comically shaggy eyebrows.

"I'm going to take a shower."

"Alright, angel. I've made a fish pie for tea."

"Thanks, Gran!"

Tamsyn walked up the steep, narrow staircase to her bedroom, followed by Mo, who still looked like she was hoping for a walk, sighing when Tamsyn headed to the shower instead.

Leaving her hair wet, she ate supper with her family, then her grandfather headed to bed for an early night. He'd be up before dawn, then driving to Newlyn to hail his crab and lobster pots.

She'd just finished blow-drying her hair when her phone rang, and she accepted Jess's video chat immediately.

"Hey, Tam! I read *Cornwall Live* online about that woman's body you found. I was dying to tell everyone that my friend was there. It nearly killed me to be discreet. Is that Morwenna on your bed?"

Jess's voice and personality filled Tamsyn's small room.

Tamsyn turned the phone to Mo, happy not to talk about the dead body, and the little dog pressed her nose to the screen.

"Hi, Morwenna! You're just a little cutie-pie, aren't you?" and Jess made cooing noises that had little Mo wagging her tail and trying to lick Tamsyn's phone.

"Ugh, she's slimed the screen," said Tamsyn, wiping the phone on her towel.

"Just as long as it's not you licking your phone because that would be weird," Jess snorted, peeling off one of her false eyelashes.

"I didn't ask what you guys did last night."

"Not much. Went to the Reef bar at Praa Sands. Everyone says hi." Jess paused, and Tamsyn sensed the unspoken words behind the casual tone.

"They still think it's weird, don't they?"

"No, it's not that..." Jess didn't sound convincing.

"I've joined the police, not a cult."

"Same thing," Jess laughed, although not entirely joking. "You should stick to arresting criminals because you murdered that joke."

"Really?" Tamsyn said, rolling her eyes. "You've been waiting to say that, haven't you?"

"Maybe," Jess admitted with an innocent look. "Whatever. So, show me your uniform, PC Poldhu."

Tamsyn grabbed her helmet and put it on her head at a jaunty angle.

"Very impressive – goes with your towel," said Jess.

"I know, right?" Tamsyn laughed.

"But ... you're okay?" Jess asked, her expression worried. "I mean, after finding a body and everything?"

How could she answer that? *Yes, I'm fine; everyone dies. No, I'm sad; everyone dies.*

She tried to find a middle ground, tried to find the words to explain to her oldest friend how she was feeling.

"Yes ... I'm really okay. It's hard to explain, but I feel like I was helping. I mean, being part of a team that's going to find out who she is and what happened to her ... like I'm doing something that matters, you know?"

"Unlike selling houses?" Jess said sharply.

Tamsyn was surprised at her tone.

"No! You know I don't mean it like that," Tamsyn replied quickly, frowning at Jess's outburst. "I think it's great that you get to be at the start of people's lives: new house for a new baby, or getting married, or a new job..."

"Or a new divorce," Jess added with a wry smile. "Don't forget that."

Tamsyn felt forgiven, smiled and raised an eyebrow, then remembered that she had some other news for Jess.

"Oh God, I forgot to tell you earlier – guess who works at my police station? Chloe Rogers!"

"No! That biznach?"

"I couldn't believe it when I saw her."

"Frickin' luck!"

"I know. She hasn't changed. She's a civilian investigator from Camborne."

"A civilian investigator? I didn't know there were any."

"Yeah, there's quite a few. I hope she goes back sooner rather than later or I might have to arrest myself for assault."

The old intimacy was back and they talked for a while longer until Tamsyn glanced at the time and saw she'd have to hurry or risk being late for her date. Truthfully, she'd rather have just gone to bed. If she'd had Ollie's phone number, she'd have cancelled, but she couldn't bring herself to just stand him up.

Jess suddenly noticed that Tamsyn had blow-dried her hair.

"Hey, you're looking foxy-doxie. Are you going out?"

"Uh yep. I got talked into a date tonight."

"What the hell? When did you have time to get asked on a date? I thought you'd been out ridding the world of crime and when I talked to you this afternoon, you didn't mention anything. How the hell did you get a date since then? Who is he? Is he hot?"

Tamsyn laughed. "Well ... he's someone we went to school with: Ollie Garrett. Do you remember him?"

"Maybe? The name rings a bell but I can't picture him." She gave a short laugh. "Anyway, it's not worth my while remembering his name because you never give any guy a chance."

"Shut up!" Tamsyn laughed. "I'm not that bad."

"Remember Harry in Year 10?"

Tamsyn cringed. "Yeah, alright, I'll admit that one."

"You said he had bad breath and a tongue like an eel."

"It was true!"

"It was ten minutes into your first date."

"My point exactly."

"We were fifteen – no guy knows how to kiss at that age," Jess pointed out.

"Don't remind me!"

"And what about all the cute surfer dudes you met when you were doing bar work?"

"What about them?"

"You never gave any of them a chance."

"Maybe because they'd hit on me Monday to Friday, then come in with their girlfriends on the weekends."

"Not all of them!" Jess objected, but Tamsyn shook her head.

"Anyway, I'm about to prove you wrong because I'm meeting Ollie at the Coldstreamer in a few minutes. You want to come along and be my wingwoman?"

"Can't. Got a thing with the oldies, but I'll call you tomorrow for a full report. I've gotta run! Have fun – don't do anything I wouldn't do," and she ended the call.

Sighing, Tamsyn pulled on skinny jeans and her favourite long-sleeved Roxy Surf t-shirt, then did a five-minute makeup routine. She wasn't *that* excited about her date.

"You look nice, Tammy. Going out?" her grandmother asked, glancing at the clock on the mantelpiece.

"Yes, a quick drink with someone I used to go to school with."

Her grandmother looked surprised but then nodded.

"It'll do you good to relax a bit even though it doesn't sound like you had much on today."

Tamsyn grimaced. She hadn't been completely honest when her grandparents asked about her first day. One of the trainers at Middlemoor had offered this blunt advice:

"Tell your mum nothing and only tell your dad half the truth – he'll halve that again when he tells her."

Or grandparents, in Tamsyn's case.

So her version of the day was that she was present at the initial questioning of a witness, helped keep a cordon, did some paperwork and drank several cups of coffee.

She gave her grandmother a hug, ruffled Mo's fur, checked she had her phone and wallet then opened the door.

Mo looked crestfallen when she realised that Tamsyn was leaving the house without her.

"I'll take you for a walk tomorrow," she promised, but a

common problem with Jack Russells was that they didn't believe in delayed gratification – *now* was much better.

Ollie was waiting for her at the Coldstreamer Inn. And from the look of him and his mates, they'd been waiting for some time even though she wasn't late.

"Tam!" he yelled over the noise. "Now we can get going."

"Going? I thought we were just having a quick drink."

"I heard about this party. It'll be great."

He leaned in for a kiss and she could smell his beer-breath. Lovely. She turned her head so the kiss landed on her cheek instead of its intended target.

"I can't have a late night, I have to be up early for work."

"One drink, one dance and I'll get you home. Deal?"

Sighing, she nodded.

"How about one for the road?" he grinned. "What you drinking?"

"I'll have a Rattler, please," she said, naming the cloudy Cornish cider that was popular with people her age.

Ollie bought the drinks and handed her a bottle as they all piled in the knackered old Mini Cooper that she'd seen him in earlier. If he'd been the one driving, she'd never have got in, but the evening's dedicated driver had been drinking plain Pepsi at the pub. She hoped it was just Pepsi.

It was a squeeze to get three adults on the backseat and Tamsyn had to sit on Ollie's knee. It was a good thing he didn't try to feel her up because she'd have been tempted to elbow him in the face.

It turned out that the party was in Penzance, so it wasn't too far if she had to walk home.

On the way over, Ollie told her about the last couple of years when he'd been living in Kent and that he couldn't wait to get back to proper surfing beaches. He told her about his new bar job at a holiday park over in Carbis Bay. And after she'd listened and finished half her cider, he finally asked her what she did.

"I'm a police officer," she said, pride in her voice.

He laughed. "No, really?"

"Really," she said, her tone several degrees cooler.

"Your girlfriend is the filth?" his friend asked obnoxiously. "Nice!"

There was an uncomfortable silence. Tamsyn remembered what her trainer had said about some people dating police officers so they could say they'd screwed a copper.

She wished she'd stayed at home. It was only Jess's dig about her dates never lasting long that made her determined to see it through.

When they arrived at the small terraced house, people were spilling out of the doors and windows, and music thumped through the walls. Tamsyn felt sorry for the neighbours. She was on edge, wondering if the noisy party would be reported and what that would mean for her if she was found inside.

Ollie offered her another drink but since she hadn't seen it being opened, she shook her head. Last month, Jess had been roofied in a club in Falmouth. One minute, she had a nice buzz going, the next she was so out of it that she couldn't stand. Tamsyn and another friend had managed to get her home. Scarily, Jess couldn't remember a thing about the whole evening. Since then, Tamsyn watched her drinks carefully and never left them unguarded. And she didn't know Ollie's friends. She didn't really know him.

He grabbed her hand and pulled her through the crowd into the living room and found a small space where they could dance, albeit squeezed together.

"It's really great to see you," he said again, resting his hands on her waist.

The music changed from drum 'n' bass to Kings of Leon *Sex on Fire* and a shout went up as everyone piled into the already crowded room.

"Yeah, great," she echoed, wishing she were anywhere but here.

They danced until they were both hot and sweaty and Tamsyn even began to enjoy herself, then Ollie asked her again if she wanted a drink – although 'asking' meant yelling in her ear so she could hear him above the pounding techno.

As they fought their way to the kitchen, that's when it happened: she saw a guy swapping a packet of powder for a bundle of notes.

Ollie saw the direction of her gaze and looked annoyed, then worried, then annoyed again.

It was obvious that the guy was dealing – she didn't know what, but as she watched, frozen, another girl came up to the same guy and another exchange took place. Tamsyn didn't know what to do. What was the right thing? What was the *safe* thing? She had no police radio, no one knew where she was, and she had no backup. This was a bad situation and she needed to leave.

"I'm going," she said, pushing Ollie away from her and heading for the front door.

"Oi, leave it out, Tam! You're not even on duty."

"I'm always on duty," she said fiercely. "I'm a sworn officer of the law, not just when I'm wearing my uniform."

"You can't report him, he's my mate!"

"Your friend is a drug dealer."

"It's just some molly! Don't be such a bitch."

"I'm leaving."

"Whatever. You're boring as fuck anyway," and he pushed her through the door and slammed it behind her.

Shaken and angry, her heart racing, she wanted to storm in there and arrest the asshole dealer. She was angry with Ollie, too. He knew she was a police officer and yet he'd still let her walk into that party knowing that his *friend* was dealing.

"Tamsyn?"

She was so angry as she stood outside the house that she hadn't been as aware of her surroundings as she should have been. When it sank in that someone had called her name, she looked up and saw a man outside a pub lighting a cigarette, the flare of the lighter casting his face into shadow, but she had no difficulty recognising Detective Inspector Rego.

CHAPTER 8

Rego took in the expression on Tamsyn's face and defensive body language.

"Are you okay?" he asked.

"I was at a party," she said unhappily, glancing back at the house as music continued to shake the windows.

He nodded, looking at her sideways to see if she'd tell him what had upset her.

"It's good to have a life outside the force," he said, his voice neutral. "We see a lot of dark things in this job – it's good to have a bit of light."

She frowned, deep in thought, and found that she really wanted to talk to someone who'd understand.

"I saw someone selling molly," she said in a rush. "Well, I think it was. I don't have any proof. And ... I didn't know what to do, so I just left."

He nodded and exhaled a thin stream of smoke from the side of his mouth. "Good decision."

"I wanted to do something, sir, but I was by myself and I didn't think that..."

"As I said, good decision. Anyway, if they know you're in

the job, they'll all be flushing the drugs down the toilet right now. I'll call it in, let uniform know. It's about time that music was turned off anyway."

He glanced across at her before continuing.

"A good copper knows his patch, it's an important advantage. Of course in your case it can be a disadvantage, too."

"Really?" she said, sounding confused. "Why's that? I thought it would be a good thing."

"Because you grew up here, you know these people, and some will try to use that to their advantage and ask for favours; others won't want to know you anymore." He grimaced and looked away from her. "Guys will want to say they shagged a copper. Girls, too. I'm not saying don't have a life, I'm only saying be aware; don't forget you're a police officer now, and that comes first. Always."

He pulled out his phone and called the Control room, giving them the address.

"Do you have the name of the dealer?" he asked. "I'll have a word, let him know his collar's been felt."

"Sorry, I don't know. I just met up with someone I went to school with and..." she shrugged helplessly. "I'm sorry, sir."

"What are you sorry for? You did the right thing. And we're off duty now – you don't have to call me 'sir'."

"Uh, okay. Um, I forgot your name."

He grinned at her. "It's Robert, Rob."

It felt weird calling him by his name, so she just gave a quick smile and nodded.

"Did you take anything?" he asked abruptly.

"No!"

"Were you smoking anything?"

"No, I wasn't," she said stiffly.

"Because anything you've smoked, well, you can tell the

history of someone's drug use in their hair," he said calmly. "Was anyone smoking weed at the party?"

Tamsyn bit her lip. "I don't know. Maybe." *Probably.*

"You'll need to let your tutor know and write it in your notebook." He glanced at Tamsyn who looked sick. "The presence of cannabis can be detected up to three months after exposure even if you're not the one smoking it. I raided a cannabis factory once," he continued, his tone conversational. "Every officer got the munchies," and he raised his eyebrows at her. "You don't even have to smoke it to get high. We all had to report it to the boss."

Tamsyn gave him a weak smile.

"Things are a lot more dangerous now," he added, his tone becoming serious. "When I was a kid, it was just weed, but Spice has been a game-changer: dealers lace it with LSD or other psychoactive chemicals. Half the time they don't know what the hell they're dealing and they don't care. This stuff can cause giddiness, hallucinations, anxiety..." he seemed to be ticking off a mental list. "It can cause high blood pressure, convulsions, organ damage – and if you're really unlucky, it can trigger schizophrenia in some people. Or you can just die." His voice hardened. "And people think weed is no big deal, that it's harmless, a victimless crime, but they're wrong. That cannabis factory we raided was an ordinary house that belonged to a nice old couple who'd rented it to someone who seemed legit. But when they got the house back, electricity and water had been stolen from their neighbours, all the carpets and flooring were wrecked – completely unsalvageable – and most of the interior walls had been removed which meant the roof was sagging dangerously and the whole building was on the verge of falling down. Holes had been punched through the remaining walls and floors – it was a miracle the house was still standing, but so well insulated that we'd never have found the 'hot' house with thermal imaging. The old lady collapsed in tears and the man had a heart attack." He paused. "They couldn't claim on their insurance because the house had been used for illegal activity and they hadn't done sufficient checks on the man renting it. That house was their nest egg – they lost everything. And what people don't like to think about is that the money moves up the line to fund organised crime: Class A drugs, people trafficking, money laundering."

Tamsyn swallowed nervously as his voice rose, and Rego made a conscious effort to lighten up.

"Don't worry about the party," he said in a more even tone. "Tell your tutor that you were there but left when you saw what was going on. It'll be on record that I called it in. You'll be fine."

She took a deep breath. "Okay. Thank you."

They walked in silence for nearly a minute until Rego spoke again.

"Do you live near here?"

"Near-ish – in Gulval. It's about ten minutes away."

"I'll walk you home."

"That's okay, I walk home by myself all the time."

"Yeah, well, I don't want to have to spend the night worrying about whether or not you got home safely," he replied, and Tamsyn didn't think she could argue with him even though she didn't need his help.

Rego didn't mention that he was concerned by the possibility of a dealer following Tamsyn home.

"What are you doing here anyway?" she asked him, then pulled a face when she realised how she sounded.

"Had my *greeze* at a pub but my brain won't quiet down," Rego tapped his head. "so I came out for a walk."

At a time like this, a detective's hours were definitely not nine to five. There was a saying that you weren't a real detective until you had at least one divorce behind you. Rego refused to believe that was in his future.

He smiled at Tamsyn.

"And it's no bad thing to get to know the area. They've got me a room at the Premier Inn by the station."

"I guess. But ... your grease?"

He laughed. "*Greeze* – it's Bermudian slang for a nice meal."

"You're from Bermuda? I thought you were from upcountry."

"My mum is from Bermuda but I grew up in Manchester, if that's where you mean by 'up country'."

He took a last drag of the cigarette and dropped it on the pavement, stubbing it out with his heel.

"You shouldn't leave cigarette butts," Tamsyn rebuked him. "Seagulls think it's food and it can choke them."

He stared at her solemn expression then bent down to pick up the butt and chucked it in a bin.

"Better?"

She nodded in satisfaction and he had to withhold a smile.

"I'm trying to quit anyway."

Tamsyn chewed her lip.

"Can I ask you something, sir, Robert?"

"I think I like being called Sir Robert," he teased as Tamsyn's cheeks turned pink. "Sure. What do you want to ask?"

"Are there any new leads since the press release went out?"

His smile disappeared.

"One possible ID which we're checking out, and DC Forshaw is going through the last three days of the *Scillonian*'s passenger lists."

Rego didn't think the victim had fallen from the ferry, but he needed to be thorough and eliminate that line of inquiry.

He fell silent, and Tamsyn had the feeling that there was something he wasn't telling her.

"Can I ask about the autopsy?"

"The *post-mortem*, yes. White female aged between 25 and 40, slender, underweight the doctor said, possibly malnourished. No track marks but we're testing for drugs and alcohol."

"It's sad that nobody has missed her yet," Tamsyn said softly.

Rego neither agreed nor disagreed.

"The Coroner will be all over me until we identify her," he admitted.

"What if nobody calls in? She might not even be British."

"What makes you say that?" he asked, his interest sharpened.

"We get a lot of foreigners come over to pick the daffodils in January and February, and farmers have casual labour in the summer and harvest time."

"What about this time of year?" Rego asked.

"Yeah, I guess. There are always some, especially in hospitality. There were loads before Brexit and Covid, but they're coming back again now. I think more in the summer though. What will we do if she's not British?"

"We'll check her fingerprints against the national database first. We do have dental records so we can use those once we have an idea who she might be."

"Isn't there a national database for dentists, as well?" she asked. "You always hear about dental records being checked."

Rego smiled in the dark, his teeth very white under the streetlamps.

"'Fraid it's not that easy. No, we don't have a national

database for teeth. We have to have an idea who the victim is first, then ask their dentist to compare."

"Oh."

"And since you mentioned Brexit, it's become harder to get access to records from Europe. But we can go to the NCA and Interpol to see if any missings have been reported."

"What about DNA?"

"Samples have been taken but it could take a couple of weeks to get those results, even on rush. And if she's never been arrested, there's nothing to compare them with anyway."

Tamsyn stopped outside her home.

"This is me. Thank you for walking me home, sir."

Rego gazed at the quaint little cottage and smiled.

"No problem. Night, Blackpool."

"Blackpool? Really?" Tamsyn laughed and Rego smiled as he turned to head back towards Penzance.

"Sir! Robert?" Tamsyn chewed her lip. "Why do you think she wanted to kill herself?"

There was a short pause before he replied.

"She didn't."

Tamsyn turned to face him.

"How...?"

"You know you can't talk about this, don't you?"

"Yes, sir."

"The pathologist believes she bled to death."

"She was stabbed? I didn't see..."

"Her tongue was cut out."

Tamsyn drew in a sharp breath.

"That's horrible! Why would anyone do something like that?"

Rego's voice was grim.

"To stop her talking. As a punishment. Maybe even as a warning to someone else. We need to pursue all lines of inquiry, but there's definitely something symbolic in cutting out a tongue."

"Was ... was she alive when it happened?"

Rego thought of the quantity of blood found in the victim's lungs.

"We believe so," he said carefully.

"She was murdered?"

Rego took his time answering.

"Could she have survived if she'd received immediate medical attention? Probably, yes. Can I prove that the intent was to kill her? No." *Not yet.* "Do I believe she was left to die and her body dumped at sea?"

He paused and met Tamsyn's appalled gaze.

"Yes."

CHAPTER 9

Rego's wife once asked him how so many people could get away with murder. He answered that of the 710 people murdered in the UK last year, three-quarters of those crimes resulted in someone being charged, and some of the other investigations were still ongoing.

Cassie had argued that 25% was still a lot of murderers who had got away with it, and Rego didn't disagree. There were cases where there was no evidence and no witnesses; sometimes the investigation was screwed up. The truth was, if you didn't score a viable lead in the first few days, years could pass and no one was ever brought to justice.

The first 48 hours in a major investigation were the most critical. Although sometimes, in places where there was a high volume of the general public – like a station or a shopping centre – that timeframe could be compressed to much less because people were likely to move through more quickly; witnesses or suspects disappeared into the crowds. And anyway, after 48 hours, witnesses' memories began to fade, blur, or even be confused with another event. He'd experienced all those situations, and then it was down to the detective's skill and doggedness to determine fact from fiction.

Rego was now fourteen hours into this case with the murder having taken place as much as 72 hours earlier.

But at least there were leads to follow up.

Tamsyn was still thinking about her late-night conversation with DI Rego. And even though she was exhausted, she'd tossed and turned, her mind rehashing everything she'd seen, heard and learned. She lay awake with her eyes wide open and her mind whirring, ignoring her need for sleep, despite the fact that she had to be ready to start the early shift.

For the second night running, Mo left, grumbling about her own doggy sleep being disturbed – as if she didn't nap during the day anyway.

When Tamsyn did finally fall asleep, ugly images chased her across the landscape of her dreams: her friends walking away as she called their names, her father disappearing into the mist, waving goodbye, always goodbye.

The phone alarm woke her at 5.30am and she shot out of bed like she'd been electrocuted. She'd slept maybe two hours. Even so, a surge of adrenaline and nerves shot through her.

Mo joined her in the kitchen and Tamsyn turfed her outside, hoping that today wouldn't be the one when Mo decided to go exploring through the gap in the fence. But the little dog trotted back in and flopped down in front of her empty food bowl, her eyes silently following Tamsyn's progress around the kitchen as she filled the kettle and put three bags in the teapot.

Dawn was still an hour away, and only a thin, grey light struggled to reach through the tiny cottage windows, set deep into thick granite walls. But there was no doubt that spring had arrived, and soon the hordes of holidaymakers would descend again, starting at Easter, peaking in August, and vanishing after half-term in October.

Tamsyn was surprised to hear her grandfather moving about. First light was usually the time he'd be landing his catch at Newlyn. She'd hoped to avoid any more emotional scenes after yesterday's start, but it looked as though her grandparents had other ideas.

Wanting to be here again today as she got ready for work would cost her grandfather money they could ill afford.

"Morning, Tam," he said, his voice a low rumble as he clomped down the stairs. "Had your breakfast?"

"Not hungry," she said, giving him a weak smile.

"Just nerves," he nodded. "You were like that the first week when you started school. Seems like only yesterday." He gazed at her critically. "You're too skinny."

She shook her head at the familiar argument. "I'm a healthy weight."

He muttered something under his breath while he pottered around the kitchen, taking eggs and bacon out of the fridge and frying them together in a large, cast iron pan. When Tamsyn had her back turned to pour the tea, he gave Mo a rasher of bacon and a scoop of his eggs.

"Grandad!" Tamsyn chided gently as she glanced down at Mo scoffing the food. "It's not good for her. Or you. Too much salt."

"I had a mother, don't need another one," he grumbled, not meeting her eyes.

"The doctor said..."

"Bugger him! I'd sooner go to the vet – get seen faster, that's for sure."

Tamsyn gave up. Her grandfather had breakfasted on

fried eggs and bacon for seven decades and had no plans to stop now.

She dropped a kiss onto his white hair, breathing in the familiar scent of pipe tobacco, diesel, and fish. It should have been unpleasant but it was comforting.

"You be careful today," he said gruffly, his tone echoing her gran's the night before.

"I will. Don't worry."

"I'll always worry. Accidents can happen anytime."

They were both quiet, remembering the day Tamsyn's dad had died: the soft, silent grief of her grandmother; the louder sobs of her grandfather; her own mute shock.

"I've been trained," she reminded him lightly.

"For a couple of months! That's not long enough!" he huffed.

"You know it was longer than that, Grandad," she said patiently. "And I'm double-crewing for the first couple of weeks. I won't be by myself."

He shook his head, the lines of worry etched into his skin, tanned and leathered by sun and salt, wind and waves; concern and care deepened the sea-blue of his eyes. Tamsyn left him with another kiss and went upstairs to shower.

She started to send a text to Jess describing her date from hell, but decided to call her later instead. She needed to think about what she could and couldn't say about Ollie's friend the drug dealer.

It wasn't until Tamsyn was getting dressed that she remembered about leaving her bag of clothes and day-old sandwiches in the boot of the DI's car – she really needed to get those back.

As she rechecked that she had all her uniform and equipment, she took a moment to stare at the embossed badge in her Warrant Card, running a finger over the raised braille dots that spelled 'police'. It was proof that she'd made it, that she was a police officer, serving her community.

Her photo ID made her look like an older, more severe version of herself. Putting on the uniform meant putting on a different persona and becoming PC Poldhu. It required a mental shift that was still new and ill-fitting, and although she felt proud of her uniform, she'd also felt uncomfortable wearing it on the way home yesterday. Much better to leave and return in civvies.

By the time Tamsyn clattered down the stairs, her grandmother was in the kitchen with Mo on her lap.

"Tammy," she said, tears glistening in the bright blue eyes which Tamsyn had inherited. "We're proud of you, you know that, don't you? And we love you very much."

"Yes, Gran. I know. I love you, too."

"Here, take this," and she handed Tamsyn a small, polished stone, striped with green and grey and red. "I meant to give it you yesterday. It'll help keep you safe."

"Gran..." Tamsyn began.

"It's older than any living thing, Tammy," her grandmother said seriously. "It's Serpentine from the Lizard."

Tamsyn rolled the pebble between her fingers.

"It's pretty."

She didn't believe this supernatural stuff herself, but she loved her grandmother and tried to respect her beliefs.

"The Infinite Stone is a wonderful protector."

"Thanks, Gran," said Tamsyn, slipping the pebble into her pocket.

"Take care, angel."

"I will."

She leaned down to hug her grandmother, trying not to squash Mo.

"Your dad would have been so proud of you," whispered her grandmother, voice raw.

She hugged her grandfather again, then left quickly before they could get even more emotional.

Tamsyn loved them deeply, but she hoped that they weren't going to do this every day.

It was only a mile to the police station, so she didn't hurry, taking the long way round to walk past the harbour and see the sun rising over St Michael's Mount. She never tired of that view – it was magical, ethereal, and when mist clung to the soaring rocks, it wasn't hard to imagine a Spanish galleon sailing up with a flash of cannon and a boom echoing across the water. Tourists never tired of photographing it. But to Tamsyn, it meant home was near.

The small boats and yachts in Penzance harbour were listing to one side, resting on muddy sand as water began to lap around them. It would be hours until the tide came in and they were afloat.

Next week it would be April and the month for spider crabs. Tamsyn knew that from now until autumn, her grandfather would be spending long hours on the water. Winter was the time when pots were washed, mended and put away; pasties were eaten and pints were drunk at the Mackerel Inn, and tall tales were told.

Realising that she'd been staring at the sea longer than she'd intended, Tamsyn turned and walked quickly up the hill to the police station, arriving fifteen minutes before her second shift as a police officer began.

"PC Tamsyn Poldhu," she said to herself, and smiled.

Having her own locker made a difference, and Tamsyn began to feel like she belonged.

When she walked into the station on her second day, the atmosphere was subtly different. Yes, there were the same number of dirty cups in the kitchen and yes, the conference room was filling up as C-team prepared to handover to the morning crew, but everyone was talking about the woman found floating at Lamorna Cove.

"Jen Bolitho told me the vic was murdered," Jamie announced importantly.

He was immediately inundated with questions.

It was interesting watching Jamie in front of an audience as he described the little that he'd seen.

"And this is Tamsyn Poldhu, folks – got seconded to the DI yesterday," and he slung his arm around her in a way that seemed overly proprietorial.

Jamie's introduction opened the floodgates, and they all wanted to know about the new DI and why DC Mimi Eagling had been drafted in from Camborne.

Tamsyn kept her replies to the minimum and was glad that Jamie soon took over again, clearly enjoying being the centre of attention.

"I just seen Harry Joules from Camborne with his drone kit," said Jamie. "The new DI is the Senior Investigating Officer, and Jack Forshaw and Jen are working the case. Mimi Eagling says she's acting as Exhibits Officer and doing the analytics. I mean, normally Jack or Jen would be doubling up and doing Exhibits. Or DS Stevens. So I reckon there's something else going on – typical CID – something we're not being told."

"Like what?" asked Jason, the former Royal Marine.

Jamie didn't get a chance to answer before Sergeants Terwillis and Carter entered the room.

"Good morning, troops. Settle down. I'm sure you've all seen that we have some new faces in CID – that's because the unexplained death recovered at Lamorna Cove is now being treated as murder. DI Rego from Exeter is the SIO and DS Tom Stevens is Deputy SIO. We've been asked to assist."

He immediately started handing out the actions needed.

"Carl, Mitch, Ky, Jethro: house-to-house at Lamorna – I've emailed you a list of questions, and ask about CCTV. Use the Electoral Roll to find out which are holiday homes, and get the details of the agencies and owners. Check PND and PNC for anyone with form. Harry Joules will be out there with the drone, checking the coast path in both directions."

He glanced at Jason and Tamsyn.

"Just a reminder for our two newest officers, the Police National Computer records details of convictions, cautions, reprimands, warnings and arrests; the Police National Database records local intelligence, what we call our 'soft' intel – things like details of investigations that didn't lead to any further action. Got it?"

Tamsyn looked up from where she'd been writing in her notebook and nodded. Jason hadn't moved and looked as though he hadn't needed the reminder.

"Okay, good. So, Jason, you'll be with Andy again today. Go to the Bay Hotel in Penzance and talk to the manager, Ben Travers. Possible lead on our vic – a 32 year-old cleaner with a distinctive tattoo on her lower leg hasn't turned up for work since Friday. Tamsyn, you're with Jamie – you two are going to see the owner of the Caerlyon guest house in St Ives. Their housekeeper has been missing for the last three days – I want to know if it's connection or coincidence. Andy, Jamie, discuss the interview strategies in advance. Only one chance to get a first impression."

Tamsyn wondered if that was the student officers making a good first impression, or whether he meant it was one chance to get a first impression of the people they were interviewing, but there was no chance to ask before they headed out to pick up their patrol car.

Jamie was carrying a sports bag which he dumped in the boot.

"Where's your go-bag?" he asked, looking behind her as if he might have missed her carrying it.

"I have everything," she said, patting her stuffed pockets and vest.

Jamie shook his head.

"No, there's more you need," and he proceed to show her the contents of his sports bag.

"Statement paper with continuation sheets, exhibit labels, nitrol gloves for handling exhibits, exhibit bags of different sizes." He paused. "We used to have these fixed penalty tickets which were in self-carbonating pads, the HORT 1 tickets – totally old-school – we issued them for minor offences like dropping litter, or using a phone while driving, in some instances speeding offences, bald tyres – that sort of thing. Usually minor Road Traffic Offences and there were loads of them on the ticket, so you just have to tick the right box. Now we've switched to a D&C force-issued device, your work mobile, yeah? And they're called OSCO's: Officer Seen Conditional Offer. The offence and evidence is written out on a form which gets sent to the CATS – Collisions and Ticketing Office, and they make the decision on what action is taken, depending on the offence."

Tamsyn had learned this on her course, but hearing about how they used to do it was interesting, if a bit confusing on her first day.

She nodded and Jamie winked at her. For a moment she wondered if he was going to pat her head.

"Your go-bag is like a mini office, so there's all sorts of

different bits of paperwork you might need," and he opened the bag up wide so she could see inside.

Tamsyn smiled as she saw several Snickers wrappers, sweet papers and half a beach worth of sand, as well as all the equipment he'd mentioned.

"Besides, you might want to keep a spare shirt in case you get puked on, and a pair of wellies."

"For the puke?"

Jamie laughed. "Yeah, it sometimes feels like there's that much puke – especially at chucking-out time!"

Tamsyn thought she'd prepared properly for the day but now realised that there were other things she needed, and she really appreciated the light-hearted way Jamie had steered her in the right direction.

As he drove, Jamie chatted away about some of the weird stuff other officers kept in their go-bags, Tamsyn mulled things over. She was glad to still be part of the case, and she had so many questions. Having been there when the victim's body was recovered, she wanted to know what had happened; she wanted to find the person responsible. More than that, she knew that one day she wanted to be a detective.

When she'd been at the crime scene with DI Rego, something had clicked, and for once in her life, Tamsyn felt like she fitted. She was in the right place at the right time, where she was supposed to be – where she was needed.

Yes, in three or four years, when she was more experienced, when she'd had enough of running around, she'd go for her detective exams.

Jamie was a talker. He rattled on non-stop all the way to St Ives, telling her stories of the cases he'd worked and some of the crazy stupid things criminals did.

"He was a rugby player, a frickin' enormous prop. I

couldn't let go to get the cuffs on him, so I had to sit on him for twenty minutes till backup arrived. Bastard kept trying to bite me! Even chewed a hole through my new trousers!"

At least he could laugh at himself, but after 20 minutes of nonstop anecdotes, Tamsyn thought she preferred Rego's ease with silence.

When they were a few minutes out from St Ives, Tamsyn interrupted Jamie's reminiscing.

"So, what's the interview strategy?" she asked.

"What did they tell you at Middlemoor?" he grinned, shooting her a smile.

"Interviews are 'to obtain accurate and reliable accounts from victims, witnesses or suspects about matters under police investigation'," Tamsyn quoted from memory.

"This isn't a formal interview," Jamie acknowledged, shifting gear. "We get the facts about this woman's missing housekeeper: *who, what, where* and *when*, then go on to open-ended questions to find out why the press release about our vic made her call us."

Tamsyn nodded, and scrawled a note as Jamie threw the car around another tight bend.

"We ask for a photograph and find out if this woman has any distinguishing features. We ask to see her room, we obtain her phone number, and take her toothbrush for DNA matching. Make sure you have a couple of evidence bags with you."

Caerlyon Guest House was a rundown Edwardian villa with a cliff rising steeply behind, no parking, but superb views over Carbis Bay.

The sea glittered in the morning sunshine, the dark blue of the water turning to turquoise as it rippled across the beach's soft, white sand.

It was a view that artists painted endlessly, the perfect light of the St Ives peninsula, and a view that drew five million tourists to Cornwall every summer.

The guest side of the hotel was bathed in sun, which unfortunately highlighted the grimy windows and sticky carpet. But at the back of the hotel, the staff entrance was dark and damp, the cliff moss-covered and dripping with water.

Tamsyn knew that they'd still be fully booked come the summer.

The owner was Mandy Pryce, a woman in her thirties who had three children under the age of 11 and a partner who worked in St Albans during the week.

"We've only been here six months," she said wearily, leading them into the messy family kitchen. "We brought the kids here for a better quality of life," and she gave a harsh laugh. "But I've never worked so hard and Trev is gone four nights a week. He's shattered when he comes home."

Tamsyn wondered if she was supposed to sympathise and agree it must be hard, or maybe go and make tea, but Jamie hadn't said anything about either of those things, so she simply nodded and kept her mouth shut.

"Jowita came with the place," Mandy said. "She's our housekeeper. That's why I called you when I saw that you'd found..." she paused uncomfortably. "I think she'd worked here for about a year before we bought this place. I don't really know."

"When did you realise she was missing?" Jamie asked as Tamsyn took notes.

"Saturday morning. She hadn't started the breakfasts and I had to do them all by myself while Trev looked after the kids. Weekends are always more work because guests like to read the papers or whatever before they leave, and they always eat three times as much toast. So because Saturday is a change-over day and they take longer at breakfast, I have more rooms to clean and less time to clean them. I was rushed off my feet and Lucy had to help serve. She's ten. She's a good girl ... when she's not being a right little madam."

"And after breakfast service was finished?"

"Trev and I had to run round and do nine bedrooms, that's what!" she said angrily.

"And did you call Jowita?"

"Of course I did! But her phone was turned off." She paused. "I went in her room but the bed was made so I thought maybe she'd gone out Friday night and got lucky."

"Got lucky?"

"You know, met a guy."

"Is that something she did often?"

"She's an adult, I don't know!" Then she sighed. "No, not that I know of. But if she wasn't here at night, I wouldn't know as long as she was here in the morning. She'd never missed breakfast service before. She's a good worker," she said reluctantly.

"What's her full name?"

"Something unpronounceable."

Jamie waited without speaking and the woman flushed.

"I don't know, okay? We pay her cash in hand. It's what she wanted."

Tamsyn watched as Jamie let that fact settle, then moved on to the next question.

"Do you have a home address for her?"

Mandy Pryce looked worried but her tone was defensive.

"No. She was Polish. That's all I know."

"How old is Jowita?"

This time the woman answered more confidently.

"Twenty-seven two weeks ago. Lucy made her a birthday card."

"What's Jowita like?"

"Quiet, keeps to herself. I've never had any trouble with her."

It wasn't a ringing endorsement but Tamsyn knew how easy it was to disappear into the background if you wanted to.

"Did you ever meet any of her friends or boyfriends?" Tamsyn asked, noticing an annoyed flicker in Jamie's eyes as she spoke for the first time, forgetting that she was supposed to look, listen, learn and keep quiet.

"No," the woman said slowly. "I don't think so. She didn't go out much."

"But you thought she'd 'got lucky' on Friday night?" Jamie commented.

Mandy Pryce looked confused.

"Yeah, so? Maybe she did. Maybe she decided she'd had enough of this shit hole. I wouldn't blame her."

"Did she have a car?" Jamie asked.

"No. She walked everywhere."

Mandy Pryce didn't have a photo of Jowita and her description was so vague as to be almost useless: average height, slight build, brownish hair, eye colour unknown – unremarkable.

"Any piercings or tattoos?" Jamie asked.

"No, neither. Not that I could see," and she smirked.

Tamsyn exchanged a look with Jamie. Either Mandy Pryce didn't know about an ankle tattoo or her housekeeper wasn't their vic.

"Did she like to get dressed up when she went out?" Tamsyn asked cautiously, glancing at Jamie, and hoping that this wasn't leading the witness.

Mandy Pryce shook her head. "Jeans. She always wore jeans."

Which would have covered up the tattoo.

Jamie asked a few more questions but there didn't seem anything else, so they were taken up to see Jowita's room.

It was compact, to say the least, gloomy, but neat and tidy. A pile of washing lay folded but un-ironed on the narrow bed and there was a small TV screen attached to the wall.

Tamsyn pulled on a pair of forensic gloves as she gazed around the room, taking it all in. *Does anything seem out of place? What doesn't fit?*

She opened the narrow wardrobe, finding three pairs of jeans, a winter coat, a worn pair of flip-flops and a phone charger for an iPhone. Jamie checked the small chest of drawers and under the mattress but there was no phone and hardly anything personal in the whole room.

Tamsyn picked up the remote and turned on the TV, surprised to find a children's channel which was playing an episode of *Hey, Duggie*. She looked questioningly at Mandy Pryce.

"Lucy used to bring the twins to watch TV with Jowita," she said, twitching a shoulder irritably. "Alex and Alice – they're six."

"Does Lucy have a phone?" Tamsyn asked. "Would she have a photo of Jowita?"

"Yes, she has a phone, but I don't think..." her words tailed off. "I'll ask her when I pick the kids up from school."

Tamsyn collected a hairbrush and toothbrush in evidence bags.

"Do you think she's the woman you found?" Mandy Pryce asked. "You know ... the body?" She twisted her wedding ring on her finger and looked up at Tamsyn. "The kids miss her."

"It's too early to say," Tamsyn replied. "We do need to look at Lucy's phone though. A photo would really help us."

As they left the guest house, Jamie nodded approvingly.

"Good call on the daughter's phone. We might get lucky with that. What made you ask?"

"There was one of those plastic tiaras from Claire's by Jowita's bed. It's not something a 27 year old would wear. So that's when I thought Ms Pryce's children probably used to go in there."

"Wait, who's Clare?"

Tamsyn smiled.

"It's a shop: Claire's Accessories. There's one in Truro and one in Newquay. But lots of places sell this sort of stuff that little girls like: plastic hair clips, scrunchies, teddy bear backpacks, unicorn phone cases..."

"Right, got it," Jamie nodded.

The room had been depressing, so lacking in personality, and the glittery little tiara had stood out.

"I don't know why I turned on the TV. I just wondered what sort of shows she watched," Tamsyn continued. "It didn't look like she'd packed any clothes. I don't think she planned to be away."

"No," Jamie agreed, turning up the volume on his Airwave radio. "Looks like Jason and Andy struck out – the vic isn't the woman reported missing by the Bay Hotel." He glanced at Tamsyn. "But Jowita is looking like a possible. We need to get that photo."

"Can we go to the school now and get it?"

Jamie shook his head doubtfully.

"We'd need the mother there."

"We're not interviewing the girl, just checking her phone. Wouldn't the head teacher be enough, a responsible adult and all?"

He blew out a long breath.

"Definitely not chancing that, but I'll call it in and ask."

Tamsyn flipped through her notes. Mandy Pryce clearly knew very little about the woman who'd been living with her for the last six months, but Tamsyn thought her daughter might know more.

"We need to question Lucy," she said.

Jamie pulled a face.

"They'll probably get Jen Bolitho to do it – she's done the course."

"What course?"

"ABE – Achieving Best Evidence. Basically, it's how to interview vulnerable people and kids."

"Oh, right."

"Don't be too disappointed," Jamie said encouragingly. "You did alright in there."

"Thanks."

"Fancy going for a drink tonight?"

"Uh well..."

"We usually try and go for a drink together once a week, E-team – sometimes guys from the other teams."

"Is everyone going then?"

Jamie shrugged.

"Dunno, but I am."

"Maybe," Tamsyn said. "I'll see how I feel later. This week has been full-on already – and I have some studying to do for my course, as well."

It was a weak excuse and Jamie laughed.

"It's only your second day! Wait till you've done two lates and two night shifts in a row." His voice became more serious. "I think you should come. It's important to talk stuff out that you can't say to civvies," he said. "Get things off your chest."

As he said the words, his eyes drifted fractionally lower to Tamsyn's chest before his head snapped up guiltily.

Jamie seemed like a nice guy but Tamsyn had no interest in hooking up with anyone from work and definitely didn't want to sound like she was leading him on, so her answer was deliberately noncommittal.

"Maybe, but I'll see if..."

"Great, it's a date! We'll be at the Admiral Benbow in Chapel Street at seven – pizza and a pint."

CHAPTER 10

When Rego heard that a ten year-old girl might be able to ID the victim, he sent Tamsyn and Jamie back to St Ives to collect the mother, then to the girl's school to pick up both the girl and her phone. The mother hadn't been happy about any of it – in fact, she'd been quite vocal in her unhappiness, but Rego had persuaded her – eventually.

And it had been worth it.

The phone's message log showed hundreds of texts, Snapchat and WhatsApp messages between Jowita and Lucy, innocuous enough, but showing that the girl trusted Jowita. Crucially, there were several photographs. One picture showed Jowita sitting barefoot on her bed, a tattoo peeking out. Rego was now 99% certain that the murdered woman's identity had been discovered, plus they had her phone number. They were making progress.

Except they still didn't know Jowita's surname.

Except they didn't have her handset.

Except the only witness they had was an anxious ten year-old child.

Except that Mandy Pryce had refused to go to the morgue to formally identify Jowita.

Rego tasked DC Jen Bolitho with interviewing Lucy Pryce as soon as possible – preferably sooner. He was relieved that an appropriate PPU interview room was available. Even better, because another interview had been postponed, there was a social worker available to sit in, which was definitely a bonus. Parents could get agitated during interviews, so it helped to have a neutral third party.

More surprisingly, after Tamsyn and Jamie had collected Lucy and her mother, the girl asked for Tamsyn to be at the interview.

"You must have made a good impression on her," Rego said. "She feels a connection with you."

He didn't say that it might also be because Tamsyn was young and pretty and closer in age to the little girl than any of the others.

"Jen will lead the interview and you'll be there to take notes and come across as supportive and sympathetic. If you have a question, *do not interrupt the interview*, but write it down and pass it to Jen, or – preferably – tell her when you have a break. And don't wear your uniform: the interview will take place at the Public Protection Unit. It's designed to be as non-threatening as possible."

"Yes, sir," Tamsyn said, nervous but excited to be in on the interview with Lucy.

"These are photographs of Jowita that we've taken from Lucy's phone."

As Tamsyn stared at the picture of the smiling woman, only a few years older than herself, it all became real. This wasn't just about a crime, it was about a person. A person who'd had parents, maybe siblings, a family – maybe even children.

Tamsyn's throat tightened as she compared the woman's picture to the memory of the body found at Lamorna Cove, stripped of dignity and deprived of life. Maybe she'd been a good person, maybe she hadn't, but nobody deserved to die that way. Someone had done this to her.

Tamsyn wanted to find that person, wanted it desperately, wanted it as urgently as the cruelty of the violence chilled her.

She might have passed Jowita in the street and never known. She'd lived only a few miles away. It felt personal.

"Yes, sir," she said again, meeting the DI's eyes.

She thought she saw it in him, too, this need to find the person responsible and to see them punished.

Rego took his own car as they drove to Redruth, but Tamsyn rode with DC Jen Bolitho.

They parked side by side, and Rego remembered that he'd found Tamsyn's hold-all in the boot of his car.

"You'll probably need these back," he said with a quick smile, handing them over.

"Oh! Thank you, sir. I'd forgotten about them."

She was about to follow the DI as he strode away, when she felt Jen's hand on her arm.

"Tamsyn," Jen said carefully. "It doesn't look good, leaving your clothes in the DI's car."

Tamsyn flushed.

"I didn't have time to get a locker yesterday morning and I forgot to get them back later. That's all."

Jen nodded.

"Just be careful. Police stations are hotbeds of gossip – you wouldn't believe how people can put two and two together and come up with five."

In silence, Tamsyn stowed her bag in Jen's boot, wondering if people would gossip about her if it was Jen driving off with her clothes.

But she definitely understood the power of gossip. She was glad that Jen had handled it so discreetly – she cringed at the thought of what someone like Chloe would have made of it.

She trailed behind Jen in silence.

The Public Protection Unit was located on the outskirts of Redruth, some 18 miles from Penzance. It was an unassuming building on an ugly industrial estate. From the outside, it looked like an ordinary office building, and there were no marked cars or police uniforms anywhere. Inside, there was a small reception area, but the main interviewing suite was set up like a comfortable lounge with easy chairs and a TV. It was where they took rape victims to be interviewed.

Rego introduced himself to the social worker, then sat in the room next door where there was recording equipment, so he could watch and listen discreetly.

He saw Tamsyn give an awkward wave as she smiled encouragingly at the little girl curled up into the furthest corner of the plush settee.

"Thank you for coming, Mandy," Jen said politely to the girl's mother.

"Didn't have much choice, did I?" Mandy Pryce replied. "Look, how long is this going to take? I've got to pick up the twins at quarter past three."

"We've asked the school's head teacher to keep an eye on them, in case we run over," Jen said reassuringly. Then she turned to the girl. "Hi, Lucy," she said with a friendly smile. "I expect you're a bit nervous but there's nothing to worry about. My name is Jen and I think you've already met Tamsyn?"

Rego had been told that Bolitho had a 19 year-old son who was away at university, and he could see that she had the ability to switch on a sort of motherliness which calmed both

Lucy and Mandy, probably Tamsyn, too. It was exactly what he needed. Even though his own kids were closer in age to Lucy, he knew that his height and build could be intimidating. Maybe even the colour of his skin in rural West Cornwall.

"You're not in trouble, Lucy," Jen continued. "Your mum is worried about your friend Jowita. We're worried, too."

The little girl glanced at her mum then nodded uncertainly.

"But let's start with a couple of ground rules. Firstly, this is your interview – if you want to stop, just say stop. Okay?"

Wide-eyed, Lucy nodded.

"We can take a break whenever you like. Now, Tamsyn can get you a drink: there's juice, milk, or squash. What would you like?"

"Juice, please," Lucy replied, in a very small voice.

"And a cup of tea for Mum?" Jen continued.

Mandy nodded. "God, yes."

Tamsyn smiled at them both, trying to mirror Jen Bolitho's air of calm competence while she poured Lucy a glass of apple juice and set it in front of her then put the kettle on.

Jen continued talking as Tamsyn made three mugs of tea.

"Now, Lucy, do you know what I mean when I say it's important that you tell the truth?"

Lucy bit her lip. "I mustn't tell lies."

"That's right! Well done. So, if you took some chocolate from the fridge and then said you didn't, would that be a lie?"

"But I didn't take any chocolate! I promise!"

Jen smiled. "I know, that's okay. It was only an example. But knowing the truth is important because we want to find Jowita, don't we?" She paused. "You had some nice photos of Jowita on your phone. Did you watch TV in her room with her?"

Lucy nodded again.

"What did you watch?"

"*Bad Education, Switch, Creeped Out* ... Jowita liked *Love Island* but I thought it was boring."

"You let Alex and Alice watch *Creeped Out*?" her mum interrupted, face creasing with anger. "Is that why they've been having nightmares?"

Lucy shrank back in her seat, her arms folded defensively.

"They always follow me around!"

"Because you're supposed to look after them! I can't do it all!"

Before the row could escalate further, Jen interrupted gently.

"It must be hard for you with your husband away. Jowita must have been a great help."

Mandy shrugged, and Jen directed her questions to Lucy again.

"Tell me about Jowita. What was she like?"

"Nice," said Lucy. "She listened to me," and she shot her mum a look.

Gradually, Jen got Lucy talking. Jowita had been kind to her and they watched TV together most days after school. The hotel didn't offer evening meals, so Jowita's work was usually done by early afternoon, but from what Lucy said, it was rare that she went out in the evenings.

Her mother disagreed, apparently having changed her mind since the morning.

"No, I saw her going out a few times after the kids were in bed. I thought maybe she was meeting friends or had a boyfriend."

Lucy shook her head.

"She didn't have a boyfriend! She would have told me."

Mandy Pryce rolled her eyes.

"She would!" Lucy insisted. "Her friend called her sometimes, but he wasn't her boyfriend."

Rego's ears perked up, and Jen was on it immediately, but still sounding casual.

"Tell me about Jowita's friend," she said pleasantly.

Lucy looked trapped, as if she hadn't meant to mention that.

"I don't know," she muttered. "A man used to text her. Once he phoned her."

"How do you know it was a man?"

Lucy shrugged. "I heard his voice. "She never seemed pleased to hear from him. I thought it might be her dad."

Mandy looked as though she was going to interrupt again, so Tamsyn gently pushed the mug of tea nearer to her, distracting her long enough for Jen to continue.

"That's very good, Lucy. Can you remember what she said?"

"I think so? She said she was busy babysitting, but I'm not a baby like the twins," she said indignantly.

"Did the man speak in English?

Lucy just looked confused, so Jen quickly rephrased the question.

"Did the man have an accent like Jowita or did he talk more like you?"

"He talked like you," Lucy said abruptly.

"Like me?"

Lucy shrugged.

"Yeah, like the kids at school. Cornish kids." Her mouth turned down. "They tease me and say I talk like I'm off *EastEnders* but we're not from London," she said sounding hurt. Then her shoulders slumped. "When is Jowita coming home?"

Jen leaned forward and looked into the girl's eyes.

"We don't know, Lucy. But I promise that we'll keep looking for her. Now, can you tell me what she was wearing the last time you saw her?"

After nearly an hour, they took a short break.

Rego stood up and stretched as Tamsyn and Jen Bolitho entered the recording suite. The social worker had gone outside for a cigarette and Rego would have liked to join her.

"Good work, Jen," Rego said, trying to ignore his nicotine cravings. "And you, Tamsyn. Keeping the mother from interrupting is a job all on its own."

Jen Bolitho nodded. "I got the impression that she was worried we were going to come down on her for paying Jowita cash in hand."

"I'll leave that to HMRC," Rego said humourlessly. "When you go back in there, ask about anywhere Jowita took the kids after school. Was there anywhere in particular they used to go? Any cafés? Did she talk to anyone more than once? Did Lucy ever hear her talking in anything other than English? And I want to know more about this man that Jowita didn't want to talk to. When did this happen? Days or weeks ago? What time of day was it? And weekends – what did Jowita do on weekends?"

Jen took notes and Tamsyn copied her, then they went in for round two.

By now, Lucy was tired and a little tearful. Tamsyn opened a packet of chocolate chip cookies and pushed them forwards.

Lucy darted a look at her mum then took two. Mandy looked like she wanted to say something ... or maybe finish the rest of the packet, but she pressed her lips together tightly instead.

"Just a few more questions," Jen said encouragingly. "The man you heard Jowita talking to, how many times did you hear him?"

"Only once."

"And when was that?"

"I don't know."

"Days ago? Weeks? Longer?"

Lucy rubbed her eyes with a grubby finger.

"Maybe a few weeks?"

"Did Jowita ever take you anywhere, school, maybe?"

"No," said Mandy. "I always did the school run, well, always in the mornings. Anyway, Jowita didn't drive."

"Sometimes Jowita met me after school and we walked home together," Lucy said loudly, casting a challenging look at her mum.

"Maybe Jowita took you somewhere on the weekends, Lucy?"

"No," Lucy shook her head sullenly. "Dad comes home on weekends. I have to stay home."

"It's the only time he gets to bloody see you!" Mandy said angrily.

Jen continued calmly.

"What did Jowita do at the weekends?"

Lucy shrugged, shooting her mum another angry glance.

"What about after school? Did she ever take you anywhere when she met you? A café, perhaps?"

"We never go anywhere! We never do anything!" Lucy cried out, her eyes filling with tears.

"I think that's enough now," the social worker interrupted firmly, and Jen sat back in frustration.

"About time!" Mandy glared, reaching for her handbag.

"That's been really helpful, Lucy," Tamsyn said, pushing

another cookie towards the girl and taking one herself. "They're good, aren't they?"

"We only ever went to that stupid church!" Lucy muttered as crumbs spilled from her mouth.

They all froze. Then Jen raised her eyebrows at Tamsyn, encouraging her to keep the conversation going.

"Oh, that's nice," Tamsyn said, trying to gather her thoughts. "I like old churches, they're always so peaceful."

Lucy gave a small smile. "I like the flowers."

"Like the daffodils outside?"

Lucy shook her head. "No, the ones inside. They're really pretty."

"Did you like going in the church?"

"It was alright," Lucy shrugged. "It got a bit boring after a while, so I played *Llama Spit Spit* on my phone while I was waiting for her."

"What was Jowita doing?" Tamsyn asked.

"I dunno. She made me go inside."

Tamsyn noticed the taut expression on Jen's face, but she wasn't sure what she was supposed to say.

"So ... Jowita was outside the church? Was she making a call ... or did she see someone?"

"I don't *know!*" Lucy said, sounding annoyed. "I told you! I was inside. She was outside."

"Did that happen often?"

"I don't know. Sometimes."

"Which church was it?" Tamsyn asked.

Lucy looked at her mum. "Up the hill?"

Mandy Pryce just shrugged.

"Did Jowita ever give you anything? A present? Or..."

Tamsyn was racking her brains, but Lucy gave her a big smile.

"Yes! She gave me a sparkly tiara! She said it had real diamonds and everything."

Mandy rolled her eyes. "It was plastic and nasty."

"It wasn't!" Tears gathered in Lucy's eyes.

"Thank you, Lucy," Tamsyn said. "You've been really helpful."

In the recording room, Rego was already pulling up a map on his phone.

CHAPTER 11

Rego muttered to himself, as he studied the map, "What were you doing at the church?"

"It must be St John's-in-the-Field," said Jen Bolitho, walking into the room. "That's the only church that's uphill from Lucy's school."

At that moment, Rego's phone rang.

"I have to take this," he said, seeing that it was DCI Finch calling. "Jen, take Tamsyn and check it out. Don't ask me what you're looking for because I don't know, but Jowita wasn't there to pray."

He strode out of the room with his phone clamped to his ear.

Jen threw Tamsyn a commiserating look.

"I know you're supposed to be going off shift now..."

"It's okay. I don't have anything planned," Tamsyn said, half hoping that she'd be able to miss drinks at the pub later. "And I'm on the late shift tomorrow, so I can have a lie in. Do we need to contact the vicar?"

Jen shook her head.

"We're just going for a look-see. If we find anything, we'll call it in."

Rego waited until he was out of earshot, then answered his phone.

"Rob," said the DCI's voice. "I know you're busy with the murder, but there's been a development on yesterday's RTC: the artic had to be craned off the road and taken to St Austell."

The DCI pronounced it 'Sun Ozzle' which left Rego scrambling to keep up.

"The mechanics found a large amount of Scottish currency which they thought seemed odd, and when they couldn't contact the driver, they called us. The Scottish banknotes are a red flag, and ANPR information shows that the lorry was regularly travelling from Rotterdam to Harwich." Finch paused. "It's looking fishy. You worked on organised crime up in Manchester and have contacts with the NCA – I need you on this one. I've emailed the information."

Scottish banknotes didn't circulate in England: the banks weeded them out and sent them back to Scotland. But drug dealing was a cash business and Scottish dealers paid for their drugs in Scottish notes. The DCI was right – a large quantity being found in the lorry was suspicious, and the tramper doing a runner certainly added to that. Then throw in the fact that Rotterdam was a major container port and the Harwich route was a favourite with traffickers, and circumstantial evidence was beginning to join the dots.

"I'm sorry about this, Rob," DCI Finch went on. "I know your priority is the murder and I didn't want to have to lumber you with more, but we need your experience to keep an overview of the lorry investigation to ensure it goes in the right direction. It's beginning to look like the driver gave us a fake name and phone number."

Rego appreciated the apology but he really didn't need the distraction right now.

As he skimmed through the DCI's email, he saw that the Automatic Number Plate Recognition system showed the articulated lorry was making the journey to the UK two or three times a month, supposedly carrying a consignment of toilet rolls each time. That was a lot of toilet rolls.

"On it, boss," he paused as he programmed his car's SatNav for the garage in St Austell.

It was time to tell the DCI his suspicions.

"I don't know if it's a coincidence, but we think the murdered woman found at Lamorna Cove was Polish: Jowita, last name unknown; a housekeeper in a B&B. She had a tattoo on her ankle that's similar to ones used by the Albanian organised crime gang Hellbanianz."

"You're sure?"

No, Rego wasn't sure, but a pattern was definitely developing – one that he didn't like.

"I ran it past a colleague at the National Crime Agency, and he agreed there were similarities," Rego said cautiously. "I'll be keeping an open mind, but it's beginning to look like organised crime or a county lines gang operating down here."

There was a long silence as they both considered the serious implications of this.

"I'm going to need more evidence to get extra resources for you, Rob."

"I know, boss. But now we have the woman's first name, I'll go back to the NCA ... it could be a coincidence," he said, in a voice that implied he didn't really believe that.

"I don't like coincidences," DCI Finch said grimly. "Good work, Rob. Keep me updated."

Coincidence number two came less than a minute later

when DC Mimi Eagling called him while he was driving north.

"Boss, I've been going through local CrimeStoppers reports and one from the Neighbourhood Watch, and there's something interesting there."

"Go on," he said, accelerating past a learner on the dual carriageway.

"So, the first report that's interesting is a woman from a Neighbourhood Watch in Newlyn. She reported seeing what she described as a 'drug deal' taking place. She saw a small packet being exchanged for cash outside a pub, and one of the men involved shouted at her, which scared her away."

"What did he say?"

"Ah, here it is. The younger man yelled, 'Fuck off, you old bitch before someone gives you a smack'."

"Not very nice."

"No, she was rather shaken."

"What was the name of the pub?"

"The Mackerel Inn – it's where all the fishermen go."

"Okay, any corroboration for suspicion of drug involvement?"

"Possibly. There was a call to CrimeStoppers where a local woman claimed that there was drug dealing going on at a different pub in Newlyn, the Red Lion."

"Newlyn again. What else have you found?"

"The same woman says she found drugs in her son's wardrobe – he's 15 and goes to Mounts Bay Academy in Penzance. She says it was a white powder, but she didn't confront her son, and the 'drugs' disappeared the next day. She didn't leave a name but wants someone to go to the school. It's all uncorroborated so..."

"Right. Anything else?"

"I talked to my colleague in Camborne, and he's had word

from an informant about a Polish woman dealing drugs in the area, specifically Newlyn and Penzance."

"Polish?"

"Yes, I thought that was interesting, too. I'm trying to match it up with intelligence sources across other forces and national databases."

"Saved the best till last."

"Yes, boss!"

"Good work, Mimi. I'm heading to St Austell now but I hope to be back some time later this afternoon. Let me know if anything else turns up."

"Yes, boss."

CrimeStoppers was a charity where people could phone in, anonymously if they wished, to report a crime. If you wanted to register yourself, you could also receive a payment if you provided 'information leading to the arrest and conviction' of the perpetrator.

So far, what Mimi had unearthed was circumstantial, but as she'd said, a pattern was definitely emerging.

Drugs were seen by so many people as a victimless crime, but only until something happened: something like violence, intimidation, mounting debts.

Rego's next call was with his friend at the NCA.

"Vik, it's Rob. I have a possible ID for our murder victim – I've emailed you some photos and the deets. And I've just heard from my DCI that a Polish lorry involved in a RTC contained nearly £170,000 in Scottish banknotes. The driver's a tramper and he's disappeared. I'm on my way to St Austell to see it now."

"Scottish bank notes? Interesting."

"And that's not all. I've now got an informant talking about a Polish woman dealing drugs in the area – so far uncorroborated, but I have an analyst working on it. That's a lot of connections with Poland. You hearing anything about that?"

"Our money laundering and drug trafficking expert witnesses always ask if Scottish money has been found – they use it when they present their evidence in court. And I'm hearing that new trafficking routes are being developed through Poland."

"Why Poland? Why risk freighting drugs across Germany?"

Vikram gave a dry laugh. "Poland is the twenty-seventh easiest country in the world to do business with – it's on our government's website; makes it easier to get into the country in the first place. And there's free borders within Europe."

"Mate, my vic was Polish, too."

"You know what this is looking like, don't you?"

Rego knew. He knew all too well. He pressed his foot down on the accelerator, his powerful car leaping forwards.

Rego's first rule of detective work was don't suspect, don't fear, and don't hope for any particular outcome. His job was to observe, find evidence, record it and present it to the Crown Prosecution Service. They were the ones who took the case forwards; a judge and jury agreed the punishment for the crime.

But his second rule was one he'd learned the hard way: to block emotion. He forced himself to leave anger and pity for later. Emotions could lead to an error of judgement, a mistake, a shortcut, a break in the chain of evidence – and that never helped the victim.

Jen Bolitho drove quickly and efficiently as they took the narrow back lanes towards St Ives.

"Your first two days have been pretty full on," she said to Tamsyn with a smile.

"Yeah," Tamsyn agreed with a heartfelt sigh. "Pretty much. I hadn't expected ... well, all this."

"It's unusual, but not as much as you might think. When I first started in the job twenty years ago, murders were rare. Even four or five years ago there were only three a year." She sighed. "Now, it's more like ten a year."

Tamsyn was surprised. "What do you think has changed?"

"There's more drugs around, that's for sure. But also NHS cuts. There used to be Moorhaven for people with severe mental health problems but that closed in '92. There's Glenbourne now, up Plymouth way, but that only has two wards. It's not enough. Hospitals don't have the beds so they're discharged back onto the streets after 24 hours – too many kill themselves ... or someone else."

"That's so sad," Tamsyn said quietly.

"It's criminal, that's what it is," said Jen tightly.

She was silent for a moment, then continued.

"And you've got to remember that not all crimes are reported so your regular villain thinks he can get away with it. But another possible reason is that we're not respected the way we used to be. And a bobby on the beat is rarer than hen's teeth. It's a great way to get to know your patch, but catching criminals? If a burglary is reported two miles away, an officer on foot isn't much use." Her hands flexed on the wheel. "You'll see when you're let loose in a couple of weeks. It's funny, I get treated a lot better now I wear a suit." She paused. "And here's a tip from one woman in the job to another – you might want to rethink your makeup a bit. I know, I know, light makeup is allowed, but you're young and pretty, and the first time you go into a pub to sort out the rowdies, I guarantee they'll be yelling, 'The stripper's here!' It sounds funny, but it happened to me when I first started out, and well, nothing diminishes your confidence or credibility faster. You'll have to grow a thicker skin. Okay?"

"Okay," Tamsyn said quietly. "Thank you."

Jen nodded, satisfied she'd made her point.

As they neared the town, Jen left the country lane, turned past the fire station then sharp right and Tamsyn found herself back in St Ives for the third time that day, but now at the top of the hill, not near the sea.

The town was spread out below them in miniature, the granite buildings, cobbled lanes and scenic harbour, white sandy beaches, framed by the turquoise sea on three sides.

The church of St John's-in-the-Fields wasn't surrounded by wide open meadows as the name suggested, but a carpark edged with tall, leafy trees like the lace doilies that Jess's grandmother brought out for special occasions.

It was Victorian and faintly gothic, but built in a warm stone that glowed in the afternoon sunshine.

"Right, my money's on the wooded areas, but just to be sure, we'll check around the outside of the church first. Do you have forensic gloves with you?"

Tamsyn grimaced and shook her head.

"Sorry, no. I left them with my uniform."

Jen passed her a pair.

"Always keep some in a pocket. You never know when you'll need them."

Tamsyn tucked the gloves into the back pocket of her jeans. This was the second time she'd been told to be prepared – twice, she'd been found wanting.

She promised herself that there wasn't going to be a third time.

"And be careful what you touch," Jen advised. "Isolated

places like this can be used for midnight trysts or addicts. If you see any needles or used condoms, take a photograph and then tell me."

Walking close to the church, Tamsyn examined the ground and building as she searched clockwise, Jen going in the opposite direction. She also looked upwards, trying again to see anything that shouldn't be there. It had worked at the Pryce's guest house – maybe she'd be lucky again.

When she met Jen at the far side of the church, the older woman shook her head.

"Nope, me neither. Now we'll check the perimeter. I don't think it can be much further than that – Jowita wouldn't have risked leaving Lucy for longer than a few minutes in case she came out to see what she was doing or complained to her mum."

Tamsyn wasn't so sure about that, but she knew that without more help or an idea of what they were looking for, they would have to limit their search to the immediate area.

She continued walking around the tree-lined boundary. There was no graveyard here, just grass, trees and a fence that divided church land from a playing field.

There wasn't much to see: a couple of crisp packets and some sweet wrappers. She started to move away, too slow to take the hint her brain was messaging. She turned back – something had caught her attention. *What? What did I see?*

Between a hawthorn bush covered with tight white buds and a small yew tree, half hidden in the dappled light filtering through the trees, there was an area of flattened undergrowth.

Tamsyn bent double and peered into the shadows, then pushed further inside, her hair catching on twigs. The ground had been disturbed and was darker in colour, but it was a palm-sized, white quartz pebble that had caught her attention. How did a pebble get half a mile from the beach unless someone had put it there? Hoping she was on the right trail – and not about to dig up something a fox had stored for a snack later – she pulled on the forensic gloves and gently scraped away the loose soil.

A few centimetres below the surface was a Tupperware box, slightly larger than a shoebox, with dirt staining the lid.

Tamsyn's pulse kicked up a notch. She wondered if she should call Jen but then decided that she'd look like an idiot if it was only some kid's box of treasures.

Despite the dirt encrusting it, the lid lifted easily. Tamsyn blinked twice, shocked and exhilarated by what she was seeing.

She checked around the tin to see if there was anything else, then reversed out from under the bush. Taking a deep breath, she phoned Jen.

"I've found something."

CHAPTER 12

They'd found a gun.

It was a Beretta 9000, a small handgun, not in the best condition, with the serial numbers filed off, and a small amount of ammunition.

Rego was buzzing. The find at the church proved that Jowita was much more than the quiet, mousy housekeeper who'd befriended Lucy. His gut told him that she was involved with organised crime, almost certainly the Hellbanianz, but involved how?

He'd taken the call from Jen Bolitho when he'd been knee deep in items of evidentiary significance from the Polish lorry. They'd found a notebook but so far no one knew what language it was in. Rego had snapped a couple of samples of the writing and emailed them to Vikram. There was no sign of a phone, but there were five old SIM card holders and several top-up vouchers. Those gave locations of where they'd been purchased, and along with fuel receipts from service stations, it meant there was CCTV waiting to be mined. If they were lucky, they might even find footage of crims meeting each other.

There was a laptop cable, but no laptop. It was likely that the driver had taken it before they'd realised what he was involved in. It was a pity because Rego would have liked to see the email traffic. Not that these crims would have sent emails necessarily – they simply typed out the drafts, then the other person could use the same login and password to read the message without it ever being sent.

A forensic analysis of the lorry's digital tachograph would add more information – crucially routes and rest stops. There was a dashcam, too, and although the flash card had been wiped, it hadn't been reformatted so Rego was hopeful that it would still hold some imagery.

In addition to the Scottish banknotes, the team tearing apart the lorry had found a second concealment space in a 15kg propane gas canister. If you shook it, it still sounded like there was liquid in it, but closer examination showed a cleverly constructed space where drugs had been hidden.

Although it was empty now but they knew that drugs had been stored there because it had sent the sniffer dog wild. It begged the question: had they been delivered along the way, or were they about to be picked up?

The concealment was a clever con, because the crims knew that if a bag was seen to be handed over, it could look suspicious, but changing a gas bottle would give the impression that the driver was being replenished with gas, especially if the vehicle delivering the gas bottle had a fake stick-on sign that depicted a gas bottle company.

They were clever bastards. Clever and ruthless.

But the forensics team had a crowbar and they weren't afraid to use it. There was no part of the articulated lorry that they wouldn't know about.

Rego made sure that every member of the forensic and IT

team were prioritising the lorry, then he turned around and headed back to St Ives.

He was definitely clocking up the miles. When he'd been a young police officer in Manchester, it was quicker and easier to get around the city by bus or tram – cars always got caught up in traffic, and parking was a nightmare. It was a common sight to see uniformed officers jumping on and off public transport.

But not in Cornwall. Public transport was thin on the ground and Tom Stevens had joked that he'd end up waiting for yesterday's bus.

But it wasn't just about transport, it was a factor at the heart of the modern force. Cuts to policing were having a serious impact, local police houses shut and front line cops weren't being visible walking local areas. The old 'beat' cop had always been a valuable source of information. They would have time to stop and talk to shopkeepers and other locals, who were always up for a bit of gossip about what was going on in their street.

That connection had been largely lost, and with it, much of the public's support.

As the twilight deepened, Rego focussed on his driving. Only another couple of weeks and the clocks would change, making the evenings lighter. He could use that right now.

He could also use a break in the case.

And it looked like Tamsyn had found it.

The plastic storage container was a potential treasure trove of information. Jen Bolitho had informed him that they'd recovered a set of car keys, a small quantity of five- and ten-pound notes which was still being counted, and a burner phone. It was a basic model Alcatel that you could pick up for a few quid from Tesco. IT techs were going to have fun going through the call logs.

Forensics were all over the scene, an unhappy vicar hovering at a distance.

When Rego had spoken to Reverend Michaels, he hadn't been able to identify Jowita from the photograph they had, but he *thought* she looked like a young woman he'd seen at the church on a number of occasions, sometimes with a girl he'd thought was her daughter.

He'd never spoken to either of them but thought he'd first seen them together the previous autumn.

Rego could only imagine how angry and upset the vicar would be when he found what his church was being used for.

The gun had been fingerprinted, photographed and swabbed for DNA by a Crime Scene Investigator. Rego had been forced to wait for a specially trained 'make safe' CSI tech who was authorised to handle a firearm, trained in how to safely examine it to establish whether or not it was loaded. The Beretta hadn't been loaded, but if it had, the CSI officer would have been trained to unload it safely and package it for transportation to the lab.

It was already on its way to the National Ballistics Intelligence Service to see if it could be matched to any criminal activity.

The plastic container was being checked for fingerprints, and the banknotes would also be examined; the car keys were being analysed to find a make and model.

Jowita must have been clever and careful to have kept a car without her employers even knowing that she could drive. No registration details had turned up for anyone with the name 'Jowita' in west Cornwall, which meant either that the car was uninsured, or that she'd been using a fake name, or both. It was also possible that she'd been threatened and forced to keep the gun, phone, cash and car keys for someone else. Possible, but looking less likely by the minute.

Rego pulled into the Penzance police station's car park, noticing that there were far more cars than the previous night. CID were working late – whether his team were trying to get in his good books or simply hardworking and dedicated, he didn't yet know, but he was pleased to see them.

Climbing out of the car, stretching out the kinks in his back, he turned, trudging up the stairs to CID.

Damn, they needed a break on the vic's ID as soon as possible.

And hopefully something that linked Jowita to the missing lorry driver and the Scottish banknotes.

"Well, hell, why not?" Rego muttered to himself. "And a nice red bow to tie it all up."

"Boss?" DS Stevens said, glancing up and looking as tired as Rego felt.

"Just thinking out loud, Tom."

If this was the work of organised crime gangs, and the notebook that had been found really was written in Albanian as Rego had suspected, and he knew from his previous case in Manchester that cannabis was a major export of Albanian agriculture, but the country was also an active trans-shipment point for organisations moving hard drugs such as cocaine and heroin into Europe from Turkey or even countries in South America and Asia. He didn't think the lorry would have carried 20 kilos of hash when coke, heroin and meth were so much more lucrative. But maybe the lorry had carried both at one time or another.

Cocaine: the party drug of choice. He scowled, thinking of all the nice, middle class professionals who didn't consider that their 'recreational usage' was part of a world where a woman's tongue was cut out.

Then he reminded himself that this was all circumstantial, still just a theory. He needed evidence. He needed to work out how ... or if ... Jowita fitted into the picture. And he really wanted to know who she'd been talking to – a man that little Lucy said had a Cornish accent.

He was pinning a lot on the word of a child.

ABC, he reminded himself: assume nothing, believe no one, challenge and check everything.

He rubbed his chin, realising that he'd forgotten to shave.

It was possible that Jowita was the local liaison for dealers. But how important was she? Could sleepy, picturesque Penzance be a major distribution point for drugs? Cornwall had over 400 miles of coastline – too many places where drugs could be landed without anyone seeing them.

Yes, it was possible that Penzance was a distribution centre. But the lorry was a definite – he needed to focus on the known facts.

Rego was about to call DCI Finch with an update when his phone rang, but instead of his boss, he was surprised to see that it was his wife calling.

Working away from home wasn't easy on them as a couple or as a family, so he tried to FaceTime her and the kids each night before bedtime, but Cassie rarely disturbed him during the day, and his heart thudded as he answered.

"Hey, luv, you okay? Kids okay?"

"Patricia called around again. She's driving me insane!"

Rego withheld a sigh; it was an old argument, and one that no one was ever going to win. When he was young and dumb, he'd thought that being fought over by two women would be cool. He knew better now, especially since his wife and mother seemed to rub each other up the wrong way on a daily basis. He tried to speak calmly.

"I know she can be a bit ... but she's just trying to help and..."

"It isn't *helping* when she lets Maisie have four chocolate

Hobnobs on the way home from school, and then I've got a kid with a sugar rush who won't eat her tea; and it isn't *helping* when she lets Max play football *inside* the house when I sent him into the back garden, and he smashes a glass."

"I'm sure she didn't mean to..."

"She never does mean to!"

Rego winced as his wife's voice went shrill enough to alert dogs ten miles away.

"If you don't have a word with her, Rob, I will!"

She hung up.

He rubbed his temples and decided to call his mum later. He could almost predict what she'd say: *I'm only trying to help; Cassie doesn't appreciate me; I'm their grandmother; all children need a little spoiling.*

He remembered his old boss's words when he'd joined the force as a young and newly engaged man: *Join the Force and get a divorce.* He was determined to buck that trend.

But he had to throw off all thoughts of the impending family discussion (row) and compromise (loggerheads), because he was getting closer to finding Jowita's killer.

He strode across to DC Jack Forshaw who was working with the new DC from Camborne.

"Jack, Mimi, I want to know who are the faces for drug dealing in St Ives, Penzance and anywhere else within a fifteen mile radius. Find out which pubs they frequent, then I want you to pull CCTV footage for the last fortnight. You're looking for the victim and anyone she meets. I know it's going to be a lot of legwork, so I'll see what help I can get you. If you don't find anything for the last 14 days, go back another week and widen the search parameters. And Mimi, if you could talk to your colleagues at Camborne and find out about known dealers up there."

"Falmouth has a big student population, boss," said Mimi. "Might be worth trying around there, too."

"Okay, but start here first and then work your way out. And I want to know if any of the local faces have been seen around St Ives."

From his desk at the other side of the room, Tom Stevens looked up and raised an eyebrow.

"Locals try not to go into St Ives, and definitely not between Easter and September, boss. The parking is so bad, I swear it shortens my life by a year every time I go. A parking space was recently sold for £40,000."

"You mean a car park?" Rego asked.

"No, boss: a single parking space that was 2m x 4.4m."

Rego raised his eyebrows in amazement.

"I see what you mean, Tom. Well, we have to find her car. Where would she park it? On the street?"

Stevens shook his head. "Maybe, but it would have to be a distance from the B&B. Street parking is really difficult in St Ives and she'd have been racking up parking tickets – not smart for someone wanting to stay under the radar."

Rego took that on board.

"I'll get uniform to take a look around the streets near where she lives, and see if anything shows up. What about residents' parking?"

"There are four residents' car parks," said Stevens as he ticked them off on his fingers. "Barnoon, Porthgwidden and Island, Westcotts Quay and Wheal Dream."

Rego frowned in confusion. "There's a car park called 'Real Dream'?"

His CID colleagues shared knowing smiles.

"Uh, that's *Wheal* Dream, boss," Stevens chuckled. "'Wheal' is an old Cornish word for a mining area."

Rego shook his head.

"I didn't know I'd be learning another language when I came down here. Right then ... Jack, Mimi, check out the residents' permits just in case anything pops up." He turned to his sergeant. "What about long term car parks, Tom?"

"It would cost a fortune, but yes..."

"If she was dealing drugs, she probably was making a fortune," Rego said drily.

"Okay, we'll check the long stay car parks," Stevens agreed. "May as well check the short term ones, as well."

Rego's phone rang and he headed to the HOLMES room which was empty now the office staff had left.

"Vik, what have you got?"

"Jowita Wojciechowski, aka Jowita Nowak, aka Saemira Ruçi. Brought up by her mother five miles from the Kosovan border in a village called Bytyç – don't ask me how to pronounce that because I have no idea. Ethnically Albanian, no religious affiliations that we know of. Wanted in Poland and Spain for drug trafficking offences..." He paused theatrically. "And a cousin of Ellvana Sinani, sometime girlfriend of..."

"Dritan Domi."

"Well remembered."

"I'm not likely to forget her," Rego said ruefully, his fingers automatically going to the raised ridge on his arm where the woman had slashed a kitchen knife across his bicep. He whistled between his teeth. "This is big."

And here was Dritan Domi again – like a big, fat spider at the centre of a vast web, pulling on the threads, tightening them one by one. Yes, Rego knew his name all too well. Domi had been a lieutenant in the Hellbanianz until he'd been sent down on five counts of conspiracy to supply Class A drugs. And that was only the crimes they could prove – there were more, a lot more. Rego had been on the team that had caught him, but he knew that just because Domi was serving 21 years in HMP Manchester – Strangeways, as it used to be called – it didn't mean the crime boss no longer had power. Prisons ran on the protected and the prey; doing favours for the right people was how you survived.

"And the notebook images you sent me is a list of dates with questions that appear to be about couriers," Vik continued. "Our experts tell me that they're written in the Gheg dialect of northern Albania." He paused. "I think you've got your connection."

Rego strode back to CID just as Tom Stevens put his coat on to go home.

"Tom, we've got the victim's real name: Saemira Ruçi, and she's not Polish, she's Albanian. In fact, her cousin was in a relationship with one of the gang leaders in the Hellbanianz that I put away last year. I've had it confirmed. Can you run this and her other aliases? See what turns up."

Tom took off his coat again and sat back at his desk.

"Now we're talking."

"And I want that CCTV from the pubs now – if she's been dealing in Newlyn, she's probably dealing all over. Get her face out to teams in Camborne, Falmouth and Truro, and send it on to the brass at Middlemoor, too."

"On it, boss."

He needed to let his team know that they'd been wrong about the Polish connection – but were very, very right about how serious this case was. Where did the lorry driver fit in? Was he the one bringing the drugs in for Ruçi to distribute? It seemed probable but Rego couldn't help feeling that he was missing something.

He thought back to the victim's close relationship with the girl Lucy. Was she being groomed to sell drugs for Ruçi?

Rego wanted to listen to all the recordings for a second

time before he decided whether or not he wanted to interview the girl again. He needed to be sure.

He drew in a long breath then rolled up his sleeves. There was a lot of work to do. With Saemira Ruçi's real name, they now had proof: Albanian gangs were operating in Cornwall.

CHAPTER 13

Jen dropped Tamsyn at the Admiral Benbow just after 7.30pm. Tamsyn hadn't asked her to, but Jen already knew that each of the uniformed teams met once a week and she'd simply assumed that Tamsyn would want to go.

"It's good to get to know the people you work with," she said cheerfully. "But don't let them buy you shots – I know what that lot are like when they get going."

Tamsyn smiled. "Thanks for the tip!"

It would be good to get to know the rest of E-team, but she hadn't slept much the last two nights but. She decided that she'd stay for one drink then leave.

Jamie must have been watching for her because the moment she stepped through the door, he waved and called her name loudly.

The pub was busy but not crowded, and several people turned to stare as Tamsyn made her way across the dimly lit room with its low, beamed ceiling and cluttered, *olde worlde* charm.

"I thought you'd stood me up for a moment," Jamie said

cheerfully, "then I reckoned that no one in their right mind would do that."

"Who said Tampax is in her right mind?"

Chloe's voice came from behind her, and Tamsyn stiffened as her former classmate returned from the bar carrying a bottle of Rattler.

She rolled her eyes, not bothering to hide her irritation.

"Can't you take a joke, Tampax?" Chloe asked spitefully.

"Yes. Can you tell one?" Tamsyn shot back.

Jamie laughed loudly. "I think someone's jealous!"

"Oh, please!" Chloe snorted, "I could outshine her wearing a paper bag."

"A paper bag from 'Ho's R Us'," Tamsyn said under her breath.

Luckily, no one heard her.

"I got you a drink in, Tam," said Jamie, pointing at a glass of white wine on the scarred table.

Chloe scowled, and Tamsyn wondered if the witch was crushing on Jamie. Not that she'd ever needed a reason to be a stone-cold bitch.

Andy, one of the older members of the team, ignored the exchange and leaned forwards.

"I know you got a quick introduction this morning but you probably won't remember everyone's names since you hit the ground running. I'm Andy, and you've met Jamie; those two clowns are Carl and Jethro," he pointed at two men who both had short brown hair and were wearing rugby shirts; she wasn't sure which was which. "Jason is our other student officer, Mitch is on the Guinness, and that's Ky," he pointed at two older men of around thirty.

Tamsyn smiled and nodded as Jamie shuffled across the bench seat to make space for her.

"How are you settling in?" Andy asked.

"Yeah, good." She shot a glance at Chloe. "People have been really friendly and helpful."

"What's the new DI like?" asked Jamie.

Tamsyn hitched a shoulder. "Yeah, he seems nice."

They waited for more but Tamsyn didn't know what to say. She knew better than to admit she thought he was hot, and she definitely wasn't going to mention that he'd walked her home from that godawful party.

"He's an asshole," said Chloe. "Thinks he's better than everyone else."

There was a surprised silence then Andy shook his head. "Rego seems like a stand-up guy to me."

"Rodrigo has his little favourites already," Chloe said, smirking at Tamsyn.

Andy frowned.

"He's a copper's copper – came up through the ranks. My mate worked with him in GMP and says he's not off running to the policy handbook like some of them."

Then turned his back on Chloe, and spoke to Tamsyn.

"I heard you went over to St Ives with Jen Bolitho."

Tamsyn didn't know what to say to that either, or what she was allowed to say. She looked over her shoulder, wondering if the drinkers at the next table could hear them.

"Hey, you found a gun, right?" Jamie tossed in, looking at her half admiringly, half resentfully.

They all waited for her to say something as she took a sip of the wine.

"I'm not being funny," she answered at last, "but are we supposed to talk about ... work ... when we're in public?"

"God, you're such a teacher's pet," Chloe jeered.

Tamsyn snapped, too tired to pretend the jabs weren't getting to her. "What is your problem? We're not in frickin' nursery school!"

"Alright, everybody calm down," Andy said. "Chloe, you're bang out of order."

Chloe's eyes glittered dangerously.

"Tamsyn has a point," he went on. "We should be careful what we say. And the reason I'm sitting with my back to the wall is so I can see everyone coming in and who could be near enough to overhear us – which is no one, by the way. Anything you say..."

"Can be taken down and given in evidence!" Jamie laughed, raising his bottle in a salute.

The others were grateful to join in and lighten the atmosphere.

Tamsyn took another sip of wine which tasted slightly better on the second go and told them what she'd seen.

"We found a plastic container hidden under a bush – there was quite a lot of money in it, car keys, a phone ... and a handgun. Jen called in crime scene techs and DI Rego was on his way over when we left. That's all I know."

"Two days in the job and you find all that," Jamie said enviously. "You'll be Superintendent by the end of the week at this rate."

"Was it stashed by the murder vic?" Andy asked.

Tamsyn shrugged uncomfortably. "It looks that way."

"It's got to be about drugs," Carl said quietly – or it might have been Jethro – Tamsyn wasn't sure. "I heard that the vic isn't even Polish – she's Albanian."

"County lines," Andy grimaced, and several of the others nodded.

Drug dealers from the cities were using children and teenagers in rural areas to sell their product in schools. Low risk for the dealers and they were able to penetrate rural communities more efficiently.

"CID just put out a briefing that the vic was dealing," said

Andy, turning to Tamsyn. "And she'd made friends with her employer's daughter. Is the kid involved?"

"She's ten," Tamsyn said, feeling sick at the thought.

"That's the age they start 'em," Andy said shrewdly. "Bastards."

Tamsyn's brain spun. Had Lucy been involved? *Did I miss something?*

"I've got a friend in Border Force," said Jason. "He says they're getting more and more single-handed yachts sailing up from the Bay of Biscay and dropping off to dealers along the coast. They caught a Dutch guy near the Isles of Scilly who'd sailed a 36-footer from Portugal. The only reason they got him was because he had problems with his rigging. They found cocaine worth twenty mill."

As the others reminisced about cases they'd been involved in, Tamsyn slipped outside to make a call.

"Rego," came the crisp voice.

"Uh, hello, sir. It's Tamsyn Poldhu."

"What can I do for you, Tamsyn?"

"I'm sorry to bother you, but do you think Lucy was involved? In the drugs, I mean? I don't think ... I don't know..."

"I've been asking myself the same question," he said evenly. "So I've listened to the entire interview with her again: you asked Lucy if Saemira had ever given her anything. She said yes, and mentioned a girl's plastic tiara, the kind of thing you can pick up in Poundland or Claire's Accessories."

"You've heard of Claire's Accessories?" she asked, surprised.

Rego gave a dry laugh. "I have an eight year-old daughter – she once asked her mother if we could live in the Arndale branch." He paused. "The way Lucy answered so readily, it didn't sound as if she was hiding anything. I don't believe that

Ruçi involved her, but if we need to interview Lucy again, we can."

"Sir, do you think Ruçi would have asked Lucy to deal drugs? When she was older?"

Rego was silent for several seconds.

"We'll never know. You did well today, Tamsyn. Go and have a drink with your colleagues. Have fun."

The call ended but she stayed outside for a few moments, deep in thought. Then she pushed through the door and went back to join the rest of the team.

Finally, she began to relax, putting the last two days behind her, drinking in the laughter and camaraderie along with the white wine which tasted much better now. Chloe ignored her, which was just fine with Tamsyn.

"Well, while some of us have been playing in the big league," Andy said, raising his glass to Tamsyn, "I've been after a bunch of kids who've been out lamping. There was three of them, two still at school: titch was the lamp man, scaring a small herd of roe deer over St Just way; big brother was the shooter; and their cousin had borrowed his dad's Land Rover, except poor old dad didn't know about the 'borrowing' and reported it as having been nicked. So he was grassing up his own kid and nephews. Of course, once he realised, he didn't want to press charges for theft, but they'll still be charged with deer poaching and firearms offences anyway. The farmer whose land they were on wasn't happy either – the silly sods drove all over a field of Cornish earlies."

'Earlies' was the name for Cornish new potatoes which were small and sweet and perfect with a knob of butter. Tamsyn's stomach rumbled – she was craving her grandmother's cooking, and a slice of cold pizza at the pub wasn't cutting it.

"D'you know what gets me?" said Jethro (or maybe Carl).

"I get fed up going to the same families two or three times a week. Same people, same problems. If we could ship them off to Samson, our lives would be a lot easier."

"Nobody lives on Samson," Jamie said.

It was one of the small islands that made up the Isles of Scilly 30 miles off the Cornish coast. Some 2,000 people lived on the Scillies, but of the 140 islands, only five had permanent residents. Samson had been uninhabited for 170 years and was little more than a barren rock.

"It used to be a penal colony," added Jason. "Tourists go there now."

For some reason, Jamie found that hilarious, and his laughter was contagious. Tamsyn grinned at him and he winked back.

"I nicked a local villain for dealing coke," he said, when everyone had managed to stop laughing. "Magistrate let him out and two days later he was at Hell's Mouth, you know, those steep cliffs northwest of Gwithian? So there he is, standing on the edge, threatening to jump, and I'm staring down at the beach 300 feet below, not wanting to get anyway near that twat in case he takes me with him. He recognises me as 'the Filth what nicked me last week' and starts ranting and raving. I'm trying to calm him down, calling him 'mate' and saying 'you don't want to do it – let's calm down and have a cuppa' – and the bastard jumps! Right in front of me. We had to get the Coast Guard out there to retrieve the body."

Everyone was quiet and Tamsyn saw the weariness that Jamie tried so hard to hide behind his jokes.

"I wouldn't make a good negotiator," he continued. "I've never talked anyone down at Hell's Mouth. They always jump."

He took a swig of his cider then belched loudly.

Carl/Jethro began to laugh again, and as the others joined in, he thumped Jamie on the shoulder.

Tamsyn finally understood what these drinking sessions were all about – this was how you decompressed. This was how you coped when someone killed themselves in front of you.

An hour later, having enjoyed herself more than she'd expected and beginning to feel that she really was part of the team, she finished her wine, made her excuses and left. Andy and Jamie went with her, keeping her company as far as the train station before they all headed in different directions.

"Don't fall asleep on the train, guys," she said, smiling at them. "You'll end up in Plymouth!"

"Devon!" Jamie yelped. "Don't wish that on us!" He waited until Andy had disappeared into the station before he spoke again. "Tam?"

Her smile froze, guessing what was coming. *Please don't say it.*

"Maybe we could go for a drink sometime? I mean, just the two of us."

He said it.

"Jamie, I think you're really nice..."

He winced. "That's the kiss of death."

"You've been really helpful and I appreciate it but I don't think it would be a good idea to date anyone I work with." She looked as uncomfortable as she felt. "Things could get weird, you know?"

He gave a wry smile. "Wow, friend-zoned already?"

She tipped her head on one side. "Friends is good, right?"

He gave an embarrassed laugh. "Sure, better than nothing. See you tomorrow, Tam."

"See you, Jamie."

She watched him disappear into the station, cringing at

how awkward that had been. At least he'd waited until they were in private.

She dug her hands into her pockets and walked fast, ravenously hungry and eager to be home. And she wanted to talk to Jess. Tamsyn realised that she hadn't turned her personal phone on, and when she did, she had three missed calls from her grandmother and one from Jess. But when she tried to call her back, it went straight to voicemail. She didn't leave a message and she didn't call her grandmother because she was only minutes from home.

Gulval was quiet, and the windows of the cottage glowed behind the curtains. Tamsyn felt grateful that she had family, people who cared about her.

She let herself in, sniffing appreciatively at the aroma of fish pie – her grandmother's speciality.

Mo came racing out to greet her, and guiltily Tamsyn remembered that she'd promised to take her for a walk today.

"Sorry, scruff-bucket," she said, stroking the dog's wiry fur. "I'm on lates tomorrow, so we'll go in the morning, 'kay?"

Mo held no grudges and wound herself around Tamsyn's legs like a cat then followed her as she headed into the tiny living room.

"Hi, sorry I'm late."

Her grandfather scowled. "You should have phoned. Your gran's been worried!"

"Sorry, Gran," she said, looping her arms around her grandmother for a quick hug. "I got caught up at work, and then everyone from E-team was going for a drink after. I couldn't say no and I forgot to turn my personal phone back on. I'm really sorry."

"Just text us next time," her grandmother said gently. "We worry about you. Especially now."

"I know, I'm really sorry. Just so you know, I'm on lates for the next two days, so I won't be home until after midnight."

She hoped that her grandmother wouldn't be waiting up till the small hours because she needed her rest, and her grandfather needed to up before first light.

"Are you hungry? Have you eaten?"

"No, and Mo is looking pretty tasty right now," she said, picking up the little scruff and kissing her furry head.

"Tammy!" her grandmother laughed.

While she filled a glass with water, her grandmother took the warming plate out of the Aga and put a slightly dry fish pie in front of her.

Tamsyn had only taken a few mouthfuls when her grandfather spoke.

"I saw Bernie Ryder this morning."

Tamsyn could guess what was coming, but kept her eyes on her plate.

"Why didn't you tell me that you were there when they found that poor drowned girl? Why did I have to hear it from Bernie?"

She swallowed then took a sip of water.

"I won't always be able to tell you what I do, Grandad," she said gently. "And I didn't want to tell you what I did on my first day because I didn't want either of you to be worried about me or be upset. I spent the rest of yesterday and all of today trying to find out who she was."

She definitely couldn't tell her grandparents that the woman had been murdered. Or could she? She wasn't actually sure what she could and couldn't say to her family. But one of the Poldhu family mottos was 'least said, soonest mended'.

"Uncle George thought she might have fallen off the *Scillonian*," she added, because she had to say something.

Her grandfather bristled. "George? What's he got to do with the price o' fish? He didn't tell me you'd seen him!"

Tamsyn groaned inwardly. Somehow, she'd managed to open her mouth just to change feet.

"I told my boss, Detective Inspector Rego, that if anyone could make a guess where the body could have floated from, it would be you. We went down to Newlyn yesterday morning but you'd gone to Pirates; Uncle George was there so we asked him."

Her grandfather shook his head. "And he said she'd come off the *Scillonian* and ended up at Lamorna? Has 'e gone Bodmin?"

Tamsyn raised her eyebrows.

"No way that girl come off the *Scillonian*!" he snorted.

"Why's that?"

"Tides and currents were all wrong for the last couple of nights – she musta come from further east, nearer Lizard."

The murdered woman's ravaged face swam before her eyes and Tamsyn pushed her unfinished meal away and set the plate on the floor. Mo was delighted, wolfing Tamsyn's fish pie without drawing breath, then sat licking her lips.

While her grandmother was pottering around the kitchen, Tamsyn leaned closer to her grandfather and lowered her voice.

"You can't tell anyone this, but she didn't drown. The pathologist thinks she'd been dead for quite a few hours when her body was dumped at sea, maybe a day or more."

Her grandfather didn't look as shocked as she'd expected, but then again, he'd lived a long time and endured a lot of dark days.

"She was last seen late on Friday morning, so she was probably killed and dumped on Friday night or Saturday morning."

Her grandfather interrupted.

"It was a grounder sea late Friday night."

Tamsyn nodded in understanding, but if DI Rego had heard, he'd be clueless.

"Nobody was out till Saturday afternoon," her grandfather continued.

"When did the swell drop?"

"Not till gone six."

Tamsyn considered this. It would have been risky to dump a body in daylight. Not impossible, but...

Her grandfather obviously followed her train of thought.

"No, he'd a had to wait until Saturday night." He paused and met her gaze. "So she was murdered?"

Tamsyn grimaced and nodded as they shared a look.

"Pity I wasn't out Saturday night because I might a seen something..." his words trailed off and his eyes became distant.

"What is it, Grandad?"

He blinked twice then shook his head. "Something o' nothing," and he pressed his lips together.

Tamsyn knew from experience that whatever it was, he'd only tell her when he was ready.

"You going to talk to that boss of yours?" he asked after a short pause.

"I'm going to email him in a minute." She hesitated, wanting to say what was on her mind but unsure if it was the right thing to do. "Grandad, she lived in St Ives, for nearly two years now. I could have passed her in the street – and she was killed here."

He nodded slowly.

"And yeah, I guess someone could have driven down from upcountry to ... to hurt her but..."

"...it could be someone local who murdered her, that's what you're thinking."

Tamsyn swallowed.

"It makes more sense – someone who had a boat, a small one that couldn't put out to sea on Saturday night."

"Boats can be bought, borrowed or stolen," he reminded her.

"Yeah." She let out a long breath. "Right, well, I think I'll go to bed now. My shift doesn't start till the afternoon. I'll have a bit of a lie in then take Her Royal Scruffiness for a walk."

Mo looked up, grinning at the promise of an outing and wagging her tail.

Deep in thought, her grandfather nodded. "Awright, maid. You take care now."

"And you, Grandad," Tamsyn paused. "There are some bad people out there."

He didn't answer.

Her grandmother appeared in the living room, frowning at the charged atmosphere. Tamsyn gave her a quick smile.

"I'm going to have an early night, Gran."

"'Spec you'll be calling Jess for a chat first."

Tamsyn laughed. "Probably."

"I don't know what you girls find to talk about all the time."

Tamsyn wrapped her arms around her grandmother, acknowledging the comfort of the familiar, the faint scent of her floral perfume, the tight hug, the unspoken love.

"Get yourself off to bed then. Let little Mo out first, will you?"

Tamsyn glanced at the dog. "Come on, trouble, but don't take too long."

Little Mo sprang up, shook herself and pranced to the backdoor while Tamsyn wrapped her grandfather's coat around her and shoved her feet into his enormous rigger boots, following the excited dog into the garden.

The moon was huge and bright, casting pale shadows across the small garden – a smugglers' moon they called it in the old days. Tamsyn knew her friends would be partying on the beach, drinking, probably smoking doobies. She missed them. And she didn't.

Maybe because she'd lost her parents so young, she'd always felt older than her years. Maybe she'd grown up faster, or maybe she just didn't fit anymore, if she ever had.

Mo was snuffling around the gap in the fence to next door's garden. Tamsyn hoped that her grandfather would repair it soon so they didn't have to watch the dog when she was outside.

After ten minutes, Tamsyn decided that Mo had been given long enough to do her business.

"Come on, Mo. Time to go in."

More snuffling sounds but no dog appeared.

"Morwenna! Get your furry little backside here now!"

The dog's head popped up from beside the compost heap, looking very pleased with herself.

Back inside the cosy kitchen, Tamsyn fetched Mo's bedtime biscuit, then climbed the narrow staircase, taking the steps two at a time, Mo charging ahead.

She felt it, the changes happening in her life; felt it like it was her body and blood and bones that had changed, not just the start of a new job; felt it like it was *us* and *them*; felt it like it was more than just a job.

She'd have to be careful about what she said to Jess, and the thought made her stomach hurt.

Settling herself on the old single bed that she'd slept in since she was ten, she tapped out a quick email to DI Rego, then called her oldest friend.

"Hey, you!" Jess's grinning face filled the screen. "I've been waiting *all day* to hear how your date went? I was beginning to think you'd run off to Bristol with him. Come on, spill the beans!"

"Ugh. Worst date ever."

"It was a bust?"

"In so many ways."

As Tamsyn told Jess about the awful party and the aftermath, Jess's face crumpled in sympathy.

"What a loser! I can't believe he said that to you!"

"I know, right? Anyway, I reported it to my boss."

"You didn't!" Jess sounded shocked.

"Hey! I had to. I might even have to get a drug test to prove that I didn't take anything," Tamsyn snapped.

Jess bit her lip and was silent.

"This is serious, Jess," Tamsyn said more gently but with a hint of steel in her voice. "This is my career now. You get that, don't you?"

Jess nodded, but her eyes were questioning.

Tamsyn hoped that she wasn't going to ask what would happen if she, Jess, had weed on her or anything else. Because the answer was exactly the same as she'd said to Ollie.

When Jess didn't speak, Tamsyn knew it was up to her to break the awkward silence.

"I did get asked out by another officer," Tamsyn offered.

Jess smiled, grateful to be off the hook.

"The hot ex-Royal Marine?"

"No, another guy called Jamie. He's kind of sweet, but I said no."

"Why?"

"Like I said before, I just don't think it's a good idea to date someone at work. Imagine if we broke up and I still had to see him every day."

"Yeah, but you're only going to meet other police officers and criminals, aren't you?" Jess laughed.

She had a point.

CHAPTER 14

Rego was intrigued by the email he'd received from Tamsyn which had been sent late the previous night.

> Grandad says it was a grounder sea on Friday so the body couldn't have been dumped until Saturday. Hope this helps.

He had to do a search on Google for 'grounder sea' before he could make sense of the message, but then he understood what she was saying and its significance: when the waves were coming in so heavy you couldn't launch or land the lobster boats or any small craft, the fishing community called it 'a grounder sea'.

So, if the murderer had used a small boat, it wouldn't have been able to get out in a heavy swell – and it could explain why the victim's body hadn't been disposed of immediately – the killer or killers would have had to hide the body somewhere until Saturday night. Which made him think about the strange lividity marks on the victim's back: could she have been lying at the bottom of a boat?

Right now, that information didn't move the case

forwards, but if and when they found the boat that had been used, forensics should be able to get them crucial evidence: Locard's Exchange Principle – every contact leaves a trace.

And there was more news: whatever witchcraft the IT techs had used, they'd managed to crack or bypass Ruçi's phone passcode and were tracing the numbers she'd called, some in Spain, Poland, Germany and Albania, but many more in the UK.

He expected that the numbers would all lead to other burner phones, but you never knew – criminals weren't always clever or careful.

Intriguingly, the majority of the victim's phone traffic was with a number that was currently offline, and this was the one that Rego was most interested in. Rego thought again about the mysterious man with a Cornish accent who'd phoned Ruçi.

Unfortunately, there were so many messages and calls in the weeks before she'd been killed, it was impossible to say which number corresponded to the man Lucy had heard. In fact, bearing in mind the time of the call, either he'd made a mistake and called Ruçi on her personal phone – the one Lucy had texted her on which they hadn't been able to locate – or that something urgent had happened.

Evidence from phones was one of Rego's favourite types. As a DC and even as a DS, he'd always volunteered to be the Telecoms Officer working with IT to collect all the data a phone could offer, which was a lot. As a DI and Senior Investigating Officer on this case, he'd reluctantly handed that job over to DS Stevens.

Rego believed that the call data record on the mystery number could prove crucial for building a solid case. They just had to work out which number was the key from out of the dozens on the phone. But they'd start with the most frequently used numbers. CDR information included calls and messages made and received, data usage, and cell sites which would identify which phone masts were used and therefore chart the user's approximate location.

The application for CDR information had to be made by a Superintendent, and Vodafone was expected to respond within the next 24 hours. As soon as that came in, DS Stevens would be all over it and Operation Volt would take a giant step forwards.

What they already knew was that Ruçi's burner phone had an unregistered SIM which showed hundreds of texts over more than 18 months between her and Subject F – the letter assigned to the prolific mystery texter. Messages had come in at all hours of the day and night, referring to 'deposits' and 'transfers', giving days and times but no locations, just 'the house' or 'the water' or 'the market'. Occasionally, Ruçi had replied in the afternoons – which was probably when she was at the church with Lucy – but more often she'd made calls and sent texts late at night. Clearly, she'd had no problem leaving the hotel unnoticed or fooling the Pryce family about her whereabouts during the hours of darkness, or even the fact that she had a car.

Lucy had provided the number for Ruçi's personal phone, and Rego expected that a 'clean phone' would only have numbers for her friends, family, fast food and maybe a taxi company – those sorts of innocent numbers. Unless, unless either she'd made a mistake and used her personal phone to call a criminal associate, or a criminal associate made a mistake and phoned her 'clean phone'. If an analyst found any matching numbers, it would show that person was close enough to Ruçi to have both numbers. Thank God for software programs that helped match the data, because that was a lot of information to comb through.

Rego felt that they were on the right track and that the case was going to break soon. The trickle of information was like watching an old fashioned egg timer – it seemed slow at the start, but then intel came in faster and faster, and processing it could be become time-consuming and complex, which is where the use of an analyst and specialist software came in.

He'd worked late the previous evening reviewing the case file at the station rather than going back to his small room at the Premier Inn. As he was away from home, it made no difference where he worked, although Cassie said that he hadn't been home on time since he'd joined CID, which was probably true. So, he made the effort to FaceTime with her and the kids before their bedtime. And last night, as he'd promised his wife, he'd had 'the talk' with his mum, too. That hadn't gone well.

"Who do you think you're talking to, Robert? I'm your mother, not one of those dirty criminals! I work my fingers to the bone all my life, and this is the gratitude I get? Those children of yours is growing up wild! And I'm the one there helping your wife. Your wife! You think it easy with two growing children?"

And on, and on. But since she wouldn't accept that four Hob Nobs after school or football in the living room weren't appropriate and not what Cassie had told her, it was a one-way conversation.

Rego rubbed his forehead. Why was it so much easier interrogating hardened criminals than talking reason to his own mother? She meant well, but she was trying to make up for her own absence in her son's life by spoiling her grandchildren.

His mother had been blessed with a multi-generational upbringing in Bermuda where grandparents and great grandparents were as involved with raising children as the mother and father, sometimes more so. She couldn't – wouldn't – understand that Cassie found her constant presence intrusive and interfering rather than helpful. And Cassie had begun to resent the fact that Patricia lived two streets away while her own mother lived more than an hour away in Macclesfield.

The conversation had ended with Patricia bursting into tears, saying his father would be turning in his grave – which he doubted, since the bastard had rarely been sober enough to care one way or another – and slamming the phone down, before she remembered that didn't work with smart phones, but by then Rego had ended the call for the sake of his own sanity.

Talking to Cassie had merely led to the second ear bashing of the evening. He'd only been away from home for a week. How the hell was he going to do this for a couple of years? It had seemed like a great idea to move to the southwest for a promotion, get wider experience of policing in a rural area, learn some new skills, then head back to Manchester with a packed CV and go for a DCI's position – hopefully.

Cassie hadn't been thrilled about being a 'single parent' for large chunks of time, but she hadn't wanted to move the kids twice in a few years either. They'd agreed that he'd take the promotion and travel home at weekends; during school holidays, they'd come down to him.

Rego made himself the third coffee of the morning, trying to decide which was the worst, the Premier Inn's sachet of Nescafé or the station's: faintly flavoured hot water versus coffee strong enough to beat him in a bare knuckle brawl. Take your pick.

"Boss," said Jack, interrupting his thoughts. "We've found her!"

Rego jumped to his feet and strode across to Jack's desk. "Show me!"

Being the CCTV Officer on a case could be a thankless task. First, you had to visit all the locations on foot, looking for CCTV cameras. Then you had to find out who owned them, and if you were lucky, they could pass over digital footage. Lots of times no one knew who owned the CCTV cameras and other times they weren't working; but sometimes, just sometimes, after hours and hours of mind-numbing and bum-numbing footage, you struck gold.

"It's her!" said Jack, pointing to a frozen image of Saemira Ruçi outside the Mackerel pub in Newlyn. She was talking to a man in his early twenties and another man in a hoodie whose face was hidden.

"Wait, what's that?" Rego asked, his eyes narrowing as he squinted at the grainy image. "Re-run the tape."

A small package was passed between them, but the image was so poor that it was impossible to tell if Ruçi was handing something over or receiving it.

Jack rubbed his eyes. "I missed that, boss. Sorry."

"Run it again."

They ran the footage three more times but still couldn't be sure who was handing over and who was receiving – it was frustrating as hell.

"When was this?" Rego asked, his gaze panning between Jack and Mimi who'd also been trawling through hundreds of hours of footage.

"Thursday night, 10.47pm," replied Mimi.

"The day before she disappeared," Jack added, not wanting to be left out.

"Good, but check the timestamp – don't assume it matches real time. And for God's sake, check the date is correct."

Rego needed this piece of the puzzle, but he needed it to be right. More often than not, there could be some time slippage, especially the change from BST to GMT, and that could knock an old analogue system out by an hour; sometimes even the date could even be wrong if it hadn't been re-set correctly after a power cut.

"I've tried to find a better image of the other guy, but he keeps his head down," said Jack.

"It looks like he knows where the CCTV cameras are," Mimi added.

"Maybe," Rego nodded. "What do we know about the Mackerel Inn?"

"It used to have a bad rep, lots of fights, hard drinking and some low level drug dealing, but it's going for a more upmarket image now and doing pretty well," said Jack. "It's still the boozer of the Newlyn fishermen – they always have the funeral there when they lose one of their own."

"Is it the kind of place where there are more men than women?" Rego asked.

Jack nodded. "Yeah, definitely."

"So maybe someone would remember Ruçi," Rego said. "If she went inside at all. Jack, can you tell from the footage if she was in the pub or just meeting these men outside."

"I don't think she went in, boss, but I'll check."

"Okay, then I want you to go down there – show the photo of Ruçi and also the one from CCTV outside the pub. Mimi, I want those images emailed across to all teams to see if anyone recognises any of them. And get it sent to the Press Office ready to circulate as 'a person of interest' but they're to hold off until they hear from us again."

"Yes, boss," Mimi replied.

"Then keep looking for anyone else she's met up with."

Rego paused. "Jack, Mimi, good work," and the younger man grinned while Mimi just smiled calmly.

They all felt it, that buzz, that rush of adrenaline when the case made a leap forwards.

Rego sent the CCTV images to Vikram, in case facial recognition could bring up a name for Ruçi's contact.

Of course, it could be that the men in the photograph were only customers in the pub or guys who were flirting with Ruçi, but Rego didn't think so – the body language was too furtive, and the man in the hoodie seemed to have deliberately kept his face hidden.

He looked at the shadowy figure, wondering if this was the man who'd murdered Ruçi – or knew who had.

"I'm coming for you, you bastard."

CHAPTER 15

Tamsyn woke up sweating, suffocated by a weight on her chest.

"Ugh, get off, Mo! You're too heavy. Why are you lying on me? I swear that sometimes you think you're a cat."

She pushed Mo away and sat up.

Mo jumped off the bed and stood by the door expectantly.

Muttering under her breath, Tamsyn climbed out of bed, pulling on an old sweatshirt and pyjama pants, sliding her feet into sheepskin slippers, and yawning as she opened her bedroom door.

Mo thundered down the stairs, surprisingly loudly for a small dog.

Tamsyn followed, frowning at her phone: only 8am. She'd hoped to sleep later than that. Yawning again, she slid the phone into a pocket and followed Mo downstairs.

Mo was standing at the backdoor, her comical eyebrows expressing urgency as she shot outside then found the perfect spot to relieve herself.

Tamsyn left the door open, feeling the tentative warmth of a spring day, pleased to see that her grandfather had blocked up the hole in the fence. Mo was safe – and currently scaling the compost heap.

The house was silent for now, but Tamsyn knew her grandfather would be back soon, grumbling about the poverty of the catch and the criminally low price he was paid for crab and lobster. As a child, she'd thought he must be very unhappy, but her grandmother said that everyone needed something to grumble about, and if it wasn't that, it would be something else. It was almost a sort of white noise to her now – she missed it when it wasn't there.

She wasn't sure where her grandmother was, but rising early was in the Poldhu genes. Her grandfather put it down to generations of fishermen on both sides of the family.

Tamsyn had worked alongside him every school holiday since her father died, but the Cornish fishing industry was struggling. Thirty years ago, Stevenson's of Newlyn had the largest privately owned fishing fleet in Europe – more than thirty boats – now they were down to ten beam trawlers, and all of those were old. No one from Tamsyn's year at school had gone into fishing, and she only knew one hired skipper under the age of forty. Their local Sainsbury's stocked crab from Indonesia.

The Poldhu family fishing tradition would die with her grandfather.

Mo danced back into the kitchen, eyebrows twirling, looking pointedly in her empty food bowl then licking it for effect.

Tamsyn laughed, scooped out some dry dog food and topped it with a shaving of Cornish Yarg, a strong local cheese which Mo found irresistible.

While Mo wolfed her food, Tamsyn made a cup of tea and ate a slice of toast, idly scrolling through her phone. She read some group Snapchats that her friends had sent, flipping through photos from their night out, but Jess hadn't tried to call her again. That world seemed so far away from what she was doing, ignorant of the violence on their doorstep, but at least they were living their lives, having fun. So, why did she feel resentful of them?

A few toast crumbs dropped on the kitchen's flagstone floor because Tamsyn hadn't bothered to use a plate. Mo licked them up and stared at Tamsyn, trying to hypnotise her to drop more.

Tamsyn sighed. Mo's life was so simple: eat, sleep, cuddles, repeat. No judgement, just unconditional love.

And small hairy dogs didn't care if you dropped crumbs and talked with your mouth full. In fact, they hoped you would, because human food was so much more interesting that the contents of their dog bowl.

Tamsyn tossed the rest of her toast to Mo, then headed up to shower and dress.

Ten minutes later, she clipped Mo's lead to her collar, made sure she had her phone, sunglasses and poo bags, then headed out, her wet hair dampening the back of her jacket.

She walked briskly with Mo trotting beside her, heading to the seafront.

Penzance spread out along the shore below and up the hill towards Madron behind her. Faint wisps of mist swirled around the Mount, while silky flags fringed the Jubilee Pool, the largest seawater lido in the UK, built for a long-dead king.

Tamsyn bent down to let Mo off the lead, and the small dog bounced along the wide promenade, inspected the giant pebbles that had been installed instead of benches, greeted some other dogs, looked tempted to chase a couple of joggers, and gave the lone skateboarder a wide berth.

Tamsyn had made this walk many, many times, but today, she felt outside herself – looking the same, feeling different.

The last two days had changed her, but it was more than that – death had visited her when she was young, and when she thought of that day, it was like watching TV with the sound muted.

She remembered her grandfather, grey-skinned, his face broken with grief; she remembered her grandmother's frozen silence; and she remembered the police officers who'd come to the harbour – a man and a woman. It had been the man who'd bent down and spoken to her quietly, then taken her small hand in his and walked her out of sight of her father's cold, dead body.

She wondered who he was. It was only ten years ago so he could still be a serving officer – she might even work with him. It was a strange thought – comforting and ... just weird. Would he remember? Or did the deaths and disasters blur after a while?

And she was one of them now, the one who'd be there when people were at their most vulnerable. She was proud of that, but even with all the training she'd been given and would continue to be given, it was daunting to be the person that people would turn to in a crisis, expecting her to know what to do, expecting her to take command.

And in the last two days, she'd seen a murder victim, interviewed a scared child, found a handgun, gone on one of the crappiest dates in history, then been asked out by a colleague. She winced at that memory – she hoped she'd said enough to put Jamie off for good.

Her phone pinged with an incoming message but she ignored it, deciding to enjoy the salty air, light breeze and sun on her skin. Her grandmother's beliefs had taught her to appreciate the small things in life. And she touched the pebble of Serpentine in her pocket, even though she didn't believe in it.

At Newlyn harbour, her grandfather and George had already done a day's work: they'd unloaded their catch to stow pots and tanks next to the fish market, a large corrugated shed that dominated the harbour. Now, they were washing the mackerel scales, blood and guts off their decks and would spend the rest of the day on maintenance, Ozzie checking his pots and George mending his nets.

She let Mo off the lead as she always did, although it was strictly against regulations in the harbour, and a tourist would have been yelled at. Then she started second-guessing herself, wondering what would happen to her if someone reported a police officer breaking the rules. Although, nobody down here would do that – the fishermen were family.

"Hi, Grandad! Alright, Uncle George!"

Her grandfather glanced up from the deck of the *Daniel Day*, his unlit pipe clamped between his teeth, waving a gloved hand then continued to scrub the deck.

Down the pontoon, Uncle George jerked his head at her. "At least you're not in that copper's uniform this time."

"Better get used to it," she laughed. "I hope your car tax and insurance are up to date."

He threw her a wounded look. "Play fair, Tammy! By the way, how's your car running now? Everything okay?"

"Yeah, it's fine, thanks. How was the catch today?" she asked.

"Fair to middlin'," said George at the same time her grandfather mumbled something scathing under his breath.

George grinned and raised his eyebrows at her as they shared a smile.

"Croust time, Tammy," he said. "Stick the kettle on."

"You're getting soft, George Mason, having a kettle on your boat. It's bad luck," grumbled Tamsyn's grandfather. "You're getting to be a fine weather man."

George's smile widened and he turned to Tamsyn. "Old Ozzie is so mean, ee'd skin a turd to save a shilling."

"Ef you want to know the value of money, try and borry some," her grandfather shot back.

"You can't believe a liar when he's tellin' the truth."

"A toad is a diamond in a duck's eye."

"You mean, a duck's arse, Ozzie!"

Tamsyn started laughing as the insults flew back and forth across the narrow strip of water.

"You can't expect anything but a grunt from a pig," said her grandfather without missing a beat.

"Slow but sure, Ozzie, like the Parson's donkey."

Her grandfather stood up, stretched his back and scowled at George. "Silence is the best noise."

George shouted with laughter and Tamsyn shook her head.

"You two should go on the stage with your double-act," she grinned.

"First stage outta town," George chuckled. "Go on, Tammy, make us a cuppa with my new kettle."

"You hate my tea!"

"Better than a poke in the eye."

"Ha ha. And thanks for doing my tyres the other week."

"That kettle won't boil itself."

"Yeah, yeah."

Tamsyn lifted Mo aboard George's twenty year-old netter and went into his wheelhouse to make three mugs of tea.

Her grandfather took a Thermos flask every day but she didn't think he'd say no to a fresh brew, no matter how much he grumbled and talked about 'the old days'.

She found a packet of Rich Tea Biscuits and brought those on deck, as well.

The sun glittered on the water, and the rigging of nearby

yachts jingled, a background symphony of harbour life. Tamsyn tipped her head back and stared up at the cloudless sky. The breeze still held a bite to it and it was always cold out on the water, but this was her second home. She opened her eyes as Mo's nails clattered across the deck, pausing to sniff at the bait bucket full of ray-backs. She was as much at home aboard as on firm ground.

Tamsyn yawned, took a sip of tea then started to open the packet of biscuits. Mo immediately trotted over and sat at her feet.

They shared a biscuit, and Tamsyn pulled out her phone while she waited for Uncle George and her grandfather.

She sat upright when she read the email from DI Rego – a lot had happened with the murder investigation since she'd left work last night. She read through the list of Saemira Ruçi's aliases and bio, realising that whoever she was, she was no innocent bystander. Although it didn't mean that she deserved to be murdered.

Two images were attached to the email. Tamsyn had already seen the first one which was from Lucy Pryce's phone, but the second one was a grainy CCTV image of Saemira with two men outside the Mackerel Inn.

With a shock of recognition, she identified one of the men, 'a person of interest', as Ollie Garrett. Her face felt hot. What would DI Rego think of her if she admitted this was the guy from the party? She really didn't want to tell him but she knew she had to.

"What's the matter, bird?" Uncle George asked, swinging onto the boat. "You've got a funny look on your face – are you constipated?"

"Wow thanks, Uncle George, you say the nicest things."

Her voice was laced with sarcasm but her mind was on the photos.

She held out her phone to him and showed him the smiley photo of Saemira, or whatever her name was.

"Do you know this woman? She was seen outside the Mack Shack last week."

George peered at her phone, then took it from her in his huge paw of a hand.

"No, who is she?"

"She's the woman who was m— the woman who died at Lamorna Cove. So you've never seen her in the pub?"

"Nope, can't say's I have."

Her grandfather clambered aboard, claiming his tea.

"Do you recognise her, Grandad?" she asked, passing her phone to him.

He peered at the picture and started shaking his head. Then he paused and fumbled in his overalls for his reading glasses.

He looked again and Tamsyn's pulse quickened.

"No," he said at last, "not *in* the pub. I seen her outside the pub a few times. First time I thought she was maybe a tourist asking for directions, but I seen her again since then."

"Can you remember when that was?" Tamsyn asked.

He scratched his beard thoughtfully. "Some time last summer, I reckon. That was the first time. Twice this year, maybe."

"When was the last time you saw her?"

He pulled at his ear and put his glasses back in the bib pocket of his overalls.

"Reckon it was a month or so ago. Can't be sure."

"What time in the evening did you see her?"

"Late," he said, nodding with certainty. "Closing time."

"Thank you, Grandad," said Tamsyn eagerly. "That's really helpful. Is it okay if I bring my DI down if he wants to talk to you?"

He sighed and grumbled a bit then said he'd probably be at the harbour for no more than another hour.

Tamsyn called Mo, lifted her off the boat and phoned DI Rego.

"Sir, it's Tamsyn – I know one of the men in the photo."

CHAPTER 16

Usually, a DC would have interviewed Ollie Garrett but Rego's team was already stretched, so he decided to do this one himself – in fact, he was looking forward to it. It had taken less than an hour to find Garrett because he'd told Tamsyn that he was working at a holiday park outside Carbis Bay and there were only a limited number of those. Unfortunately, there was no duty solicitor available to attend the interview in the Camborne custody suite until the afternoon.

Rego had requested Tamsyn's presence, firstly to find out what else she could tell him about Garrett, and secondly to reassure her that she wasn't in any trouble. Although now Garret was a person of interest, Rego definitely wanted to know more about why she was at a party with him.

Tamsyn looked nervous when he found her waiting outside CID shortly after lunchtime.

He waved at her to come in.

"Take a seat, Tamsyn. Thanks for coming in early."

"No problem, sir," she said formally.

"So, tell me everything you know about Ollie Garrett."

Tamsyn cleared her throat.

"We both went to Humphrey Davy, that's the secondary school on Treneere estate, up near the hospital."

Rego nodded.

"He left in … I think it was Year 10 because his parents were getting divorced, and I saw him again on Monday."

"You had no contact with him in between? Snapchat? Instagram? Follow each other on TikTok maybe?"

"No, nothing. I didn't even remember him when he told me his name. I mean, vaguely, but I can't picture him from those days. It was five years ago, sir."

She said 'five years' like it was a century.

"And when you met him on Monday?"

"I'd been for a run and I was nearly home. An old Mini pulled up outside the Coldstreamer in Gulval, and this guy called my name."

"Number plate?"

She flushed. "I don't remember. It was an older car and made a noise like the exhaust was blown. It was dark blue with white racing stripes."

"How many people were in the car?"

"Four, but I didn't recognise any of them."

"All men?"

"Yes, sir."

"Okay, what happened next?"

Tamsyn collected her thoughts.

"Ollie said he was back living in Cornwall now, and that he'd left here when his parents got divorced. He went upcountry with his mum."

"'Upcountry' meaning?"

"Anywhere north of the Tamar, like Devon or whatever," Tamsyn shrugged. "But he said he'd been living in Kent for the last couple of years. And then later in the car was just, you know, talking about surfing, people we knew from school. Um, that's all I remember."

"And at the party, when you saw his friend dealing, did he say anything else?"

Tamsyn screwed up her eyes, trying to remember.

"I didn't know we were going to a party – we were supposed to just be meeting for a drink at my local. But as soon as I got there, he said we were going to this party in town. So we got there, and we had a drink and people were dancing ... um, he saw me looking at this guy with the bags of powder – he didn't give me a name – and I said, 'I'm going' and he said 'you're not even on duty'. I said that I was still a police officer even if I wasn't in uniform. He said, 'you can't report him, he's my mate'. I said, 'your friend is a drug dealer' and oh! I just remembered, he said, 'it's just some molly'. That's right – I'd forgotten that bit."

Rego tapped a finger on his desk. "Could the second man in the photograph be Garrett's 'mate'?"

"I don't think so," Tamsyn said slowly. "The guy dealing was really tall and skinny. The man in the photo looks shorter than Ollie."

"What did you say to Garrett when you saw the deal going down?"

"What I said before: I told him that his friend was a drug dealer. He called me a bitch and I left. That's when you saw me."

"Well done, Tamsyn. You did the right thing."

She looked relieved and Rego hoped that she'd told him everything, for her own sake.

He decided to pass on his thoughts on the subject and hope she learned from them.

"When I was a student officer, my tutor was an old-school copper. At the end of my first week, we all went for a drink together and he saw a group of kids in the pub that he knew were underage – they were friends with his neighbour's son. He didn't do anything at the time, but told me he was going to have a quiet word with his neighbour later. And then he said – and I always remember this – 'We were all young once. You're off duty now'."

Rego pinned her with a look.

"The thing is, it was the wrong thing to do. He should have told them to leave the pub immediately and reported the publican to the local licensing authority. Because we don't know where this could lead. How would you feel if one of them was injured or killed on the way home? Or one of the girls was so drunk she didn't know what she was doing or consenting to – or if she'd fallen in front of a car. Not only that, it's unprofessional; it's *wrong*." He leaned forwards. "What you did, reporting the incident to a senior officer, that was the *right* thing to do."

Tamsyn straightened in the chair. "Yes, sir."

"By the way, has he tried to contact you at all since then?"

She shook her head. "I didn't give him my number."

"Can you think of anyone from school that he might have stayed in touch with?"

"No, I'm sorry. I don't really remember who he hung out with. I barely remember him at all."

"You were at school with Chloe Rogers, right?"

Tamsyn looked as if she was sucking on a lemon when she nodded.

"Could she have known Garrett?"

"We were all in the same year so … maybe, I guess."

He gave her a penetrating look. "Do you have a problem with Ms Rogers?"

Tamsyn didn't know where to start. The girl had been a bully since primary school and had always hated Tamsyn. Jess said it was because she was jealous, but Tamsyn found that hard to believe.

"No, sir," Tamsyn said. "No problem."

Rego didn't look convinced but didn't challenge her either.

"Send her in, please, and meet me at my car in ten minutes. Take the time to go through your emails and get up to date with the crime reports. DS Stevens will be meeting us at Camborne to sit in on the interview."

"Sir."

She stood up and he glanced across at her.

Tamsyn looked like she'd rather shovel shit than speak to Chloe, but it was an order, however politely given.

A few minutes later, Chloe sauntered into his office, standing silently until Rego pointed at a chair.

"Thanks for coming, Chloe," he said pleasantly. "I understand you were at school with Oliver Garrett, known as Ollie."

"No." Her dark eyes gave nothing away.

"I've already spoken to PC Poldhu and she says that you were all in the same year at secondary school."

She shrugged. "Well, if Tamsyn says so."

"You don't remember him?"

"No."

"You're sure?"

She looked irritated. "There were 130 kids in the year, more than 30 in my house."

"And you were in the same house at school as Tamsyn, but she remembered him."

"So? She didn't have any friends so she probably spent more time watching everyone else."

Rego was taken aback at the venom in her voice.

"Is there a problem between you and PC Poldhu that I should be aware of?" he asked, his tone cool.

"No," she said sullenly. "We're just not friends."

"I can see that. Do you like your job here, Chloe?"

Her eyes widened and she gave a curt nod of her head.

"Good. And you can work with PC Poldhu without friction?"

He'd phrased it as a question but it wasn't one.

"Yes," she said, her mouth twisting.

"Okay. Thank you for your help."

He had no idea what had gone on between Tamsyn and Chloe and he really didn't care, but he didn't want personal grudges to get in the way of performance either.

He made a note to read Tamsyn's police application as well as Chloe's most recent appraisal.

Tamsyn was waiting by his car, as instructed.

"Right, let's go and see what Mr Garrett has to say about his dubious friends."

He pressed the key fob and Tamsyn slid into the passenger seat, quietly buckling her seatbelt.

Rego reversed out of the parking spot then waited until they were on the road before he started speaking.

"There are three objectives in the Garrett interview: firstly, find out his involvement with Ruçi – we need to establish if Ollie was a customer of hers; secondly, identify the other man in the photograph; and thirdly, identify his drug dealer friend. The interview could go one of two ways: he'll clam up and answer 'no comment' to everything – that's quite common, so don't worry about it." He gave a quick smile. "It's not evidence, but you'd be surprised how much we can learn from reading their body language when we ask questions. Or, he'll try to play down how much he knows them and give us the 'I only just met them' line. In a way, I'm hoping that's what he does, because then I can confront him with the fact that he described this drug dealer as his 'mate' to you." His smile widened. "Of course, there's a third possibility – that he tells us everything we want to know and ties it all up with a pretty red bow."

Tamsyn didn't smile.

"What do you want me to do, sir?"

"You'll be outside: watch, listen, take notes. If you think of a question, write it down and have another officer bring it in to me. I'll decide later whether or not I want Garrett to see you."

She swallowed and nodded. "Yes, sir."

Suddenly she sat upright.

"Oh my God, I forgot to say! I showed Grandad that photograph of Saemira Ruçi, right? And he remembers seeing her at the Mack Shack – I mean the Mackerel Inn at Newlyn. I'm so sorry! I completely forgot when I recognised Ollie."

Rego was irritated – he could have done with that information several hours ago.

He used the in-car phone and called Jack Forshaw.

"Jack, I want you to go and talk to..."

"Ozzie Poldhu," Tamsyn whispered.

"Talk to Ozzie Poldhu about seeing the murder victim at the Mackerel Inn. I want as much information as possible about times and dates. And Jack, he's PC Poldhu's grandfather."

"I'm sorry I forgot," she said again when he ended the call.

He nodded. "Jack will talk to your grandfather. Right now, we have to interview Garrett."

"Have you arrested him?" she asked in a small voice.

"No. At this stage, it's a voluntary interview, an interview under caution. Garrett has been asked to be present and he indicated that he wanted a solicitor with him. I'll invite him into an interview room, but tell him that he's not under arrest and is free to leave the station if he so chooses. There's no record on him, so if this is his first brush with the law, he'll want to get it over with as quickly as possible. If he's not as innocent as he's pretending, he'll stay anyway because he'll be worried that by getting up and walking out, he'll be arrested, which then means that the custody procedure kicks in and he'll spend some time in a cell, and there will be a significant delay in getting out."

He glanced across at her.

"I've emailed you the interview plan, so read it through now."

The rest of the journey passed in silence.

CHAPTER 17

Tamsyn and Rego entered Camborne station from the staff entrance. Tamsyn wasn't sure how she felt about Ollie knowing that she was there and she hoped that the DI wouldn't need to mention it.

She was left to watch from the viewing room while Rego and DS Stevens met Ollie and his solicitor in the front office.

Ollie's solicitor was an older woman with an expensive looking trouser suit and John Lennon glasses. She introduced herself as Annabelle Hoskins.

Rego and Stevens shook hands with both of them.

"First of all," Rego said, his tone confident and calm, "I want to ensure that Mr Garrett understands this is a voluntary interview." He turned to Ollie. "Thank you for coming in so promptly. And I'd like to remind you that you're not under arrest and are free to leave at any time."

Ollie nodded but looked uncomfortable, sweat breaking out on his upper lip.

"Can I offer you anything to drink?" Rego asked politely. "I need to have a chat with Mrs Hoskins first."

The solicitor declined a drink but Ollie asked for water

and drank down the whole plastic cup in one go while he was waiting.

In the viewing room next door, Tamsyn clutched her notebook, leaning forward to hear what the DI said to Ollie's solicitor.

"Thanks for coming in on short notice, Mrs Hoskins."

"Not a problem, DI Rego. May I see the pre-interview disclosure documents?"

He handed her a sheet of A4 paper printed on both sides and she skimmed it quickly, raising her eyebrows a couple of times. Tamsyn had already seen the document and knew it listed the topics that would be covered in the interview. She also knew that the DI's softly-softly approach wouldn't be for long.

"Mrs Hoskins, your client has been invited into the police station today as we suspect he is involved in drug dealing. He is not under arrest and he is free to leave the station."

"Inspector, has my client been under surveillance?"

"At this stage, I have given you appropriate disclosure to enable you to talk to and advise your client. I will explore each topic as the interview progresses."

She nodded, then looked down at the sheet of paper again, and Rego continued, reading word for word what was written on the pre-interview disclosure.

"I have information that your client was at the Mackerel Inn public house on Thursday 22nd March where a suspicious meeting was held where a drug deal is suspected to have occurred. We will ask your client questions about his involvement in that offence, and ask him to account for any persons he met on that evening. We will ask your client to provide the telephone numbers of any phones he has access to or used."

"Anything else, DI Rego?" she asked, peering over her glasses at him.

"I have information that on Monday 26th March, your client was at a party at 23 Leskinnick Place, Penzance, where a person was seen to exchange a package which was believed to be a controlled drug. Your client appeared to acknowledge it was a drug and was closely associated to the person making the drug deal. We will ask your client questions about his involvement in that offence. We will ask your client to provide any information about the identities of the person making the exchange at the house party."

Mrs Hoskins made a few notes then asked to speak to Ollie about the disclosures.

Tamsyn knew that anything said between a solicitor and their client was classed a legal privilege and was conducted in private, so now all they could do was wait.

Rego and DS Stevens joined her in the viewing room, discussing how they were going to conduct the interview.

Then Rego turned to Tamsyn.

"So, the way we're going to do this is with phased disclosure. We'll be holding back some facts, hoping that Garrett will trip himself up with lies. At this stage, he doesn't know about the CCTV footage from the Mackerel Inn. I'm going to start by asking about the drug dealing at the party." He gave her a quick smile. "And Garrett has drunk a fair bit of water by now, so he'll be wanting a toilet break. He'll think he's finished and will relax a bit more – then we'll start part two, got it?"

"Yes, sir."

They had to wait twenty minutes before Mrs Hoskins indicated that she was ready for the interview to proceed.

Tamsyn watched as they all took their seats and DS Stevens pressed the 'record' button.

Everything was recorded digitally into a cloud-based system. No tapes, no discs, and at the end of the interview, Mrs Hoskins would be given a unique reference number where she would be able to access the cloud from her office computer and download her client's interview.

Tamsyn leaned forward as Rego began.

"The time is 4.15pm on Wednesday 28th March at Camborne Police Station, Detective Inspector Robert Rego and Detective Sergeant Tom Stevens attending. Please identify yourself for the purpose of the tape, including your date of birth."

Ollie's voice shook slightly and his eyes kept darting towards his solicitor.

"Ollie, um, Oliver Garrett. My birthday is 1st August."

"Annabelle Hoskins, solicitor, DG Law."

DS Stevens read the caution.

"You do not have to say anything, but it may harm your defence if you do not mention when questioned something which you later rely on in court. Anything you do say may be given in evidence."

Rego's face was impassive as he stared at Ollie. "Do you understand the caution?"

Mrs Hoskins replied for Ollie.

"I've explained the meaning of the caution to my client and he understands."

Rego nodded, his eyes still on Ollie. "Mr Garret, I'll remind you that you are not under arrest and you are free to leave the station at any time."

Ollie relaxed a fraction. It wouldn't last for long.

Rego didn't even glance at his notes.

"We suspect that you may be dealing controlled drugs in the local area. Can you tell me your involvement in your drug dealing activities?"

Ollie's Adam's apple bobbed up and down as he tried to swallow.

"No comment," he said, his voice raspy.

Rego glanced at DS Stevens indicating for him to take over.

"I understand you have recently returned to Cornwall," DS Stevens said pleasantly, continuing the questioning. "When did you come back?"

Ollie licked his lips.

"Three weeks ago. Well, nearly four. At the beginning of March."

"Why did you come back to Cornwall?"

Ollie glanced at Mrs Hoskins who simply nodded.

Gaining confidence, Ollie replied clearly.

"I got a job as the marketing manager at Pedrick's Camping & Caravan Park in Carbis Bay."

"Where are you staying?"

"I've got a lodge on the site."

"And who do you live with?"

"A couple of the chefs that work there, Sam and Alfie."

"How much do you earn, Mr Garrett?"

"I don't see why..." he began, then changed his mind. "I get £20,000, just about, but I get free accommodation."

Rego glanced at DS Stevens, then resumed leading the interview.

"Last Monday, I believe you were at a party, where we believe controlled drugs were being supplied. What can you tell me about that?"

Ollie licked his lips again and swallowed.

"I don't know anything about any drugs."

"Whose party was it?"

"I don't know. I just heard there was a party. Lots of people were there. I didn't really know any of them."

"How did you hear about the party?"

"I think someone at the pub mentioned it?"

"One of your friends?"

Ollie paused. "I don't remember – it could have been."

"I'll need their names and addresses."

"I only know their first names..."

"That will do for now."

He pushed his notepad towards Ollie who picked up the pen with obvious reluctance and scribbled the names but Rego only glanced at the short list.

"Who was dealing drugs?"

"No comment," Ollie said, sweat breaking out on his forehead.

"What type of drugs were being supplied?"

"No comment."

"Were you dealing drugs?"

"No!"

"Who was?"

"No comment."

"Were they your drugs that were being supplied?"

"No comment."

Ollie's face was slowly turning red, as if he was sitting under a space heater. His earlier confidence had completely evaporated and he looked like he was going to be sick.

"Where do you get your drugs from?"

"No comment."

Rego paused, leaning back in his chair.

"Ollie, I know it's your right not to say anything, but this is your opportunity to give us your side of the story. If you haven't supplied any drugs, please tell me; it's your opportunity to provide an account."

Ollie was silent, glancing at his solicitor for guidance. She gave a small nod of her head but he just frowned at her.

"Who was at the party, Ollie?"

Ollie didn't answer, his eyes glued to the table in front of him as he pushed his finger against the grooves and dints from previous 'persons of interest'.

Neither Rego nor Stevens filled the silence.

Tamsyn looked up as a uniformed officer she recognised slightly came into the viewing room.

"Your new DI knows what he's about."

"Sorry, what?"

"I saw you earlier in the week. You're new, aren't you? I'm Harry, Harry Joules. Drone pilot and a useful fly-half though I say it myself. You free for a drink later?"

"Just, er, what did you mean about Inspector Rego?"

He sat down next to her.

"Your crim is practically pissing down his own leg. See, he's answering all the non-relevant questions, but saying 'no comment' to the important ones about his involvement in crime."

"Okay, so?"

"So, if it went to trial the prosecuting barrister would make a big play on that, and probably the Judge in his summing up. With the usual old lags who've been up and down here more times than an umbrella on a bank holiday Monday, 'no comment' interviews are 'no comment' from start to finish because their briefs know that the Judge or barrister will be onto it and it can work against them. But some suspects, like your boy here, they can't help themselves … they start off all confident and 'no comment', but look at your DI – he's an old hand. He's just sitting there, pretending to read that file. Meantime, fella over there is expecting the questions to come quickly, but your DI is making him sweat. I bet you a pint of Rattler that your boy will break first. Look at his brief, she knows what the DI is doing; she's probably rolling her eyes under those ugly glasses."

Rego repeated the question. "Who was at the party, Ollie?"

Ollie shook his head then blurted out, "They're just people. I didn't know them."

"I'd advise you not to say anything else," said Mrs Hoskins.

Harry grinned at Tamsyn. "Got him! Told you."

"We have a witness who saw you at the party," Rego said as if there'd been no delay in Ollie's answer. "You appeared not to be bothered by the fact that drugs were being supplied; is that because they were your drugs?"

"What witness? Who?" his eyes narrowed and he glanced towards the one-way window where Tamsyn was hidden from view.

Even though she knew he couldn't see her, she flinched and Harry threw her an amused look.

"So, we on tonight? Quick drink after work? Or maybe a long one?"

Tamsyn tore her attention from the interview and gave Harry a regretful smile.

"Oh, sorry, I can't. I'm on lates."

He looked disappointed and stood up to go. "Another time then?"

"Sure," she nodded distractedly. "Maybe."

"Great! I'll hold you to that. See you around."

Ollie sat back in his chair, his arms folded and a belligerent expression on his face.

"No comment."

Rego glanced at DS Stevens before continuing the questioning.

Tamsyn wondered how many of these exchanges were

real and how many were planned theatrics just to ramp up the tension for Ollie.

"I want to ask you some questions about a second incident at the Mackerel Inn public house on Thursday 22nd of March," Rego said calmly. "Do you know where the Mackerel Inn is?"

"No comment."

"Have you been to the pub recently?"

"No comment."

"When was the last time you went there?"

"No comment."

"What time would you normally go?"

"No comment."

"Who would you go with?"

"No comment."

"Have you been dealing drugs at the Mackerel Inn?"

"No comment."

"Were you at the Mackerel Inn on 22nd March?"

"No comment."

"Who did you go with?"

"No comment."

"Who did you meet?"

"No comment."

If Rego was frustrated by the 'no comment' answers, he didn't show it.

"Was any meeting pre-arranged?"

"No comment."

"How was the meeting arranged? By phone? Did you set up the meeting? Did you use your phone to set up the meeting?"

"No comment."

"What is your phone number?"

"No comment."

The questions continued: *where is your phone? Did you go to the Mackerel Inn by car? Was it your car or someone else's? Did you hand anything to anyone? Did you receive anything? Tell me what you handed over.*

Ollie continued to give 'no comment' answers. Finally, Rego looked up from his list of questions.

"If nothing illegal took place, please tell me now, because you haven't got anything to hide."

"No. Comment."

Ollie sat back, a smug look on his face.

Rego glanced back at his notes.

"Mr Garrett, we have CCTV footage which shows you and another man wearing a hoodie outside the Mackerel Inn public house, where a package is being handled by a female. Who is the man with the hoodie?"

Ollie glanced nervously at his solicitor. This time she shook her head.

"No comment."

"Is he a friend? What's his name? How do you know him? Is he a drug dealing associate? Who is the woman in the picture? How do you know her? Is she a drug dealer? What's in the package that's being handed over?"

The questions came thick and fast and Ollie sat in stunned silence, as if he'd only just realised that this was a lot more serious than he'd first thought.

"Ollie," Rego said slowly, "If it's nothing illegal, this is your opportunity to tell me now. By saying 'no comment', it raises my suspicions that you're involved in illegal activity. Look at the facts: it's late at night, you met outside the pub in a dark corner that you didn't realise was covered by CCTV; you are outside for a brief few seconds where you meet up with this woman and a package is handed over. It doesn't look to me like a social meeting, or a meeting where you chanced to meet a friend or cadge a fag. What was this meeting about?"

Ollie swallowed and licked his lips.

Rego leaned forward, his voice confidential.

"Are you scared of anyone, under any sort of threat if you provide an account?"

Ollie's eyes widened and he glanced compulsively at his solicitor who raised her eyebrows.

"I need to be sure that you're not being intimidated or being made to deal drugs through threat of violence, because if you are," Rego continued persuasively, "if you tell us what's going on and are truthful, we can protect you. So again, I will ask you, tell me what that meeting was about."

This time he slid the CCTV photograph in front of Ollie and his solicitor. Ollie paled and turned a ghastly green as he studied the grainy black-and-white image.

Rego pressed on.

"We will find the man in the hoodie, Ollie. Do you think he'll talk? Do you think he might implicate you?" He paused, but Ollie seemed incapable of speech. "This is your final chance, right now, to tell me who was behind the drug dealing at the party. If it's not you, tell me whose drugs they were, and provide a full account to me about the circumstances of your meeting outside the Mackerel Inn, what was being exchanged, and who were the people you met."

There was a long silence; Ollie didn't even say 'no comment'.

Rego turned to DS Stevens. "Do you want to ask some questions?"

Stevens shook his head.

"Perhaps Mr Garrett would like a break to go to the toilet?"

Ollie nodded quickly, relieved to have the excuse to get up and leave the room.

Rego looked at his wristwatch. "The time by my watch is 17.27, and I'm terminating the interview."

DS Stevens escorted Ollie to the toilet and Rego opened the door to Tamsyn's room.

"I expect you need a break, as well."

"Oh," she said, surprised. "Okay, thank you."

Tamsyn hurried to the bathroom, but when she came out, she immediately bumped into Ollie who glared at her.

"Bitch! You did this! You stitched me up! You're a fucking grass!"

Horror then anger rushed through her.

"You did it to yourself, dickhead!" she snapped, and walked away hurriedly.

Tamsyn was furious – with Ollie, with herself, but mostly with Rego.

She stormed back into the viewing room where he sat flicking through his notes.

"Sir! You wanted Ollie to see me, didn't you?"

He raised his eyebrows. "Yes, I did."

"But ... you *used* me!"

His gaze hardened and Rego shoved his chair backwards as he stood up abruptly.

"Get over it, PC Poldhu. If you can't deal with this, you'll never make a copper, because you'll have to face a lot worse than the likes of him."

She stood in silence, stunned and hurt as he strode through the door.

He reappeared in the interview room where Annabelle Hoskins was making notes on a legal pad.

"There are a few questions I want to ask about another

matter, if your client doesn't mind bearing with us for a short time."

"Something else you want to disclose, DI Rego?" she asked crisply.

"At the conclusion of the last interview, I showed your client a still image of three people outside of the Mackerel Inn public house at 22.47 hours on the 22nd of March. One of the persons in that image we say is your client. The female in the image we believe is a woman known as 'Jowita', who has a number of aliases but that her real name is Saemira Ruçi. Saemira has been murdered. We want to ask your client a few more questions about his association Saemira and any knowledge of her murder."

"I see," said Mrs Hoskins, peering over her glasses with a grave expression. "I will speak to my client."

Ten minutes later, everyone trooped back into the interview room and the procedure began again with Rego giving the time and date, Ollie and the solicitor identifying themselves, as before. Once again, the caution was read out and Rego asked if Ollie understood it.

He nodded and muttered an affirmative.

Rego ploughed on, seeming neither tired, frustrated nor anxious.

Ollie, on the other hand, was sweating freely, and his right knee was jiggling uncontrollably.

"At the conclusion of the last interview, I showed you a still image captured at 22.47 hours on 22nd March outside of the Mackerel Inn public house in Newlyn. There are three people in that image: we can clearly see that one is a male, which we say is you. There is a person wearing a hooded top, and a female which is Saemira Ruçi. Saemira is dead, she has been murdered: did you kill her?"

Ollie sucked in a shocked breath.

"No! I didn't. I didn't even know she was dead till just now. I don't know anything about that! I swear!"

"Again, I will ask you to account for that meeting."

After that, Ollie couldn't answer Rego's questions fast enough.

"Okay, okay. Look, it was just some weed, yeah? No big deal. I smoke a doobie now and then, that's all. Everyone does it. A friend of a friend told me that if I go down the Mackerel of a Thursday evening I can score, right? It was just some weed! I didn't kill anyone!"

"Did you know Saemira?"

"No! I didn't even know that was her name."

"Did you know her by another name?"

"No, I mean yes. He just said that there was this Polish woman called Jo who he knew and that she got him good weed, right? Maybe some spice, I don't know."

"Then how did you know who she was at the pub?"

"He said she had long brown hair, and I just thought she looked ... I mean, I said, 'Are you Jo?' and she nodded and asked what I wanted."

"Was it a drugs transaction?"

"Just weed! I only gave her twenty quid."

Rego met Ollie's eyes and Tamsyn almost felt sorry for him. Almost.

"Ollie, I've already asked you in the previous interview a series of questions about this meeting, but now the level of seriousness is off the scale and I would like you to account for the purpose of that meeting, going back to when you very first met the woman we call Jowita, through to the very last time you saw her, going into as much detail as possible."

Rego then began to repeat every question and Ollie answered them all.

"I just like a smoke now and again; maybe some E if I

want to go old-school. A bit of molly sometimes, but not that much. Just sometimes, with friends. So I was at this pub in Gulval. I'd only been back in Cornwall a couple of weeks and I met up with some people I used to go to school with. One of them, Adrian, had this mate called Spider who he said could hook me up with whatever I wanted. I don't know his real name and I only met him twice, once at the Coldstreamer and again at that fuckin' stupid party. But he was the one who knew about this Jo woman. I met her at the Mack Shack that night and gave her twenty for some weed. That was the first and last time I ever seen her."

Tamsyn swallowed hard. It was such a familiar story. She'd done her share of partying; she felt cold at the thought that it could have been her sitting in that interview room. She'd never thought ... she'd simply never thought what it meant, how it all connected.

She felt sick with shame.

"And the man who was with Saemira?" Rego asked Ollie. "Had you seen him before or since?"

"No, never. He was a scary dude. Just the way he stared, you know?"

"Did he speak to you?"

"No."

"Did he speak to Saemira?"

"Yes, but I didn't know what he said. It sounded like Russian or something. I suppose it was Polish. But ... but I got the feeling like he was in charge. I could be wrong, I don't know. It just felt like he was telling her to do something."

"Can you describe him?"

"I don't know. It was dark and I only saw him for a second."

"Would you be prepared to work with a police artist to give us a description of him?"

Ollie nodded reluctantly.

An hour later, Rego wound up the interview having wrung every tiny detail from a scared and cowed witness.

"Ollie, you have just admitted buying a small amount of cannabis. I don't intend going through the custody procedure and we can deal with this by way of a caution, if you choose to accept a caution. That means you won't be placed in a cell, but as possession of cannabis is a recordable offence, you will have your fingerprints, photograph and DNA taken, which will stay on record. I'll have a member of the custody staff finalise the paperwork."

Ollie glanced at his solicitor who nodded.

"Yeah, okay," he said weakly.

Rego glanced up towards where Tamsyn sat in silence.

CHAPTER 18

Rego sent Tamsyn back to Penzance with another uniformed officer as he continued to question witnesses. Ollie's friend 'Adrian' had been found quickly, and DC Eagling said that 'Spider' was a face well known to Camborne officers. It took another couple of hours to find him, but by then, Rego was on a roll.

Kevern Moyle, aka 'Spider' was a tall, skinny man in his early thirties, wearing a dirty beanie pulled low over his bald head, and a Cornish flag tattooed over his left bicep.

His rap sheet was longer than both arms put together: 51 previous convictions for 104 offences, including supplying Class A drugs. When uniform searched his Alverton flat, they'd found nine wraps of heroin worth over £100 and one wrap of crack cocaine. Three years ago, he'd been sentenced to two years in prison, suspended, so it would only be cooperation on the murder investigation that would keep him out of prison this time.

As soon as he opened his mouth to confirm his name and date of birth, Rego was struck by Moyle's strong Cornish accent – the long vowels and missing syllables were a dead giveaway.

When Rego had asked for his date of birth, Spider had responded, "Madder do it?"

Tom Stevens translated.

"He means, 'it doesn't matter, does it'."

Rego wondered if Moyle could be the mysterious Subject F, the man that Lucy had overheard with Saemira Ruçi. But the evidence showed that all Moyle's calls went to her burner phone, not the number Lucy and the family had used; and he didn't seem to do much of anything until the evenings.

Rego had his doubts that Moyle was Subject F but couldn't rule him out either.

But no matter what questions Rego asked, or how many times he pointed out that Moyle was looking at prison time, he never said anything other than 'no comment'.

Rego leaned in, invading the foot and a half of Moyle's space. It was a subliminal part of an interrogation, then you leaned back when you got what you wanted.

It wasn't working today.

"He's scared," Stevens said as he and Rego discussed what to do next. "As soon as he saw that CCTV image, he clammed up tighter than a goose barnacle."

Rego didn't know what a goose barnacle was but he got the general idea.

"Maybe, but the Hellbanianz have a very efficient structure. When one of their low level dealers gets picked up, he's told to plead guilty so it only goes to Magistrate's Court – a lesser sentence and his family is looked after in the meantime. It's a successful business model. Moyle knows he'll only get a couple of years, and if he keeps his mouth shut, he'll be well paid."

"That's why he isn't talking?"

"Maybe," Rego sighed. "Either that, or he knows the other man well enough to be scared even though he's not working for him."

"Spider's a junkie," said Stevens. "He won't like being locked up."

"We'll hold him for the maximum allowed, let him sweat, then question him again. But he needs to be seen by a healthcare professional and monitored by the custody staff more frequently, if not constantly. Make sure he was one of our special toilets."

Rego knew that detainees such as Spider often concealed drugs in an orifice, so he wanted the man to be given a special toilet which captured the drugs on their eventual exit. Kinder Eggs were a favourite, but drugs concealed inside the anus could take up to 36 hours to pass. Special measures were required for this, and medical staff deployed just in case the packaging ruptured and the detainee's life became at risk.

"I'm certain Moyle recognised the guy in the hoodie," Rego continued.

Stevens nodded.

"Yeah, and whoever he is, Moyle is definitely scared. Boss, we've had the police artist sketch back from Garrett – it could be the guy in the hoodie."

Rego enlarged the image on Stevens' phone.

"Maybe."

It wasn't as much as they'd hoped, so they decided to head back to the station. Rego was just pulling into the car park at Penzance when his mobile rang.

"Boss, it's Jen. Where are you? I've got news and you're going to like it: we've found the lorry driver on CCTV."

"I'm back at the station now. I'll see you in CID in one minute."

He took the stairs two at a time as Stevens puffed behind him.

Jen Bolitho was at her desk and gave a bright smile as they walked into the office.

"Boss, we've traced the route the driver took from Harwich and have got CCTV of him at the docks, and cameras on the M25 pick him up five times heading west. He stops at Potters Bar services, three times on the M4 at Reading, Chieveley and Leigh Delamere, and twice on the M5 at Gordano and Exeter."

"That's a lot of stops," Rego commented.

"Yes! And each time he gets a delivery of a propane bottle – but from different gas companies – all legit in theory but I'd bet my son's new X-box that those deliveries aren't the real companies." She paused to draw breath. "But look at his sweatshirt – see that logo? I reverse-imaged it and that's Klub Kukësi, a football club from Kukës in Albania. Kukës is only forty miles from Bytyç where Ruçi is from." She stumbled over the pronunciations. "But that's not all!" she said, her excitement barely suppressed. "The logo on his sweatshirt looks like an eagle and..."

"And a football, yeah. And?"

"Now look at the hoodie the guy from outside the Mackerel Inn is wearing!"

Rego peered at the two images, his pulse kicking up. The CCTV image was grainy, and only in Hollywood could the image be 'cleaned up' and digitally enhanced. He looked closer.

"It looks like..."

"It's the same logo, sir, I'm sure of it!" Jen announced with quiet satisfaction.

Rego looked again. It would have been impossible to pick

out the logo from the pub's CCTV, but it certainly looked similar: the shading where the eagle and football were positioned was similar. It wasn't conclusive and probably wouldn't stand up in court, but Rego felt it in his gut, and looking around at the faces of his new colleagues, he saw it in their eyes, too: the man outside the Mackerel Inn with Ruçi was the missing lorry driver.

"Jen, I want his face circulated to all forces, and I'll get onto the NCA now. Jack and Mimi, keep looking at CCTV images for him in the hours leading up to arriving at the pub and the hours after leaving. I want to know where he's been and where he went." He nodded at his DC. "Good work, Jen. Very good."

She beamed at him and Mimi high-fived her.

Rego sat at his desk which was already piled high with paperwork and files. He made a list of things he needed to do: email the lorry driver's image to Vikram; update his DCI and the Super; Ruçi's car still hadn't been found; he needed Tom to chase Vodafone for the data from her burner phone; he needed to circulate intel about the lorry driver to the relevant police forces where he'd stopped on the way to Cornwall and ... Rego paused, a thought occurring to him: what had the driver been doing while driving from Harwich? Had he been distributing drugs or collecting payments?

"Fuck!" he swore softly, giving himself a mental slap.

He picked up the phone and called Traffic.

"Sergeant Goff, it's DI Rego from Penzance. About that artic RTC at Crowlas ... which way was the lorry heading: north or south?"

He tapped his fingers against his desk while he waited for the answer.

"It was travelling upcountry, sir," came the reply. "The

driver said he'd delivered an order of toilet rolls to Lidl in Wherrytown, near Penzance. The wagon was empty at the time of the collision."

Rego thanked the sergeant and laid his phone on the desk. So what did that tell him? The wagon was empty – no drugs – but Scottish banknotes to the tune of £170,000 had been found along with £43,000 in English notes. Why had no drugs been found? It didn't seem likely that the driver would have had time to retrieve hidden drugs after the accident. But the dogs had definitely found traces. Did that mean that the driver been delivering drugs from the continent and collecting payments at the same time? Was Ruçi a local dealer? Had the driver been the one who'd killed her? His lorry was still in the police garage, so how had he left the county? The simplest thing would have been to take the train – so Rego needed to get someone onto CCTV at the station. It was also possible that he'd taken Ruçi's car. Or had he been killed along with Ruçi? Would another body be washing up on a Cornish beach?

Another worrying thought occurred to him: maybe the driver had been collecting his merchandise from Penzance and the lorry was empty because something had gone wrong. Maybe Ruçi had been killed because she'd lost or stolen the drugs. Rego frowned. She'd have to have pretty stupid – or desperate – to do that. But then again, most criminals weren't known for their high IQs.

The slow drip of intel had turned into a torrent. His team were working hard to sift through it all, but it was up to Rego to manage the flow of information and then to connect the dots. God, what a case for his first as inspector.

Rego wasn't a man much given to doubts but right now, the pressure felt close to being overwhelming.

His mobile rang again and Vikram's name flashed up.

"Vik, what have you got for me?"

"You're going to like this, buddy. I've found your driver: Besnik Domi, younger brother of Dritan Domi."

"Jesus!"

"Yeah, I know. Domi junior, aka 'Tehu' which translates as 'the blade'. He's a nasty piece of work – an enforcer with the Hellbanianz. A knife is his preferred method of torture – hence the nickname. NCA would very much like to get our hands on him."

"Join the queue," Rego said with feeling. "I've just got to find the bastard."

"But it's odd," Vikram went on. "Besnik Domi has stayed in Albania since before you had his brother sent down. He's run the family business from his home in Tirana, Albania's capital. We haven't clocked him doing any deliveries in person since pre-Covid."

There was silence as both men considered the possibilities.

"So what was different about this trip?" Rego asked, thinking out loud.

"Either he wanted to check out the supply route himself," Vikram said, "or maybe look at new supply routes..." he paused. "Or..."

"Or what?"

"Or it was personal."

"Saemira Ruçi. The way she was killed, that wasn't an execution: that was personal."

"But what would make it personal?" Vikram pressed. "The Hellbanianz are criminals, but it's *organised* crime – not chaotic and out of control. They're businessmen, and killing someone like that was bound to be a giant red flag."

"You're thinking that she did something that personally pissed off Domi. Like what?"

"Buddy, she had her tongue cut out – he thought she was talking to someone."

"Well, it wasn't us," said Rego.

"Then who?"

"Good question."

CHAPTER 19

Tamsyn was double-crewing with Sergeant Terwillis for the rest of her shift. It was the first chance she'd had to spend any time with the officer in charge of all the students and she was feeling a little nervous, especially as he'd suggested that she drive. It was also the first time she'd driven a patrol car since her training at Middlemoor.

At least she was familiar with the road and made sure she kept to the speed limit. Her sergeant had watched as she moved the seat and rear-view mirror to suit herself and she'd also checked that the petrol tank was full, even though the last officer to use it would normally have filled it up.

When she shoved her go-back and wellingtons in the boot, she also checked it had two road cones and a 'road closed' sign, as well as other pieces of equipment that an officer might need.

Her fob key recorded the mileage in the car's digital log, then she followed the cockpit drill, adjusting the wing mirrors and making sure she knew where the lights, fog lamps and siren were located. She knew it, and she knew that she knew it, but checking helped steady her nerves.

Sergeant Terwillis was a large man, heavyset, comfortable in his own skin. A trimmed moustache edged his tanned face, and he exuded calm competence. Tamsyn wondered if she'd ever feel like that.

A slight cough rattled his chest, reminding her that he'd been off sick the day she'd started.

"So, how are you settling in, Tamsyn? It's been a hectic couple of days for you so far."

"It's been good, thank you, sarge. Really interesting."

They were driving to St Ives to tell the Pryce family that the body found at Lamorna had been formally identified from the fingerprints.

"What would you say has been your biggest challenge so far?"

Tamsyn pressed her lips together, unsure what to reply.

"I'm not looking forward to telling Lucy – that's the Pryce's little girl – I'm not looking forward to telling her that 'Jowita', as she knew her, is dead," she said at last. "She really liked her ... and I think Saemira was kind to her."

Sergeant Terwillis nodded. "I won't lie – it's one of the hardest things you'll do in the job. That's why we have the training to fall back on. So what will be your approach?"

"Me?"

"You have a relationship with the girl and her mother," he reminded her. "So, yes – I want you to take the lead on this. I'll be there to back you up. Now, what were you told about handling this type of scenario?"

Tamsyn mentally scrolled through her training.

"I knock on the door, introduce us and ask Mrs Pryce to allow us inside. I'll try to ensure that she's sitting down. I'll tell her that a body has been identified as the woman she knew as Jowita Wojciechowski – I don't mention the aliases, do I?"

The sergeant shook his head.

"I say that she was found at Lamorna on Monday, and that we're treating her death as suspicious."

"Anything else?"

"Um, I have to be clear about what's happened but keep it brief, and ask if there's anyone she wants us to call on her behalf. We stay with her until a friend can come and be with her."

"Anything else?" he repeated.

Tamsyn racked her brain. "I don't think so."

"You express your regret about the death."

Tamsyn's cheeks flushed.

"Sorry. Of course I'll do that."

She side-eyed him as he nodded.

"It's easy to forget when you're intent on delivering the facts, but it's one of the most important things. People will remember this moment forever: your words matter."

Tamsyn took a deep breath. "Yes, sarge. Sorry."

"You'll be fine."

The streetlights had just come on when Tamsyn drove up to the guest house, and the Caerlyon's windows glowed jewel-like in the dusk.

"The family live around the back," Tamsyn croaked, her mouth dry.

"After you."

Tamsyn swallowed then squared her shoulders, leading Sergeant Terwillis to the back door.

"Tamsyn," he said quietly, his voice stopping her. "Take your hat off."

He removed his own cap and tucked it under his arm as Tamsyn did the same.

Then she knocked twice, so softly only a bat would have heard her. She pulled a face, then knocked again, far more forcefully than she'd meant.

There was a short pause and then the door opened.

It was Lucy.

The girl's eyes widened at the sight of Tamsyn and Sergeant Terwillis.

"Have you found Jowita?" she asked.

Tamsyn attempted a smile but it was probably more like a grimace.

"Hi, Lucy. Is your mum or dad in?"

"Dad's away. Mum's put the twins in the bath."

"Could you get her for us?"

"She gets cross when she's busy."

"It's important that we speak to her, Lucy. Could we come in?"

"I'm not supposed to let anyone in."

"That's ... a good thing," Tamsyn said, feeling flustered. "Could you get her for us, please?"

Lucy headed for the stairs, leaving the door wide open. But then she stopped.

"Did you find Jowita? Is she coming home?"

The expression in Tamsyn's eyes must have said it all because Lucy's little face crumpled and hot tears spilled down her cheeks.

Without thinking, Tamsyn crouched down, and Lucy flung herself into her arms, knocking Tamsyn's hat to the floor then holding on tightly, as if she never wanted to let go.

Sergeant Terwillis moved silently to pick up Tamsyn's hat as the child sobbed with abandon, then walked to the bottom of the stairs.

"Mrs Pryce," he called, "it's the police. Can you come down, please?"

The woman appeared, peering over the bannister, red-faced, her t-shirt soaked down the front.

"What the hell's going on?" she shouted.

"Could you come down, please?" Sergeant Terwillis repeated.

There was a shriek from the bathroom and Mandy Pryce rushed away.

Tamsyn stared helplessly over Lucy's heaving body as Sergeant Terwillis quietly shut the front door and sat on the edge of the sofa.

With Lucy still welded to her, Tamsyn moved awkwardly from a crouch to kneeling as the child's tears dampened her uniform. She met her sergeant's eyes, and his gaze softened, his expression agreeing that no amount of training prepared you for a child's grief.

Finally, Mrs Pryce reappeared with two pink-faced, damp-haired children in mismatched pyjamas.

Terwillis rose to his feet. "Mrs Pryce, I'm..."

And that was as far as he got.

"Is it about Jowita?"

"Yes, I'm sorry to have to tell you that..."

"Was she the body you found?"

Lucy collapsed against Tamsyn again, her shrieks even wilder.

"Mrs Pryce," Sergeant Terwillis said firmly, "can we speak in private? Not in front of the children?"

"What? Oh, okay, but I'll have to put the kids to bed first. Lucy, take the twins upstairs while I talk to the police."

Lucy didn't look capable of standing, let alone looking after her brother and sister.

"Perhaps there's someone you can call to help, Mrs Pryce," Sergeant Terwillis suggested, casting a meaningful glance at Lucy.

Mrs Pryce followed the direction of his gaze then shrugged tiredly.

"There's nobody," she said, towing the twins upstairs with her.

Lucy's crying was quieter now, her grip on Tamsyn's neck loosening. As the child nestled against her, Tamsyn kept one arm around her thin shoulders. Upstairs, they heard a TV being turned on. It sounded like cartoons.

It was another ten minutes before Mrs Pryce came downstairs again.

"Lucy, go up with the twins," she said wearily.

"I want to hear," Lucy cried, her voice raw.

"I don't think..." Tamsyn began.

"No!" Lucy said, her chin jutting out. "She was *my* friend!"

"Upstairs now!" Mrs Pryce yelled.

"I hate you!" Lucy screamed then stormed from the room.

Mrs Pryce didn't react, and when Tamsyn glanced at Sergeant Terwillis he raised his eyebrows and gave her an almost imperceptible nod.

Tamsyn cleared her throat.

"Mrs Pryce, I'm sorry to have to tell you that Jowita is dead. She was found at Lamorna Cove on Monday and we identified her from her fingerprints."

Mrs Pryce sighed. "What do I do about her stuff? Her clothes and that?"

Tamsyn paused, trying to recalibrate because this wasn't the script she'd practised.

"We're trying to identify her next of kin but it might take a while so..."

"Because I'll have to clear her room," said Mrs Pryce. "I'll need to get a new housekeeper. I can't do it all myself."

"Perhaps you can box it up and store it..."

"Can't you take it?" the woman asked. "Isn't it evidence or something?"

Sergeant Terwillis answered. "We'll forward you an address when we have one."

Mrs Pryce looked like she was going to argue but then she slumped in her seat.

"Poor cow," she said.

As they left the guest house, Tamsyn breathed a sigh of relief.

"You did well in there," said Sergeant Terwillis. "It's never easy when a child is involved."

"I don't think Mrs Pryce even cared," Tamsyn replied. "She seemed more worried about who was going to do the hoovering for her."

"Looks can be deceiving," he said. "No two people have the same reaction to death."

"I feel so sorry for Lucy."

Sergeant Terwillis climbed into the patrol car, his bulk making the chassis sink a fraction on the passenger side.

"Probably the first time she's known anyone who died," he agreed quietly. "But you were good with her. She'll remember that."

It felt like a heavy weight of responsibility, but Tamsyn was glad she'd been there for Lucy, too.

She'll remember me, thought Tamsyn. *She'll remember me the way I remember that officer who looked after me when Dad died.*

With two hours still to go before the end of her shift, Tamsyn felt drained. Sergeant Terwillis had told her to drive to McDonalds where they could talk about the evening, drink some bad coffee, and write up their notes.

But before they'd taken more than a sip, they were called to a fight outside Wetherspoon's.

As they hurried to the scene, pulling up outside the pub,

Tamsyn saw a large group of men yelling at each other, lots of raised voices, some pushing and shoving.

Nervously, she ran her fingers over the incapacitant spray.

"You won't need that," said Sergeant Terwillis.

"How do you know?"

He tapped the side of his head.

"Experience. Come on, Tamsyn, time to practise your conflict resolution skills," he said dryly.

Several of the men slunk away when they saw the patrol car, and a couple of others ducked back inside the pub, but a core of seven remained outside, red-faced and shouting abuse at each other and at the two officers.

"Just make steady progress, but don't rush to the fight. You'll be going to loads and loads of these, drunken mates fighting over football or some girl. It's usually handbags at dawn, and most of them get worse injuries playing rugby at the weekend." He gave her a small smile. "I will guarantee that no one will make a complaint. They'll all be mates again tomorrow and laughing about who can take a punch and who can't. As long as no one makes a complaint and there's no damage, no harm done." He saw that she was nervous and spoke more seriously. "You'll learn, Tamsyn, we've all been there – even an old sweat like me – and you *will* know when we have got to get to a fight quick. For now, just take names and addresses, if they give them ... I'll probably know most of them anyway, and you'll get to recognise them, too."

His knowing eyes scanned the small crowd.

"Call it in to Control," he said to Tamsyn, "and get an ambulance for that one." He pointed at a man who was sitting on the kerb, bleeding from a head wound.

Then he climbed out of the car and headed towards them. Tamsyn followed close behind, talking breathlessly to Control.

"Now then, lads," Terwillis said mildly. "Let's get you out of the road before someone is run over."

"Fuck off, pig!" one man mumbled, but kept his eyes down when Terwillis turned his head to stare at him.

"We've got an ambulance coming for your friend," said Tamsyn, pulling on a pair of disposable gloves, hoping she didn't get blood on her new uniform. It was still damp from Lucy's tears.

But the fight seemed to have gone out of the group, and most of them went back to their pints and ciders in the pub. Terwillis chatted pleasantly to the two men who stayed outside, keeping one eye on Tamsyn as she checked on the injured man. She was relieved that she didn't know any of the people involved. One day she probably would.

When the paramedics arrived to take over, Terwillis and Tamsyn went inside to talk to the pub staff. As there hadn't been any damage, and the man with the head wound insisted that he'd fallen over, there wasn't much for them to do except make sure that closing time didn't bring any more incidents.

"So, how was your first night with a bit of real policing?" Sergeant Terwillis smiled at her as she drove them back to the police station.

"I'm not sure I could have dealt with that pub fight by myself," Tamsyn said honestly.

"Maybe not right away, but you will," he said. "Confidence is the key and most of the time people *want* the police to sort it out, even if you get a lot of verbal from them. It's working out which ones are all mouth and which ones are going to kick off, and that comes from experience. You stayed calm, you did alright."

"Thank you, sarge," said Tamsyn.

"Bikers and Travellers are the ones I've been to where there's been blood and snot all over the place," Sergeant

Terwillis reminisced, "but nobody makes a complaint. It was like part of a good night out for them. And when I was based at Plymouth, the squaddies, sailors and bootnecks were all the same: as long as nobody was really hurt and the Red Caps or shore patrol didn't find them before getting back to barracks, it was part of life."

Back at the station, Tamsyn finished up her notes, joined in the handover briefing to the next shift, and changed into her jeans.

It was gone 1am and she was tired but too wired to sleep. She turned down Jamie's offer of a lift home and decided to walk back via Newlyn harbour. She wanted to see if her grandfather was there and how his interview with DC Forshaw had gone. She was annoyed with herself for forgetting to tell the inspector that her grandfather had recognised Saemira aka Jowita. She was also angry that she'd lost her temper with Ollie and been unprofessional. It was a good thing no one else had heard her call him a dickhead. How many times had she been told that she had to stay calm in all situations? She'd let Chloe get to her the night before, too.

I need to toughen up – that's what the DI had told her.

It had been a full-on day with so many highs and lows. She was proud of how she'd helped Sergeant Terwillis with the pub fight, even though not much had happened in the end. Although she had helped the guy who was bleeding – sort of helped him.

Her thoughts strayed back to Lucy, and she wondered how she was doing. With everything they'd learned about Saemira Ruçi, aka Jowita Wojciechowski, aka Jowita Nowak, the gun she'd hidden, her involvement with an international drug ring – it was hard to square that with the woman who'd been Lucy's friend. She hadn't asked Lucy to cover for her or try and get her into selling drugs at the primary school or anything illegal that they were aware of; she'd been kind to a lonely little girl. Although that might have changed in time. After all, it was a textbook example of grooming.

The roads were almost empty now, and even Newlyn harbour, which was open 24/7, seemed quiet. But at first light, the fishermen would be heading out, and the fish market opened at 4am, with buyers online from all over the country going to work as the fish were weighed and graded.

She could see the green sector light on the tip of North Pier, and a light flickered on in the ice house. Two red lights indicated Mary Williams Pier, and opposite those were where the leisure craft tied up. Her grandfather's punt wasn't at its mooring, and the Old Quay was completely empty. It was thought to be around 600 years old – nobody was really sure but the *Mayflower* had stopped there in 1620 to take on water on its way to the New World. She'd done a project on it at school.

North and South Piers had been added in Victorian times and the Mary Williams Pier in 1980. Tamsyn's grandfather had been there when Queen Elizabeth II had officially opened it. There'd been a photograph of him meeting Her Majesty in *The Cornishman* – the framed photograph hung over the mantelpiece at home now.

The harbour was all so familiar to her. It was as much home as the cottage in Gulval.

She saw that *Mari-morgans* was still tied fast down the pontoon, but there was no sign of Uncle George.

Disappointed, she headed home, alone with her thoughts. She sent a quick message to Jess to see if she was still awake, but there was no reply.

When she finally reached the cottage, she kicked off her trainers and curled up under the duvet with Mo at her feet.

CHAPTER 20

Rego was awake early, his mind churning. Instead of heading straight to the station, he'd gone for a run along the promenade, the dawn light turning it pink and grey, then wheezed his way back through the subtropical Morrab Gardens promising himself that he was going to give up smoking, and still managed to be at his desk shortly after 7am.

With his halo shining, he promised to treat himself to a fish supper tonight – Tom Stevens had recommended Frasers in Wherrytown.

But when he opened his emails, all thoughts of what he'd be eating 12 hours from now disappeared. The National Ballistics Intelligence Service firearms lab had sent in their report – the gun found at the church had been used at two gang-related shootings in east London, one of which had been fatal. Forensics also confirmed that Ruçi's fingerprints were on the weapon. It didn't mean that she'd been the shooter. Rego was well aware that guns were handed around and often shared within a gang. Apart from anything else, with multiple sets of fingerprints on a weapon, it made it almost impossible to be certain who had fired the gun and when. Yes, you could swab a suspect for gunshot residue, but with something that was the consistency of flour, it typically only stayed on hands for a few hours. And even then, if someone had washed their hands or had even just been putting them in and out of their pockets, these actions could render a negative test result. And sometimes third parties were persuaded or coerced to hide a weapon for safe keeping.

He read through the NABIS report of where the handgun had been used before, found out the names of the MIT officers in charge then emailed them saying that the weapon had been recovered and the circumstances pertaining to it.

NABIS coordinated all firearms criminality in the UK. They would get intelligence from firearms, shell cases or bullets recovered and manage the database of forensic examinations. Cartridge cases could be matched by looking at firing pin strikes on the primer or indentations made by the ejector. There were tens of thousands of entries on the NABIS database, which grew exponentially every year.

The call data records still hadn't come through for the burner phone, Ruçi's personal phone, or any of the other numbers that they wanted to trace. Frustratingly, Ollie Garrett's number hadn't been listed on the victim's burner. Spider Moyle, on the other hand, he hadn't been so lucky. When uniform had searched his house, they'd found his mobile wrapped in the sort of waterproof pouch that surfers used, and hidden in the toilet's cistern; the CDR call detail record was also being sought. It helped hugely to have a handset as there was so much more data to analyse including texts and WhatsApp messages – as well as fingerprints to prove that he'd used it. Even so, he was still answering 'no comment' to every question.

Tom Stevens had done a preliminary dive through Moyle's handset and had printed off various conversations between Moyle and Ruçi. Now IT were going through it to try and retrieve what had been deleted.

It had become apparent that Spider was a major distributor for Ruçi but Rego thought that there were probably others. After all, the Hellbanianz were savvy businessmen, so it seemed unlikely that they'd put all their eggs in the basket of a junkie like Moyle.

Interestingly, several conversations between Ruçi and Moyle mentioned delays and the 'product' being unavailable; Tom Stevens had been trying to match that intel with the movements of Domi's impounded artic from ferry records, but so far, the data wasn't matching up.

Next, Rego read Jack Forshaw's interview with Tamsyn's grandfather. It had thrown up two additional sightings of Ruçi outside the Mackerel Inn going back to before Christmas, but the old man had been vague on dates. He had, however, identified Spider Moyle as having been there at the same time as Ruçi on at least one occasion, which was good news for the CID team. But it also meant that there was a lot of extra CCTV footage for DC Forshaw to wade through – hours and hours of it. Mimi Eagling was helping, but with the analytics and exhibits included in her workload, most of it fell to Jack. It was the kind of work that sent you cross-eyed after a few hours. But it was important: Rego wanted to know who else the woman had been talking to, who she'd been dealing with.

So far, they hadn't found any footage at all of Ruçi near any of the pubs in St Ives: nothing at the Lifeboat or Sloop Inn, nothing at the Balcony Bar. Rego had also pulled in help from officers in Camborne, but there was no trace of Ruçi anywhere other than Newlyn and the Mackerel Inn. Either she'd avoided being caught on CCTV and hadn't known there was any outside that pub, or they simply hadn't been lucky enough to find the footage yet. Another possible reason occurred to Rego – perhaps she only ever dealt from Newlyn. Odd, but not impossible.

Vikram had emailed additional intel on Besnik Domi, confirming that the mobster rarely left Albania, and with the exception of this trip, Vikram hadn't found any information that he'd left the country at all since before lockdown. Of course, it was possible that he'd travelled under an assumed name, but NCA and Interpol had been keeping a pretty close eye on him since his brother's arrest, and there hadn't been any long gaps of time when they'd lost track of him or didn't know his whereabouts.

So why had he broken his routine with this trip to Cornwall? It was possible that he'd been scouting new routes, but given that Besnik's elder brother had been in a relationship with Ruçi's cousin, Rego still favoured the idea that this was personal. Unfortunately, gut instinct wasn't admissible as evidence.

If the timing had been different, Rego would have thought that Domi junior had come to avenge Ruçi, but that wasn't the case. Which made him question whether Domi killed her? And if so, why?

Damn, he needed those phone records – he felt sure that they held the key.

He emailed Tom Stevens about chasing up Vodafone asap – that was now urgent. And he wanted another crack at Spider Moyle. Perhaps a night in the cells would have made him more cooperative.

Rego knew that he had to get better at delegating, at being the boss, the one who managed the workload.

Gritting his teeth, he worked his way through the hundreds of emails that had dropped into his work account. Just because this case was kicking their arses, it didn't mean he could take his eye off what else was going on across his new patch. So he sat and read through all the reports that uniform had sent in over the last few days, as well skim reading through the other cases that CID were working on, not just at the Penzance station, but for the whole of Devon & Cornwall Police. There had been two fatal RTCs – a motorcyclist on the A30 and a student on the Penryn bypass; a case of arson on a housing estate in St Austell; and a brawl involving squaddies and bootnecks in Plymouth.

Next, he scanned a memo on an important Exeter Chiefs rugby match that would require extra policing later on in the month. He made a note to read up on how D&C had policed the G7 Summit a couple of years back. He remembered that Manchester had sent extra officers: in fact half of the UK's police seemed to have been drafted in to keep all those expensive Heads of State with their heads attached.

God, so many emails! But he persevered. He needed to understand the area and where the crime hotspots were.

One report caught his eye: CID up in north Cornwall were dealing with a celebrity stalking case in a small village between Polzeath and Rock. Rego's eyebrows shot up when he read the name.

Tom Stevens came in while he was still reading, glancing over Rego's shoulder at his computer screen.

"Morning, boss. Yeah, we get a lot of that. Lots of second homes down here – all the stars." His eyes went dreamy and his voice softened. "I met Kylie Minogue once when she was filming a pop video – she was lovely."

"Got you spinning around, did she, Tom?"

"Nah, the music's shite, but she's 'ansome."

Tamsyn woke to the sound of a spade turning over soil in the garden. She yawned and stretched, feeling Mo's warm weight pinning the duvet to her legs.

The small dog didn't seem in any hurry to get up, so Tamsyn enjoyed some early morning snuggles with someone who wasn't going to judge her.

Eventually, she rolled out of bed and trudged down the stairs, finding her grandmother in the vegetable garden.

"Morning, Tammy! Sleep well, angel?"

"Pretty good, Gran. I didn't see you yesterday."

"Only a month till Beltane – I've been busy with the girls."

Tamsyn smiled. She knew that her grandmother's 'girlfriends' were all in their seventies and eighties. They were a funny bunch of old witches.

"The police interviewed Grandad about that poor murdered woman," she said, straightening her back. "He wasn't happy about it."

"Not happy that he was interviewed or not happy that he'd seen her?"

"Both, I reckon. It's a terrible thing, terrible." She studied Tamsyn's face. "How are you holding up?"

"I'm fine, Gran," said Tamsyn, pouring a cup of stewed tea from the pot and settling on the back doorstep. "I mean, it's horrible what's happened, but I feel like I'm really making a difference, you know? Or at least part of a team that's making a difference. I know that the police get a bad reputation..."

"I've told the neighbours that you're a civil servant," said her grandmother. "I was going to say you worked in a bank, but your grandfather thought that was worse."

"Seriously? Wow, thanks!"

She looked to see if her grandmother was joking – it was hard to tell.

"Anyway, the whole team are working really hard to find out what happened. The DI is putting in 12 and 14 hour days."

Her grandmother smiled.

"You like him, don't you? I don't blame you – he's a nice-looking young man."

"Gran! When did you see him?"

"The night he walked you home. I thought then he was a real gentleman. You should invite him for tea."

"Oh my God, no! He's my boss! And married and ... just no!"

Her grandmother shrugged. "I'm only being neighbourly, him being a foreigner and all."

"He's from Manchester," Tamsyn said, rolling her eyes.

Her gran laughed. "Anywhere north of Truro is foreign to us. Well, maybe north of the Tamar. D'you know, my grandmother was born when Queen Victoria was still on the throne, and she talked about going to England when anyone crossed into Devon. She didn't leave Cornwall her whole life. Oh, she might have gone to Plymouth once."

"Really?"

Some of the kids Tamsyn had been at school with couldn't wait to go and live in Bristol or even London, but Tamsyn was happy here. Who wouldn't want all these beautiful beaches, the sea and sky and just so much space?

Mo jumped onto Tamsyn's lap.

"Alright, fur ball. Let's go and have some breakfast."

As she shared her toast with Mo, Tamsyn read through the dozens of emails and briefings from the station. She almost missed the reference to times when Ruçi and Spider Moyle had complained about the supply of drugs drying up, but then she read it more thoroughly, something niggling at her.

"I wonder..." she muttered out loud.

Mo cocked an ear but lay back down again after a few seconds.

Tamsyn sent a quick email to Jen Bolitho asking for the exact dates when Spider and Ruçi had been messaging about supply problems.

It would probably take a while for Jen to get back to her, so she finished her breakfast, pulled on shorts and trainers, then took Mo for a run up through the fields, around Kenegie and back past the Carn. Mo wasn't much of a fan of these long runs, preferring to sniff at her leisure and chase rabbits on occasion, but she kept Tamsyn company, and was happy to flop down in the garden afterwards.

While Tamsyn was in the shower, Jess had messaged.

Pub tonight?

Tamsyn had to text back that she was working. Hopefully, they'd catch up later on in the week.

By then it was late morning and Tamsyn's grandfather arrived back from the harbour. She heard his old Rover coughing diesel fumes as he parked outside the cottage. It was a miracle that car was still running but he refused to get rid of it. Tamsyn suspected it was because he could fill it up cheaply with red diesel which was legal for boats but definitely not legal for cars. She definitely didn't want to know for sure because then she might have to report her own grandfather. She knew that some of the old farmers had been known to run their cars on chip fat to avoid paying duty. You could always smell those ones as they drove past.

He parked on a wedge of scrubby grass next to her tired Fiat Uno.

Her grandfather teased her for having an 'Eye-talian' car, and said that FIAT stood for 'fix it again, Tony'.

By the time she was dressed, he was in his usual seat at the kitchen table. He glanced up at her from *The Daily Mail* when she came down the stairs.

"This what you're calling morning now, Tammy?"

"Leave her be, Ozzie," her grandmother said tolerantly.

"I've been out for a run," she said, bending down and planting a kiss on his white hair.

"Practically lunchtime," he grumbled.

Tamsyn sat at the table scrolling through her phone, pleased to see that Jen Bolitho had replied. She read the message, sucking her teeth and frowning at the dates.

Then something fell into place. She leaned forward, her mind going a hundred miles an hour. She searched on her phone and started scanning through the last three months of weather reports. It had seemed a long shot but now...

"Grandad, remember all that bad weather we had at the end of January and the beginning of February?"

"I'm not likely to forget," he scowled. "It were blowing south-easterly for nearly three weeks – couldn't barely get out the harbour for even longer."

"That's right," she said, almost to herself. "That's right. And it was bad again at the beginning of this month, wasn't it?"

He nodded, studying her face. "'Sright. Madder do it?"

"Just an idea..." she said vaguely. Then she glanced at her grandmother. "Don't bother with lunch for me, Gran, I'm going into work."

"But you're not on till three, luv! You've got to eat..."

"I need to do a few things first," she said, grabbing her phone and heading out the door.

Mo slumped sadly, her hazel eyes fixed on the front door as it slammed shut.

"You'll see her later," Tamsyn's grandmother said, scratching Mo behind her ears.

When Tamsyn arrived at the station, only CID seemed to be staffed – everyone else was out on duty.

Nervously, she approached DI Rego's desk and waited for him to notice her. Finally, he looked up.

"Tamsyn, hello. How are you?"

"Oh fine, thanks, sir. Um..."

"Yes?"

"You know those dates when Saemira Ruçi and Spider couldn't get any drugs?"

"We're assuming they were talking about drugs, but yes, what about them?"

"Well, I've had this idea. I mean, it might be rubbish but..."

He pointed at the chair opposite him.

"Go on."

"Okay, so I was wondering why Saemira was meeting Spider at the Mackerel Inn and not in St Ives. At first I thought it might be because people would know her in St Ives because she lived there. But what if it wasn't that? What if it's because of the harbour?"

"What do you mean?" Rego asked, his dark eyebrows pulling together.

"Well, St Ives harbour is tidal, right? It's got a large hand-line fleet and there are about 20 boats, most single-handed, so they catch mackerel in the bay; some hake, turbot, cuttlefish. But you can't launch at low tide, so you can't use it 24 hours a day. Newlyn is dredged so it operates around the clock.

There's nearly a hundred fishermen there every day – 600 boats a year, although two- or three-hundred residents' punts – probably about a hundred working regularly. It's the biggest fish harbour in the UK."

Rego listened attentively, intrigued. Her voice had grown stronger and her face was more animated now.

"Newlyn's harbour protects boats from the prevailing south-westerlies," she went on, "but when the wind blows from the southeast, it's really choppy and difficult for small boats to get out. Dangerous for anything under 35 foot. And even with a bigger boat, you'd really have to know what you're doing." She looked down at her phone. "So I checked the dates when Saemira and that Spider guy couldn't get their stuff..." She glanced up at Rego. "And all the dates fit with the bad weather when we had weeks of south-easterlies – Grandad couldn't get out for three weeks or more at one point – and he's the best there is. So I just thought that maybe ... I thought it might be important."

Rego sat back in his chair, then pinned his eyes on her. "Are you sure? About the dates?"

"Yes, sir. I asked Grandad and I checked the weather reports twice – I'm sure."

Rego tapped his fingers on the desk, his mind racing.

"So I wondered," Tamsyn said, chewing her lip. "Maybe the reason Saemira used the Mack Shack is because the drugs were landed at Newlyn Harbour."

Rego turned away from her and called out to his CID colleagues. "Briefing room! Now!" Then he spun his chair around and grinned at Tamsyn.

"Well done."

CHAPTER 21

For the first time, Tamsyn didn't feel nervous standing in front of other police officers and explaining her idea to the CID team. She'd spent all her summers helping her grandfather – she knew the sea's rhythms and pulses, wind and the water, almost as well as any fisherman.

But she still felt relieved when DS Stevens clapped and gave her a wink, and Jen Bolitho gave her a thumbs up. They all nodded, energised by this new piece of information.

"Tom, get on to the harbour's manager at Newlyn," said Rego. "I want a list of the boats that have regular parking spots there and are too small to go out in bad weather; if they were large enough to go out, there wouldn't have been a supply problem."

"Clint Brady is the Harbour Master. He's from up your way," said Stevens.

"Manchester?"

"Newcastle."

"Practically next door," Rego deadpanned. "Tell Mr Brady that you'll be dropping by for a chat – and get the harbour's CCTV for the 72 hours around the vic's known dates."

"The office is on North Quay," Tamsyn offered, "but Jonas Jedna is the night watchman. I mean, they call him 'security staff' but really he's just there to collect the mooring fees. He patrols two or three times a night, so he'd be a good person to talk to about who is moored regular and who's down the pontoon ... I mean ... if you think..."

She hoped that she wasn't coming over like some pushy know-it-all.

"Thanks, Tamsyn," Rego said. "You've been a great help."

Tamsyn hesitated for a moment but everyone was now heads down and working, so she left the busy CID briefing room that was buzzing with activity, and went to the kitchen. It was the usual mess of half-drunk coffees and crumbs everywhere. Sighing, she filled the washing up bowl with soapy water, cleaned and scrubbed until the room wasn't such a health hazard.

She couldn't help the need to create order where chaos reigned – and if she admitted it to herself – was probably one of the reasons she'd joined the police in the first place.

She made herself a cup of instant coffee in the much cleaner kitchen, then started working through her textbooks for her Police Constable Degree Apprenticeship course and updating her student officer portfolio.

She was unpleasantly surprised when Chloe came in to get a coffee refill. Tamsyn glanced up, but when she saw who it was, she didn't even bother to say hello, simply carrying on studying, although still aware of the dark cloud of heavy silence that Chloe seemed to drag with her.

Chloe gazed around at the spotless surfaces, her eyes drawn to the rack of drying mugs, plates and cereal bowls.

"Who are you trying to impress, Tampax? Brown nosing Rodrigo, are you? I bet he'd like that."

Tamsyn looked up from her books, met Chloe's eyes, but just shook her head and decided to ignore her.

"I bumped into Ollie Garret last night," Chloe went on, lowering her voice as if they were two old friends sharing a secret. "He bought me a drink and we got talking about school and other stuff. He had some very interesting things to say about you." She paused for effect. "He says you're a skanky blonde cunt who fitted him up and now he's going to lose his job because of you." Her voice became louder. "Why do you have to be such a bitch?"

Tamsyn leaned back in her chair.

"Is your asshole jealous of the shit that comes out of your mouth?"

Her tone was conversational as Chloe gaped at her.

"Ollie made his own choices, same as you, same as me," she continued, her voice hardening. "He's friends with some not very nice people. So if you're cleverer than you look, you'll stay away from him. And while you're at it, stay the fuck away from me, too."

It took Chloe several seconds to think of a comeback.

"Bitch!" she said, storming from the room – without her coffee.

Tamsyn deducted points for lack of originality and took a sip of her own tepid drink. Another encounter with Chloe hadn't been on her to-do list this afternoon. But it bothered her that Chloe had been talking to Ollie Garrett. She wondered if she should tell someone, but then decided she didn't need any more of the drama which Chloe seemed to thrive on.

As her shift was about to start, she stowed her textbooks in her locker and changed into her uniform. She was getting used to it now, and felt real pride every time she pulled up her long hair into a neat bun and checked the equipment on her utility vest.

Today, she was double-crewing with Jamie again, who grinned and winked so much, she wondered if he had something in his eye.

Their first job would be to check out all the car parks in St Ives, then foot patrol around the residential areas near the Caerlyon guest house, searching for Ruçi's car.

"This is the fob, so it should save you some time," said Sergeant Carter, handing the key to Jamie. "Look for a car with a build-up of leaves on it or under it, also rubbish blown against the wheels, a windscreen that's not clean – anything that says 'abandoned car' to you."

"Sarge, this is going to take forever!" Jamie complained, then saw the look on Sergeant Carter's face, and backtracked a few paces. "Is it the best use of resources?

"No information is useless, Smith. You don't know when it will come in handy." Carter clearly wasn't interested in hearing anymore complaints. "Beep it around and see what flashes up. You're looking for an older model Ford Focus, registered between 2003 and 2005. Have a chat with the locals – see if anyone has noticed a car hanging around that shouldn't be there."

Jamie pulled a face has they headed out.

"Don't know why we've pulled such a wanky assignment," he said, shooting her an aggrieved look. "I thought you were their star pupil."

Tamsyn shrugged. "Sounds alright to me, walking around St Ives on a nice afternoon."

"You'll learn, Padawan. You'll learn." He sighed and gave her a half-smile. "You'll end up getting asked for directions by all the tourists because nobody can ever find the Tate. And the business owners will complain to you about the stupid things visitors do. You get hot, the stab vest is uncomfortable, and you've got no chance of having a quick coffee without being interrupted half-a-dozen times. And even if you have so much as a bottle of water, someone will ask if you haven't got anything better to do than stand around having a drink."

Tamsyn raised her eyebrows but didn't say anything.

Jamie didn't offer to let her drive, and she soon tuned out his running commentary on Plymouth's chances against Port Vale this coming weekend, and his bemoaning the fact that AFC Bournemouth was the nearest premier league club which was 200 miles away in Dorset.

Tamsyn's family had always followed rugby, so she didn't know much about football and cared less.

Besides, she liked knowing that Cornwall was a long way from anywhere, at the very end of the country; she liked the fact that it was one of the few counties in England without a motorway. Up until 2013, it hadn't had a university either, although she had to admit that having the Tremough campus was an improvement because it made tertiary education cheaper for locals.

She loved that Cornwall had its own language, with a history that was more Celtic than Anglo-Saxon. She loved the surf and the beaches and the space. She couldn't imagine living in a city. Visiting Bristol or London was okay; Christmas shopping in Plymouth with her grandmother was bearable – but actually living in a city? No way. Something else that separated her from many of her former classmates.

She pulled her mind back to the job, cutting across Jamie's verbal stream of consciousness.

"Shall we do Barnoon and Porthgwidden first?"

"Why those?" he asked, sounding grumpy.

"They're the largest – I just thought it would be a good place to start."

Jamie didn't argue, which seemed like tacit agreement. So, it surprised her that they ended up at Westcotts Quay first – with all of its seven parking spaces to investigate.

Tamsyn could see straightaway that none of the cars were Fords, but decided to check for CCTV on foot, leaving Jamie to do a nine-point turn, trying to ease their patrol car out of the narrow space without losing a wing mirror.

Tamsyn found a lone CCTV camera, but a hanging wire made her think that it probably wasn't working. She took a quick video with her phone in case there was anything she wanted to look at later.

Jamie was sweating by the time he'd managed to turn the car without scraping the paint.

"I should have let you drive," he said with feeling, and Tamsyn laughed.

Next, Jamie drove them to Wheal Dream with its 22 spaces. This car park had CCTV, and Tamsyn took a photo of where it was positioned so that DS Stevens as Telecoms Officer could try and track down ownership later. That should be straightforward, seeing as it was a Council car park.

There were two Ford Focuses, but both were newer, and neither the fob nor the key worked on either.

Porthgwidden and the larger Island car park were next to each other and had one of the best views in St Ives overlooking the picture-perfect white sandy beaches. The tiny chapel of St Nicholas stood on a grassy promontory high above, with the lookout station for the National Coastwatch Institution a short distance below.

It was peaceful and serene and beautiful – and transformed from what had been the town rubbish dump until it was given a makeover in the sixties. Her grandfather said that the smell with an onshore wind had finally persuaded the council to pay for the redevelopment.

But finding the missing Ford was a bust in both car parks.

"Barnoon next?" Jamie suggested, sounding as discouraged as Tamsyn felt.

"Sure, why not? We can..."

Something caught her attention, a flutter of paper at the edge of her vision. She almost dismissed it as a pile of litter until she went closer.

Crouching down, she pulled on a pair of disposable gloves and took an evidence bag out of her pocket.

"Jamie, look at these. What do you think?"

Someone had thrown away two parking tickets – probably just pulled them out from under the windscreen wipers and dropped them on the ground.

"Can you do a PNC check for this number plate?"

Tamsyn read out the number and Jamie tapped it into his phone.

"Read it again, Tam. I think I took it down wrong."

But a second attempt gave the same result.

"Okay, that's weird. It says the car that got this parking ticket belongs to a 97 year-old woman living in Alderley Edge in Cheshire." He pushed his cap further back on his head. "Unlikely, but I guess we can check."

Tamsyn tapped in a query, scrolling through the data. The result surprised her.

"According to this, Margaret Beth Evans died two months ago and the car is subject to probate before being sold."

They looked at each other.

"Cloned plates?"

"Definitely looks like it."

"What are the dates on the tickets?"

Tamsyn checked the paperwork.

"Last Saturday and Sunday."

"The day after the vic was killed." He nodded slowly. "I'll call it in. And we need to find out who has the CCTV for this car park." He held out his hand and she high-fived him. "Nice work, pardner."

CHAPTER 22

It took a frustratingly long time for the CCTV of Porthgwidden car park to come back the next day. When it did, it showed Ruçi driving a silver Ford Focus at 19.08 on the Friday evening, then leaving on foot with a backpack over one shoulder.

She had no idea that she'd be dead within a few hours.

The first parking ticket was issued late afternoon on the Saturday, and the second on Sunday evening.

At 01.23 on Monday morning, another car had arrived and dropped off a man with the build of Besnik Domi, although they weren't able to see his face. If it was him, by then, he'd discarded the distinctive hoodie.

Rego leaned over Mimi Eagling's shoulder, watching the tape run backwards and forwards as they tried to pick up more clues.

"It looks like the other car is deliberately staying out of sight," he said, frustration in his voice as they stared at the screen, only able to glimpse the headlights shining a pool of light onto the road.

"Reckon the driver knows that car park has CCTV?" Mimi asked.

"Possibly. It's the kind of thing a crim would be on the lookout for."

Rego rubbed his eyes, debating how to prioritise his resources and personnel. Ideally, he'd like to know exactly where Domi – or whoever had been driving Ruçi's car – had gone next. Maybe it was a long shot, but with the number plates that had probably been cloned, it seemed like one worth pursuing, although he'd already had three of his officers glued to computer screens looking at hours and hours of CCTV footage, and they were still searching for a sighting of Ruçi at other pubs in the area.

Domi could have left Cornwall in Ruçi's car if he'd been the one to kill her, although that fact was far from being established, so cameras on the A30 might have picked him up. And at that time on a Monday morning, there wouldn't have been much traffic, so it ought to be fairly quick to check the footage. And maybe it would be worth looking as far as the M5 at Exeter, if Domi had decided to avoid main roads for a while.

He knew that criminals often travelled on FOG's – Fraudulently Obtained Genuine passports. Crims submitted a passport application with their own photograph but someone else's details. It was scarily easy to do – all they needed was some willing person who wanted to make a few quid and let them use their details. Which meant that Domi could have left the country and they'd never even know.

But at least they had other leads to follow up.

Jack Forshaw had pulled a late shift and gone to the harbour to interview Jonas Jedna, the night watchman.

"Not that chattiest bloke I've ever met," said Jack, sarcasm lacing his voice. "I thought hell was going to freeze over before I got a whole sentence out of him."

Rego was interested.

"Boss, no one checks in on him that regular – a night watchman would have plenty of scope to move around the harbour without anyone knowing."

"What exactly did he say to you?" Rego asked.

Jack pulled out his notebook.

"He said, 'Awright, boy. Where's you to?'"

"Pardon?"

Jack grinned. "It's a Cornish thing – we call everyone 'boy' instead of 'mate', I guess. And he was asking what I was doing there."

Rego wondered if he should buy a dictionary of Cornish slang. And good to know that being called 'boy' wasn't a racial thing: he'd wondered.

"Would he have time to take a boat out while he was working?" Rego asked thoughtfully.

Forshaw hesitated.

"Risky, but not impossible."

"So what do we know about Jedna?"

"Bit of a loner. He's a local – born and brought up in Mousehole – knows his boats. Did his 22 in the Army in REME, including two tours of Afghanistan; left with the rank of Staff Sergeant. I checked PNC and he's got two cautions for being drunk and disorderly. But those were both five years ago and nothing since. He's been working as night watchman for three years now."

"Okay, I want him in for a formal interview, Jack. Anything else?"

Forshaw nodded then handed over a piece of paper.

"The Harbour Master sent over a list of small craft which

were permanently moored there that wouldn't have made it out in bad weather."

His tone was strained, and when Rego ran his eyes over the paper, he could see why: Tamsyn's grandfather's boat was on the list.

Rego mentally ticked through what he'd learned about the fishing industry since he'd been in Cornwall. When he'd gone to the harbour, Ozzie Poldhu's boat had been one of the smaller and older boats. Stood to reason that he didn't make much money from crab and lobster, especially at his age. Was he getting an income from an illicit source?

Rego hoped he was wrong. It was never easy when a copper's personal life became part of an investigation.

Tom Stevens interrupted his thoughts.

"Boss, we've got the CDR from Vodafone on the vic's number," he said. "I'll start going through it all now."

"About bloody time," said Rego. "Well done for keeping on them, Tom. Let me know what it flags up asap ... or sooner. Start on the burner and then her personal phone. Any data usage that points to online banking? And work with Mimi – I want all that information fed into the analyst charts."

"On it."

Rego knew that this information was going to be crucial in building up a picture of Ruçi's movements. The handset itself gave them information about the numbers called, when, and the call's duration, as well as texts, WhatsApp and Snapchat messages – they'd already been working on that; but the CDR would tell them where Ruçi had been when she'd made those calls and sent those messages. Rego was hoping that this would narrow down the areas to search for CCTV to see who else she'd been meeting.

Most criminals knew about burner phones these days, but they still made mistakes, calling girlfriends and boyfriends, and sometimes even food delivery services. It wasn't unusual to find Domino's as one of the most frequently called numbers. Maybe it was weed giving them the munchies? And even if it was a new burner, there was a good chance that there'd be links from their older phones.

The CDR information sent from the phone provider was hundreds of pages of data that all had to be checked, crosschecked and referenced.

Rego had done this job himself and knew how time-consuming it would be. But then again, few complex crimes could be solved quickly; not many people walked into a police station and said, 'I done it, guv. Send me to prison.'

The method Rego had been taught was to start with the top ten most used numbers, then expand out. There was a lot of information to cull – starting with billing, including where and when top-up vouchers had been bought.

The crims didn't even have to make a call. Mobile phones worked by constantly hunting for the next cell area where it would lock on. This gave an approximate location for the person with that phone. If another phone that you were interested in 'mirrored' the location of the crim's phone, then it was a reasonable assumption that they were meeting, and that was then evidence.

One of Rego's colleagues had worked on a case where a group of migrants had been found illegally entering the UK. So they had 27 phones with 27 lots of communication with the people who'd organised their transportation.

It had required a huge amount of patience and concentration, and the translator who'd worked on the case had been overwhelmed, but at least they'd caught and jailed the people-smugglers involved. Some of them.

People smuggling – was that part of the key to this case? Rego spun his chair around and called across to Jack Forshaw.

"Jack, have you found any sign that Ruçi had an online bank account?"

"No, boss. Nothing."

"Then how were they moving the money around?" he said to himself. "In the lorry?" Then out loud, "Get onto Clint Brady at Newlyn Harbour – I want CCTV of the boats going out after the bad weather on the list of significant dates. I know, more CCTV, but this is how we're going to catch this killer – good, solid detective work."

"Sir, there are CCTV volunteers at Launceston – maybe they could help?"

Jack sounded a little desperate. Rego knew how he felt – he'd been craving a cigarette for at least two hours, but he'd promised Cassie he was giving up.

"Yep, great idea. Get onto them to see if they've got some resources to help us, but I'll need you to stay on this yourself, as well. Work with Tom on locations where we know the victim made calls – get CCTV and find who she met. I want to know who she talked to, who she saw."

Jack gave a resigned nod and picked up the phone.

Rego surveyed his team, pleased with the way they were working together. His DCI had described Tom Stevens as 'a safe pair of hands' and Rego was impressed with his calm capability. The man was a good fifteen years older than Rego, and he wondered why his DS had never applied for his Inspector's exams. One day, when he knew him better, he'd ask him.

They worked solidly for the rest of the day on the victim's phone and CCTV footage, putting in the long hours, hoping to get a break on the case.

Rego was just thinking about packing it in for the evening and getting those fish and chips that had been calling his name, when Tom Stevens knocked on his door.

"Have you got a minute, boss?"

"Sure, come on in."

Tellingly, Stevens closed the door for privacy, then took a seat opposite.

"I've been looking at CCTV from the harbour during the times when the vic and Moyle had been discussing shortages. Well, we've identified several small boats that we've seen going out shortly after the bad weather..."

"Okay?"

Stevens grimaced.

"The thing is, boss, there's one small boat that crops up on every single one of the dates in question."

"Go on."

"And it belongs to Ozzie Poldhu, Tamsyn's grandfather."

That was not what Rego wanted to hear.

"Are you sure about this?"

Stevens nodded, his face expressing a mixture of concern and sympathy.

Rego sighed and rubbed his forehead.

"Okay, we'll need to bring him in for questioning. And I'll need to talk to PC Poldhu. Do we know where she is?"

"Bryn Terwillis is the student's tutor, he'll have her timetable."

Rego decided to walk down and see the sergeant as a courtesy. Besides, Tamsyn was under his supervision, so he needed to be informed if there was a problem.

He found Terwillis eating a sandwich at his desk. He started to stand up when he saw Rego.

"No, it's okay – finish your sandwich, sergeant. I just wanted to have a word with you about one of your students: Tamsyn Poldhu."

"Is there a problem, sir?"

Rego closed the office door and pulled up a chair.

"Possibly. What do you make of her?"

"From the little I've seen, I'd say she's sharp, observant, hard-working ... a little lacking in confidence, but that'll come with experience. I'd say she has the makings of a good copper. So, what's the problem?"

"I need to bring her grandfather in for questioning on the Saemira Ruçi case."

"Ah."

"Yes."

Rego went on to explain why he wanted to talk to Tamsyn's grandfather, and how the CCTV clearly showed his boat going out at the times when they suspected smuggling was taking place.

"I will be interviewing a couple of other fishermen, but so far, Ozzie Poldhu is the only one who fits all three of the time slots that we're looking at."

"That's not good."

"No, it's not. I'm going to keep the interview as informal as possible but there's a chance that it might become more formal. I want to tell PC Poldhu myself rather than her hear about it after the fact."

"And she won't be able to have anything to do with the case either."

"No."

"Sir, cards on the table: is there any suspicion that PC Poldhu is involved in any illegal activity?"

"No," Rego said, then paused. "Not at this moment. But I do need to talk to her."

Terwillis nodded. "Let me check the duty roster. Okay, she's on nights today and tomorrow, so she'll be in for the briefing handover but I'll ask her to come in early and..."

"Unfortunately, I need to interview her grandfather this afternoon."

Terwillis grimaced. "Well, I could call her – ask her to come in now."

"Thanks," Rego said as he stood up. "Don't tell her why I want to speak to her – and if you could just keep this between us for now. Once I've interviewed Mr Poldhu, well, it'll be entered into HOLMES and then it will be common knowledge, but as I said, I will be interviewing other fishermen from Newlyn, so hopefully we can keep this low-key and need-to-know for now."

"Of course, sir. And could I ask to be kept informed of how the interview goes with her grandfather?"

"Yes, I'll do that. Thank you, sergeant."

Rego was heading back to his own office when his phone rang with a call from DS Stevens.

"Boss, Ruçi's car has been found."

"That's great news! Where?"

Rego was expecting to hear that it had been found in London or Dover or Calais – somewhere Domi would have dumped it prior to heading back to Albania.

"Marazion, in the car park for the community centre."

For a moment, Rego was speechless, and he had to revise his thoughts quickly. The murder victim's car had been found a stone's throw from St Michael's Mount – a favourite destination for tourists and members of the National Trust looking for a cream tea.

But then again, just because somewhere was scenic, it didn't mean there was no crime. As he was learning.

"Any CCTV?"

"Nope. Sorry, boss."

Rego was disappointed but he was fairly sure his team would be relieved not to have to sit through even more hours of blurry digital images.

"Okay then, let's get over there to retrieve the vehicle: full forensic lift, a secure garage, samples and photographs – the works. And because we believe it's on false plates, look at the VIN number to identify its correct number and where it was stolen from."

"Yes, boss."

"As soon as there's any news, I want to know it."

Before he'd even finished the call, he heard Mimi Eagling trying to get his attention and looking more animated than he'd seen her for a few days.

"Boss! I've got something, too."

Probably a new pair of glasses because you've been scanning CCTV for three days non-stop.

He looked over her shoulder at the computer screen.

"I've got footage of the victim's car," she said, excitedly.

"Where and when?"

"Newlyn Harbour, Saturday 24th March. Look at the time-stamp: 02.23."

"Just a few hours after she was killed!"

"Yes, and look at this..."

She clicked on fast forward, then paused over an image of a man bending over the boot of the car. He'd parked in a deep pool of shadow and his face was hidden by a baseball cap.

Rego squinted at the image. It didn't look like Domi who was short and wiry; this was someone tall and thick-set. Rego watched the screen as the man pulled out something bulky and heavy that he struggled to carry. It was wrapped in bin bags and tied with a piece of rope.

"That could be a body, sir," Mimi pointed out.

Although the video had no sound, Rego could see the ends of the rope whipping around in a strong wind. Their theory had been that poor weather had kept the murderer from disposing of the body – it looked like they were bang on with that.

Then he remembered that had been Tamsyn's theory – a theory that could possibly implicate her own grandfather. And he didn't know what to make of that.

"Can you see which boat he goes to?"

"No, sir. He goes out of screen ... then we pick him up again six minutes later heading back to the car. It's dark and he keeps his head down, so we don't have much to go on. He gets in the car and drives away – we can't see the number plate or which direction he went either. He's avoided all the CCTV and night vision security." She paused. "If that was the vic, it's a pretty ballsy move to leave a dead body on a boat like that."

"Agreed. Get the Harbour Master to give us a list of all the boats that were in the harbour that night – small ones are the priority, but I want to know everyone who was there."

"Already done it, sir," she grinned at him. "There were eleven boats under 12 metres that night. Nine of them were local fishermen, and two were visiting yachts which took refuge from the storm: *Coleraine Queen* owned by a Kevin Coyle from Northern Ireland; and *Magio de Machico*, owned by a Portuguese national living in Madeira named Aderito de Jeles." She paused. "Madeira is off the coast of Africa."

Vikram had mentioned drug routes coming to Europe from North Africa – was this a possible link?

"Find out if either of those yachts have visited Falmouth, Newquay or..." Rego struggled to think of any more Cornish fishing ports, "...or anywhere else relevant."

"I'll check with the harbour masters."

"And find out if either of those yachtsman are on our databases."

"Boss."

"And Mimi – well done."

She gave a pleased smile as she headed back to her digital searches.

Rego's phone alarm reminded him that Tamsyn would be in shortly. He needed a moment to put his thoughts in order, but when he returned to his office, she was already waiting for him with the same eager and alert expression he already associated with her. And looking so very, very young.

She wasn't in uniform as her shift didn't begin until that night, and he regretted that he'd had to deny her a lie-in after a late shift, but that was the nature of policing: birthdays missed, anniversaries forgotten; hell, most relationships ended up taking second place once you were on a case. Of course, it wasn't always like that ... just mostly.

She smiled as she sat down, and he felt like a shit for doing this to her, especially as the connection between 'product' shortages and bad weather had been her idea.

Unfortunately, he now had to consider the possibility that she had some ulterior motive for mentioning it, maybe even deliberate misdirection. Maybe not, but he had to at least consider that she might not be as entirely squeaky-clean as she seemed. And he hated that.

"Tamsyn, thank you for coming in early. Again."

She smiled.

"No problem, sir."

"The thing is," he said, choosing his words with care, "your suggestion about a possible link between bad weather and the shortages mentioned on the victim's burner phone, it's thrown up several avenues of inquiry that we'll need to follow up."

"Oh, that's great!" she said, looking pleased. "I mean, it was just an idea, so I'm really glad that ... I'm really glad."

Rego withheld a wince.

"Yes, so we have a list from the Harbour Master of smaller

craft with moorings at Newlyn, and we also have CCTV which shows the boats heading out after the severe weather, as discussed."

She nodded, still looking interested and engaged, still not recognising that she was about to hear bad news.

"We'll be talking to all the owners of those boats." Rego looked down, as if checking his notes. "And one of the people we'll be interviewing is your grandfather."

He could see the exact moment that she understood what he was saying.

"You ... you want to interview Grandad?"

"Yes. I'm going to invite him to come in for questioning this afternoon."

"But ... he didn't do anything. He wouldn't. Not drugs. No way."

"At this point, it's just an informal interview."

Her expression cleared a little. "You want to eliminate him from your inquiries."

"That's a good place to start," he said.

She seemed to take what he was saying at face value, which made him feel worse.

"DC Forshaw already talked to him at the harbour," she said, as if he needed reminding.

"Yes, but now I need to talk to him about specific times and dates – now that we have them."

"Oh, okay." She paused. "Grandad can be a bit ... difficult ... especially with strangers. But he doesn't mean anything by it – it's just his way."

"Noted," said Rego. "But until we have eliminated him from our inquiries, you can't have any active role in this murder investigation. I'm sure you understand."

"But, sir..."

He met her gaze, his own expression unyielding.

"You're not allowed to have anything to do with this case, and you can't talk to your grandfather about it. If we find out that you've been talking to him, then as a minimum, you will be investigated for gross misconduct, but the likelihood is that you would be arrested and interviewed for perverting the course of justice. If you're found guilty, you'll be looking at a lifetime ban from the police. Do you understand, Tamsyn?"

Her mouth fell open and she blinked several times.

Rego hoped she wasn't going to do anything awkward like cry. But she simply stood up from her chair.

"Thank you for telling me, sir. Can I go now?"

"Yes. Thank you for coming in."

She gave him a terse nod and left the room.

Rego watched her for a moment, then picked up his phone to call her grandfather.

He was not looking forward to this interview with Ozzie Poldhu. Forshaw said that the old guy had been grumpy and bad tempered when he'd talked to him at the Harbour Master's office, and even Tamsyn had warned him that her grandfather could be 'difficult', so asking him to come and be interviewed in a custody suite would be like asking a Manchester United fan to cheer for City.

He debated briefly whether or not to have a more informal chat in Penzance, but then he thought that it wasn't fair to bring him to Tamsyn's workplace – so Camborne it would be.

CHAPTER 23

Ozzie Poldhu was waiting in the reception area at Camborne police station when Rego went to bring him down to the interview room. The old man looked like a character from a previous century with his white beard, bushy eyebrows and heavy knitted sweater. His face was tanned and creased like an ancient atlas, and there was something almost biblical in his watchful silence. Only the strong aroma of diesel and pipe tobacco that clung to his clothes brought him into the twenty-first century. His arms were crossed defensively across his body, and he scowled at anyone who looked his way. The bright blue eyes that seemed to run in the Poldhu family, glittered with anger and humiliation.

"Mr Poldhu, I'm Detective Inspector Robert Rego and this is Detective Sergeant Tom Stevens. Thank you for coming in. First of all, I want to ensure that you understand this is a voluntary interview."

"Is it now?" he growled, his Cornish vowels as long as the southwest peninsula, the consonants almost completely swallowed. "I was under the impression there was nothing voluntary about it."

"No, you're not under arrest and are free to leave at any time."

"Right, that's me off then! Wasting my time, as if I haven't got enough to do."

"Mr Poldhu," Rego said quickly. "We will be interviewing other users of Newlyn Harbour who match the criteria for our inquiries, and it will be much better in the long run if you talk to us here and now today. I arranged for your interview to be at Camborne instead of Penzance in consideration of your granddaughter."

That was stretching the truth slightly, but he could see the old man wavering. Rego knew that he was being disingenuous for using Tamsyn to get her grandfather to talk to him.

"Can I offer you anything to drink?" Tom Stevens asked politely. "While we wait for your solicitor."

"Not much of a choice, is it?" the old man said angrily. "I'll have tea. Strong – don't just show it the teabag, let it brew."

"No problem. Milk? Sugar?"

"Splash o' milk," he said grumpily. Then he looked up and met Rego's gaze. "And I won't be needing no bleddy useless solicitor neither."

Rego was surprised. It had been a while since he'd had anyone come to a police interview without a solicitor.

"We can appoint one for you if you don't have your own."

Ozzie waved him away.

"Let's just get on with it so I can get out of here and back to work."

"Are you sure? You want to do an interview without a solicitor?"

"I've already told you, boy."

"Well, if at any time you want us to stop and get a solicitor, we will."

"How many times have I said no? Reckon you must like the sound of your own voice."

Rego nodded and led the way to the custody suite where the interview would be recorded.

Tamsyn's grandfather sat heavily in a chair and waited, his white eyebrows pulled together in a fierce frown.

"Mr Poldhu, I need to caution you," said Rego and proceeded to read out the legal requirement. "You do not have to say anything, but it may harm your defence if you do not mention when questioned something which you later rely on in court. Anything you do say may be given in evidence. Do you understand?"

The old man scowled at him, his frown deepening, the anger apparent on his face. Angry enough to kill somebody?

"Mr Poldhu, do you recognise the woman in this photograph? I am showing Mr Poldhu a photograph of Saemira Ruçi, also known as Jowita Wojciechowski."

"Yes, I seen her."

"Where was that?"

"Outside the Mack Shack a couple of times. I told Tammy this a'ready," he growled, "and that other fella you sent to talk to me. I never saw her inside, always out, and always late at night. I never spoke to her, never knew her name. Saw her with some scruffy layabout. I don't know 'is name neither."

"Did you ever see this woman at the harbour?"

"No."

"Are you sure?"

"Iffn you's going to repeat everything, we'll be here till Christmas. Get on with it, Mr Inspector."

"I have to tell you that Jowita was murdered."

The old man didn't react.

"Mr Poldhu?"

"I guessed as much."

"Why do you say that?"

"Because," Ozzie replied, "you wouldn't make this much fuss over an ordinary drowning."

He said it with such certainty, such grim finality that Rego suddenly remembered that Poldhu's own son, Tamsyn's father, had drowned. It was sad, but he needed to move the interview on.

"Are you aware of how Jowita died?"

"I assumed she was thrown overboard left to drown," he said, sounding puzzled.

"She did drown, Mr Poldhu, but not in the sea. Her tongue was cut out and she drowned in her own blood."

This time Rego did get a reaction. It was hard to tell, but he thought the old man looked shocked.

"My question, Mr Poldhu, is about whether or not Jowita's tongue was cut out with a fish filleting knife?"

The old man's face contorted with disgust, and finally he spat out the words.

"I wouldn't know, boy." He shook his head, his voice so quiet it was hard to hear him. "I can't believe it. Not here, not Newlyn. This is my *home*."

It struck Rego that this interview may have set in motion an event where Tamsyn's grandfather would want to speak with or meet the person who was involved in either drug trafficking or Jowita's murder. Rego thought that if Ozzie Poldhu was involved, he'd be calling that person or persons after this interview. Rego really loved phone intel – although he still wanted to be wrong about Tamsyn's grandfather. But he had a duty to explore all reasonable lines of inquiry.

Rego changed tack and produced another photograph.

"Is this your boat?"

"Yes, that's the *Daniel Day*."

"Did you go out fishing on Friday 20th January? I'm

showing Mr Poldhu a CCTV image of his boat leaving the harbour at 4am that morning."

"How am I supposed to remember that? That's my boat, so I reckon I must have."

"And there'd be a record of your catch at the fish market?"

Ozzie shifted on his seat.

"Yes." He paused. "Sometimes, I keep some for a few friends."

"Is that usual?"

"I reckon."

"I'm showing Mr Poldhu CCTV from Thursday 16th February. Is this your boat?"

"Yes."

"And do you remember what you caught that day?"

Ozzie stared at him.

"Know much about fishing, do 'ee?"

"Not really."

"Lobster season is from June to August, and the best months to catch lobsters are May to October. But then there's a short run of large females inshore in January and February. So no, I don't remember what I caught, but I do know that it would have been worth my while to hail the pots."

"Hail the pots?"

"Bring in the lobster pots and traps."

"And you sell direct to customers?"

"No, we're not allowed to do that. Reg'lations."

Rego tapped his pen on the desk.

"But it happens sometimes?"

"I wouldn't know."

"Could you give me a list of your regular customers?"

"I could."

"That would be helpful, thank you."

Tom Stevens passed the old man a notepad and they

watched as he slowly wrote a list of restaurants from Land's End to London who bought from him, his flowing, cursive script heavily incising the sheet of paper.

"Thank you," said Tom Stevens.

"Now, this is another image of your boat, the *Daniel Day*, on Sunday 26th March," said Rego. "Do you remember that?"

"Yes. Do you want to know what I had for breakfast, too?"

"No, that's not..."

"Four rashers of bacon, two eggs, two slices of fried bread and a cup of tea. Ah, hang on a moment, it may have been two cups of tea."

Rego let the old man's irritation die down before he asked his next question.

"Did you take your boat out the two nights before, Friday 24th or Saturday 26th?"

The old man's bright blue gaze flickered.

"Not the Friday, no, I didn't. It was roaring like Cudden, wouldna you, sou'-sou'-east – had been for weeks: *wind from the east, fishing least; wind from the west, fishing best.* But I've been having problems with my spark plugs, see. So I was off the water Saturday as well, so for those two days, there was no catch even though it was coming up to a neap tide."

Rego paused, wondering about the significance of the fact that Poldhu hadn't been out either of those nights. The pathologist had been certain that the victim's body had been dumped on the Saturday night.

"I was worried I wouldn't get to my pots in time," the old man mumbled.

"Time for what?" Rego asked.

Poldhu scowled at him.

"Lobsters are the gardeners of the sea, but with your crab in a confined space, they'll eat anything and everything. When we land 'em, we snip the claws so they can't be at each other. I had to get to my traps in time to stop the crabs from trying to eat each other."

Rego was mentally crossing another type of seafood off his *must try* list.

"So, for two whole days, you didn't take your boat out at all?"

Ozzie stared at him inscrutably.

"Reckon you don't know much about engines either, iff'n you think you can start 'em without spark plugs."

"Did you go out on the Sunday night?"

"No."

"Why not?"

The old man looked embarrassed, but eventually answered gruffly.

"I wanted to see Tammy off in the morning."

Rego must have shown his surprise, because Poldhu leaned forward. "You got children, inspector?"

"Yes."

"Then you know."

They both leaned back in their seats and Rego considered what he'd learned. He also remembered that the morning the body had been recovered, Tamsyn's grandfather couldn't be found at his boat because he'd gone to buy new spark plugs. He wanted to know if the old man had actually bought any – that would be easy to check.

"Do you have a receipt for the new spark plugs?"

"'Spec I got it somewhere, but if you think I'm lying, ask Barney over Pirates – he sold 'em me."

Rego made a note, then tapped his pen on the desk, wondering where that left the investigation. He glanced up to see the old man staring at him. Was he involved? Was he looking into the eyes of a killer?

He glanced at Tom to see if he had anything to ask, but received a subtle shake of the head.

"Thank you for answering these questions, Mr Poldhu. We may need to re-interview you if new evidence comes to light."

The old man muttered something under his breath and pushed his chair back.

"I also have to tell you, Mr Poldhu," Rego said seriously, "that I have already spoken to Tamsyn about this interview."

The old man's face darkened, his eyes stormy.

"As a sworn officer, she isn't allowed to discuss this case with either you or your wife. If we find out that she has been talking to you, she'll be investigated for gross misconduct, or arrested for perverting the course of justice. That could lead to her being dismissed from the force, and a lifetime ban from the police anywhere in the country."

Ozzie Poldhu's eyes blazed with fury.

"Don't you threaten me with your mealy-mouth lawyer words! Tammy is a good girl, an honest girl! She joined the police to do her bit and you ... you...!"

The old man was momentarily lost for words. But then he slammed his gnarled hands down on the table, thrusting his face forwards.

"You do your worst, Inspector Big Mouth, but you leave my granddaughter out of it!"

Then he heaved himself up and stamped out of the room, slamming the door behind him.

Rego wanted to be wrong about Ozzie Poldhu, and he didn't want to believe that Tamsyn was involved. He didn't want to, but he definitely had to consider the possibility.

Rego glanced at Stevens who raised his eyebrows and closed his notebook.

CHAPTER 24

It had been a long nightshift and Tamsyn had already attended six incidents while she'd been double-crewing with Mitch Rogers. At 32, he was one of the older men on E-team. He was slightly shorter than Tamsyn, but with the build of a rugby prop and the demeanour of a man who'd heard it all and seen it all – the kind man you knew you could rely on.

Starting at midnight, they'd gone straight to the first of their six call-outs, all involving excessive alcohol, leading to a couple of fights, one suspicion of vandalism, loud music at 3am, and two domestic incidents.

Tamsyn had watched and learned as Mitch managed to de-escalate each situation with a few well-chosen words and a friendly but professional demeanour. No one had been arrested, no one cautioned.

The seventh incident came in two hours before the end of the shift.

"Right, Tamsyn," said Mitch. "We've had a call about a vulnerable man suffering from Alzheimer's, gone missing from his daughter's home. Let's go."

The daughter had phoned 999, frantic with worry

because her father was obsessed with a nineteenth-century mineshaft near their home. Apparently, he'd been a tin miner at South Crofty before it closed more than twenty-five years earlier, and his daughter was afraid that he might try to climb over the flimsy fencing and fall in. She couldn't go and look for him herself because she was baby-sitting her granddaughter.

They drove slowly through the deserted streets that led to the old mineshaft, looking at every front garden, under every tree and along every driveway.

They'd gone nearly a mile, without seeing anything when Mitch finally spotted him.

"Over there," he said, pointing at an elderly man who was standing on a grassy roundabout, clearly lost and distressed.

"He must be freezing," Tamsyn murmured, taking in the man's pyjama bottoms and bedroom slippers, his naked chest concave, his shoulders hunched with cold and fear, the world a vast and confusing place.

"It's a good thing that it's early in the morning and there isn't much traffic on the road yet," said Mitch. "The old boy could easily have been knocked over and killed before making it off the roundabout. Right, let's go and check on him – get him into the patrol car and warm him up."

"Do we need paramedics?"

"Let's just get him in the car first," said Mitch, already climbing out.

But when the elderly man saw them, his distress increased. He stared at Mitch, then started moaning, shaking his head and rocking on his feet.

"You try," Mitch said, backing off a few paces and handing Tamsyn a blanket that he'd pulled out of the boot. "Just keep talking to him quietly. See if you can get him over to the car."

She remembered what Sergeant Terwillis had told her about appearing non-threatening and decided to leave her hat in the patrol car.

"Hello, are you Alec? I'm Tamsyn. Your daughter Helen has been very worried about you."

That seemed to be the wrong thing to say, and the man started shouting but she couldn't understand the words.

"Are you cold? Would you like to borrow my blanket? I know it's spring now, but it's still chilly."

Slowly, so slowly, she drew nearer, talking to him quietly, saying anything that came into her head, telling him all about fishing at Newlyn, all about Morwenna and the mischief she got up to, until finally she was able to wrap the blanket around his thin shoulders and get him calm enough to sit in the back of the patrol car so they could take him home.

The daughter flung the door open as they pulled up and was yelling before she'd taken a step.

"Where the hell have you been, Dad? I've been so worried! You've got to stop doing this! It's doing my head in."

The old man cowered and the woman burst into tears.

They were both surprised when the father put his arms around his daughter and said, "There, there, Hells Bells. There, there."

Mitch ushered them all inside and finally the woman was calm enough to thank them for finding him.

Mitch gave her the demential helpline number for the Alzheimer's Society, and then they quietly left her to her own despair.

As they drove back towards the station, Tamsyn remained silent and Mitch glanced across at her.

"I know. We can't solve their problems but we stopped that old boy from getting hurt tonight. Count it as a win."

Tamsyn nodded slowly. "Do you think she'll call that helpline?"

"She might. We'll probably never know."

Tamsyn thought of her own grandparents, fit and healthy in their early seventies, but they wouldn't always be that way. Time caught up with everyone eventually.

It had been upsetting to see that old man so scared and confused, but at least it had been the last call of the night, so after that they were able to go back to the station to type up their reports – and something else for Tamsyn to put in her student portfolio.

As she changed out of her uniform, she felt lightheaded because she hadn't eaten and her body was sagging with exhaustion.

Unfortunately, Chloe was leaning on the desk in reception when Tamsyn was heading out. She definitely didn't feel up to a run in with Bitchtits, as she'd privately nicknamed her.

Jamie was there too, looking equally tired, but possibly a tad more energised than Tamsyn because he was taking a moment to appreciate Chloe's assets – both of them on display in a shirt that gaped open when she leaned forward.

Chloe obviously relished the chance to take another swing at Tamsyn, because her eyes lit up with malice when she saw her.

"Well, well, well – not the station's sweetheart anymore, are you? I heard that your dodgy Grandad was interviewed and they're probably going to re-interview him under caution."

Tamsyn's anger surfaced quickly. She hadn't known that piece of information that Chloe seemed to think was juicy gossip.

"Not so whiter than white now, are you?" Chloe sneered. "Although maybe you've got a thing for darker meat."

Tamsyn assumed that was a dig at DI Rego but right now, she only had the energy to care about her family. She continued to stare at Chloe, the anger draining away with the worries that crowded in, worries she'd been able to put out of her head while she'd been crewing with Mitch.

"Give it a rest, Chloe," said Tamsyn tiredly. "You're not impressing anyone with your attempt to win bitch of the year."

Jamie frowned, his gaze flicking between the two women.

"They're interviewing several of the Newlyn fishermen," he said, but Chloe shook her head.

"That's what they're saying, but her Grandad is the only interviewee entered into HOLMES." She smirked at Tamsyn. "Things aren't looking so rosy for you, are they? Perhaps you'd better forget about pretending to be a police officer. Why don't you go home and polish your surfboard?"

Tamsyn curled her lip.

"You wax a surfboard, not polish it. Dickhead."

And she walked out of the station.

Jamie rushed after her.

"She was just winding you up. She didn't mean anything by it."

Tamsyn gave him a cynical rise of one eyebrow.

"I don't know what you've got against her," he muttered.

"Me? What *I've* got against *her*?" Tamsyn shook her head in disbelief.

"I know she can be a bit..." even Jamie struggled to find the right words to describe Chloe. "But she's alright when you get to know her."

"Only someone with a penis would think that."

Jamie's mouth dropped open, gaping like a grouper fish, and Tamsyn left him standing in the staff car park as she strode home. He seemed like a nice enough guy but so frickin' clueless.

She walked faster, hoping he wouldn't try and catch up with her, but the truth was that after her conversation with DI Rego the day before, she was worried. And if Chloe was right about none of the other fishermen being interviewed...

She needed to find out what the hell was going on.

Which was going to be a problem now that she'd been warned off the case.

Tamsyn walked home in a daze, tiredness, concern and confusion all swirling around in her brain, making it impossible to decide what she should do.

She couldn't even talk to her grandparents about it, and she'd always been able to talk to them about everything.

It almost made her want to avoid going home, but she couldn't because that wouldn't be fair to any of them.

But as she reached the cottage, she saw her car. Someone had put a brick through her windscreen and spray-painted the word 'grass' across the bonnet.

Tamsyn was furious and then felt sick. She took a photo of the damage and was wondering what to do when her grandmother came running out of the house.

"Oh, Tammy! I was just about to phone you! I came out after breakfast and saw it. We've never had any trouble here – it's a quiet village. Who would do something like this?"

Tamsyn had her suspicions. The graffitied word 'grass' was the clue – it was what Ollie had called her when she'd run into him at Camborne station.

And that wasn't all. Chloe had said herself that she'd been talking to Ollie Garrett. Ollie was connected with Spider and who knew who else – there weren't many corners of the country where you couldn't buy some weed or a few wraps these days. It was a growth industry, she thought bitterly.

Besides, Ollie already knew that she lived in Gulval – it wouldn't have taken more than a two-minute online search to find the Poldhu family.

"Probably just kids," Tamsyn lied. "They heard I'd joined the police or something. It's a pain, but don't worry about it, Gran."

"But I do worry!" her grandmother cried. "I worry all the time!"

Her grandmother turned and angrily walked into the kitchen, gazing unseeingly as she leaned over the sink.

Mo came trotting over to see Tamsyn, but even she seemed dispirited, her tail drooping. Tamsyn crouched down to give her a back scratch, then scooped the little dog into her arms.

Her grandmother turned to face her.

"What are you going to do?"

"I'll report it and get in touch with my insurance." She forced a weary smile. "I might ask the neighbours if they saw or heard anything."

"It must have happened after Ozzie went out. And I didn't hear a thing. Anyway, Miss Nellie nextdoor would have been straight on the phone to the police if she had," her grandmother frowned.

"I'm sure you're right," said Tamsyn, deliberately downplaying it.

"I'm sorry, angel. I didn't even ask! How was your night shift?"

"Yeah, it was fine. Grandad gone to work?"

"Why wouldn't he?" her grandmother asked stiffly.

Then she dipped her head, her white dandelion hair hiding her eyes.

"I shouldn't take it out on you, Tammy, but what they're saying about him! And now your car. It's so unfair! As if he'd ever even think about..."

"Gran, I can't talk to you about that," Tamsyn interrupted. "I could lose my job."

Her grandmother's eyes flashed with anger. "You *know* he's innocent! You *know* it's nonsense what they're saying about him!"

"Of course I know that," Tamsyn said quickly. "I just can't talk about it."

"Can't you do something then? Now you're one o' them?"

They stared at each other across the kitchen, and Tamsyn didn't know what to say that would help.

"Let them do their job, Gran," she replied at last. "They'll see that Grandad didn't do anything."

Then she turned and climbed the narrow staircase, Mo still in her arms.

Shit, I hope I'm right.

A shiver ran through her, and Mo whimpered.

Chloe had been right about one thing – Ozzie Poldhu was the only fisherman from Newlyn that Rego had interviewed personally, because he was the only one who fit all the criteria. And unfortunately, Poldhu hadn't been able to give Rego any reason to rule him out of their inquiries – if anything, the opposite was true.

Clint Brady had explained to Rego that all fishing boats were required to have an iVMS, an in-shore vessel monitoring system fitted – a transponder that reported their position every two hours. Problem solved? Not quite, because currently the system only applied to boats over 12m, and Ozzie Poldhu's boat was smaller than that.

Which put him right in the frame.

It went back to the theory that the problems Ruçi and Moyle were having with supply must mean that whoever was bringing in the drugs, Subject F perhaps, must be using smaller boats – or a smaller boat.

Rego listed out the questions he needed answered:

1. Who had killed Saemira Ruçi?
2. Did the CCTV show the killer taking her body to Newlyn Harbour, and if so, where had the body been kept?
3. Who was 'Subject F'? Ozzie Poldhu? Jonas Jedna? A third party not yet identified?
4. Where was Besnik Domi?
5. Was Tamsyn Poldhu involved in any of this?

Rego massaged his temples, something he did habitually when he was thinking, even when he didn't have a headache.

There was one date that didn't fit in with Ozzie Poldhu being involved with Saemira Ruçi – and that was the night her body had been dumped. Poldhu had been having trouble with his boat's spark plugs and it hadn't left the harbour that night, nor the following night because he'd wanted to see Tamsyn off to work on her first day. More than one person had commented on his not being there because it was his usual day for selling his catch. Which left three possibilities: Ozzie Poldhu wasn't involved; another fisherman was involved; or Poldhu was working with someone else.

Somehow, Rego didn't think it was the last option; he couldn't imagine that grumpy old geezer working well with anyone else.

Rego wanted Tamsyn's grandfather to be innocent. Unfortunately, the evidence didn't rule him out. Poldhu might not be teaming up with anyone – he might simply have taken someone else's boat that night.

Rego moved on from that question and thought about the other evidence that they'd gathered.

Traces of blood had been found in the victim's car – AB negative, a rare blood type that was the same as Saemira Ruçi's. Only 1% of the UK population had AB negative blood, and in Albania it was 0.9% – Rego had checked. The blood still needed to be DNA matched, but Rego was confident that it belonged to the victim.

He reviewed what he knew: Ruçi had been murdered, location unknown; two unidentified suspects had entered the St Ives car park, retrieved Ruçi's car, taken it to an unknown location, then transported the victim's body in her own car to Newlyn Harbour, where the body was kept for up to 12 hours before being disposed of at sea.

Then he reviewed what he believed: the body had been shuttled from the murder site to the harbour in the victim's car; a local fisherman had been working with Ruçi and Domi to distribute drugs in the southwest; Domi had murdered Ruçi to stop her from talking – the symbolic cutting out of her tongue.

They didn't know who she'd been talking to – because it wasn't the police or any of the law enforcement agencies, so had she been negotiating with other criminals wanting to take over the business? That would be a very risky strategy, but it could have happened. He decided to run that idea past Vikram, who had a nationwide overview of organised crime gangs.

Rego stared at his computer as if the answers would jump from the screen.

Where had Ruçi been killed? He felt sure that the CCTV Mimi had found showed the body being brought to Newlyn Harbour. But according to the pathologist, there would have been a lot of blood at the murder site, and they hadn't found it in the boot of the car.

Three drop locations had been mentioned on Ruçi's burner phone: 'the water', 'the market', 'the house'. Where was this house that had been mentioned and who did it belong to?

Somehow Rego couldn't picture Ruçi parking up outside Tamsyn's cottage in Gulval – the whole family would have had to be involved. Rego didn't buy it.

Okay, so someone else – but who? Rego wondered if it would be worth having another go at Spider. The man definitely knew more than he'd said so far.

Rego decided to set that up as soon as possible.

He glanced across at his small team. Tom had gone to the harbour again to ask questions about Ozzie Poldhu's activities on several other dates of interest and to check his sales for those days. Jen Bolitho was off sick with shingles and no one expected her back for at least a fortnight. The timing couldn't have been worse when they were already short-staffed. As for DC John Frith who was recovering from having his appendix removed, Rego hadn't even met him yet, although apparently he was hoping to be back at work in a week.

Rego hoped that this case wouldn't be running on that long. He felt like they were making progress – and he wanted to nail Domi. It would be a real achievement to get scum like that off the streets. He could share a cosy prison cell with his lowlife brother.

Jack was concentrating on Ruçi's CDR, Mimi was feeding all the intel into her analysis charts, and support staff from Bodmin, Launceston and Truro were still looking through hundreds of hours of CCTV for sightings of Ruçi and/or Domi.

Information from Ruçi's burner phone had been prioritised and they'd been able to identify a number of known local druggies who subsidised their own use with some dealing on the side. They were all small-time, but between them it added up to a lot of petty crime. They'd also been able to 'mirror' several of the numbers so they'd be able to look for more CCTV footage of where the dealers were meeting. It was tedious but it was that kind of laborious, painstaking work that got results.

Vikram was particularly interested in the overseas numbers Ruçi had used, and Rego was glad to have a substantial amount of intel to pass to his friend.

"Boss," Mimi gave a quick knock on his open door and immediately stepped inside. "I've started on Ruçi's personal phone and there's really not much on there. The only overseas number she used frequently belongs to her mother in Albania, but I've found hundreds of WhatsApp messages between the victim and the little girl Lucy Pryce – even more than the girl had kept – lots of memes and jokes about the family, messages about when she was picking her up from school."

"Grooming her?"

Mimi pulled a face.

"I'd say so. Lots of little digs about the mother, lots of affection to Lucy, telling her she's pretty and smart. I think that little girl would have done just about anything for Ruçi. So yeah, I'd call it grooming – it was only a matter of time before she'd asked her to do something else, something illegal *for her friend*."

Rego's own daughter was only two years younger than Lucy Pryce and his son two years older. He hated the thought that someone might try to use either of them like that. How did you warn kids and keep them safe without scaring them? How did you stop criminals pretending to be their best friends and taking advantage of them, of using them, of grooming them for criminal activity – or worse?

"There's only one number of real interest," Mimi continued, "and that was an incoming call at 15.57 on Tuesday 7th February, lasting 34 seconds."

"Too long to be a wrong number so..." Rego realised that Mimi was grinning at him. "What?"

"Boss, it matches one of the contact numbers on Ruçi's burner phone – she had the number listed under the name '*Gaforrja*'. I looked it up on Google Translate: it's Albanian for the astrological sign Cancer. And cancer is..."

"The crab – maybe a fisherman?"

Someone who caught lobster and crabs.

"I think this *Gaforrja* character could be our Subject F – it's the only call Ruçi received that fits with what Lucy Pryce told us."

"We're putting a lot of faith in the word of a ten year-old girl. What do we know about the number?"

"Ruçi was the only person the user called. And there weren't many of those, even on the burner: mostly text messages sent at night about setting up meetings. No time given, so maybe they always met at the same time?"

"Maybe."

"The last text sent by this user was on the Thursday before Ruçi died. We know that it instructed her to meet the next day at 'the market'. We also know that she read it."

"You say 'instructed': did you get the impression that the user was the one in charge, the boss?"

Mimi thought about this.

"You know, now you mention it, the tone changed over the last three months. At first it was 'can you' and 'will you', then it changed to a couple of words: 'the house' or 'the water'. Maybe the balance of power was changing."

"Maybe," Rego repeated. "Or maybe they just knew each other better."

"Yeah, but what if this whole thing is about crims falling out?"

Rego nodded. The theory had legs.

"Definitely worth considering, but let's get all billing and call data for the number attributable to *Gaforrja*. Get it processed as an 'Urgent' – priority one." He paused. "I'm wondering where 'the market' would be. If that was the last text sent on the day before she was murdered, it could well be significant, and it could be the place she was lured to and then killed. It would make sense if they were talking about the fish market at Newlyn."

"Maybe," she said, not looking convinced, "but isn't there a load of CCTV all around the harbour, as well as night-vision cameras? If that was the meeting place, we would have found something by now."

Rego disagreed.

"At least one person worked out how not to be seen – if that was the victim's body we saw being carried from the car."

"Yes, that's true," she said, still sounding uncertain.

"So, where else are you thinking? We know that Ruçi had to work in the guest house every morning, so if the fish market is out and a farmer's market is unlikely due to the timing..."

"They have craft fairs at Porthleven Harbour on Tuesdays, Thursdays and Saturday afternoons," Mimi offered.

"Feels too public."

They both paused, thinking, then Mimi smiled and said, "Marazion! That's where her car was dumped, right?"

"Marazion has a market?"

"No! Marazion *is* a market."

"I'm not following you."

"It's what the name means in Cornish – *Marghasyewe*, Thursday Market!"

Rego nodded but remained sceptical.

"It seems unlikely that Ruçi would have known that."

"I agree," said Mimi, "but if we're right about Subject F being a local, he'd have known it!"

"It's a possibility," Rego agreed, "but we want to stay open-minded on this. What else do you know about this number?"

"Burner, and it's been off since Ruçi was killed."

"Stay on it, Mimi. I want to know everything about that number for the last year."

"Already got Jack working on it," she said.

As she left the office, Rego's mobile rang.

"Vik, I was going to call you," he said. "I've got some Albanian numbers from Ruçi's burner phone, as well as Spanish, German and Polish. You want to run them?"

"Definitely! Thanks, Rob. But I'm calling about something else. Not sure if it's connected with your case but the timing is interesting. We've had intelligence that a yacht we've been watching for a while has crossed the Bay of Biscay. We attached a beacon to track it, but it only pings a location every ten hours. We thought it would turn east and head for Jersey, but it hasn't turned up there. It could be that it's on its way to Ireland, but our friends at Border Force think it could be heading to Cornwall." He paused. "The yacht's owner is a person of interest to us, but we don't believe he's the one sailing it. So it's possible it's an entirely innocent yachtsman who just happens to be connected to a known player, which would make it another of those pesky coincidences that neither of us believe in. My boss is going to ask the Royal

Navy for assistance so we can use their long range radar, but we'll definitely have a Border Force cutter there anyway."

"When is this yacht estimated to be in British waters?"

"If it has crossed the Channel, it would be with you tonight," said Vikram. "I'm emailing you the information now. Because of all the attention Newlyn has been getting lately, they don't think that will be the destination but we're keeping an open mind on that."

"They don't want a patrol car at the harbour?"

"No, too visible. Use an unmarked car for surveillance. If Newlyn is where the yacht's heading, we're just going to let it happen. The Fishery Protection Vessel will patrol up the north coast, and we've got the Coastguard going east along the south coast. They're hoping to find out where this yacht is going: watch but no interception – yet. We won't get another location until 6am tomorrow morning, so it's going to be a bit of a long shot. This guy is definitely trying to travel under the radar." He paused. "Mate, do you still get seasick?"

Rego groaned.

CHAPTER 25

Tamsyn wasn't used to sleeping during daylight hours, and even though she was bone tired, her brain was wide awake.

CID seemed so certain that Newlyn Harbour was at the centre of this, and Tamsyn herself had pointed out that neither Penzance nor St Ives were dredged so their harbours could only be used at high tide. But that left plenty of others, such as Falmouth, and even more places you could anchor off the coast within easy reach of a quiet beach or stretch of coast path.

What weren't they telling her? What didn't she know? Jen Bolitho might have given her a heads up, but Tamsyn had heard that she was off sick. She didn't know anyone else in CID well enough to ask them, and she definitely couldn't ask the inspector, no matter how friendly he'd been to her before – their last meeting had been terrifying.

She suspected that Jamie would tell her anything she asked, but given that he was friendly with Bitchtits, that definitely wasn't a good idea either.

Mo was curled up by her hip, happy for any excuse to

snuggle with her favourite human, and she opened one eye at Tamsyn's restlessness.

Forcing herself to lie still, Tamsyn practised relaxing her muscles one by one, until she slipped into an eerie, dream-lit world where the horizon grew dark and shadows crept at the corners of her eyes. She dreamed that she was back at Lamorna Cove, but when she looked down to see the body, her father's blank gaze stared up at her.

Tamsyn woke with a start, her hands shaking as she wiped sweat from her face. It wasn't even lunchtime and she'd slept less than three hours.

She stumbled out of bed anyway, showered and sat at the kitchen table. And even though her stomach felt hollow, she had no interest in eating.

Mo watched from her own bed in the corner by the Aga, looking disillusioned when she realised that Tamsyn wasn't eating, cooking, or dropping even a single crumb.

They both heard Ozzie's car pull up at the same time. Mo trotted to the front door to greet him, but Tamsyn sat frozen in her chair. She still didn't know what to say to him.

"Alright, Tammy. Any more tea in that pot?"

"No, but I'll make you a fresh one," she said, sliding out of the chair and glad to have something to do.

He sat at the kitchen table, hands the size of hams wrapped around the mug of tea that she made for him. He looked exactly as he'd always looked, as immutable as the granite he seemed carved from.

She was mesmerised by those hands, so strong, so capable, the hands that had always caught her when she fell.

"I'm sorry, Grandad," she said at last.

For a moment, he was silent, then he laid one of his heavy hands on top of hers.

"Nothing to be sorry for, maid. Nothing at all."

The words she was desperate to say were trapped behind a wall of bureaucracy and the fear that Inspector Rego would find out.

Her grandfather squeezed her hand.

"Have you eaten?" he asked.

"No, I'm not hungry."

"You're too bleddy skinny. I'll do us a fry up."

She gave him a wry smile.

"Didn't you have a fry up for breakfast?"

"The caff sells 'all day breakfasts' – if it's good enough for 'em, it's good enough for me."

And Tamsyn knew it was the only thing he could cook.

He set up the frying pan and soon the sizzling sound of frying bacon and sausages filled the small kitchen.

Tamsyn felt happier now she knew that her grandfather didn't blame her. She turned to look at Mo; the little dog was sitting up in her bed, fixated on the movements of the frying pan. She looked like she'd turn a cartwheel for the chance of a piece of bacon. Ozzie was happy to oblige, and dropped half a rasher in her bowl.

She plucked it out carefully, and trotted back to her bed where she licked every speck of grease off it before eating it one happy gulp and looking up for more.

Tamsyn's appetite returned and she tucked three crispy rashers between two wedges of bread, smothered them in tomato sauce and took a huge bite. The salty goodness made her realise that she was hungry after all.

It had always been like that for her – if her grandfather was alright, then the world would still turn.

She was still intent on working her way through the doorstep of a sandwich when her grandmother returned, giving Ozzie a cool eye as he enjoyed his second breakfast of the day, shaking her head and muttering to herself as she dropped a kiss on his head and plumped down at the table, helping herself to her husband's food.

"Getting busy out there on the roads. Emmets coming down for their Easter holidays," she commented.

Tamsyn smiled. This was normal. This was how things always were around this table. She watched as her grandfather filled his pipe with tobacco, taking pleasure from the preparation, then strolling outside to enjoy smoking it by himself in the back garden.

Tamsyn turned to her grandmother.

"Will you be starting your cleaning job again, Gran?"

"Yes, missus left a message saying she'll be down on Maundy Thursday, and that the house was to be ready for guests."

To supplement their income, Tamsyn's grandmother did cleaning for a wealthy couple who had a second home nearby. Four or five cleaning jobs during the tourist season – which seemed to be longer each passing year – meant a world of difference to the family fortunes.

Tamsyn was happy that she'd be able to help out more now she was earning a good salary. Maybe both her grandparents could cut their hours a little. Then she frowned ... assuming she stayed on as a police officer and didn't get fired before she'd finished her probationary period.

Her mood took a darker turn. She'd wanted to be a police officer since she was a kid – if she didn't have that, she didn't know what she'd do.

After lunch, Tamsyn drove out to Praa Sands to spend an hour surfing. The wind was a northerly, meaning it was offshore on the south coast, and the only time Praa's beach break was really good.

Mo came with her but stayed at the edge of the water,

watching Tamsyn as she chatted out back with some of the local surfers she knew, then caught wave after wave before riding the last one to the beach. Then she treated herself to a hot chocolate with whipped cream and marshmallows at the Reef beach bar, and Mo was allowed to lick some of the cream off Tamsyn's finger.

Feeling more chilled than she had since she'd started in the job, Tamsyn stopped at Café Sisu to pick up a batch of the world's most wonderful triple-chocolate brownies to take into work the next day. Then she spent the drive home over-thinking whether it would make her look like she was trying too hard.

Her grandfather was watching the local news when she came in, but immediately switched it off.

"Heard some talk down at the harbour."

"Oh yes?" said Tamsyn, her mind on other things.

"Customs officers are out in the Channel," he said.

Tamsyn frowned. "You mean Border Force?"

"Yep, saw it meself. Heard they're searching east toward the Lizard, and up the north coast as far as Newquay."

"I wonder what they're searching for?"

Her grandfather raised an eyebrow.

"Oh," she said, feeling foolish. "Right."

"Police have buggered off," he said, giving her an almost-smile.

"That's a relief," she laughed a little awkwardly.

"I did the shopping while you were out," her grandmother said from the kitchen. "Fancy making your special Shepherd's Pie for tea?"

"Sure, why not. It'll make a change from fish," Tamsyn teased.

Her grandmother popped her head into the living room and smiled.

"We could have George over," she suggested. "I haven't seen him for ages."

"He was talking about running some new lines over Carn Gawas this afternoon," her grandfather grunted. "I tole him he wouldn't catch much there but he was all for trying it. He's prob'ly back by now empty handed."

Something pinged in Tamsyn's brain.

"Was there anyone else at the harbour?"

"Only Jonas Jedna coming on for the night watch."

Tamsyn sat up straight. They'd been looking for a fisherman all this time, but Jonas had never been questioned as far as she knew. He did his nightshift and went home again, rarely stopping to chat to the fishermen. He was known as a loner.

Tamsyn realised that Jonas fit the profile completely. He had access to all the boats, including her grandfather's; knew who was in, who was out, who was landing the best catch, and if there were any visitors and where they were from because he was the one who collected the fee for staying overnight.

But she couldn't be sure. She couldn't go around accusing people without evidence.

"What's the matter, angel?" asked her grandmother. "You look like you've seen a ghost."

"No, no ... just something I thought of." She looked across at her grandfather. "Is Uncle George there by himself?"

"Jus' him and Jonas, like I said."

"Does he know about what you heard?"

"Couldn't say."

"Do you think Jonas knew that you'd been interviewed by the police?"

Her grandfather scowled.

"Thought I'd take out an advertisement in *The*

Cornishman in case anyone there was anyone who hadn't heard."

And it wasn't just the fishermen who'd known – as Chloe had pointed out, the information was in the HOLMES database, which meant that every officer on the case and at the station knew about Tamsyn and her grandfather, which meant all those people had access to their home address and the fact that Ozzie Poldhu could be found at the harbour most nights.

Tamsyn rubbed her forehead. Then again, any number of people at the harbour could have seen her grandfather talking to the police. Jack Forshaw had even said that they'd used a room in the Harbour Master's office for an informal chat; the more formal interview at Camborne was a matter of record. She hated that he'd been subjected to that, and she resented that Inspector Rego had thought her grandfather could be mixed up in this, no matter that the evidence had been compelling. She still didn't understand exactly what had happened because no one would tell her.

"Lots of us was supposed to be interviewed," her grandfather said bitterly. "But I'm the only one they talked to."

He hadn't recovered from it either.

"I guess anyone could have seen Inspector Rego and the other police down at the harbour," Tamsyn said after a short pause. "You know what they're all like for gossip down there," and she gave a weak smile which only her grandmother tried to return.

But only one person there has a granddaughter who's a police officer.

None of them said it, but they were all thinking it.

"Look, I'm worried about Uncle George," said Tamsyn, biting her lip. "You said yourself that he's down there alone and he could get caught up in all this ... whatever this is ... if we don't warn him. I mean, I could be wrong."

"But George don't have nothin' to do with it, Tammy," said her grandfather. "Why'd anyone bother him?"

"Maybe no one will bother him," Tamsyn agreed cautiously.

"They bothered you alright," her grandmother threw in furiously.

Tamsyn hated that her grandmother was right, but at that moment, she was downright terrified to think that Jonas Jedna could be linked to Saemira Ruçi and Besnik Domi. Domi was a killer – it wouldn't matter to someone like that if Uncle George was in the wrong place at the wrong time.

"I'll call him," her grandfather said calmly. "Just to let him know to watch his back. Don't worry, maid. George can handle hisself."

Her grandfather picked up his mobile phone, the one he complained about having in the first place because he'd 'never needed one before'.

His blunt fingers stabbed at the buttons on his ten year-old clamshell, and it seemed as though they all held their breath while the phone rang. And rang, and rang, and rang.

"He's not answering his phone, the stupid bugger!" Tamsyn's grandfather groaned with frustration.

"Is it ringing or going straight to voicemail?" Tamsyn asked worriedly.

"Going straight to his message," her grandfather replied, staring balefully at the phone. "Useless bleddy thing!"

Tamsyn tried calling from her own phone but with the same result. A horror film of images rushed through her mind's eye, and all she could think of was Saemira's violated body tossed into the ocean, just human jetsam.

She knew that she was being emotional, irrational even,

which wasn't the best state of mind for making good decisions. There was no reason to think that Uncle George would be in danger, and her superiors, the experienced officers, they'd decided that Newlyn was no longer a priority. Her grandfather had already said, *the police buggered off.* Tamsyn knew she should leave it to CID – everyone said that Inspector Rego knew what he was doing, even if he was a foreigner.

But they don't have family here.

And it won't hurt to check.

CHAPTER 26

Tamsyn reached for her coat from the hook by the door.

"Are you going out? What about your Shepherd's Pie?"

"I'll make it tomorrow, Gran."

"But where are you going?"

"Newlyn," she said, hunting for her car keys.

"Not by yourself, you're not!" her grandfather huffed, hauling himself from his chair so quickly, she heard his knees click.

"You don't need to come with me, I'm a police officer," she reminded him.

"You're my granddaughter!" he shouted, his face creased with worry.

"Ozzie, go with her," her grandmother urged quietly.

"I don't have time for this!"

Fear and frustration made Tamsyn curt as she headed for the front door, tapping out a brief text to let DI Rego know where she was going. She didn't want to phone him in case he told her not to go – he wouldn't understand that Uncle George was *family*.

But when she saw her decrepit old Fiat with its shattered windscreen, she could have howled with frustration. Instead, she ran back to the house, grabbing the keys to her grandfather's ancient Rover, then flung herself in the driver's seat and wrenched the key in the ignition, swearing as the engine failed to catch.

A second later, her grandfather was opening the passenger door and squeezing his heavy frame into the seat.

"Grandad..."

"Don't!" he snapped, his expression fierce.

Tamsyn grimaced then tried the engine again and this time it coughed to life.

The car leapt forwards, but a flash of white raced in front of her wheels, and Tamsyn slammed on the brakes, her heart hammering as she realised that she'd nearly hit Mo.

"I'll get her!" Ozzie yelled, flinging open the door so the little dog could jump in.

Mo squeaked in protest when he squeezed her too tightly.

"Why are you bringing her?" Tamsyn yelled.

"Quicker'n leaving her behind."

Tamsyn shook her head and gunned the engine.

Fear was infectious, and she could feel it clawing inside her.

Please be alright. Please be alright. Don't take someone else I love.

Was it praying?

Tamsyn wouldn't have admitted it because she'd sworn off God and any sort of faith after her father died, but right now, at this moment, she had to believe in something that would keep her family safe.

The roads weren't busy and they were at Newlyn Harbour in minutes.

Tamsyn didn't even bother parking properly in a

designated bay but abandoned her grandfather's car and jumped out.

The harbour was eerily quiet: too late for day trippers, too early for fishermen, and too dark for tourists.

The silence seemed ominous as they hurried down the jetty towards the pontoon where Uncle George kept his netter, and only Mo's nails clattering on the wooden boards could be heard above the pounding of Tamsyn's heart.

If Jonas Jedna was there, he hadn't come out to see them.

The *Daniel Day* and *Mari-morgans* were tied up opposite each other, as they always were – George's fifty foot ring-netter berthed with the larger boats. Tamsyn's grandfather swung himself aboard ducking into the wheelhouse.

"Not here, Tammy! Check the..."

"Alrite, Ozzie," came George's voice. "Where you to, boy?"

Tamsyn sagged with relief as she saw Uncle George unharmed, hands stuffed in the front of his yellow overalls.

"Are you okay?" she asked breathlessly, her heart still slamming in her chest.

He nodded at her, eyebrows raised. "Proper job, me."

Tamsyn's knees felt weak, and she slumped down onto an empty fishing crate.

"We've been so worried!"

"Why's that then, bird? Where's the fire?"

She ran her hands through her hair, not sure where to start.

"You didn't answer your phone."

"Didn't know I had a curfew," he said slowly. "Anyways, I lost my phone a few days ago. Musta dropped it overboard or summat."

"It's not safe here by yourself," Tamsyn said seriously.

He outright laughed at her.

"Not safe? I've been here man and boy, and the on'y thing that scares me is the way you women's minds work!"

Tamsyn ignored the jibe and decided he should know everything, because that way he might take her seriously. The inspector had said she couldn't discuss the case with her grandparents – he hadn't said anything about Uncle George.

Even as she rationalised it to herself, it sounded like a lame excuse, but she ploughed on.

"That body the police found last week, you remember? She was murdered. I've been working on the investigation – well, not much – helping out a bit. Anyway, she was connected with a drug ring from Europe, probably Albanians. We think they've been using small harbours all up and down this coast – my DI says it's because the big container ports have so much security now. So they're targeting smaller places like Newlyn."

Uncle George snorted in disbelief and her grandfather looked truly shocked.

"That sounds a bit farfetched, Tammy. You been watching too much Netflix."

Tamsyn gave an embarrassed laugh.

"Yeah, I know! But it's true. Grandad and I were worried that you might be walking into something dangerous here by yourself. I even texted my DI about it! He'll think I'm such an idiot."

George nodded.

"You'd better tell him it's a false alarm then."

"Oh my God, he could be on his way! I'll text him now."

She pulled out her phone, wondering again if she should call Inspector Rego to explain, but feeling like too much of a fool already.

She sent the text then shoved the phone back in her pocket.

"Have you seen Jonas Jedna?" she asked.

"Jonas, no? Why would I? You know he never talks to anyone 'less he has to." He frowned at the expression on her face. "Why are you worried about him?"

Tamsyn hesitated to tell him, but she'd already told him more than she should have so what did it matter if she told the rest, as well.

"There's this really scary Albanian gangster called Besnik Domi. He's seriously bad news and he's been seen in this part of Cornwall, outside the Mack Shack even! We thought he'd left Cornwall, but now we're not so sure. There's a possibility that he was in Marazion."

"There's a criminal hotspot," Uncle George joked. "'Specially the prices they charge in them tourist shops."

He wasn't taking her seriously, but that didn't matter: all that mattered was he was safe.

"Tell me about it," she laughed, thinking of the quiet little town by St Michael's Mount, all cobbled streets and quaint shops that sold fudge and pasties. "Anyway, that doesn't matter. At first, we thought that the criminals had been using Newlyn – we just don't know if anyone has been working with them from here."

Uncle George looked bemused.

"And you think Jonas Jedna is involved?"

"I know, it's crazy, right? I can't believe it's anyone we know. I mean, who'd do that? But I was wondering if there were any new faces around."

Uncle George chuckled.

"New faces! Listen to you sounding all official like a policeman, Tammy."

"Well, I am a police officer now," she reminded him with a rueful smile that faded quickly. "You need to be careful, Uncle George," Tamsyn said seriously. "Anyway, CID have moved their focus to some of the old smuggler beaches like Rinsey and Prussia Cove, and further afield like Helford Passage, and up the north coast toward Newquay. We think they might be using smaller boats that they can land on the coast without needing a dredged harbour, although that's just a theory." She reddened because it was *her* theory. "But honestly, I think it's only a matter of time before they try to use Newlyn because it's easier, and especially coming into the summer when we've got a lot more tourists so more people using the harbour – it would be hard to keep track of everyone. Um, you probably shouldn't tell anyone else what I've said." She paused. "You haven't seen any strangers about, have you?"

George shook his head.

"No, only your Inspector. He's not from around here, is he?"

Tamsyn narrowed her eyes.

"Please don't say anything racist or I'll have to arrest you."

Mo barked loudly, her shrill yapping making Tamsyn jump.

"Oh my God, Mo!" Tamsyn gasped, clasping her hand over her heart.

"Probably seen a rat," said Ozzie.

Mo wouldn't stop barking, her piercing cries echoing over the water.

"Better quiet her down, Tammy!" grumbled Uncle George. "She'll disturb half the town and ole Jonas will be over here making a fuss."

"Morwenna! No!" Tamsyn said crossly, but the little dog wouldn't stop barking, the intensity only increasing. "Noisy little mutt," Tamsyn sighed, standing up to grab her. "Mo, come! Now!"

There was a yelp followed by a whimper.

Tamsyn rushed forwards, half tripping over the crate she'd been sitting on as Mo shot out from behind the boom, whimpering, tail firmly between her legs.

Tamsyn swept the terrified dog into her arms, feeling the wiry fur all over for an injury.

"Were you bitten?"

A shadow separated itself from the darkness and Tamsyn stumbled backwards, only just catching her balance as Mo wriggled in her arms and resumed the loud, incessant barking, her small body rigid.

The shadow came closer and Tamsyn felt all the blood rush from her body as she came face to face with lorry driver who'd disappeared: the man now known to be Besnik Domi.

CHAPTER 27

Domi's pale eyes glittered in the moonlight, but the face that had been clean-shaven in the CCTV images was now covered with thick stubble, and he wore a beanie pulled low over his ears.

Tamsyn said the first words that came into her head.

"Besnik Domi, I'm arresting you for the illegal importation of a banned substance and ... and..." her mind went blank.

There was no evidence that he'd killed Saemira Ruçi, even if it's what they believed.

He cocked his head on one side, a small smile doing nothing to soften the cruel planes of his face.

"I am?"

"Yes! I'm a police officer."

He shrugged.

"And that is a police dog?"

He glanced at Mo whose hackles were up and all her fur standing on end, making her look like an angry puffball.

"No, but...

"And you are too pretty to be a police officer."

"I ... I ... well, I am."

Even as she said it, she knew that she sounded ridiculous. She *was* ridiculous.

"Have you ever arrested anyone before?"

"That's not the point!" she stuttered.

"I don't think I want to be arrested today," he said, taking a menacing step towards her. "So I will say no."

"We have to get going!"

The hurried words came from Uncle George and Tamsyn nodded, automatically backing up so she was next to him.

Mo's lips peeled back revealing sharp canines, and her eyes narrowed as she focussed on the mobster, a fierce growl rolling up from her throat.

Tamsyn put her down carefully, then pulled out her phone, backing away from Domi who was still advancing, but Uncle George bumped her arm, and the mobile slipped from her fingers, clattering onto the deck.

She started to say something but her grandfather was on his feet, scowling at Uncle George.

"You fool!" he snorted. "You bleddy stupid fool!"

"Shut up, Ozzie," said George, his face tense.

Tamsyn couldn't make sense of what she was seeing, what she was hearing. She stared at George, confusion slowing her movements.

And finally Tamsyn saw what her grandfather had already seen: a gun tucked into the top of George's overalls, a gun that he was now pointing at Tamsyn. This wasn't right – it simply wasn't where her brain had organised him to be.

Everything happened in less than a second as her grandfather threw himself forward, knocking George over, and Tamsyn screamed as the sound of a pistol shot echoed across the harbour.

Ozzie fell as if in slow motion, his eyes rolling upwards

when his knees hit the deck. Then he toppled sideways, unmoving, as blood soaked his white hair, spreading across the deck and draining lazily from the gunnels.

"Ozzie! Why did you have to do that?" George cried out as he gazed down at the man he'd called a friend for forty years.

Tamsyn was on her hands and knees.

"Grandad!" she whispered, shock stealing her breath. "Oh my God! Grandad!"

She crawled towards him, slipping in his blood, but George gripped her shoulder, yanking her backwards, holding the gun in his other hand.

"You shouldn't have come here, Tammy," he hissed, his voice grim. "You shoulda minded your own business."

"You shot him!" Tamsyn's voice was shrill with horror. "You killed him! He was your friend and you killed him!"

She gasped, gazing up at him, this man, this man she'd known her whole life.

"Why?"

He didn't reply, but she already knew the answer. It had been staring her in the face and she'd been too blinded by love, too certain of loyalty to see it. It wasn't Jonas Jedna, it never had been.

Who else knew how and when to foul Ozzie's sparkplugs then replace them with good ones? Who else knew the trick of making the *Daniel Day's* cranky old engine spring to life? Who else knew exactly how to place the blame on Ozzie? Who else in the whole harbour would they have trusted beyond reason? Who else would she never suspect? Never in a million years.

She was too shocked to fight him as he dragged her into the wheelhouse, pushing her to one side where she collapsed in a heap.

Her hands were red with blood and they shook as she held them out like Lady Macbeth.

It's my fault it's my fault it's my fault. The words thundered through her head, drowning out her harsh gasping cries.

She curled into a tight ball on the hard floor of the wheelhouse and waited to die.

"We need to leave," she heard George say urgently. "Someone could have heard that shot."

The Albanian's voice sounded almost bored.

"You English are soft – no one here knows what a gunshot sounds like. But yes, my friend, we should go. Drop the old man over the side. Weight him down properly this time, no more mistakes. Then the girl."

A tiny part of her still hoped, still believed that George would refuse to kill her.

But he didn't.

Weight him down. That's what Domi had said. He'd been referring to Saemira, Tamsyn felt sure of it.

Oh God.

"I know what you're thinking," George said to her, his voice almost beseeching until it gradually hardened. "Why did I do it? Well, why wouldn't I? That's what you've got to ask yourself. Fish all played out, government left us to drown after Brexit – all their promises were lies."

Domi smiled, clearly entertained by a rant he'd heard before.

"And I thought you made your money from the Hellbanianz for the last ten years, my friend, but it was stinking fish all the time."

Ten years. Ten years?

"You've been working for them for ten years?" Tamsyn

asked, looking up slowly, a terrible thought planting roots in her soul. "It's ten years since Dad died."

George wouldn't or couldn't meet her eyes, busying himself with starting the engine and making ready.

"You bastard," she whispered. "You complete and utter shit of a human being. You murdered your best friend." Then she filled her lungs and screamed at him. "You murdered my father!"

He whipped around, trapped, his eyes feral.

"No! No, I never. It was an accident. If he'd just kept his mouth shut, I would have seen him right. I'm not the first and I won't be the last. We could have done something, the two of us! He thought buying a ring-netter was enough. He thought small, he couldn't help it. That's why your mum left. Did you know that? Danny always said he didn't need much. He was a fool! But there was no better seaman 'cept Ozzie himself. We could have made real money for a change! But he was just like Ozzie. Stubborn! Too prideful, too..."

"Too honest!" Tamsyn spat the words out.

George didn't reply for several seconds, only the low throb of the engine filling the silence.

"I'm sorry, Tammy. I didn't mean for it to happen. It was an accident. But once you're in, you're in. There was no going back. I did what I did to protect you, to protect all your family."

"Fuck you, *Uncle* George! You're a liar, and a coward and a murderer, and I'll see you rot in prison!"

Tamsyn burned with rage, almost destroyed with hatred and the need for revenge. She wanted to kick and bite and scream and feel her nails tearing into his flesh.

George turned away from her, the conversation over, but Domi clapped, an ironic round of applause.

"She has fire," he said with a smile that made Tamsyn's skin crawl. "Perhaps I'll keep her."

"I'd rather die!" she snarled.

He lifted one shoulder. "That is the other choice."

"Stop arsing about and cast off," George interrupted. "Time we's going."

Domi gave Tamsyn another assessing look, then jumped off the boat and started casting off the lines that attached the *Mari-morgans* to the pontoon.

"George!" Tamsyn begged. "Uncle George ... leave him here. I'll speak up for you if you just stop now! I'll say that you didn't mean to hurt Grandad, that Dad ... that Dad was an accident. I'll say that you've helped my family since he died. The police are on their way now – leave Domi here! They'll arrest him and we'll be safe. Please, George."

He couldn't quite meet her eyes, but his expression was regretful.

"I can't, Tammy. They'd kill me."

"So you'll let him kill me instead?"

He turned away from her again and it felt as if her last shred of hope had been surgically removed from her heart.

"They'll find Grandad's car," she said. "They'll know what happened."

George shook his head.

"No, Tammy. They'll find ten wraps of cocaine under Ozzie's spare tyre with yours and your Grandad's fingerprints all over the car. And underneath the jack in the boot of your Fiat, the police will find a hundred tabs of Ecstasy. They'll assume you were involved, you and Ozzie both. They'll think it was all you. And when you disappear..."

She slumped to the floor, her knees beginning to throb from when she'd fallen to the deck.

The engine roared and Tamsyn felt the hull shudder as the boat chugged out of the harbour.

When Domi crowded into the wheelhouse, she tried to scramble away from him but there was nowhere to go. George's gaze was fixed on the gaping mouth of the harbour's entrance and he wouldn't even look at her, but the Albanian squatted down close beside her, amusement dancing in his cold gaze.

"You see? I said you would not arrest me."

"The police know all about you," Tamsyn said, her voice wobbling, so afraid she thought that she might wet herself.

"It doesn't matter," he said indifferently. "They won't find me. By the way, I must thank you for that list of all the other places that they're looking for me. Very helpful."

Tamsyn fastened her gaze in the far corner, refusing to look at him. She wouldn't give him the pleasure of knowing how scared she was, how utterly without hope.

But he gripped her chin, his fingers digging into her skin and forced her to look into his eyes.

Tamsyn couldn't help the tremors that racked her body. Was this how he'd killed Saemira? She'd had finger marks on her jaw, too.

"Maybe I'll take you with me – you'd be surprised how much I can get for an Englishwoman. And I've had a lot of expenses on this trip. Although the truck I lost is worth more than you."

He shoved her dismissively and she fell to the deck. Tamsyn lay there, winded then struggled to lift her head, as if the heaviness in her soul weighed her down.

"I'm not English, I'm Cornish," she whispered as she stared up at him. "And you can go to hell,"

"Perhaps. But you first."

CHAPTER 28

Rego was frustrated.

And feeling nauseous.

Why the hell had he thought that being a DI in a county where there was 400 miles of coastline was a good idea? When just stepping onto this boat had made his stomach lurch and salvia pool in his mouth. Well, it was anyone's guess because he had no clue.

Everyone else seemed to be enjoying themselves, he thought sourly as he leaned over the side of the small boat, hoping he looked nonchalant, not like he was about to revisit his lunch.

Nope, too late. His stomach lurched upwards and Rego was violently sick. He felt as if his entire insides were trying to surge up his throat. He hung over the side, wheezing, his eyes watering.

"It gets better, boss," said Jack Forshaw, looking annoyingly healthy, a recruiting poster for the RNLI.

"What does?" he coughed, wiping his mouth with his hand.

"The seasickness," Forshaw replied cheerfully. "Even Nelson got seasick for the first few days of a voyage. O' course, he wasn't Cornish either."

Rego didn't even bother to try and answer.

They'd already searched four small pockets of remote beaches framed by towering granite cliffs that apparently smugglers had used before Napoleon had even thought of taking on the British at Trafalgar, but when Rego had asked where they were and had received the reply 'Piskies Cove', he was fairly sure that the crew were taking the piskie out of him.

His phone vibrated in his pocket and he struggled to pull it out from under his bulky lifejacket.

Fighting with his borrowed overalls and heavy slicker, he finally managed to extract his phone.

Two texts from Tamsyn had come in together, and he wondered if it was her signal that was spotty or his own.

Trying to read the small print made the seasickness worse. He closed his eyes and clamped his jaw shut.

"If you focus on the horizon, sir," said Forshaw, gesturing into the darkness, "it'll help."

Rego grit his teeth, snarling out a response that had the younger man backing away, as far as was possible in a boat that was less than 6m wide.

"Firstly, DC Forshaw," Rego said, churning out words like a concrete mixer, "I'm trying to read a text; and secondly, it's night time – there is no horizon."

"Sorry, boss," the young DC muttered, shuffling even further away.

Rego felt too ill to regret his sarcasm.

As he squinted at his phone, his stomach gurgled and he had to swallow down a mouthful of bile. He didn't miss the amused glances exchanged by the crew.

The boat slowed as they rounded a small headland, and Rego risked glancing at his phone again.

"Bloody hell," he swore, making Forshaw look across and ask a question, probably against his better judgement.

"Problem, boss?"

Rego grimaced.

"PC Poldhu has taken it into her head to go to Newlyn Harbour. She wants to check on her Uncle George. What the hell was she thinking? Until Domi is caught..."

Rego was too furious to finish the sentence.

There was CCTV at the harbour, a surveillance team were on their way, and the night watchman, plus who knew how many fishermen getting ready to go out. She'd be safe enough.

But ... they hadn't caught Domi or Subject F who still remained unidentified. They didn't even know if either man was still in the country. They weren't certain that anything would happen tonight, despite the NCA's latest intelligence, and being out here at night scouring the numerous small coves that made up Britain's southwest, it was all beginning to feel like searching for a needle in a haystack.

With rubbery fingers, Rego typed out a short text telling Tamsyn, no, *ordering* her to go home, and to message him when she got there.

Then he changed his mind and decided to call her and give her the bollocking she deserved. He put his phone on speaker so he could hear over the helmet he'd been forced to wear. The phone rang three times then stopped.

He called her again, but this time it went straight to voicemail.

A sliver of unease worked its way down his spine.

Was she deliberately avoiding him? Or was there another reason that her phone had been turned off.

He contacted the Control room, yelling too loudly into his phone as he asked them to radio PC Poldhu, or failing that, to speak to the surveillance team at Newlyn, or the night watchman. And if that failed, they'd have to send up a bloody great flare.

While he was waiting for their response, he was surprised to receive a call from DC Eagling. He loosened his helmet, wedging it uncomfortably between his knees

"Mimi, I'm with the Coastguard; now's not a good time."

"Boss, I think this might be important – I'm fairly sure it is."

"Okay, shoot."

"So, I finished with the vic's burner phone because that was the priority, and I finally got around to working through the list of calls from her personal phone – and there's one call that stood out – received from George Mason, a fisherman down at Newlyn."

"Mason?"

Rego was surprised and felt like he'd missed a step somewhere. Tamsyn had introduced the man as her 'Uncle George'.

"I met him," Rego said tersely. "He's related to Ozzie Poldhu, I think. Or a good friend." He paused. "Just the one call?"

"Yes, during the day – 15.27 on the 17th March."

"A week before Ruçi disappeared. Did she ever call his number?"

"No, but they talked for nearly three minutes."

"Not a wrong number then."

"I doubt it, boss."

"Just like her burner phone."

"Exactly the same."

"Thanks, Mimi." He paused. "So, it was Mason all along."

"I think so, boss."

But what about the Poldhu family?

He ended the call just as Control got back to him: they couldn't raise either Tamsyn or the night watchman and the surveillance team weren't yet in place but were on their way.

Now Rego was seriously worried. Was Tamsyn involved? Had she and her grandfather misled him from the start? Then he thought of all the ways she'd helped the investigation ... or had she? Was it luck or prior knowledge that led her to the Tupperware box at the church? Luck or knowledge about how weather conditions affected the drug supply business? No, that last one didn't fit – it had pointed the finger right at her own grandfather.

Rego hated doubting her because it meant he was doubting his own instincts – instincts that had kept him alive in the job for fourteen years.

He scrolled through his contacts and called Tamsyn's home.

The phone was answered by an older woman. "Hello?"

"Good evening, this is DI Robert Rego. Am I speaking to Mrs Poldhu?"

Rego was using what his wife called 'your nice police voice'. It came instinctively these days and was designed to be formal but non-threatening, used mainly with victims or vulnerable witnesses.

"Oh! Hello, Inspector. Are you with Tamsyn and Ozzie?"

He paused.

"No, in fact I was hoping you could tell me where she is ... where they are."

He tried to keep the concern out of his voice because he could already hear it in hers.

"They went to find George at the harbour. George

Mason, that is. He was our son's best friend. Tammy calls him 'Uncle George'. Sorry, I'm running on. I'm just so ... well, Tammy was worried he might be in trouble. He wasn't answering his phone, see."

"How long ago was that, Mrs Poldhu?"

"About twenty minutes. I thought you were them calling. I'm worried, Mr Rego."

Rego was worried, too. But it wouldn't help to admit that.

"I'm going to send a patrol car over there just to check. I'll call you back when I've heard from them. Or if they contact you first, please call me on this number." He started to reel off the digits when she interrupted him.

"Oh, just a moment, I need to find a pencil."

He heard her put the phone down, and while he waited for her to find a pen and paper, he clamped his hand over the microphone and whisper-yelled at Forshaw.

"Jack! Code Zero to the harbour – no sirens. PC Poldhu isn't responding to her phone and she doesn't have her AirWave with her; also, the night watchman isn't answering his phone. I don't like it. Units to be alert for Domi. And get Armed Response on standby."

"They've gotta come from Bodmin, boss," said Forshaw. "Seventy minutes, tops."

"Are you serious?" Rego was flabbergasted. "Seventy minutes for *rapid* armed response?"

Forshaw nodded.

"Jesus!"

"But we could ask the MoD plods out at Culdrose to help," Forshaw suggested.

MoD Plod was the slang name for Ministry of Defence Police who patrolled Royal Naval Air Station Culdrose at Helston, twelve miles east of Penzance.

"Whatever you need to do to get them there, do it!"

Forshaw pulled out his phone and sent the urgent requests via Control.

Tamsyn's grandmother came back on the line, saying that she had her pencil and paper ready. Keeping his voice calm and controlled, Rego reeled off his direct number. She scribbled it down then read it back to him. He was about to end the call, when her she spoke again, her voice trembling.

"Please, Mr Rego. They're all I have."

He sucked in a deep breath.

"I'll do everything I can, Mrs Poldhu. Try not to worry."

He ended the call then checked that help was on its way to the harbour from the landward side.

"Boss," said Forshaw, his voice tight. "I spoke to Culdrose's Silver Commander on the MoD police team, an Inspector Mike Pearson – he's sending two ARV's and his Bronze Commander Sergeant Ed Bladen. ETA, fourteen minutes." He glanced at his watch. "Thirteen."

Rego nodded his approval then raised his voice over the sound of the ILB's engine and spoke to the Officer in Charge.

"Ryder, how fast can this thing go?"

"Top speed is 35 knots," Ryder replied, frowning over his shoulder as Rego re-fastened his helmet. "Why?"

"I think that one of my officers, Tamsyn Poldhu, and her grandfather are in serious trouble. How quickly can you get us to Newlyn Harbour?"

Ryder's expression hardened.

"Six minutes," he said. "Hold on."

The ILB leapt forward and Rego was almost jerked off his feet. He held on with both hands, spray lashing his face as he was tilted back. It seemed impossible that anyone could steer the bucking craft as it raced across the black water towards the lights of Newlyn. The sea that had seemed so calm and flat just minutes before now tossed them around like a cork as the 200hp engine propelled them forwards, bouncing and skittering across Mount's Bay.

He had no idea how fast 35 knots was, but it felt like they were flying through a hurricane.

And still, it wasn't fast enough.

CHAPTER 29

They were only half a mile out of the harbour when Tamsyn felt the boat begin to slow.

Domi looked surprised too, frowning at George.

"Why are we stopping?"

"Just picking up some travelling money," he said.

He drew up next to one of his own orange buoys with a green flag on the top, hooked it out of the water and pulled on the rope, hand over hand, lifting a lobster pot from the sea. But instead of crustaceans, Tamsyn saw a heavy waxed bag wrapped in layers of cellophane, and from the shape of it, she was guessing it contained bank notes.

He kept hauling on the rope and a second lobster pot thumped onto the deck. He was going for a third pot when Domi pulled out a small but lethal-looking knife, cutting the rope with a fast, upward slice.

"We don't have time!" he snarled.

Mason clenched his fists, his face dark with anger.

"That was my savings!" he bellowed. "I needed that!"

"Too bad," said Domi indifferently. "Now get back in there and drive this thing."

Cursing under his breath, Mason did as he was told.

"So that's how you did it," Tamsyn breathed. "We were looking for strangers bringing drugs into the harbour, but it was you all along. Business as usual. Maybe even Grandad's pots, as well." She laughed cynically. "We always wondered why you carried on crabbing when you were doing so well with ring-netting. But this way you could visit the pots any time and no one would think twice about it." Realisation caught up with her. "And you used the *Daniel Day* to do it, didn't you? That's what all those problems with Grandad's sparkplugs were about! It was you making sure that you had use of his punt whenever you wanted, wasn't it?"

Mason didn't even bother to deny it and smiled at her proudly. "Tha's right, so they would never come looking for me if they found anything they shouldn't. But the police round here are too dozy to even suspect a thing," and he shot her a scathing look.

Tamsyn swallowed painfully.

"Because you were family. Grandad trusted you. We all trusted you. Grandad would never..."

Her words faded away as her throat closed up.

She couldn't see where her grandfather was lying, but she knew he was out on the deck. *He'll be cold without his oilskins*, she thought. *Colder than death.*

"Anyway, you're wrong," she said dully, pushing tangled hair out of her face. "We know all about yachts coming up the Bay of Biscay with drugs from Turkey and North Africa. We were close. We would have got you sooner or later."

George shrugged. "Madder do it, I'm done here. I'm not going back."

Domi shot him a sharp look.

"What?"

"I'll take you to the rendezvous, but I can't go back now."

"That's not what we agreed."

"Yeah, well, plans change," said Mason as he glanced at Tamsyn. "You know that."

"Going to live in Albania, are you, *Uncle George*?" Tamsyn asked, derision in every syllable.

"I was thinking Spain," Mason replied. "Costa del Sol, that'll do me. I've got enough money to disappear." He glanced at Domi. "I can set up for you there. Maybe Portugal – Costa Verde is nice. Start again. We can make it work."

"I will consider your offer," Domi said coolly.

Tamsyn ignored the Albanian and directed her words to the man who'd betrayed her whole family.

"I'll find you," she said quietly. "I'll find you and I'll arrest you and I'll see you in prison for the rest of your life. And I'll never forgive you."

Domi chuckled quietly.

"He can't afford to let you live, little girl. He killed your father, he killed your grandfather, and now he'll kill you." He grinned at her. "He must really hate your family."

Her gut churned. *Stay alive! Say something and stay alive!*

"I didn't tell you all the places they're looking for you," Tamsyn said hurriedly, a cold sweat breaking out across her body as she lied through her teeth.

Domi's gaze narrowed. "Tell me now."

"Why should I? You're just going to kill me anyway."

He stared at her, his icy blue eyes entirely without emotion.

"But I can make it quick, or I can make it painful." His upper lip lifted. "You choose."

Tamsyn's intention had to been to keep him talking but she felt completely out of her depth.

"Why did you kill Jowita or Saemira or whatever you call her?"

"Because she stole from me," Domi said, his mouth tilting into a cruel leer. "She thought that because my brother was fucking her cousin that this would protect her. No one steals from the Hellbanianz and lives." He folded his arms across his chest. "That would be bad for business."

Tamsyn frowned.

"How did she steal from you? We found her stash in the churchyard and there was only a little bit of money in it, less than £2,000. There was no online account on her burner phone, and her personal phone wasn't used for online banking either. We know you took her car so if the money wasn't there, where is it? We don't have it – the police never found any other money." She paused, seeing that Domi was listening. "There were no drugs either." She shrugged. "Maybe she had another hiding place."

Domi exploded, grabbing her by the hair and dragging her across the deck until they were face to face.

"You're lying! The bitch stole my money and now the police have it!"

"We don't! We didn't find any money."

"Where's my money?" he screamed, spittle hitting her face.

"I don't know anything about your money! I promise."

"You're lying! I know you're lying. You police found it!"

"We didn't! All we found were Saemira's phone, gun and car keys. That's all! Almost no money! No drugs!"

"Then you took it! You and your grandfather. Tell me now, or I will cut off your fingers one by one until you tell me!"

"I can't tell you what I don't know!" she screamed.

Domi let her fall to the deck and was silent, his fury shutting off as if someone had flipped a switch.

She scuttled away from him, crouching by the side of the

wheelhouse, watching him warily. He was frowning and staring out to sea. George was keeping both of them in sight, squinting out of the corner of his eyes, but he did nothing to help her.

Tamsyn massaged her scalp where he'd torn out a clump of hair by the roots. If she could only keep him talking...

She edged away from George so he couldn't hear her over the sound of the engine.

"Why did you kill Saemira?"

Domi shrugged.

"She wouldn't tell me where the money was."

"I bet she was scared," Tamsyn said quietly.

"Of course!" Domi sneered, his eyes lighting up at the memory. "They're always scared."

"But she didn't tell you want you wanted to know."

Domi scowled. "No."

"Maybe she didn't know."

His eyes clouded and he frowned, deep in thought.

"Did you kill her at the harbour?"

"No."

"Then where? It must have been somewhere private."

He smiled at her, as if amused by her questions.

"Does it matter?"

"Yes, it does."

He shrugged but didn't answer.

"Why did you cut her tongue out?"

"She was a snitch. What is it the Americans say? Snitches get stitches and end up in ditches. Do you English say that, too?"

Tamsyn ignored his question.

"Are you sure that she was a snitch? Who did you think she was talking to?"

Domi scowled.

"To the filthy pigs," and he spat on the deck.

Tamsyn was surprised.

"No, she wasn't. We had no idea. We didn't know anything about Saemira until we found her body. Nobody even knew she was in the UK."

"You're lying!" he snarled.

"I'm not. Why would I? I've got nothing to gain and everything to lose. When you killed her, you made a giant mistake. We had no idea who was handling the distribution," and she shot George a vicious look which bounced off his broad back. "We didn't know anything about Saemira. Who told you she was talking to us?"

Domi's eyes narrowed and his gaze swung slowly toward George. Tamsyn saw the exact moment that realisation dawned in the Albanian's mind.

"You! You told me that Saemira had been skimming money and talking to the pigs," Domi shouted. "You told me this!"

Tamsyn saw George's hands clench on the wheel.

"She was! I confronted her about it and she started making up all sorts of lies."

"The police didn't know anything about her!" Tamsyn yelled, seeing her chance to sow the seeds of mistrust between George and Demi. "If money was missing, it wasn't Saemira who had it."

Mason swung around and tried to hit her, but she managed to duck, and he was forced to clamp his hand back on the wheel as the choppy waters made the boat lurch.

"Why did you let this man kill her? Or did she find out something that you couldn't afford to have known? Oh my God! It was you, wasn't it, Uncle George? She found out you were the one skimming. You made sure she couldn't talk and didn't even have to do it yourself!"

"Shut up!" he yelled. "Just shut up, Tammy! Jowita, I mean Saemira, she said she'd had enough of skivvying in a hotel for minimum wage. She wanted to start enjoying the money."

"Like you, you mean?" Tamsyn shot back. "You enjoyed the money, didn't you, George? You bought *Mari-morgans* ten years ago and we all wondered how you did it, but you said you'd cashed in Aunty Marie's life insurance policy after the divorce, but that was a lie too, wasn't it?" She turned to Domi. "Saemira couldn't tell you where the money is because she didn't know! She had no idea what you were talking about. We kept asking ourselves *why* Jowita had been killed. Who had she been talking to? We didn't know – the police didn't know. You were played! You know how much a new ring-netter like this costs? One million pounds. One million! Is that what you paid him nine years ago? Is that what my dad's life was worth?"

Domi's head swivelled between her and George.

"She's lying!" George bellowed. "She'll say anything to save herself! I bought this second-hand..."

"It's still worth at least half a million," Tamsyn yelled. "I asked Grandad. He was pleased for you, George. Pleased! He said he was glad you were doing so well. He loved you like a son and ... and ... you killed him! You shot him!"

All the rage that had been burning inside her ignited, and she threw herself at George, knocking him forward over the wheel, his hands slipping, making the boat list to one side.

Domi leaned across and slapped her hard, making her gasp.

And then all hell broke loose.

Mo came charging out from where she'd been hiding, sinking her sharp teeth into Domi's leg.

He screamed and tried to shake her off, but she hung on as

he swung her from side to side. Finally, he kicked toward the door of the wheelhouse and her skull hit the frame with a loud crack. Dazed, the little dog slid to the deck, then tried to stand, shaking her head, her movements unsteady.

Domi swore in his own language as he clapped his hand to his calf, and when he pulled it away, his palm was covered in blood. He swore again, then pulled out a gun and pointed it at Mo.

With a scream of fear and fury, Tamsyn charged at Domi, knocking his arm so his shot went wide. She scooped Mo from the deck, jumping overboard with the little dog in her arms, plunging into the silky black sea.

The shock of cold water made her lungs contract and she lost hold of Mo. Her arms beat a frantic tattoo as she tried to find her.

Bullets peppered the water, and Tamsyn dived beneath the surface, expecting a bullet to slam into her at any moment. She used long, even strokes to pull her deeper into the darkness, forcing herself to stay under as long as she could, all those of years of surfing making her part of the ocean, at ease in her element.

She swam underwater, further and further away from the boat.

When she had to surface for air, Domi was watching for her and she heard his shout of anger, and then more shots were raining down into the sea.

She duck-dived again, swimming deeper and deeper into the inky darkness.

Even under the water, she could hear the ring-netter's engines, but at last it sounded as if the boat was moving away from her.

When her lungs were burning and screaming for oxygen, when she couldn't hold her breath any longer, she surfaced, gasping for air and coughing out seawater from her raw throat. The *Mari-morgans* was fading into the night as George and Domi headed out to sea.

They'd won and she'd lost, but at least she was still alive.

"Mo!" she screamed, hoping to hear the dog out there, somewhere nearby. "Morwenna!"

She listened intently, ignoring her chattering teeth, hearing the sound of the waves, but no bark, no small dog.

"Morwenna!"

But the silence was profound and little Mo didn't answer her desperate cries. All she could hear was the restless ocean slapping against her icy skin.

Chilled to her soul, with her body becoming numb, Tamsyn turned, orienting herself in the intense darkness, only just able to glimpse the lights of Newlyn Harbour more than a mile away.

Tamsyn felt small and exposed with pitch black seas churning around her. She made herself push away the fear, sealing it deep inside and forced herself to think, to calculate, to survive.

Cold air extracts heat from the surface of the human body twenty-five times faster than that carried away by air of the same temperature. The core body temperature will continue to fall until the person is removed from the cold water. At 10°C, the survival time is 1-2 hours.

It was too cold, too far, too hard, and Tamsyn had already lost too much.

I'm sorry, Grandad. I'm sorry I couldn't save you.

But then she remembered how he'd thrown himself in front of the bullet that was meant for her; she remembered how he'd glared at George, the anger and fury and betrayal.

One mile from the harbour, the swim would be fairly easy. Two miles out, and the current became a problem, the distance to shore meant that it was at the limit of what was possible, what was survivable.

Tamsyn knew that her chances were slim to none. She knew she would probably die.

She began to swim.

CHAPTER 30

Rego's hands had seized up as he desperately hung on to the bucking boat. He could see the lights of Newlyn harbour, one green and two red, as they approached the entrance. He didn't know what they meant: the maritime code was a world apart. His stomach lurched again in protest.

Then he spotted the flashing blue lights from a couple of patrol cars and felt relieved.

But Ryder shouted something over the engine's roar, and the boat swung around. Rego felt as if his arms were being wrenched out of their sockets as he lost his footing, his hip colliding painfully with something hard.

"What are you doing?" he yelled, as he scrambled to his feet.

Ryder shouted something and Rego cursed the helmet's radio as it crackled but he couldn't make out a single word.

He gesticulated wildly at the harbour but Ryder kept shaking his head and pointing out to sea, obviously shouting something.

Finally, two words broke through the roar of the engine,

the static filling his helmet, and the sound of the waves slamming against the side of the boat.

"Tamsyn Poldhu!" Ryder yelled. "Tamsyn Poldhu!"

The ILB sped back out to sea, and they were soon engulfed in the darkness. Rego had no idea how Ryder managed to navigate because it just looked like an endless ocean of black.

The journey seemed to go on forever, and Rego's body was battered and cold as he lost sense of time. But then the engine's roar began to ease, and Rego saw that they were circling a large fishing boat. He immediately recognised it at as the *Mari-morgans*, but he couldn't see anyone, and a cold sensation washed through him.

If Domi was on board, he'd have his knife with him and probably a firearm – and they'd just left their armed response team in the harbour.

Rego prised his hands from the grab handles that he'd been welded to, rubbing his frozen fingers to try and get some warmth into them.

Ryder tried to raise the boat by radio, but when there was no reply, he unhooked a loudhailer to call the vessel. Rego winced at the volume of the sound that came out.

"*Mari-morgans*, this is Falmouth Coastguard. Turn off your engine and prepare to be boarded!"

There was no response, and the ring-netter continued to chug onwards, neither speeding nor trying to evade them.

Ryder repeated his command with the same result.

"A container ship radioed in that they'd seen the *Mari-morgans* but they couldn't raise her. The captain said they nearly ran her over when she didn't get out of their way. He thought she might be on automatic pilot."

The men peered into the darkness, blinking as the boat was flooded with their high-powered searchlights.

"I can't see anyone in the wheelhouse," said Ryder. "I don't like the look of this. Matt, I'm going to send you over and then we're going to put a line across."

The young officer nodded, preparing to board the larger boat.

Rego could have argued that this was now a police matter, but he knew that he didn't have the skill to cross safely between two moving vessels, even if his stomach had cooperated. And he has absolutely no idea how to drive a boat. He glanced at Jack Forshaw but decided to leave the boarding to the experts.

As Ryder inched the ILB closer, the fishing boat bumped against their hull. It took two more tries to get close enough to board her safely.

Rego watched as the crewman scrambled aboard the other boat, disappeared from view for a second, then they saw him heading to the wheelhouse.

He cut the engine, then tossed a rope across.

The two boats bobbed together in silence, then the young crewman yelled over to them.

"I've got an injured man here with a bad head wound. He's lost a lot of blood. Shit! It's Ozzie Poldhu! I can't find a pulse."

Ryder swore softly, then raised his voice.

"Anyone else? A woman?"

"Just Ozzie, sir."

Ryder exchanged a worried look with Rego.

But Rego wanted to see the boat for himself. It took him three tries to climb across, and only then when the young officer, Matt, grabbed him by his life jacket and hauled him aboard ignominiously.

Rego recognised Ozzie Poldhu immediately and knelt next to the old man, desperately trying to find a pulse. His skin was cold and very pale under the tan. Rego saw the amount of blood and swore – Ozzie had been shot in the head.

But then, he felt the faintest flutter under his fingertips. He wanted so badly for Ozzie to be alive that he thought he'd imagined it, but then he felt it again.

The old man was clinging to life, however weakly.

"I've got a pulse here!" Rego yelled. "He's alive!"

Ryder immediately turned to his radio and called it in.

Rego nodded and gave a quick thumbs up to acknowledge that he'd heard, cursing his malfunctioning radio.

He tore off his helmet and clamped his phone to his ear as he called Control for an update.

Ozzie's car had been found at the harbour. It was empty, badly parked, but locked. Rego didn't know what that meant.

The night watchman had been found unconscious, but woke up before the ambulance arrived. All Jedna could say was that he'd been hit from behind. It was a miracle that he'd been allowed to live.

When the MoD Police had arrived, there was no sign of Domi, not that Rego had expected to be that lucky – not after the clusterfuck that had been this evening's operation.

He watched as Matt rummaged through the *Marimorgan*'s first aid kit and found a blanket which he handed to Rego to wrap around Ozzie. Then the younger man taped a gauze pad to Ozzie's head wound, his expression grim.

Rego looked around, trying to see if there was any other blood, or any sign that Tamsyn had been there.

He could see splashes of blood on the other side of the wheelhouse. He had no idea if it came from Ozzie or not, even though there were two separate areas of blood spatter. It would take forensics to sort that out.

Tamsyn had been on this boat with her grandfather, he felt sure of it.

What had happened here? He didn't want to think that the blood could be hers.

Rego had many questions but he knew one thing: there was no way that Tamsyn would have left with the man who'd shot her grandfather unless she'd been forced to, unless she had to. So where the hell was she?

He crouched next to the older man and gently held his hand.

"I'll find her, Ozzie. I promise you I'll find her."

But even as he said the words, he knew he shouldn't make promises that he couldn't keep.

It was another twenty-five minutes before the air ambulance arrived, lowering a stretcher and then whisking Ozzie away.

Border Force and the Coastguard were searching the area around where the *Mari-morgans* had been found – searching for bodies.

Rego had spoken briefly to the armed response team from Culdrose who'd been stood down, and thanked them for their help.

He dreaded telling Mrs Poldhu that her elderly husband was clinging to life by a thread, and that her granddaughter was missing. He ordered a patrol car to her cottage that would take her to the hospital in Truro.

He stared out at the cold, black ocean.

"Where are you?"

CHAPTER 31

It was hard to keep going, hard to keep her limbs moving. She was so cold that her body no longer felt like it belonged to her, and Tamsyn began drifting, almost willing to let go, to float away. And then the pure rage she'd felt for *Uncle* George and Besnik Domi surged through her, giving her the strength to go on.

When she'd seen the helicopter pass overhead, she thought she'd been saved, but it flew away, leaving her alone in the darkness, and all her shouting and waving had done nothing except expend precious energy, making her death a little more certain.

This would be a taxing swim even wearing a wetsuit to protect her from the biting cold, but without it, she knew that she wouldn't be able to keep going much longer. The only thing in her favour was that the tide was coming in, so at least she didn't have to fight against the current.

She was tired of fighting. She was just so tired.

She felt hollowed out, empty, and the slow embers of rage began to cool as hypothermia crept over her, claiming her, leaving her confused.

Slowly, too slowly, she realised that she'd made a mistake by trying to swim all the way – she should have found a buoy and held onto it. There must be one close, there must, but she was too tired to think clearly. So tired...

Ryder steered the ILB back towards Newlyn. Following behind, Ryder's second in command, Matt, was sailing the *Mari-morgans*. Crime techs would have a field day with that boat.

Rego was staring out to sea when he saw something floating in the water by a marker buoy. No, not some*thing*, some*one*.

He grabbed Ryder's shoulder and pointed into the darkness.

"I thought I saw something. Turn the boat around."

"What did you see?"

Rego shook his head. "I'm not sure. I thought..." he strained his eyes into the darkness but couldn't see what had caught his attention.

Ryder turned on the boat's powerful searchlight, and they both saw her at the same time – Tamsyn's blonde hair like a beacon. Her eyes were closed but when the searchlight swept over her again, she seemed to squint up at them, and then she raised one hand in the air.

"My God!" Ryder swore, then swung the ILB towards the buoy, slowing as he got closer so the wash didn't go over her and make her lose her grip.

Rego and another crew member leaned down to pull her aboard, both men straining, the angle awkward and Tamsyn too weak to help them.

Finally, Tamsyn flopped onto the deck, shaking with cold,

and a crew member draped a foil emergency blanket around her shoulders.

"It's okay, Tamsyn. You're safe now," said Rego. "You're going to be okay. We'll get you to hospital. Do you have any injuries?"

She shook her head, but tremors ran through her body as Rego crouched down next to her. It was several moments before she could speak, and when she did, her voice was a painful croak.

"He killed Grandad! He killed him."

"No, I've seen your Grandad and he's alive. They've taken him to hospital."

"He's alive?"

"Yes."

"He's alive? You're sure?"

Rego didn't want to tell her that Ozzie had taken a bullet wound to the head. He didn't want to tell her that it would be a miracle if the old man survived.

"Yes," he said gently. "He's alive. Did you see who shot him?"

But Tamsyn couldn't speak. The tears came slowly at first, and then more desperately. Rego tucked the blanket around her, then held her in his arms.

Her skin was so pale it seemed luminous, and her lips had turned blue. Her speech was slurred and she was shivering uncontrollably. Rego knew these were all the signs of hypothermia.

He called for a second blanket and pulled that around her more firmly, trying to warm her with his own body heat.

Rego was used to the emotional intimacy that came with finding someone at their most vulnerable, but this was different. She was one of his officers.

He held her in his arms and prayed that she'd survive this.

All sorts of things could break a police officer, wear them down, make them give up, and Tamsyn hadn't even had the chance to grow a thicker skin. She was so young.

And although Rego had questions, so many questions, he needed to give her a moment. But Tamsyn spoke first.

"Did you get him?"

"Who?"

"Domi!"

"Besnik Domi?"

"Yes!"

"Besnik Domi shot your grandfather?"

"No! That was George. He was waiting for us at the harbour. He forced us to put out to sea with him. Well, they both did."

"Wait a minute – George Mason and your grandfather were on the boat with you?"

"Yes!"

"Tamsyn, we found your grandfather on George Mason's boat, but there was no one else there."

"But ... no one?"

"No."

"Where did they go?"

"We don't know."

She frowned in confusion, as if what Rego was saying wouldn't sink in. "And George wasn't there either?"

He hesitated for a fraction of a second then decided to tell her what they'd found.

"No. But there was a lot of blood, and I don't think it was all from your grandfather." Rego paused. "I'm sorry, but it doesn't look good."

Tamsyn sat up straight, her blue eyes bright and piercing.

"No! You've got it all wrong. George was the one distributing the drugs for Domi. He was there when Saemira was killed. They kept her body in the boot of her car, then George dumped it overboard. I thought Jonas Jedna was in on it, but now I don't know."

"Tamsyn, it's okay. We know about your uncle. And we've found the night watchman. He has a slight concussion, but otherwise he'll be fine." He paused. "I'm sorry about your uncle."

"He isn't my real uncle," she said, her voice brittle. "He was my dad's best friend. At least, that's what we'd always believed. But he killed my father, too. He admitted it. He'd tried to get Dad to deal drugs with him but Dad wouldn't do it. George said it was an accident ... but he admitted it all, he killed him."

"George Mason?"

"Yes!"

Rego didn't know what to think. For a time, he'd been so certain that Ozzie had been the one dealing drugs for the Albanians, and that Tamsyn had been dragged into it either to help Ozzie cover things up, or worse. But now, with what she said and what they'd found, it shone a completely different light on things.

"You still think I'm involved, don't you? Me and Grandad!"

Rego didn't answer immediately. He wanted to believe her. He wanted to believe that neither she nor her grandfather were involved.

"I can prove it," she said, as if she'd read his mind. "I can prove it all. He left the drugs and money in his lobster pots!" she rubbed her head with both hands as if forcing her brain to work. "He did it right in front of me, not that far from the harbour. Less than a mile! Anyone could have seen him but they'd just see him doing his job. Grandad always wondered why he bothered with lobsters when he made so much money ring-netting." She gave a bitter laugh. "Now we know why. Grandad used to tease him about his bad luck with lobsters and that he'd forgotten how to bait a trap."

Rego didn't say it, but finding George Mason's lobster pots only proved that she knew where they were.

"We should check his other lobster pots," she said, sounding more animated. "He didn't have had time to check them all because..."

"Because what?"

"George was taking Domi to a rendezvous, that's what he said. They were in a hurry."

"Did he say where?"

"No."

Rego repeated the information to Ryder so Border Force could send out a vessel from Falmouth and try to find Domi. He felt certain that this was the mystery yacht that they'd been searching for. The reason they hadn't found it in any coves or harbours was because that had never been the plan. Mason had been taking Domi to a rendezvous point somewhere in the Channel.

"Morwenna bit him," Tamsyn said. "He had blood on his hands."

"Who's Morwenna? Is she a dealer?"

Tamsyn gave a brief smile that soon faded.

"No, she's my dog. She knew that Domi was hiding on the *Mari-morgans* and she sniffed him out. I think he kicked or her or hurt her because she started barking like mad. Then ... then after George ... after he ... with the gun ... she was scared, so she hid. But when Domi slapped me, she jumped on him and bit him in the leg. She was so scared, but she tried to protect me anyway."

"I'm sorry, but we didn't find a dog."

Tears filled her eyes.

"No, I know. When Mo bit Domi, it gave me the chance to get away. So I picked her up and jumped overboard with her. But I lost her in the darkness. I couldn't find her! I tried and tried! And I kept calling her name, but I couldn't find her. She saved my life and I let her drown."

The tears came faster now, and Tamsyn sobbed with a hopeless, empty sound.

Rego tightened his arms around her, his face set in a grim line.

They were nearing the harbour when she spoke again.

"Someone put a brick through my car window," she said sleepily.

"What?"

"And spray-painted 'grass' on the side."

"When was this?"

"When I got home from work."

"I'll look into it."

"Doesn't matter," she said, as her eyes closed. "Nothing matters."

There was an ambulance waiting at the harbour, and Tamsyn was helped inside.

As the doors closed, she called out to him.

"Sir?"

"Yes?"

"Can you get fingerprints if something has been underwater?"

He took his time replying.

"It's possible. Sometimes. But in seawater? I don't know."

"Will you find out? Because Grandad and I can take you to all of George's pots – we'll find the evidence. I know we will."

The ambulance doors closed, and Rego couldn't tell her

that the chances of any either of those things happening were remote.

He followed behind in one of the patrol cars, working the phone as he drove.

"Vik, sorry, I know it's late."

His friend's voice was rough with sleep.

"Seriously, Rob? It's three in the morning! This had better be important. My wife will kill me if the sleep deprivation doesn't get me first."

"I'll make it up to you, buddy. Listen, I need a quick lesson in latent fingerprints: can they survive underwater?"

Rego could almost hear the computer that was Vikram's brain ticking over.

"Yes, we've done tests with fingerprints on glass and metal that were submerged. We had some good results with cyanoacrylate, but that was in stagnant water. And as you're in Cornwall, I'm guessing you're asking about seawater."

"Yes, and it's urgent."

"You can get lucky, but generally the movement of the water causes attrition which washes off the prints."

"Bottom line?"

"It depends on how the package has been handled. I can fast track it, but it'll take at least a day. If you're lucky."

Rego swore. "That's it? There's nothing else you can do?"

"That's already a longshot. But if there were multiple layers of plastic wrap, for example, there might be fingerprints inside that could be retrieved. We've had some good results from swabbing the grip-seal on Ziploc bags. We'll check for fibres and DNA, too."

By the time Rego arrived at the hospital in Truro 35 minutes later, he knew a lot more about the recovery of fingerprints. He'd also started the investigative process on George Mason. He wanted to know whether he or his ex-wife had ever taken out an insurance policy – the one he'd supposedly cashed in to buy his boat; he wanted to speak to the previous owner of the ring-netter and find out whether Mason paid by cash, cheque or bank transfer; and he wanted to check the tall tale of a win on the Football Pools.

The man's story had changed more than once, and that alone was suspicious.

But a suspicion wasn't evidence, so in the morning, he'd get a forensic accountant going through Mason's bank accounts, and comparing his apparent wealth to that earned from fishing.

And, crucially, he needed to get the lifeboat to check the rest of Mason's lobster pots out in Mount's Bay, in case any of them contained either drugs or illicit earnings. He also needed Tamsyn to pinpoint, if possible, where Mason had recovered two lobster pots of 'travelling money'. He hoped for Tamsyn's sake that they could find them. He hoped they had George's fingerprints all over them.

And not Tamsyn's or her grandfather's.

CHAPTER 32

Tamsyn was taken to A&E where they stripped off her wet clothes, pumped warm fluid directly into her veins via an IV line, and monitored her heart.

Rego was allowed to sit with her when her colour began to return to normal.

A normal colour: that was a loaded phrase. He looked down at his own skin, so dark compared to Tamsyn or his father; so light compared to his mother. He pulled out his phone, scrolling through photos of his two beautiful children, with their caramel skin and dark, dark eyes. He missed them, he missed his wife, he missed being part of a family and wondered again if taking this job had been the right thing to do.

He glanced at Tamsyn and found her watching him tiredly, her eyelids drooping.

He was about to say something when there was a flurry of activity and an older woman came rushing into the cubicle, her white hair a dandelion around her head, her eyes wild.

Rego stood up to introduce himself but she flung herself at Tamsyn, stepping perilously close to the IV line.

"Tammy! Oh, Tammy-tam! What have they done to you, my angel?"

She took Tamsyn's hand and kissed it over and over again.

"I'm alright, Gran," Tamsyn mumbled, trying to hug her grandmother with one arm. "How's Grandad?"

Her grandmother slumped into the chair that Rego had vacated.

"They've taken him to the operating theatre. They don't know..."

Her lips trembled and Tamsyn squeezed her hand.

"When they told me you were here, too, I couldn't believe it!"

"Grandad saved me," Tamsyn whispered, the words cracked and hoarse. "When George pulled out a gun, he jumped in front of me."

"What? I don't understand. You mean *our* George? Why did he have a gun?"

"He isn't *our* George," Tamsyn cried. "He never was. He fooled us all. He was a drug dealer. He's the one who shot Grandad."

Her grandmother's mouth dropped open in shock.

"And Mo's dead, Gran," Tamsyn said, her voice dropping away. "She drowned and I couldn't find her, I couldn't save her."

The two women clung together and Rego felt he was intruding, but he needed to stay and hear all of this.

"Oh, Tammy!" her grandmother cried. "Oh my darling angel. We'll light a candle for your grandfather and one for little Mo."

Then she seemed to see Rego for the first time.

Tamsyn looked in the same direction, as if she'd forgotten he was there.

"Gran, this is Inspector Rego. He's the one who pulled me out of the sea. He saved my life."

Rego was taken aback when the woman threw herself at him, hugging him fiercely. She reminded him of his mother, the effusiveness, the physicality, and he gently patted her back.

"Thank you," she said into his chest. "You promised me you'd save her and you did. Thank you! Thank you! Thank you! We'll never forget this."

She spoke with the unconscious 'we' of a long-married couple. Rego mustered an awkward smile.

"I'll leave you two alone now. Tamsyn, we'll talk in the morning." He glanced at his watch. "Later in the morning."

"Yes, sir." Then she called after him. "Rob!"

He turned as she said his name.

"Thank you," she said. "For everything. Thank you."

He nodded and walked away.

Tamsyn closed her eyes, her hand still clasped in her grandmother's. So many images floated through her brain, so many questions, but it was hard to focus.

As if from a great distance, she heard her grandmother praying.

"Wrap thee in cotton,
Bind thee with love,
Protection from pain,
Surrounds like a glove,
Brightest of blessings,
Surround thee this night,
For thou art cared for
Healing thoughts sent in flight."

When Tamsyn woke hours later, pale grey light was filtering into the ward, and something was beeping.

Her grandmother was asleep in the chair, her neck at an uncomfortable angle and her mouth open.

She looked exhausted, and absent the energy that usually animated her mobile features, she looked older and careworn.

Tamsyn felt guilty for adding to her worries. Would any of this have happened if she hadn't joined the police? No, because she wouldn't have known what was going on with Domi and the smuggling operation; she wouldn't have insisted on going to the harbour last night; and Morwenna ... dear little Mo. Another casualty lost to the vastness of the ocean.

A nurse hurried over and switched off the beeping machine.

"Your IV fluids have all gone through now," she said. "I'll unhook you in a moment."

"That would be great because I really need to go to the bathr—"

But the nurse had already hurried away, and Tamsyn was left with an empty IV bag and the cannula still in her arm.

Her grandmother sat up slowly, and Tamsyn could hear her joints creaking and cracking.

"How are you, angel?"

"I'm okay. Tired, but okay. Did you sleep?"

"Yes, I didn't mean to," her grandmother said guiltily. "I meant to go and sit with Ozzie." Her lip trembled. "He'll think I've abandoned him."

"He'd never think that," Tamsyn said with certainty. "He knows you love him. A love like yours doesn't need words."

Her grandmother shook her head.

"No, Tammy. You always need to say the words – people aren't mind-readers, and we all have doubts. You got to say the words, too. Remember that."

"Alright, Gran. Let's go and see him and you can tell him yourself." She frowned at the cannula. "I just need to get this thing out first."

It took longer than either of them wanted, and Tamsyn was desperate to use the toilet by the time a nurse rushed over, took out the cannula and put a small sticking plaster over the wound.

Tamsyn hobbled to the bathroom feeling as if every muscle had been scooped out and replaced with jelly. Once she'd washed her hands and splashed some cold water on her face, she began to feel a little more human, but so tired, so very tired.

Her grandmother was waiting for her impatiently with Tamsyn's clothes in a plastic carrier bag. But they were still sopping wet and smelled unpleasant.

She had no choice but to wear the cold, wet trainers, but as she pulled them out, the little pebble of Serpentine that she'd kept in her pocket rolled free.

"Look, Gran," she said quietly, holding it in her palm.

Her grandmother's tired blue eyes met her own and they shared a look, a moment, a feeling big enough to fill the room.

"Let's go and see Grandad. We can give him this," said Tamsyn.

She had to make do with the ungainly hospital robe that was big enough to wrap around her twice, and squelched behind her grandmother as they made their way to the Critical Care Unit on the second floor of the Trelawney wing.

But the door was locked and there was no one around to ask to open it. Despondent, they sat outside for a while until a passing nurse took pity on them.

"Visiting hours are 10am till 8pm," she said, then glanced at their dishevelled state. "Well, perhaps just a quick peek."

Ozzie Poldhu lay in a hospital bed with white bandages

wound around his head, and his eyes taped shut. His weathered skin seemed paler, and gnarled blue veins stood out on the back of his hands. His chest was bare, and he looked old and vulnerable.

Tears burned behind Tamsyn's eyes and she had to put a hand over her mouth to stop from calling out.

Her grandmother stood at the side of his bed, staring down at him as she took his hand in hers.

"Ozzie, my love, we're both here, me and Tammy. We love you and we want you to come back to us." She looked across at Tamsyn. "Tell him, angel. Tell him we need him to come home. He'll hear you."

Tamsyn had her doubts, but if it was what her grandmother needed, then she'd do it.

"I'm here, Grandad, and I'm okay. I'm okay. I'm okay because of you. Gran's right – we need you to wake up and come home." She glanced at her Gran, who nodded at her to continue. "Morwenna, Mo, she ... she saved my life, Grandad, but I couldn't save her. I'm so sorry. I'm so sorry. We need you, Grandad. Please wake up."

Tamsyn couldn't say anymore, her throat had tightened and tears were threatening again.

"You listen to our granddaughter, Ozzie Poldhu," said her grandmother, taking over smoothly. "We've been married 51 years and I can't do without you now, you stubborn ole bugger."

Angrily, she wiped the tears from her face and when she looked at her husband, her gaze was fierce.

"You come back to me, Ozzie! You hear me? You come back – it's not your time."

Shortly after that, the nurse hustled them away.

"How's he doing?" Tamsyn's grandmother asked her. "The truth, please."

"The doctor will talk to you after she's done her rounds. You can wait here."

And the nurse pointed at a row of uncomfortable plastic chairs.

"There's a vending machine just outside."

But they didn't have any money to buy food or drinks. Tamsyn had nothing at all. She kept a digital wallet on her phone and never carried cash. George had thrown her brand new iPhone overboard, and it was currently at the bottom of the sea, a toy for the fish.

Her grandmother had left the house with just her door keys.

So they sat and they waited.

Finally, the doctor arrived in a flurry of blue scrubs and stethoscope, but was swept into the CCU, and they didn't see her for another 45 minutes.

When she came out, she introduced herself.

"Mrs Poldhu? I'm Dr Michelle Cooke. I've just been to see Oswald..."

"We call him Ozzie."

She gave a kind smile. "Ozzie is doing very well. Has anyone explained to you what's happened?"

They shook their heads and instinctively held hands. The doctor dragged a chair across the floor and sat beside them.

"Ozzie has a skull fracture caused by a bullet hitting his head with force. I have to say, he is an incredibly lucky man because the bullet didn't penetrate his skull. But he does have a compound depressed skull fracture which means that some of the broken bones have pressed inwards. That caused pressure on the brain and a small bleed."

"Like a stroke?" Tamsyn's grandmother asked, her voice weak and scared.

"It can be a little like that. We had to operate to lift these broken bones off his brain to relieve the pressure. But the surgery went very well and his vital signs are looking very positive."

"Will he wake up soon?"

"At the moment, Ozzie is in an induced coma. This is the best way to let his brain heal. When we feel he's strong enough, we'll gradually reduce the medication until he wakes up." She smiled sympathetically. "That won't be today, so I suggest you go home and get some rest. We'll call you if there are any changes."

She stood up to leave and Tamsyn's grandmother gazed up at her wordlessly.

"Thank you, doctor," said Tamsyn.

The doctor smiled again and walked away.

They sat in silence for several minutes and then Tamsyn's grandmother shook her head hopelessly.

"I always said that man had a thick skull." She tried to smile but it wobbled around the edges. Then she looked at Tamsyn. "We need to get you home to rest. A long hot bath, a cup of tea, then bed."

That sounded wonderful, but ... how were they going to get there? They had no phone, no money, and Tamsyn didn't even have proper clothes to wear.

Footsteps echoed down the long corridor and Tamsyn felt crying all over again when she saw who it was.

PC Jamie Smith was striding towards them, out of uniform, and a huge grin on his face.

"Tam! They told me I'd find you here? How are you? I'm here to take you home. Is this your gran? Hey, Mrs Poldhu! I'm Jamie, but you can call me your white knight, ready to rescue damsels in distress – and to bring them clothes." He winked at Tamsyn. "Got them out of your locker at the station."

"You don't have the key," Tamsyn said, her brain slow to catch up.

"Didn't need it," he grinned. "Shall we go?"

He talked all the way back to Gulval and Tamsyn didn't roll her eyes once. His aimless chatter had made her grandmother chuckle, and for that she would be eternally grateful. She felt guilty for having thought so dismissively of him before.

He looked tired too, and she realised that he must have come straight from his night shift to bring her and her grandmother home. She'd never forget this kindness.

As his car pulled up to the kerb outside their cottage, he saw her car's shattered windscreen.

"Bloody hell! What happened to your car?"

"Vandals," she said with a wide yawn.

He frowned at the word 'grass' and started to say something when Tamsyn's eyes focussed on the front door. It looked like someone had left a bag of wet wool on the doorstep.

But then Tamsyn cried out and threw open the car door, running to the cottage and falling to her already bruised knees.

A dirty, damp and bedraggled Mo jumped all over her, wagging her tail and licking the tears from her face.

Tamsyn crushed the small dog in her arms, holding the tiny body against her.

"Oh my God, Mo! Oh my God! I couldn't find you! I tried and tried but I couldn't find you. You were all alone and you saved yourself! You clever, brave girl! I love you so much! I'll never call you scruff-bucket again!"

Mo squirmed in her arms, trying to get closer, trying to press her small, wet, doggy-smelling body against Tamsyn, as if no one in the world mattered more.

And even though Tamsyn didn't think she was cut out to be a police officer, and even though her faith in the world she thought she lived in had been shattered, and even though everything had changed, maybe, just this once, Tamsyn believed in a higher power.

CHAPTER 33

Rego was exhausted and very tempted to give in to the waves of tiredness washing over him. He'd snatched a few hours' sleep after he'd left the hospital, but his brain kept creating lists of urgent jobs, so in the end, fuelled by bad coffee and a Mars bar, he'd gone back to the office and got stuck in.

DS Tom Stevens was in early too, looking bleary eyed and determined to be fully caffeinated, drinking cup after cup of coffee until Rego was worried he'd have to peel him off the ceiling.

The whole team had worked late and then Rego had dragged himself back to his hotel room, only to do it all over again the next day, and the next and the next.

Each day brought a mountain of new intelligence that had to be waded through. Phone records from all the contacts on the various burner phones were providing a mine of information on the local crims, as well as several further afield.

Forensics were stretched thin with a team at George Mason's house, another going over Tamsyn's car and her grandfather's car; the *Daniel Day* and the *Mari-morgans* had been put on trailers and were on their way to a sterile garage where a specialist team would be looking for fingerprints, blood, gunshot residue and evidence that drugs had been on board. Rego also wanted to know if Ruçi's body had been kept on either boat. They thought they'd matched the lividity marks to an area at the stern of Mason's boat. It was still to be confirmed, but it was looking likely.

The Super was pressing Rego to have a forensics team at the Poldhu residence as well, and for Tamsyn to be suspended from duty, but so far Rego had held off on both of those, but if the evidence pointed in that direction, then he'd have to.

For now, Tamsyn was officially on sick leave.

Rego had his own problems, although they were insignificant compared to Tamsyn's. The whole situation had developed quickly so he wasn't worried that he'd be criticised for things that were out of his control, but he might have to explain why he hadn't sent Tamsyn to a different police station as soon as there had been a suspicion that relatives of hers had been involved in the Ruçi case.

There would be a review of the intelligence and decisions he'd made, all of which had been recorded in his policy book. The on-going document included everything that he'd done and the reasons that he'd made those decisions. He was confident that he'd followed the national decision-making module guidelines: gathering information and intelligence, assessing threat and risk to develop a working strategy, considering powers and policies, identifying options and contingency planning, and constantly reviewing those decisions. At the heart of it was a guiding standard of ethics and professional standards that informed every officer's decisions.

But questions were always asked, and when it came down to it, Mason was missing and Domi had escaped.

Rego was beginning to suspect from the quantity of blood they'd found that wasn't Ozzie's, that Mason was already dead. Even so, they had enough to issue a warrant to arrest both of the suspects, and details had been circulated in the UK on the PNC that Mason and Domi were 'wanted for interview'. It was a longshot, and Rego believed that Domi was probably on his way back to Albania and swilling down Smirnoff or Rakia, or whatever they drank over there.

They had a long list of dealers and users that were going to find themselves face to face with arrest warrants, too. It would put the local drug trade out of business, at least for a while.

The Harbour Master at Newlyn had given Rego a list of the areas where Ozzie and George Mason had fished, with a description of the buoys and flags they used. Rego had passed this information to the lifeboat team and so far, they'd found five live lobsters and a number of small crabs – all had been thrown back in the sea and the pots retrieved for analysis. But there were still many more to find.

A Border Force cutter had hunted for the yacht that Domi was supposed to be rendezvousing with, but the search had been fruitless; it had slipped past them in the dark and had pinged near Cherbourg, then turned around and headed back to Portugal. He had to assume that Domi was now travelling overland to Albania.

Rego rubbed his bloodshot eyes. He needed to know what had really happened on the *Mari-morgans* – he wanted to take Tamsyn's word for it but he couldn't.

He'd been pleased that PC Smith had volunteered to go and fetch Tamsyn and her grandmother from the hospital that first morning. She'd made a big impression on E-team, and they were all worried about her.

His phone rang – it was DC Jack Forshaw who was heading up the search team at George Mason's house.

"Sir, traces of blood have been found at Mason's place. Forensics say that it was a large blood spatter, apparently from a serious wound. The blood type is the same as Ruçi's but we won't know if it's an exact match until we can get DNA results back."

"I want that fast-tracked," said Rego.

"It'll be at least a week, boss." He paused. "But it's looking like this is the place where the victim was killed."

"Good work. Anything else?"

"A collection of kitchen knives as well as knives from his boat – forensics will be testing them all for blood, uh, human blood."

Rego thought about Domi's nickname, 'the knife' and suspected that he'd have used his own weapon for reprisals. The whole thing had seemed personal from the moment Domi decided to take care of business himself.

"The sniffer dog has been having a field day," Forshaw added. "She's indicated on just about every room in the house, but all we've found so far is a couple of baggies of weed."

"What about a phone? There must be one – get a digital dog on it, if necessary."

Rego knew that colleagues in Exeter had worked with the FBI to set up a programme for dogs to detect electronic storage devices, sniffing out the chemical compounds found in a circuit board. One of his success stories back in Manchester had been when a digi-dog had found a Pepsi can which was stuffed with SD cards.

Forshaw said he'd stay while SOCO officers continued to work the scene.

Rego was about to make another cup of awful coffee when his phone rang again.

"Boss," came Tom Stevens' voice. "A man's body has been found washed up at Nanjizal beach, not far from Land's End. Coastguard are there now." He paused. "They found George Mason's wallet in his pocket."

"Positive ID?"

"Negative. The face is too messed up. Not sure we'll get dental either – the victim was shot in the back of the head, execution style – and fish have been finishing off the rest."

It gave Rego no pleasure to be proved right. And if it was Mason, it added another murder victim to Domi's list.

"Thanks, Tom. I'm on my way."

CHAPTER 34

Tamsyn felt strange being back at the police station. It was the first time she'd been there since everything had happened, since her world had fallen apart. It felt as if she'd been away for months, not just ten days.

Easter had come and gone, and her grandfather had been in hospital the whole time. It had been three worrying days before the doctor had brought him out of the coma, and another week until she had finally agreed that he was well enough to go home. A neighbour had driven Tamsyn and her grandmother to the hospital to bring him back to the cottage. His Rover and her old Fiat hadn't yet been released from forensics.

Officially on sick leave, Tamsyn didn't know when she'd be going back to work ... or if she'd be going back at all.

But when she walked into Inspector Rego's office and sat down in the chair opposite him, she didn't feel nervous, just numb, as if nothing would ever matter again.

"Thank you for coming in, Tamsyn. I know this has been a difficult time for you."

She didn't even bother to reply, just watched him

watching her, seeing the wariness in his normally warm brown eyes.

She wondered if any of them would ever trust her again, because if they didn't, she had no future in the police force. Even though she wasn't sure of anything else, she was sure of that.

"Tamsyn, a man's body was found at Nanjizal beach two days ago. We have now positively identified that man as George Mason."

She drew in a sharp breath, but kept her eyes on spot somewhere above Rego's left shoulder.

"He … the victim … died from a gunshot wound to the head."

She nodded, but still didn't look at him.

"Was he?" she said rhetorically. "Was he a victim?"

Rego chose not to answer that.

"It has also been confirmed that Besnik Domi has returned to Albania."

Tamsyn gave a harsh laugh.

"So he's got away with it – he's literally got away with murder. Twice. Saemira Ruçi and George." She shook her head. "Probably others, right?"

"An international arrest warrant has been issued, and an application for extradition has been made but it's a long process. Governments don't like extraditing their own nationals."

"Like I said, he's got away with it."

Her mouth twisted in disgust.

"Kevin Moyle aka 'Spider' refused to talk, but he's going to do time anyway," Rego continued.

Tamsyn nodded without much interest.

"I also need to inform you that we found George Mason's fingerprints on the tyre jack in your car's boot, with more than a hundred tabs of Ecstasy hidden underneath." He paused. "With a street value of approximately £3,500."

"Bastard," she said softly.

"We did not find any of your fingerprints on either of the packages. Neither did we find your fingerprints on the jack."

"Did you find any prints at all?"

Rego shook his head.

"Not on the jack, no. We suspect that Mason attempted to wipe his fingerprints from everything he touched when he hid the drugs. Do you know how he managed to get access to your car?"

"I needed two new tyres," she said quietly. "My MOT was a month ago and two of the tyres wouldn't have passed. George said he'd sort out a couple of re-treads for me and that he'd be cheaper than Kwik Fit. We were laughing about it. I was grateful."

Rego sighed.

"It may have been what gave him the idea to plant drugs in your car and implicate you if he needed a quick getaway. Equally, he may have planned this much earlier. He was careful – just not careful enough."

He saw her expression harden as she clenched her jaw, the struggle with her emotions as she learned the full extent of Mason's betrayal.

Rego spoke carefully.

"It seems that Mason went out of his way to provide himself with an exit strategy that implicated you and your whole family. His fingerprints were found all over your grandfather's boat, but also his car, including the steering wheel and gear stick – and your grandmother said that Ozzie would never have let him drive it, although he'd frequently been a passenger. More tellingly, all the drugs we've recovered so far have Mason's fingerprints on the wrappers and on the

Ziploc bags, but your grandfather's fingerprints – and yours – are completely absent." Rego looked up from his notes. "That was the one piece of false evidence that Mason wasn't able to plant. We also have started looking at his financial records..."

"And I know you looked at Grandad's bank account, too," she said accusingly.

"Yes, we did, and we found no evidence of any unusual activity. But as for Mason, however, he wasn't fully able to launder his illegal gains, although he did his best to mask the true extent of his wealth and his crimes. The NCA have been able to link him to at least two off-shore accounts and suspect there may be more." He frowned. "We may never know the full extent of the network he established over the last ten years. But it was the mistakes he made at the beginning that enabled us to unravel part of the story."

She nodded, still unable to look at him.

"The blood found at his house in Marazion is a match for Saemira Ruçi. We also found remains of women's clothing that had been set alight in a dustbin. We might find some DNA, but we're not hopeful about that. Neither have we found a match for the knife that killed Ruçi. We know that she was killed at Mason's house – but proving who did it will be difficult if we don't find the weapon."

"She was killed in his house? I've been in that house! Loads of times."

"I know. We found your fingerprints."

She fell silent.

"It would seem that Mason began planning to disappear at least three years ago, and we think that's when he started using your grandfather's boat."

"So you don't think anymore that Grandad was involved?"

Her voice was still soft, but held a quiet fury that her rigid body and fisted hands transmitted loud and clear.

Rego cleared his throat.

"We have been able to establish that on at least three occasions this year, your grandfather's boat was used when we have evidence that he was elsewhere: his GP's surgery confirmed a back injury that left him with severe sciatica rendering him unable to walk, certainly not well enough to go fishing; he used his credit card to buy petrol at a supermarket at a time when his boat had left the harbour; and on a third occasion, he was seen in Cadgwith singing with other fishermen, I believe."

"Is that enough to clear his name?" she asked fiercely.

"Yes, it is. All charges have been withdrawn. He'll receive a letter saying that he's been released from the investigation."

"And an apology?"

"It was a legitimate line of inquiry," Rego replied calmly, "so no, I'm not going to apologise for doing my job."

Her jaw was still clenched but she didn't challenge him on that.

"And what about me? Do you believe that I had anything to do with what Mason was up to?"

He suspected that it was easier for her to think of him as 'Mason' than 'Uncle George' – that was too painful.

"As you know, we've looked at your call data record and we can find no connection with Mason beyond what you had already told us. We believe that so far as Mason's waterborne activities go, he was acting alone."

"Does that *clear me*, sir?" she pressed.

He leaned back in his chair, frowning at her. It all depended on how serious he wanted to make it. The whole thing could leave a question mark over Tamsyn for the rest of her career. But he'd seen some potential in her, and he didn't believe she was involved.

"I explicitly told you not to get involved in the investigation. And I know why you did what you did, but it wasn't the right thing to do. I understand that you believed Mason's life was in imminent danger and that you were doing your duty. But you chose not to call me or anyone else on the team. You sent me a text message instead – one that I didn't receive for several, crucial hours. You could have called 999, you could have called the station, or called a colleague. You did none of those things. You should have let the investigation play out, and if you were worried about anyone's safety, there were other choices you could have made. And in future, remember that your SIO probably won't have shared all the information on a case anyway. As it turned out, you made the wrong choice and I don't have to tell you how that was very nearly a fatal mistake. Tamsyn, it's a learning curve for you – you acted like a civilian would do, but you're a sworn officer and have a duty to work with the team."

"Yeah, great choices on my part alright," she said bitterly, meeting his eyes at last. "I got it so wrong, so wrong. How could I not see it? For years! My Grandad was shot in the head, I nearly drowned, Mo nearly drowned – and just because I thought I was saving my *Uncle George*."

She spat out the last words, but then the fight seemed to go out of her.

"You believed that a man you thought of as your uncle was in serious danger," Rego reminded her. "You believed there was an imminent threat to his life."

She spoke softly, wearily, as if the last weeks had aged her prematurely.

"Maybe I shouldn't be a police officer," she whispered. "I've obviously got rubbish judgement."

Rego tapped his finger against the desk. She was young and naïve and hadn't thought through the process – she'd thought she was doing the right thing, but she'd panicked and made a bad mistake.

"Tamsyn, you'd been brought up to think of him as your uncle – he fooled everyone."

"Yeah."

"We're all perfect with hindsight. In future, make sure you have all bases covered rather than just going down one track. You're only twenty – you're going to mistakes. We all do and we've all been there. Use this experience to make you a better copper."

"In the future? You're not firing me?"

"No."

She met his gaze but was still frowning at him.

"Do I have a future as a police officer? Will anyone want to work with me; will they trust me?"

"Everyone at this station, everyone in this force knows the truth about what happened here: no one will blame you."

She gave a cynical smile.

"But no smoke without fire, right, sir?"

He thought she was probably correct about that and only time, lots of time, would make people forget.

"One other thing, we found a spray can with Ollie Garrett's fingerprints on it near your cottage. He admitted to vandalising your car."

"So, it was Ollie."

"I'll need you to make a formal statement and then I'll pass it up to CPS for them to make a decision."

She was still frowning.

"You said I should use this experience to be a better police officer. How? How do I do that?"

"I guess I'm saying, don't take things at face value. Look

for patterns of behaviour, look for things that don't quite make sense: analyse, understand, report. But most of all, look after yourself. Your own safety and your colleagues' safety comes before anything else, trust me on this. Catching a suspect may make you look good but don't forget that these things can also usually be solved in slow-time. It is *never* worth risking lives – especially your own." He paused. "You'll make a good officer, Tamsyn, but it's not a race – you don't have to know it all in one week or one month or even one year."

"I don't feel like I'll ever know it." She looked up at him, her expression so raw. "How can you trust anyone? How can I trust anyone ever again?"

Her words held all the pain of someone whose loyalty had been abused, whose trust had been destroyed, whose heart and soul would never fully recover from the damage done by George Mason.

"Few people are all good or all bad," Rego said at last. "For what it's worth, I do think that Mason cared about you and your family ... he just cared about himself more. And as for trusting someone, it will take a while but eventually you'll find someone who deserves your trust," he said, feeling the painful inadequacy of his answer.

"I don't know if I can do this ... the job," and she shuddered. "All this ... this darkness. How do you do it, sir?"

"Because I have a family," he said quietly. "I have two children: Max is twelve and Maisie is eight. I have a wife and a mum. And when I get scum off the streets, I'd like to think I make the world a better place for the people I care about." Rego smiled self-consciously. "And it's a good career with a great team behind you."

She was silent, as if processing everything he'd said. Finally, she looked up.

"I'm not going to tell Gran and Grandad what Mason said, about my dad, I mean."

"It's your call," Rego replied carefully. "There's no evidence and it's unlikely there ever will be after all this time. But," and he waited until she met his gaze, "but he did confess his crime to a sworn officer – that carries a lot of weight."

She gave a bleak smile. "Yeah, right."

Rego continued to study her.

"And you've told me, so I'll have to include it in my report," he said, after a short pause. "The end of investigation report won't be made public, but now that we've had a chance to search Mason's house, we may come up with evidence that could re-open the case into your father's death."

He didn't think it was possible for her to become paler, but he was wrong.

"A cold case review would decide if the original inquiry had missed anything. Tamsyn, you'll have to decide what you tell your grandparents, but I'd encourage you to be open with them – secrets like Mason's, they only have power when they're a secret."

"Is that everything, sir?" Tamsyn asked, her face smooth, a blank mask of indifference.

Rego leaned back in his chair.

"Sergeant Terwillis will be speaking to you formally, but you'll be back on E-team next Monday."

She nodded again and looked as if she wanted nothing more than to get the hell out of there.

A random thought occurred to Rego.

"Tamsyn, do you know when George Mason's birthday was?"

She looked startled.

"His birthday? June 29th. Why?"

"What star sign is that?" he asked, although he'd already guessed.

"Cancer. Why do you want to know that?"

"That's the sign of the crab, isn't it?"

She gave him a weird look.

"Yes?"

He shook his head.

"Idle curiosity." Then he leaned towards her. "Just take the bollocking for disobeying orders ... and you owe me a beer. It's forgotten about – none of this will be mentioned again, not by me. You'll be alright, Blackpool."

"Sir."

She didn't meet his eyes or acknowledge his nickname for her, leaving his office in silence.

Rego slumped in his chair. Seeing an eager young copper get the stuffing kicked out of her, well, it was just shit.

This time tomorrow, he'd be with his family again. He needed to see his wife, he needed to spend time with his kids – he needed to be around people, around life – not all this ugliness, not all this death.

He sent a few emails, squared the papers on his desk, and got ready to get the hell out of Cornwall.

CHAPTER 35

Tamsyn didn't want to go home. Instead, she sat and stared at the sea, but it didn't bring its usual comfort. She shivered as she stared at the cold, grey water.

Containerships crowded the horizon and small fishing boats chugged in and out of Newlyn harbour. If she looked hard, she'd know every single one of them, know who owned them, who was at the tiller, who were married, who were divorced, who had kids that she'd gone to school with. But did she really know them? Could you ever really know anyone?

Her phone rang and she saw that Jess was calling her again. She didn't answer and let the call go to voicemail. She didn't know what to say to her, didn't know how to begin.

Besides, there was something she had to do first.

When she put her key in the front door, she heard Mo's excited bark of welcome. She bent down to pick her up, feeling the warmth of the small, firm body wriggling in her arms, the wet tongue on her cheek.

She carried Mo into the tiny living room where her grandfather was sitting in his usual chair. A neat, white bandage was taped across the top of his head, yellowing bruises spreading out across his left temple, but his eyes were as bright and blue as ever.

"Tammy," he said.

That was all, but she felt her throat begin to tighten.

"Gran, can you come and sit down," she called into the kitchen. "There's something I've got to tell you both."

"What is it, angel?"

She waited until her grandmother was sitting, her face lined with fear.

"It's about George."

"I don't want that man's name in this house!" her grandfather bellowed, his face reddening dangerously.

"I know," Tamsyn said tightly. "But there are things you need to know."

"More things?" her grandmother asked, her chin quivering.

"Yes."

Tamsyn didn't want to do this. She didn't want to hurt them anymore. She didn't want them to know the extent of George Mason's betrayal, but Inspector Rego was right – the truth would come out sooner or later, and it was better that they heard it from her first.

She tried to conjure up an image of her father, but it was hard – he seemed so far away. The photograph of him on the mantelpiece was more real than the few images in her head. There were flashes, but she was never sure if they were things her grandparents had told her which had gradually become her own memories.

Mo looked up at her with a worried expression, as if sensing Tamsyn's distress.

She took a deep breath, but when she spoke, her voice shook.

"I don't know when or where George met up with the Albanian gang, but it was at least ten years ago."

No one spoke. No one moved.

"You knew that after the divorce, George had money worries, but when he said he'd cashed in Aunty Marie's life insurance policy, that was a lie. There was no insurance policy. And there were no wins on the Pools either. He lied. He lied to all of us. It's looking likely that the criminals helped him buy the *Mari-morgans* and once he'd accepted their money, there was no turning back. They owned him. They probably held it over him or threatened him to make him do what they wanted. And what they wanted him to do was to bring in drugs to the UK." Tamsyn paused, picking her words carefully. "So he did what they told him to do. The drug gang would send boats, yachts, whatever, across Biscay and drop off the drugs in George's lobster pots." She looked directly at her grandfather. "And for the last three years at least, he used the *Daniel Day* to collect the drugs."

Her grandfather's knuckles turned white as he gripped the arms of his chair, the blue veins standing out like rope.

"All those times you had engine trouble was because of George. He was trying to cover his tracks so that if anyone started to suspect anything, they'd suspect you instead, Grandad. He hid drugs in your car and in mine. If anyone started sniffing around, he'd created the perfect scapegoats. He'd been planning to make it look like we were the guilty ones. And he'd been doing it for years."

"He did that to you?"

Her grandfather's voice was choked with shock, anger, outrage, disbelief and pain. So much pain.

"Yes. He did it to both of us. But there were other things he did, too. He'd been stealing money from the Albanians. I don't know if he was just greedy or stupid or already planning to disappear, but he put the blame on a woman called Saemira Ruçi. She was living in St Ives and working with the gangsters, too. And when the gang realised money was missing, George blamed her and stood by while she was murdered. He stood by and he did nothing. He even helped dump her body. And that's who we found in the sea at Lamorna Cove."

Her grandmother gasped. "I can't believe it!"

"The thing is," Tamsyn said, licking her lips as the sickness in her stomach grew, "this all started ten years ago. George told me ... he said that he'd wanted Dad to join him in getting the drugs. Dad said no."

She watched as her grandmother put her hand over her eyes, as if hiding from the blow that was coming.

"Dad said no..." Tamsyn repeated. "And then ... and then he fell overboard and got tangled in his nets."

Ozzie grasped his wife's hand in his as tears began to trickle down his hollow cheeks.

"George told me it was an accident, and maybe it was. But George didn't save him. He was there and he didn't save him. He let Dad drown."

Both her grandparents were openly weeping, holding tightly to each other.

"And George would have stood by while Domi killed me, too." Tamsyn closed her eyes briefly. "I wasn't going to tell you," she whispered. "I didn't want to hurt you even more – but they're talking about maybe reopening the case into Dad's death. If they find new evidence, they will. I didn't want you to find out like that. I'm sorry."

Her voice broke.

"I'm so sorry."

Rego finished his report and packed up his few personal things from Penzance police station. He was heading home for a much-needed, long weekend break with his family. He was looking forward to spending time with Cassie and the kids – and his mum, of course. He had some bridges to build there. But first, he wanted to check on Tamsyn and see how she was doing before he left.

After their last conversation, he'd come back from his lunchbreak to find her handwritten letter of resignation on his desk. Instead of following procedure, he'd slipped it into his pocket. He needed to talk to her before she did something she'd come to regret.

He pulled up outside the cottage in Gulval and knocked on the door. Tamsyn's grandmother opened it.

"Oh, Mr Rego," she said, attempting a wan smile. "Tammy isn't here but please come in."

She showed him into the living room where Ozzie was sitting in his overstuffed armchair, white gauze and tape covering the line of surgical stitches across his head.

"How are you, Mr Poldhu?"

"Been wanting to see you," the old man said gruffly. "You sit down, boy."

Rego sat on the edge of the settee and waited.

"You saved our Tammy's life," said Ozzie.

"It was a team effort."

Ozzie shook his head slowly.

"No, Bernie Ryder told me. It was you what saw her clinging to one o' the buoys. He hadn't seen her, but you did. You saved her." His voice deepened with emotion. "She's all we've got, Mr Rego. I'll never forget what you did and I'm in your debt. So, thank you."

He strained to stand up, his balance uncertain, then held

out his hand. Rego shook it, and an understanding passed between them.

They both sat down as Tamsyn's grandmother carried in a tray with a pot of tea and three cups. Her gaze flitted between them and she nodded.

"How is Tamsyn?" Rego asked.

"Taking it hard," she murmured, blue eyes blurred with tears.

"Did you know she was thinking about resigning from the police?"

The elderly couple exchanged a look.

"She hasn't said anything to us," said Tamsyn's grandmother. "She's hardly talked to us at all. But this morning..." she shook her head, wiping away tears. "This morning, she told us all about George ... and about our son. I won't lie, Mr Rego, this last shock has hit her hard. Well, all of us. And I don't think she's talked to anyone since the night it all happened. Her best friend, Jess, has been calling but she hasn't spoken to her either. She's bottling it all up inside. It's not good for her, Mr Rego, but we don't know how to help her when she won't talk to us. But I'm not sure she's cut out for being a police officer – she's not as tough as she tries to look."

"She's stronger than she knows," said Rego with certainty. "And I think resigning from the police would be a mistake for Tamsyn. So I'm returning this," and he laid the letter of resignation on the table.

Ozzie looked at it but didn't touch it.

"Tell her that I hope she comes back to work," Rego began. "When she's ready. Tell her to call me..."

"We don't want her being in the police," said Ozzie, but his voice lacked its usual conviction, and he glanced at his wife. "It's not safe."

Rego didn't need to point out that the worst danger had come from the man that Tamsyn had called her uncle.

"I think she should come back," Rego said carefully. "And there's a job waiting for her. She'll make a good copper."

"I don't know, Mr Rego," said Tamsyn's grandmother. "George was *family*. We believed in him – Tamsyn believed in him. I don't know if she can go through all that again..."

She shook her head, her hand to her lips as if trying to force the words back inside.

"It's not an easy job," he said honestly. "There will be other challenges, lots of them, but there won't be another George Mason."

"If only we'd..."

"No," Rego said gently. "It's not your fault. Don't let his lies have that power. Don't let him do that to you. Not anymore."

"Thank you, Mr Rego."

She looked up and nodded slowly.

"We have a saying: *Birds fly, honour dies, but love lives forever.*"

Rego had never heard that proverb before, if it was a proverb, but he knew he'd be thinking about those words later.

"Do you know where Tamsyn is?"

"It's offshore at Gwithian."

For the first time since he'd walked into the cottage, Rego smiled. He knew what that meant now, although he'd not heard of either the term or the place until he'd come to Cornwall.

EPILOGUE

What is it about the ocean? Why are we bewitched by that wide expanse of blue and grey, why does it mesmerise us so?

Tamsyn watched the long, Atlantic rollers tumbling onto the beach, the sky swollen with granite clouds and the sun glinting fitfully.

Her mouth was dry and tremors racked her body. She hadn't been back in the water since that night, since she'd nearly died, and since she'd learned the truth about George Mason. Her lip curled in a sneer: *Uncle* George – a murderer, a drug dealer, a liar – a monster hiding in plain sight.

His lies, his betrayal, it had all taken so much from her – her belief in him, in herself, and soiled her memories of childhood.

"I'm not going to let you take the sea away from me, too. I won't let you!"

Only Mo was there to hear the bitterness in her voice.

Tamsyn's fingers felt thick and uncoordinated as she fumbled with the zip on her wetsuit. Her legs were rubbery and she couldn't stop shaking. Even so, she tucked her battered surfboard under her arm and stared out across the grey expanse.

She'd never been scared of the sea: respected it, yes; feared it, no.

Now everything had changed.

But she wasn't going to let the fear win. Not now.

Not ever.

Mo sighed heavily, and Tamsyn leaned down to ruffle her wiry fur.

"Look after my stuff, scruff-a-lot. I won't be long."

Mo lay down on Tamsyn's towel, resting her head on her paws, her expression mournful at being abandoned.

Tamsyn didn't have it in her to smile, not yet, but if anyone could change that, it would be Mo.

She stared at the walls of water as they charged towards the beach. She'd spent her whole life swimming and surfing and playing in the water. She'd always loved the sea ... now, a part of her never wanted to be near the water again.

Her hair tangled around her face as she stared at the horizon.

"I won't let you take this from me, too," she whispered again. "I won't let you."

She took a step forward, letting the water swirl around her feet, then slowly waded out through the foam, feeling the first bite of cold water around her thighs.

When the sea reached her waist, she jumped onto the board belly down, and began to paddle. A five-foot wave started to break over her and she duck-dived through it, her heart missing a beat as the cold water closed all around her. Then she was through and popped up on the other side.

Her confidence was slow to return and the surf was pumping on the north coast, the gusting wind making it choppy. Muscle memory helped her cut through the water with long, fluid strokes, duck-diving another set of waves that towered over her.

The waves were ragged but powerful, and the salt water poured from her hair and face as she emerged into the light again.

After duck-diving twice more, she was beyond the breakers, and swung her legs to either side of the board, sitting astride, eyes closed, feeling the slow rise and fall of the swell beneath her, the tentative sun on her face, a breeze stirring her wet hair.

She'd made it.

The tears came slowly and silently at first, like the loss of innocence, the loss of childhood. For the first time, she allowed herself to feel everything. George Mason had been there her whole life, her father's best friend, and he'd betrayed them all. The grief that she'd hidden away spilled out of her, the shock, the fight for survival, the cold breath of death.

Her shoulders shook as she cried and cried, her tears mingling with the salt water ebbing and flowing around her.

And something inside her hardened, born of a new determination that the Masons of this world couldn't hide in plain sight – she wouldn't allow it. She'd do her job and find the evidence that would convict men like him.

She didn't yet understand that when your broken heart mends, it is harder in all the damaged places.

She screamed out her anger, fury burning her from the inside. Despite what her grandmother's beliefs taught her, Tamsyn didn't think that George Mason had suffered enough. Dying was too easy compared to living with his crime, paying for what he'd done. He should have paid more, suffered more.

She listened to the sea lapping against her board, the distant shriek of seagulls echoing across the water, and wiped away her tears impatiently. Staring out toward the blurred line of the horizon, she waited for a set to come in and carry her away from her thoughts. And finally, she felt the first whisper of peace since that night.

On the beach, Mo had sat up at the sound of Tamsyn's screams and trotted to the water's edge, whining softly, too afraid to follow her.

From a distance, Rego watched, wishing there was something he could do or say to help. But there was nothing. All coppers knew what she was feeling – the rage that bad men could do bad things, that the innocent paid, and that good officers paid with bad dreams, too much booze and broken marriages.

He'd shared a pot of tea with her grandparents then headed up to the north shore, following the directions he'd been given to the scrap of land that surfers used for a car park. Only one surfer was out today and he'd recognised her immediately.

He walked down the beach, his lace-up city shoes sinking into the soft sand.

Mo turned around at his approach and stalked back to the towel, guarding Tamsyn's things jealously.

Cautiously, Rego sat next to her and the scruffy little dog relented as he stroked her fur, leaning her small body against his.

"Sorry I haven't got any treats," he said, and Mo gazed up at him, frowning. "She'll be alright," he said, hoping, believing it was true. "She's strong."

He watched Tamsyn as she caught a wave, paddling hard, then leaping to her feet in one swift motion, crouching down slightly, working the wave to get the best ride.

Rego thought she'd ride it all the way to the beach, but as soon as the wave's momentum began to slow, she spun the board around and lay flat, stroking through the water and back out to the line-up.

He lit a smoke and watched her for several more minutes until his cigarette had burned down to the filter, then he ground it out in the sand, put the stub in his pocket and headed back to the car.

Mo watched him leave in silence.

And when the waves began to drop and Tamsyn had finally surfed enough, all she saw were his footprints in the wet sand.

ACKNOWLEDGMENTS

Huge thanks to DCI HB for the inspiration, and also to WDC Wendy Batsford (retired) for being a kickass woman in the job, when policing for women in the '80s was really tough.

Also to DS Dave Stamp (retired), Student PC RF, and Teresa Bouldon (rtd) for sharing their insight and experience of Devon & Cornwall Police. Also to PC Will Bray for allowing me to shadow him for a day of Lay Observation in D&C's 'ride-along' scheme – thanks for the blue-light run!

Thanks to Mark Finch and Mike Hudswell for information on tides and currents, and what happens to a body in the ocean; to Sam Hyland for advice on ring-netters (because he built one, just like the *Mari-morgans*); to Jemma Cavill for information on the working harbour of St Mawes; to Stone's Reef for supplying the caffeine, and Sisu for the dangerously good chocolate brownies; and to Rob 'Cookie' Cooke for details about the operations of Newlyn Harbour, local fishermen and the lifeboat, on which he spent 27 years as a volunteer. He really should write his own book...

Thanks to Andrea Rego for lending her and Ozzie's names to the story, and for all things Cornish, including 'madder do it', the delights of thunder and lightning (golden syrup and Cornish clotted cream), and the importance of a grounder sea; and to Michelle Cooke, Mimi Eagling and Jack Forshaw for the name-borrowing.

Thanks to Sharkfin Media for the website and technical help (much needed).

To Steven Keogh, former MIT Scotland Yard for his very useful book *Murder Investigation Team: How Killers Are Really Caught*.

And to Coby Llewelyn: friend, editor, reader - who told me that Tamsyn needed a Jess in her life. Of course, she was right - she usually is.

About Berrick Ford

More than 30 years in a major metropolitan police force followed by a number of years in covert policing and the National Crime Agency, together with a love of Cornwall, bring together the talents of Berrick Ford in a series of exciting, dramatic and realistic detective novels.

COMING SOON...

DEAD MAN'S DIVE – A Cornish Crime Thriller #2

It started as a date with a diving instructor, but when Tamsyn finds a body during a wreck dive off the Cornish coast, her work-life balance is in serious jeopardy.

Who is the mysterious diver with the Cyrillic tattoos, and why has nobody reported him missing? Is this an accident or evidence of organised crime, and why are fingers pointing towards the military naval air station of RNAS Culdrose a few miles away?

Tamsyn is just a student constable so DI Robert Rego is brought down from Devon to take over the case. He's missing his family in Manchester and gets seasick just looking at a boat.

But this crime is bigger than both of them, and the pressure isn't just to solve the case ... but to forget about it completely.

DEAD RECKONING – A Cornish Crime Thriller #3

When Besnik Domi, the feared enforcer for organised crime gang the Hellbanianz, is extradited to the UK, Tamsyn has to face the man who tore her family apart, and DI Rego has to make sure that the case against the killer is watertight.

The evidence against Domi is strong, but when threats are made against both their families, Tamsyn and Rego have to choose: justice or vengeance.

www.berrickford.com

DEAD MAN'S DIVE

CHAPTER 1

She hadn't thought she'd feel safe with the vast weight of water above her, but she did. She felt peaceful. She felt content. She listened to the sound of her breathing and watched the colourful shoals of fish darting around. She felt at home in the element in a way she hadn't in months.

Adam drifted closer, signalling to her, his bare hands eerily white in the water. He brought his thumb and forefinger together to make a circle: *Are you okay?*

Tamsyn ran through a mental checklist: breathing, regular; ear pressure, equalised; bubbles showing that her dive set was working correctly. She took another slow breath, then returned the 'okay' signal. He responded with a thumbs down, indicating that they should continue their descent.

Tamsyn controlled her breathing the way she'd been taught and a slow stream of bubbles trickled from her regulator, the only clue which way was up. The sound of her breathing was louder now.

She followed the shot-line, sinking slowly. At ten metres, Adam checked again that she was okay, then he pointed downwards again and they began their final descent, the light muted now, the sense of isolation amplified.

It felt so strange to stand on the seabed looking up, up, up towards the sky, the sun sparkling on the surface so far above her.

The thought was unnerving, so she concentrated on admiring the silvery pilchards swooping past her like starlings of the sea. Ferns grew in clusters, roots clinging to rocks, their green fingers waving gently.

A sea slug, the size and shape of a cucumber, idled past, making her gasp in surprise. The sudden rush of bubbles was a reminder to stay calm, to breathe evenly.

Adam finned towards her, checking on her again.

He was an experienced diver, the club's instructor, her dive buddy and maybe boyfriend, but at that moment, Tamsyn wished she were alone in this silent world: no words, no talking, no responsibilities, just drifting on the current.

Adam signalled her again, pointing in the direction of the dark, hulking shadow behind her.

For more than a hundred years, the SS *Mohegan* had lain at the bottom of the sea, broken across the treacherous Manacles rocks, within sight of the spire of St Keverne's church on Cornwall's Lizard peninsula.

In just 22m of water, the *Mohegan* was a popular diving spot and often used by sub-aqua clubs to give less qualified divers their first experience of a wreck dive.

Adam had been excited for Tamsyn to see it and promised that there were souvenirs to be had. Divers regularly brought up crockery and pieces of pottery.

"And I've got a friend who says it's haunted," he'd laughed.

Tamsyn had returned his smile because that's what he expected, but the thought made her uneasy. People had drowned here and not all the bodies of crew and passengers had been recovered: essentially, they were diving a grave site.

With her first glimpse of the huge wreck, the brass portholes drifting into view, she felt as if she were travelling back in time. Tamsyn wondered who had looked through these small windows and whether they'd felt death hovering the night of the wreck.

The huge cargo hatches were like empty eye-sockets and Tamsyn paused as the outline of the ship's hull stretched into the darkness, visibility decreasing quickly as their swim fins stirred the silt around them.

Slowly, keeping her breathing at a normal rate, she followed Adam as he finned the length of the wreck, pointing out the engine and massive boilers resting on rocks encrusted with maerl, a red seaweed with a hard, chalky skeleton.

When she saw bright anemones swaying alongside a family of sea urchins, she wanted to smile. With the mouthpiece in place, she couldn't, but she wanted to.

The feeling of contentment lasted until Adam reappeared out of the gloom, holding something in his hands. She couldn't see what it was, but he seemed pleased and placed it in his mesh dive bag, then pointed back the way they'd come toward the shot-line, telling her to start her ascent.

As she followed him, she ran through the calculations: how many times she needed to decompress at 6m intervals, and at the correct pace.

She almost swam into Adam when he suddenly reared back, his legs and arms thrashing wildly as blood bloomed in the water. An enormous conger eel had darted from the wreck, latching onto Adam's left hand. Bubbles spewed from his regulator as he screamed in pain. The needle-sharp teeth sank deeper, and Tamsyn could see the fear and panic in his eyes. She reacted without thinking, grabbing a rock and hitting the creature as hard as she could. Again and again, she used every ounce of strength, but her blows were slowed by the water. Adam punched the creature with his free hand and smashed its body savagely against the crumbling hull.

Finally, the eel let go, gliding backwards into its underwater lair, the unblinking black eyes seeming to stare at Tamsyn as it retreated.

Something brushed past her arm and she wheeled towards it, the rock still clenched in her hand.

But it wasn't the eel and it wasn't Adam.

Another body was suspended inside the wreck: lifeless, dead.

And then she did scream, or tried to.

She spun in the water, gasping, stirring up more silt until the world disappeared. She was hyperventilating now and no longer knew which way was up.

Her brain was in neutral, unable to function. Just a single certainty: *I'm going to die.*

When something grabbed her arm, she thought her heart would stop. But it was Adam, the puncture wounds visible on his hand, his little finger hanging by a thread.

He signalled upwards with growing urgency.

Tamsyn finned too fast, shooting up, using too much air. Adam followed, his damaged hand trailing blood behind him.

He was still holding her arm, dragging her down and she was desperate to shake him free. He signalled urgently with his damaged hand, and she remembered that she had to stop, had to decompress, had to wait five, agonisingly long minutes until it was safe to continue.

Adam's movements became slower, almost lethargic, and she realised he was going into shock. She grabbed his cylinders' harness and towed him upwards to the final decompression stop: waiting, counting and praying that she was doing it correctly because their lives depended on it.

When Tamsyn's head finally broke the surface, she tore her facemask away, gasping fresh air in heaving lungfuls. Adam was beside her, his face contorted and his eyes glassy.

But they weren't safe yet.

The weather had changed in the short time they'd been underwater, and the dive boat rocked from side to side, the waves growing rougher as the seconds passed. Tamsyn cursed Adam's cavalier decision to continue the dive with just the two of them after his friend cancelled, and her weakness for going along with it. She knew better. For God's sake, she knew better than to trust the sea.

She yanked off her fins and hurled them onto the deck, struggling to hold onto the boat's dive ladder as she was dunked into the sea, then whipped back, her ribs slamming painfully against the metal rungs.

It took three tries before she managed to clamber aboard and flopped onto the deck. She rolled onto her belly, and tried to find Adam in the surging water. He'd gripped the bottom rung with his good hand and had managed to shed his weight belt and swim fins, but didn't have the strength to pull himself up. She stretched out as far as she could over the boat's side, but she couldn't reach him. She needed a rope or...

Her eyes lit on the boathook used for docking. If she could just hook it around his harness without smacking his skull...

The hook clanged off Adam's cylinders five times before she managed to hook her prize. The dive boat tugged against its anchor, lurching wildly, and Tamsyn fell to her knees, but she didn't drop the boathook.

Using the last of her strength, she heaved Adam onto the deck like a neoprene-clad tuna.

His skin was pale under the tan, his lips blue, and his

breathing fast and shallow. She didn't know if it was shock or hypothermia.

"Adam! Where's the first aid kit?"

He mouthed something, but she couldn't hear him and he looked as though he was on the verge of passing out.

The first aid kit must be in the boat's wheelhouse. She lurched towards the small cabin, saw the white cross on a green background, and ripped open the plastic container. Grabbing a bandage and foil blanket, slipping and sliding across the deck, she managed to strap his hand tightly.

Adam groaned faintly and blood oozed through the white cotton. She wound the emergency blanket around his shoulders and positioned him so he couldn't be thrown out of the boat.

It would have to do.

Tamsyn ran back to the wheelhouse and picked up the radio, turning to channel 16.

"Pan-pan! Pan-pan! Pan-pan! Falmouth Coastguard, Falmouth Coastguard, Falmouth Coastguard. This is Tamsyn Poldhu with the dive boat *Heart of Lowenna*. We're two POBs, anchored 50m southwest of the *Mohegan* at 50.02.38 degrees north, 05.02.26 degrees west. I have an injured man – conger eel attack – and he's bleeding heavily from his hand. One finger is ... in bad shape. Can you send the rescue helicopter? Over."

The reply was almost immediate.

"Pan-pan *Lowenna*, pan-pan *Lowenna*, pan-pan *Lowenna*, this is Falmouth Coastguard, Falmouth Coastguard, Falmouth Coastguard on channel one-six. Message received. That is negative on the rescue helicopter, negative on the rescue helicopter. We'll send the lifeboat from Falmouth. Over."

"Falmouth Coastguard, this is *Lowenna*. Negative to the

lifeboat, repeat negative to the lifeboat. It will be quicker for me to head or Porthoustock – eta nine minutes. I've started the engines and am en route. Can you get paramedics onsite? Over."

"Do you need assistance to get to Porthoustock harbour? Over."

"Negative, Falmouth. Eta eight minutes. Over."

"*Lowenna* this is Falmouth Coastguard. Understood. An ambulance is on way to the harbour. The lifeboat will be sent to shadow you. Over."

"Understood, Falmouth. Over and out."

Tamsyn gripped the wheel and pushed the throttle forwards, increasing the speed as much as she dared in the choppy waters.

The little boat bounced and skittered across the waves, slamming down into the trough then lurching up into the next set. She couldn't risk looking over shoulder to see how Adam was doing.

Wind whipped her wet hair across her face and she shivered uncontrollably. Eight minutes seemed to take a lifetime.

As she neared the shingle beach, two elderly fishermen waved to her from the stone silo on the wharf, ready to grab the lines as soon as she could throw them ashore. She guessed that they'd heard her emergency call and had rushed to help.

There was no sign of the ambulance.

She was coming in fast and knew she should slow the engines, but a quick glance told her that Adam was unconscious.

The little boat roared into the harbour, breaking the five knots speed limit, then she slammed the throttle into reverse, and tossed a rope to the waiting men. They caught it skilfully, quickly securing *Lowenna* against the harbour buoys and boarding the boat.

"Poldhu? You Ozzie's granddaughter?" one of them asked as he squatted down next to Adam.

"Yes, that's right. I'm Tamsyn Poldhu," she said, her voice tight with strain.

"Thought so," the other one nodded. "I'm Jack and that there is Clemo."

"'E's awright, maid. The boy just fainted. Nasty bite though, bleeding like buggery – 'e might lose that finger."

The man sounded philosophical: life at sea was a dangerous business. Tamsyn could hear her grandfather's voice in her head: *the ocean gives and the ocean takes away.*

She crouched down next to Adam, taking his uninjured hand in hers, feeling its icy coldness.

His eyelids fluttered as the men undid his harness, removing the rest of his scuba equipment, and the faintest colour returned to his cheeks.

"Sorry," he whispered, giving Tamsyn a wry smile. "More exciting than I'd planned."

Tamsyn leaned closer, so the two men couldn't hear her.

"Did you see the body?"

His forehead wrinkled.

"What?"

"Another diver. He was dead."

"What?"

"You didn't see him?"

"No, nothing." Adam gave her a faint smile. "I said it was haunted."

Tamsyn didn't reply and was relieved when she finally heard the wail of sirens.

"The ambulance is here, Adam."

"Come with me?" he asked weakly.

"I'll take *Lowenna* back to Falmouth and pick up your car. I'll only be an hour behind you."

"But..."

"I'll be fine," she said, deliberately misunderstanding him. I've been around boats my whole life. I'll be okay. And I'll get our stuff so you've got some dry clothes when I pick you up at the hospital."

She suspected that his hand would need surgery, but she didn't tell him that.

The paramedics took over then, climbing onto the boat and lifting Adam ashore by stretcher.

"I'll see you later," Tamsyn called reassuringly, but Adam didn't reply.

She waited until the ambulance had left the harbour, then turned to the two old fishermen.

"I really appreciate your help."

"Don't you fret, maid. Regards to your grandfather."

They waved away her thanks and helped her cast off.

It was 40 minutes to Falmouth.

She tried to phone her boss but got his answering service.

"This is DI Rego. Leave a message and I'll get back to you."

"Sir, it's Tamsyn Poldhu. I've found a body."

Available to read now!

FORENSIC FILE

In each edition of my monthly newsletter, I'll cover a topic of interest from the forensic files.

Topics covered so far:

Fingerprints

More correctly called 'finger ridges', these are formed on a foetus by six months, due to the movement of amniotic fluid, and even the fingerprints of twins aren't identical.

Digi dogs

Search dogs have been trained to locate drugs or explosives, but they can also be trained specifically to sniff out technology such as laptops, mobile phones, USB sticks and even SIM cards. First trialled in the UK by Devon & Cornwall Police, with assistance from the FBI.

Learn more on my website and sign up for the monthly newsletter www.berrickford.com